Blood of Dragons

PRAISE FOR THE PILLARS OF REALITY SERIES

"Campbell has created an interesting world... [he] has created his characters in such a meticulous way, I could not help but develop my own feelings for both of them. I have already gotten the second book and will be listening with anticipation."

—Audio Book Reviewer

"I loved *The Hidden Masters of Marandur*...The intense battle and action scenes are one of the places where Campbell's writing really shines. There are a lot of urban and epic fantasy novels that make me cringe when I read their battles, but Campbell's years of military experience help him write realistic battles."

—All Things Urban Fantasy

"I highly recommend this to fantasy lovers, especially if you enjoy reading about young protagonists coming into their own and fighting against a stronger force than themselves. The world building has been strengthened even further giving the reader more history. Along with the characters flight from their pursuers and search for knowledge allowing us to see more of the continent the pace is constant and had me finding excuses to continue the book."

—Not Yet Read

"*The Dragons of Dorcastle*... is the perfect mix of steampunk and fantasy... it has set the bar to high."

—The Arched Doorway

"Quite a bit of fun and I really enjoyed it. . .An excellent sequel and well worth the read!"

—Game Industry

"The Pillars of Reality series continues in *The Assassins of Altis* to be a great action filled adventure. . .So many exciting things happen that I can hardly wait for the next book to be released."

—*Not Yet Read*

"The Pillars of Reality is a series that gets better and better with each new book. . .*The Assassins of Altis* is a great addition to a great series and one I recommend to fantasy fans, especially if you like your fantasy with a touch of sci-fi."

—*Bookaholic Cat*

"Seriously, get this book (and the first two). This one went straight to my favorites shelf."

—*Reanne Reads*

"[Jack Campbell] took my expectations and completely blew them out of the water, proving yet again that he can seamlessly combine steampunk and epic fantasy into a truly fantastic story. . .I am looking forward to seeing just where Campbell goes with the story next, I'm not sure how I'm going to manage the wait for the next book in the series."

—*The Arched Doorway*

"When my audiobook was delivered around midnight, I sat down and told myself I would listen for an hour or so before I went to sleep. I finished it in almost 12 straight hours, I don't think I've ever listened to an audiobook like that before. I can say with complete honesty that *The Servants of The Storm* by Jack Campbell is one of the best books I've ever had the pleasure to listen to."

—*Arched Doorway*

ALSO BY JACK CAMPBELL

THE LOST FLEET

Dauntless
Fearless
Courageous
Valiant
Relentless
Victorious

BEYOND THE FRONTIER

Dreadnaught
Invincible
Guardian
Steadfast
Leviathan

THE LOST STARS

Tarnished Knight
Perilous Shield
Imperfect Sword
Shattered Spear

THE GENESIS FLEET

Vanguard
Ascendant

PILLARS OF REALITY

*The Dragons of Dorcastle**
*The Hidden Masters of Marandur**
*The Assassins of Altis**
*The Pirates of Pacta Servanda**
*The Servants of the Storm**
*The Wrath of the Great Guilds**

THE LEGACY OF DRAGONS

*Daughter of Dragons**
*Blood of Dragons**
*Destiny of Dragons**

NOVELLAS

*The Last Full Measure**

SHORT STORY COLLECTIONS

*Ad Astra**
*Borrowed Time**
*Swords and Saddles**

available as a JABberwocky ebook

Blood of Dragons

The Legacy of Dragons
Book 2

JACK CAMPBELL

JABberwocky Literary Agency, Inc.

Blood of Dragons

Copyright © 2017 by John G. Hemry

All rights reserved

First paperback edition in 2017 by JABberwocky Literary Agency, Inc.

Published as an ebook in 2017 by JABberwocky Literary Agency, Inc.

Originally published in 2017 as an audiobook by Audible Studios

Cover art by Dominick Saponaro

Map by Isaac Stewart

ISBN 978-1-625672-93-3

To Sarah Damario, whose spirit sings bright and strong.

For S, as always

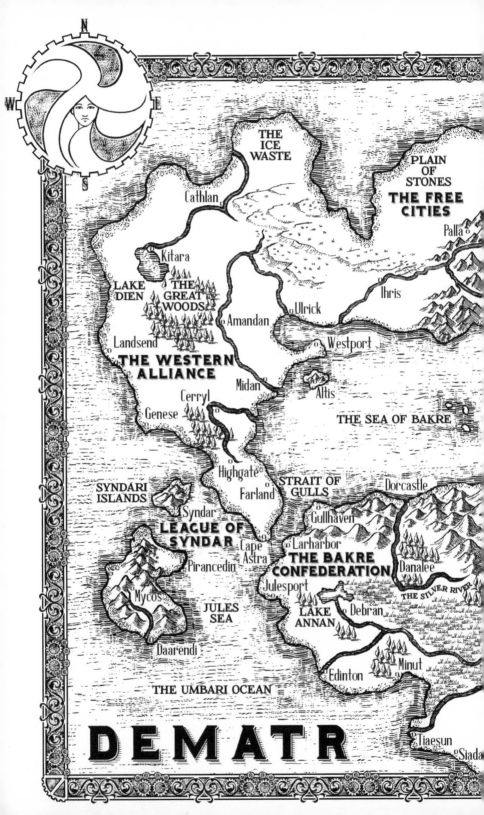

ACKNOWLEDGMENTS

I remain indebted to my agents, Joshua Bilmes and Eddie Schneider, for their long-standing support, ever-inspired suggestions and assistance, as well as to Krystyna Lopez and Lisa Rodgers for their work on foreign sales and print editions. Many thanks to Betsy Mitchell for her excellent editing. Thanks also to Robert Chase, Kelly Dwyer, Carolyn Ives Gilman, J.G. (Huck) Huckenpohler, Simcha Kuritzky, Michael LaViolette, Aly Parsons, Bud Sparhawk and Constance A. Warner for their suggestions, comments and recommendations.

CHAPTER ONE

K ira!"

Seventeen-year-old Kira of Pacta Servanda paused with her saber held in a guard position and yelled a reply. "I'm busy fighting!"

She shifted to attack, beating aside the blade of her opponent.

He managed a riposte that almost got past Kira's parry.

Without pausing, Kira ducked inside his attack and stopped with her blade poised near his neck. "Yield?" she asked, breathing hard from the duel.

Jason of Urth laughed, spreading his arms in surrender. "Okay, dragon slayer, I lost. What's my penalty?"

"Kiss me."

"That's no penalty."

She was lost in the feeling of Jason's lips on hers when someone nearby made a loud throat-clearing sound.

Kira jumped back, glaring at her mother. "A little privacy?"

Master Mechanic Mari of Dematr, the woman known to her world as the daughter of Jules, pirate queen, dragon slayer, the woman who had raised and led the army that freed their world from the domination of the Great Guilds and since then used her vast popularity and moral authority to prevent further wars, looked around at the open land surrounding their home, waving toward the sea coast visible to the south. "You're in our yard, Kira. The patrols around the house could see you. Passing ships could see you."

"I was just giving Jason a lesson in sword fighting."

"Yeah. Sword fighting," her mother said with a glance at Jason, who was looking at the ground, embarrassed. "It seems to be going pretty well. Listen, you know we've got a big dinner tonight. You two need to be ready for it."

Kira held out her own hands in mock surrender. "We'll stay out of the way," she promised.

"No, you won't. Both of you will attend the dinner, and the discussion afterwards." Mari paused to look around again, her dark Mechanics jacket open so that the pistol holstered underneath it could be seen. Kira had rarely seen her mother without the weapon. While loved by the great majority of the population of the western parts of her world, Mari still had plenty of deadly enemies who needed always to be guarded against.Kira had a similar pistol, and a similar holster that she wasn't wearing at the moment. She had grown up knowing that her mother's enemies would also target her if given the chance.

"Dress is casual," her mother said. "This is just a gathering of friends who happen to have tremendous political power. Don't wear your Lancer uniform, Kira.""I thought Queen Sien was one of the guests."

"She is, but you need to be present as my daughter, not as one of her officers, even an honorary one. We're keeping this informal. Asha has already arrived. She's—"

"Over that way with Father," Kira said. "I could feel it when she got here."

Her mother didn't say anything, watching Kira with concern, then shook her head. "Dinner. Be ready. On time."

"Yes, Lady Mari," Kira said. "The wish of the daughter of Jules is as good as an order."

"I only wish my own daughter really felt that way." Her mother smiled, then walked away.

Kira waited until her mother was a good ways back toward the house. "I wonder what that's about?"

Jason scratched his head. "Have you been part of the group at your mother's dinners before?"

"No. Or maybe just the dinner and not the discussion afterwards. Queen Sien is coming, and Mage Asha is already here, and Master Mechanic Lukas. I heard Jane of Danalee will be here, too. There must be something very important they want to talk about."

"Who's Jane of Danalee?"

"President of State of the Bakre Confederation, second only to President in Chief Julan. And there's Aunt Alli and Uncle Calu, too, since you came down here with them. Has it been all right, staying in Danalee with them? I wish you could be here all the time."

"Me, too," Jason said. "But not if I had to live in the same house with you as sort of a brother."

"That would be too weird," Kira agreed. She sat down in the grass, her sword across her lap, waiting while Jason joined her. "You don't mind having to attend as well?" she asked.

"Not if your mother needs me there," Jason said, laying his own saber over his legs. "Your parents have been so great, accepting me the way they have, and taking time for me even with all their responsibilities."

"They know that you're important to me, Jason," Kira said.

"How important?"

She gave him a disapproving smile. "You're not supposed to push. It's only been six months since you got left on Dematr. But I will tell you that I am pretty sure that I'm getting to like you more every day."

"In that case," Jason said, grinning, "I can't wait for tomorrow."

"Do you have any regrets? About staying on this world?"

"With you? No."

"What about not counting me?" Kira asked.

"No," Jason repeated. He looked at the world around them. "I wanted to stay here, remember? On Earth, I was an unhappy kid who had never done anything with his life and never expected to do or be anything, with parents who spent half their time putting down each other and the other half putting me down. Here...besides you—and it's really hard not to count you—I'm seen as sort of special, and I get to see steam locomotives and sail on sailing ships and ride horses with that cavalry unit you belong to and see a world that isn't overcrowded and over-tired, and meet people like your mother and father."

Kira looked at him, remembering that not much more than six months ago she would have flared with rebellious and insecure anger at mention of her mother. "I can understand wanting to escape the control of those awful parents of yours, but being with me isn't all sunshine and flowers. I mean, you almost got killed, too, a few times. And I've got Mother's temper."

"You're worth it," Jason said, smiling at her.

"Stop it. But not until after you've kissed me again. Then we need to go into the house and start getting ready. Father still can't read a clock, but when Mother says *on time*, she means it."

Conversation during dinner kept to mild topics. Questions to Jason about far-off Urth that he patiently answered, talk about local events in Tiae and the Bakre Confederation, the latest weapon designs in Master Mechanic Alli's workshops, and reminiscing about some of the less stressful events during the war against the fallen Great Guilds. Kira stole glances at the others as she ate. All of the Mechanics wore their customary dark jackets over nice but not fine shirts and the sturdy trousers of engineers. The dark jackets had once symbolized membership in the Guild that Mari had destroyed, but Mechanics still took pride in wearing the distinctive garment. The Mages, her father Alain and Asha, wore traditional Mage robes. Queen Sien was in loose trousers and shirt, a long coat over them, like any citizen of Tiae might wear. President Jane of Danalee's working suit was the nicest garment at the table. As her mother had said, this was simply an informal gathering of friends, the sort of friends who had immense power to direct the course of the West and thereby much of the world of Dematr.

Afterwards, they went into the living room to talk. Everyone settled back in their seats on one of the sofas or chairs. There weren't enough to go around so Kira and Jason sat on the floor in one corner of the room, Kira feeling both excited and intimidated to be part of such a group. "Let's start with the Imperial ships on their way to Tiae," Kira's mother said. "Lukas, I understand you have some inside information."

Master Mechanic Lukas, old but still sharp, was one of the most experienced Mechanics in the world. Any Mechanic he didn't personally know was probably known to someone else he did. Lukas rubbed his brow as he thought before speaking. "Yeah, Mari, the Gray Squadron. That's the name the Imperials are giving the five ships that are conducting supposed 'friendship visits' across the Sea of Bakre before heading south into the Umbari and visiting more ports in the Confederation and Tiae."

"How good are the ships?" Queen Sien asked.

"Good enough. Metal hulls and decks. Most of the stuff on them is state-of-the-art for what we can reliably build now. They've each got two boilers feeding into a single stack, and from what I hear enough coal storage for them to be able to go from the Sharr Isles to Tiaesun without refueling."

"That's a long haul," Mari said.

"Yeah. I imagine they'd be scraping the bottoms of the coal bunkers by the time they got here." Lukas shrugged. "They're the pride and joy of the new Imperial fleet. Everyone knows the so-called friendship visits are actually aimed at intimidating every place they stop. And they are pretty intimidating. One medium-heavy gun in an enclosed mount on the bow and two medium-caliber guns, one in an open mount forward and the other on the stern."

"That's enough to be trouble," said Master Mechanic Alli.

"Yup," Lukas confirmed. "Individually, they're no match for the big gun ships being built by the Confederation and the Alliance. But all five of those new Imperial ships together would give the two Confederation big gun ships a tough battle." He smiled at Alli. "I had a look at the *Julesport*, Alli. You did some fine work on the heavy guns on those ships."

"I have some great people working with me," Alli said. She grinned. "Of course, I'm pretty good myself."

Her husband, Mechanic Calu, leaned forward. "How good are the Imperial guns?"

"Nothing to match Alli's work, but good enough. You wouldn't want to tangle with all five of those ships. Which is why the Empire is sending them around to overawe everyone."

"The Imperials are getting more aggressive," Mari said. "It's been building. The Imperial legions have always been tough opponents, and now all the front-line legions are fully equipped with rifles. The last time I talked to Camber he told me that sentiment in the Empire is growing that they lost the War of the Great Guilds because of some tricks by the West and a loss of resolve by the legion commanders."

"They took hideous losses at Dorcastle," Calu said. "I'll never forget seeing all the bodies that hadn't been collected yet. I still get nightmares about that."

"I'll trade you for my nightmares about Dorcastle," Mari said.

"No, thanks. My point is, how can anybody in the Empire pretend that didn't happen?"

"They remember the losses, Calu. What they call the heroic losses, which they increasingly claim were caused by the actions of the legion generals at Dorcastle. They blame the defeat on betrayal, saying that without that the legions would have triumphed."

"Huh." Everyone turned to look at Jason. "I'm sorry," he said.

"What is it?" Kira's father asked. Master of Mages Alain, arguably the most powerful Mage in the world, and the wisest as far as Kira was concerned. "Tell us your thoughts, Jason."

"It's just like history back on Earth," Jason said, with an anxious look at Kira that she replied to with an encouraging smile. "There was something called World War One. Millions of dead, and one of the countries that started it got beaten. But a generation later, that same country helped start World War Two, because they decided they hadn't really lost. Their armies had been somehow betrayed."

"How many died in the World War Two?" Alain said.

"A lot more millions," Jason said. "Tremendous devastation. I mean, the guys who started it paid a horrible price, but so did other countries."

Queen Sien nodded in understanding. "They did not forget the losses in the first war, but they convinced themselves a second try would end differently. This is what the Imperials are heading for?"

"It's crazy," Calu objected. "If the Imperials attack anybody, Mari will call for action and everybody else will come down on them. The Imperials could beat any country in the west individually. But they can't win if the Confederation, the Western Alliance, the Free Cities, and Tiae combine forces. I'm no military expert and I can see that. And they will combine forces under Mari's leadership."

"You have identified our vulnerability in the west," Sien said: "Mari. If she is not there to unify us, old rivalries and new fears might prevent a combined response until the Empire achieves the gain it seeks."

Kira stared at Mari, worried. "They're going to go after Mother again?"

"That might have been their plan once," Jane said. "To somehow neutralize the daughter. But things have grown more complicated for the Imperial plotters."

Jane of Danalee had been Bakre Confederation President of State for eight years. As a veteran of the siege of Dorcastle, one of those who had stood on the last wall with the daughter to halt the Imperial legions despite impossible odds, Jane could be sure of being reelected as long as she wanted the job.

"Something important has changed," Jane added. "Kira."

Everyone looked at her. Kira, wishing that she knew a way to sink through the floor and out of sight, tried to hold her expression rigid, since she had no idea how she was supposed to react.

"If you had asked me about Kira's status in the Confederation a year ago," Jane said, "I would have told you that many people had hopes that she would in some small way be able to fill the shoes of the daughter if Mari was no longer able to do so. But there was also skepticism and concern. Aside from her youth, she is not Mari. She did not hold the wall. She is not the daughter of the prophecy. If Kira had called for the army in the name of the daughter, had asked for joint action in the name of the daughter, there would have been confusion, uncertainty, delay, and debate."

Everyone else nodded in agreement, their eyes on Jane now, while Kira looked around at them, uncomfortable at being the subject of the conversation and trying to guess at the thoughts of the others.

"But," said Jane, "after the events surrounding the visit of the ship from Urth, perceptions of Kira have altered dramatically. She is a dragon slayer, one who did the deed in hand-to-hand combat, surpassing even her mother in that. The stories of what she did at sea keep growing in stature. She was seen facing down the people from Urth alongside her mother and father. And, judging from the stories being passed around, while she was in hiding from the Urth ship Kira seems to have encountered half the population of the Confederation, the Free Cities, and Ihris, all of whom claim she acted with all the courage, grace, wisdom, and common touch that her mother is famous for."

"Jane," Kira's mother sighed. "Let's keep it real."

"That's your reputation, Mari. And now to some extent it's Kira's as well. The world hasn't fully embraced her as a successor to you, but it is a lot closer to doing so. If you were out of the picture, and Kira called today, the army might hesitate, but I believe it would come and answer to her. The Bakre Confederation would listen, the Free Cities would listen, and even the Western Alliance would likely be swayed."

"Tiae would also answer," Sien said.

Kira swallowed nervously, reaching to grasp Jason's hand with her own. The idea of most of the world listening to her, doing as she asked, was almost overwhelming.

Queen Sien's gaze went from Mari to Kira. "The Empire will have noticed that change."

"Exactly," Jane agreed. "Which means those in the Empire who want war know that they can't just try to neutralize the daughter. They also have to neutralize Kira, or she could become the new daughter and frustrate their plans."

"Which explains the renewed push for an engagement with an Imperial prince," Mari said. "There's no attempt at subtlety. The Empire wants Kira engaged to Prince Maxim and they want it now. There's a clear message that if the world wants peace, the daughter should agree to the arrangement, and if she does not, it will be her fault if a major war erupts. But they're also still trying to persuade her. The presents the Empire is sending Kira keep getting bigger."

"And more embarrassing," Kira added. "That jeweled bracelet they sent last month! Who would wear something like that? It was big enough to serve as armor for my lower arm!"

"Did you write them a nice note when you sent it back?" Alli asked, grinning.

"I told them again to stop sending me stuff! The Imperial household has been sending me gifts since I was born. You'd think by now they'd have figured out that gaudy jewelry and expensive clothes are not the way to impress me!"

Mari shook her head. "Jane, Camber has told me that he is advising the emperor that renewed war would be folly, and that Kira is very unlikely to change her mind about marrying into the Imperial household."

"Camber is old," Jane said. "So is the emperor. What they say and what they believe has less and less impact. The likes of Prince Maxim are operating with more freedom. Maxim has gathered support in the Imperial household by promising to elevate the Empire in its rightful, superior, place in the world now that the Great Guilds can no longer restrain it."

Lukas also shook his head, frowning. "I can't be the only one here who's heard that the remnants of the Mechanics Guild inside the Empire are also pushing for war. They want the common people to kill enough of each other to give the Guild a chance to reclaim power over the world."

"That's insane," Calu commented. "Technical knowledge has become too widespread, and the commons would never accept the Guild's control again."

Queen Sien shrugged. "Those who want something badly can easily convince themselves that even the most foolish plan could work. And we saw in Tiae that those who believe they have lost much are willing to risk everyone else losing much more in the hopes that they can climb to the top of the rubble of whatever remains. What of the Mages?"

Mage Asha made a small gesture of uncertainty. "The majority continue to explore new wisdom. Others cling to the past, but we have no information that they have gathered around new leaders. Those who favor the old wisdom fight bitterly among themselves, even though their hatred for Master of Mages Alain and the daughter of Jules has not faded."

"But will they willing aid the Empire?"

"Their services may be bought, but they also hate imperial arrogance and being ordered about by commons. Such Mages will willingly help sow the seeds of chaos among commons and Mechanics, but Mage Dav has heard nothing of any single effort that gathers those Mages hostile to the changed world,"

Jane nodded, one hand rubbing her arm where it been badly injured during the war. "The remnants of the Great Guilds cannot be discounted, but for now the real power still lies with the Empire's forces and powerful imperials like Maxim. All of them know the biggest obstacle facing them is the daughter, and now also the daughter of the daughter. Like it or not, Kira has surely become involved in Imperial plans."

"Kira just turned seventeen a few months ago," Mari said, frowning with unhappiness.

"She is also the daughter of you and Alain," Queen Sien observed. "At seventeen, I was dealing with some extremely serious challenges, Mari."

"I'm not you, Your Majesty," Kira said. "I'm not my mother."

"You have proven yourself to be a worthy daughter of your father and your mother," Sien said. "The question is, how can we convince the supporters of Prince Maxim that any plan aimed at you and your mother cannot work?"

"They can't think I would ever agree to marrying Maxim!"

"You are officially unattached," Sien said. "As long as you are free of commitments to another, they can imagine that they could come up with a way to convince you or force you to marry Prince Maxim."

Kira shuddered at the idea, aware that the others in the room, powerful people with immense experience in the world, were watching her. Not indulgently, but with the interest of people expecting her to say something worth listening to. It almost rattled her too much to keep speaking. "What if I made a public statement that I would never marry into the Imperial household? That I thought doing so would, um, compromise my mother's impartiality and any future position I might have?"

"In most cases, that would be wise," President Jane said. "But with you, that denial would be regarded within the Empire at least as proof that you wanted to marry into the Imperial household."

"What?"

"You have to understand, Kira. You're evil."

"I'm evil?"

"I've been trying to warn people about her for years," Mari commented. "Nobody believes me."

Kira made a face at her mother as the others laughed.

"In all seriousness," Jane continued, "you know who many Imperials think you are and who your mother is."

"Mara?" Jason said without thinking, then cringed as Kira bent an angry look at him and Mari sternly shook her head his way.

"Yes," Jane said. "She Who Must Not Be Named In This Household. The undead courtesan allegedly seeking to reestablish her role next to the Emperor's throne, once again pulling the strings of power as she did long ago, and with an endless supply of young men available to feed her appetites, their blood keeping her young and beautiful. The Imperials believe that everything you do and say is in the service of that goal."

"How can insisting I don't want that mean that I do want it?" Kira said.

"You're evil! Just because they can't explain or understand your plans doesn't mean you aren't plotting to do something evil!"

"Then why does Maxim want to marry me?"

"Because he claims that he can control you and neutralize you, just as Emperor Maran supposedly once did with...you know who," Jane said. "By binding you under his control, he will ensure that the Empire is safe from you."

"He claims to be a new Maran, and they are painting Kira as a threat," Alain said. His voice was impassive, in the way of a Mage, but Kira could still sense the underlying anger and worry that her father couldn't hide. "An active threat to the Empire."

"Of course. The last thing they want is for Kira to become well regarded within the Empire. And you know Imperial thinking. You are with them, doing as they command, or you are against them. There is no middle ground."

"Perhaps war at this time would not be the worst outcome," Sien said. "If the Empire intends war, we should force it upon them on our terms."

Mari shook her head. "You know how powerful the Empire is, and what war can do."

"I have far too much personal experience with it," Sien said. "But I also have personal experience with what happens when those intending harm are not countered before they grow even more powerful."

Master Mechanic Lukas, lounging back in his seat, looked at Alain. "What do the Mages think? Are there any prophecies or visions?"

Alli laughed. "Master Mechanic Lukas, you are one of the last I ever expected to ask about that."

"I'm a practical man, Master Mechanic Alli," Lukas said, "which means if I see something that works, I don't deny the evidence just because I can't figure out how it works. I work with it."

Alain answered. "I have been speaking with Mage Asha since she arrived. She brings word of many visions that have been told to Mage Dav. There is...confusion."

Asha nodded, her expression solemn. "Normally, foresight offers images that are consistent. What one Mage sees, others will see as well, if they have connections to the same people or events. But now visions come and contain clashing images. One Mage sees something that seems clear, but another sees something far different. Sometimes the same Mage sees images that contradict."

"Why?" Mari asked. "What's changed?"

"Many of the images have one person in common. My uncle, Mage Dav, believes the answer lies in that person." Her eyes, as brilliant and striking as ever, settled on Kira.

A moment of startled silence followed Asha's words. Kira looked at her father, seeing the worry in his eyes.

Mari spoke with the forced calm that Kira knew meant her mother was very upset. "What has Kira been seen doing? What's happening to her?"

Asha paused before replying. "Many…difficult…things."

Kira inhaled sharply, the sound breaking through the renewed silence that followed Asha's statement. "I would have liked hearing about that before now."

"The visions cannot all happen," Asha said. "Some see her in the Imperial court, in the robes of a consort."

"They see *what*?" Mari demanded. "Alain, why wasn't I—"

"He was just told." Asha's eyes were on Kira again. "Others see her…entering the next dream."

"Dying?" Kira barely got out. "I'm going to—"

"These are not things that will be," her father broke in. "They are things among many. They cannot all occur. Other visions show Kira happy and well, crowds cheering her, or simply living her life. In a boat, for example."

"Her future is entangled with the Empire," Asha warned. "But how that will work out is impossible to say. Nothing is clear. Jason is also seen. Sometimes."

"What's being seen of Jason?" Calu asked, concerned.

"The same. Many possible futures, some good, some bad."

"H-how bad?" Jason asked.

Asha's eyes rested on him. "As bad as the worst of Kira's."

"What about the good ones?" Alli said.

"As good as the best of Kira's. And many that show alternatives between those two. But many are…difficult."

Queen Sien looked from Kira and Jason to Alain and Asha. "This is not how I have been told foresight works. What does it mean?"

"I think," Kira's father said, speaking slowly, "it means that normally the choices of an individual matter in what may come to pass. What they choose to do. But their choices are limited by who they are."

"How does that explain things?" President Jane asked.

Alain's eyes rested on Kira. "If someone contains more than one potential, if someone can act in different ways that no other could, it would create differing possibilities. If she makes use of one set of choices from one…aspect of herself, futures would flow from that. If she makes use of choices from another aspect, different futures could come into being. And if she somehow can draw on both aspects, mingling possibilities, the futures become mixed and uncertain."

"What are you talking about? I'm sorry, but I don't understand what could make Kira so different in terms of her possible future actions."

Mari sighed. "Kira, there are two people here who aren't aware of something important about you. I would like to tell them, but only if you're all right with that."

Kira looked up at the ceiling, reluctant but knowing that her mother would not have asked without good reason. "If you think you need to."

"Lukas, Jane, this is something that's been kept to just a few of us. I have to ask that you not share it with anyone else. We're talking a major secret regarding my family that must not be revealed." They both nodded in agreement. "Kira has manifested Mage powers."

Lukas frowned. "I saw her practicing with her pistol earlier."

"Yes. She's primarily a Mechanic. But she also has some Mage powers."

Jane leaned forward, studying Kira, as Kira tried not to flinch from that examination. "That's what you meant, Alain? That Kira could act as both a Mechanic *and* a Mage? I can see how that would create a unique set of problems in predicting her actions and outcomes,"

"It creates very different possible actions and outcomes," Alain said. "But how is it possible?"

"We don't know," Kira's mother said. "The differences between the way someone with Mage powers has to view the world and the way a Mechanic views the world are, as far as we know, so vast as to be completely incompatible."

"What powers are we talking about?" Jane's eyes were still fixed on Kira, as if some outward sign might answer her question.

Kira answered, not liking the sense of being a curiosity on display. "Some foresight, in different forms. I can sense Mages and spells being cast. And once I was able to overlay a small illusion on the world. That's all."

Jane shook her head in amazement. "I've heard some rumors that Kira displayed Mage powers during the incidents involving the ship from Urth. But everyone I know of is discounting those rumors, especially the Mages, because Kira has been publicly demonstrating Mechanic skills." She looked at Asha. "Have either of your daughters shown this?"

Asha shook her head in turn. "No. Devi leans toward the Mechanic arts. Ashira has growing Mage powers. Neither can do both."

"It's not causing you any problems?" Lukas asked Kira.

Kira smiled reassuringly. Gruff old Master Mechanic Lukas had always had a soft spot for her, and Kira had always returned those feelings. "No. I've been fine. The powers have been…I guess *quiet* is the right word, for the last few months. They're still there. I've been working hard with Father on ways to block my…my Mage presence from the awareness of other Mages."

This time Asha nodded. "I could not sense you at all when I arrived, Kira. I asked your father if your powers had vanished."

"Really? Thanks. But, uh, no, it hasn't caused any problems."

Jason spoke up, frowning. "Um, Kira, you did seem kind of disoriented a couple of times when you used them."

"I was really exhausted, Jason. That's all."

Kira noticed everyone giving her more concerned looks and wished that Jason hadn't gotten over-alarmed again.

"What do you mean by disoriented?" Lukas asked Jason.

"Kira seemed to have trouble understanding me, or knowing what to do. It only lasted for a real short time."

"That does sound like extreme tiredness."

"See?" Kira said. "I'm fine."

"Is there anything besides Kira that the foresight visions have in common?" Queen Sien asked.

"Many visions show war," Asha said. "And in those visions both Mari and Kira appear prominently."

Mari ran both hands down her face. "Haven't Mages been seeing the possibility of war, and me appearing prominently, for the last twenty years?"

"Yes."

"What about mountains? Has Kira been seen in the mountains? Alain had a vision six months ago of her and Jason being chased through mountains somewhere."

"Yes," Asha said. "Visions have seen her in the mountains, on open lands, on the sea, in the sea, in the air, on a horse, walking, climbing, falling…"

"The girl gets around," Alli said. "Just like her mother."

"We cannot say which of these future visions actually portray events which will happen. Kira's nature has made the future too hard for even foresight to see clearly."

"You know," Kira said, "this isn't my fault. I'm not messing with the future on purpose."

"We know that," her father reassured her. "But your unique nature has created a unique mix of possible outcomes."

President of State Jane spread her heads imploringly. "A lot hinges on what Kira does or does not do. Do the visions offer the slightest clue as to what *we* should do?"

"No," Alain said. "Anything we do because of them could be exactly the wrong thing."

"Then why not try to disrupt the Empire's plans?"

"I think that would be wise," Kira's father said.

"Without unduly exposing Kira," Mari added.

"I have some ideas," Sien told the others. "I would like to discuss them one on one."

"All right," Mari said. "Let's…" She paused, looking toward Jason and Kira. "Jason? Is there something you need to say?"

He looked around, uncomfortable. "What about me?" Jason asked. "What should I do?"

Kira's mother smiled at him. "No matter what happens, what Kira will need the most is someone she can trust, someone she can count on, standing beside her."

Jason nodded. "I'm there."

"And if there is war?" Sien asked.

"Oh, yeah—what if Tiae goes to war?" Kira asked. "I can't be neutral if that happens. There's all this talk about me taking over for Mother, but I'm a citizen of Tiae."

Queen Sien looked at Kira's mother, who sighed and nodded. "We'll talk about that later, Kira."

"You and Sien already have some agreement? If my queen is all right with it, then I'm sure it will be fine. Queen Sien knows what she's doing."

"We'll talk about it later."

The older and wiser heads began having quiet conversations among themselves while Kira and Jason sat for a while longer, then went off to pretend to talk about other things while their thoughts remained centered on the earlier discussion. Jason stood by the window in Kira's small bedroom, she sitting on the bed, just as it had been six months ago when she hardly knew him and could barely tolerate him. "Why do you have to be involved in this?" Jason asked. "In danger again and everything?"

"Because my mother is the daughter of Jules and my father is the only Master of Mages," Kira said. "It comes with being me, with being their daughter."

"That's not exactly fair, Kira."

"Believe me, I spent plenty of time bemoaning my fate," Kira said. "You may remember hearing some of that. Excuse me, I do not need that look on your face. I was not that bad. But I've realized that if I didn't try to fulfill my...my obligations, that would be a decision to not help when I could help, to not do a job that maybe no one else could do. I can't do that, Jason. I have to try if there's a chance I can make a difference."

He nodded, looking resigned. "I remember that girl I met who kept telling me she wasn't anything like her mother. What was her name again?"

"Hey, you fell in love with her!"

Jason smiled. "Yeah, because even though she thinks I'm delusional, I really am in love with who she is. And this is part of her, part of you. I guess we're both stuck with it."

She gazed back at him, somber. "You're not stuck with it, Jason. You don't have any obligations to me. It's a choice."

"Then I am choosing to be stuck with it. Stuck with you," he said.

Kira grinned. "Lucky me. Thanks."

When Kira heard the others starting to leave, she ran down to help see them off as their carriages and coaches pulled up, the horses rested and ready for the trip to the train station in Pacta Servanda. Queen Sien, smiling as Kira saluted her but giving off an odd sense of saying goodbye in more ways than one; Lukas, giving Kira a quick pat on the shoulder; Jane taking Kira's hand and thanking her formally.

Alli and Calu shook their heads as Jason walked toward them. "You're not coming back to Danalee with us," Calu said.

"Huh? Why not?"

"Duty calls, and it's calling your name." Calu smiled fondly at Jason. "We've enjoyed having you."

"I'm staying here?" Jason said, confused.

"Don't get your hopes up," Alli said, fussing with his collar. "You and Kira are still underage. Give me a hug goodbye and get back inside."

"You guys have been so great," Jason said. "I don't know how to—"

"Just keep being who you are," Calu said. "And stay in touch."

When the others had left, Mari looked at Asha. "Are you staying the night?"

"If I may. Master of Mages Alain and I still have much to discuss."

"Go ahead, Alain. I'll talk to Kira. Jason, could you wait upstairs? You'll be staying in the guest room again."

Kira, wary, followed her mother into the kitchen, where Mari sat down and looked at her. "Why do you want to talk to me alone? Did I do something wrong?" Kira asked.

"No, dearest, you did great. Here's the idea we came up with. We need to disrupt what the Imperials are planning. A lot of that planning is surely focused on you. A public announcement that you were committed might not be believed and would be seen as a blatant attempt to rule out Imperial ambitions for you—"

"Imperial ambitions for me?"

"I know that sounds weird. I'm sorry." Mari studied her daughter while Kira waited, feeling awkward. "It's clear that the Imperials think they can still get their hooks into you. Maxim is staking his prestige on getting you. But, if it becomes obvious that your interests are firmly and genuinely set in another direction, it should throw off their plans and give us a chance to undermine Prince Maxim's position."

Kira eyed her mother suspiciously. "My interests? What direction?"

"Jason."

"Mother, I really like him. But...I still don't know if *love* is the right word."

"That's all right," Mari said. "You don't have to change that. All that matters is what the world sees. Your father and I, along with you, were already planning to go down to Tiaesun for the formal reception associated with the visit of Prince Maxim and the Imperial ship squadron. Jason is going to come as well."

"Really?" Kira said, elated. Suspicion rose again. "Really?" she asked in a different way.

"While we're there, you and Jason will go out together, be seen being happy together, buy each other jewelry in public where lots of people can see—"

"*What?* Buy each other jewelry? Mother, that is a serious sign of commitment!"

"You and Jason will know that it doesn't mean that. But Jason came from Urth. There are a lot of stories about him helping you last year, about how he saved you during that storm at sea and helped you fight your way out of Kelsi, and how he decided to stay on this world. A lot of people know he's been spending time here with you."

"You mean our enemies," Kira grumbled.

"No, I mean a lot of people. Including the Imperials. Word will get around very rapidly about you two if you're acting like a pair in public. It will be obvious that you may not be officially committed, but you are very much tied to someone else and could not possibly be interested in Prince Maxim under any circumstances."

Kira stared at her mother. "Whose idea was this?"

"Actually, Sien was the first to think of it."

"Great," Kira said. "My own queen has been plotting to embarrass me."

"That's another thing. It's time you knew," her mother said. "Sien is not your queen."

"Yes, she is." Kira shook her head at her mother. "I'm Kira of Pacta Servanda. Pacta Servanda is in Tiae. Sien is the queen of Tiae. She is my queen."

Her mother took a deep breath. "Your name is not Kira of Pacta Servanda."

Kira realized that she must have been staring at her mother for at least a minute, unable to speak. "What?"

"Have you ever looked at your birth certificate?"

"You know, for some strange reason I didn't think I had to in order to know my own name!"

"Your name is Kira of Dematr," Mari said.

How long had Kira spent staring wordlessly at her mother this time? "Kira. Of. Dematr."

"That's right," her mother said.

"No. That's wrong. You are Mari of Dematr. You are the *only* citizen of the world. I am a citizen of Tiae."

"No, you're not," Mari said. "The decision was made that my children would also be citizens of the world, so that I would not be influenced by their allegiance to any particular ruler or place."

"Who made this decision?" Kira demanded, feeling like the ground was shifting under her feet.

"I didn't," her mother said. "Leaders of the world. Representatives of every government. Including Queen Sien herself."

"My own queen helped with this?"

"Sien is not your queen."

"AHHHHH!" Kira collapsed into a nearby chair, her eyes locked on her mother. "How could you do this to me? I have spent the last seventeen years thinking my name was Kira of Pacta Servanda. Wait. I'm an honorary officer in the Queen's Own Lancers. How can I be an honorary officer of the Queen's Own Lancers if Sien is not my queen?"

"She gave you a waiver," Mari said. "The commander of the Lancers knows."

"The commander knows?" Kira slumped backwards. "My whole life has been a lie."

"Kira, you're being a little overdramatic."

"What else haven't I been told? You are my mother, right? For real?"

Mari nodded. "Do you think I would have stuck with this if I had a choice?"

"Oh, very funny," Kira said. She flopped her head back, staring at the ceiling. "Why wasn't I told?"

"We thought you'd be upset."

"Good guess. I am."

"And we wanted you to have a semblance of a normal childhood, a chance to be like the other kids."

"Seriously?" Kira asked, sitting forward to look at her mother. "Normal childhood? What part of normal childhood had bodyguards accompanying me when I went to a classmate's birthday party, and testing my piece of cake before I got to eat it, and opening all the presents to screen them before the birthday kid even got to see them, and a security sweep of the neighborhood that included Mages? I was eight years old, and for some weird reason I didn't get invited to many more birthday parties after that."

"That was overkill," her mother conceded. "You got to go to a lot of Gari's and Andi's birthday parties, and Ashira's and Devi's, and—"

"Mother, I am trying to wallow in the misery of this betrayal!" Kira got up. "Fine. My life is a lie and everyone I know has been plotting against me."

"I'm glad you're keeping a sense of perspective about this," Mari said.

"And now I will go tell Jason that he is going to Tiaesun to show off to everybody that he's my boyfriend. My really, really serious boyfriend who is going to make a completely spontaneous and private gift of jewelry to me in front of as many spectators as possible. Oh, and tell him my name isn't what I thought it was."

Her mother grimaced apologetically. "Kira, we're also going to need you and Jason to put on some public displays of affection."

"What does that mean?" Kira asked, wary again.

"Holding hands, hugging, kissing—"

"You said public. We're supposed to do that with people watching us?"

"As many people as possible," Mari said.

"I hate you."

"You'll get over it. Dearest, you know we wouldn't ask this of you, and of Jason, if it didn't seem the best way to short-circuit the Imperial plans and their march toward war."

"So now you're trying to make me feel guilty for getting upset," Kira grumbled.

"Yes. How's it working?"

★

Naturally, Jason didn't get it. "You're a citizen of the world? Cool."

"That is not cool," Kira informed him. "Neither is us making a public spectacle of ourselves."

"So I'm being invited to go to Tiaesun—"

"It's not an invitation, Jason. Invitations can be turned down. You're going to Tiaesun."

"Okay. What exactly are we going to be doing?"

"You will very publicly buy me jewelry, and I will very publicly buy you jewelry, and we'll…kiss and stuff."

"We like to kiss and stuff," Jason said.

"Not in front of crowds of people watching us, we don't!"

"And this will make the Imperials think we're serious about each other?"

Kira made a face. "It's supposed to make them think that we can't wait to turn eighteen and marry each other."

Jason stared at her. "Marry?"

"Not really," Kira said. "We just want the Imperials to think we are privately engaged, without making an official public announcement which would obviously be an attempt to influence them, because if they think their plans to neutralize me and to neutralize Mother can't work because of you—" She stopped speaking, staring at Jason as a terrible realization hit. "If the Imperials think you are standing between them and their plans, they'll target you!"

"Target me? Like, assassination target me?" Jason asked.

"Yes, target you like assassination target you!"

How could her mother and her father and Queen Sien have missed that?

They hadn't missed it, Kira suddenly understood.

Jason was to be bait, dangled before the Imperials in the hopes that arrogant Prince Maxim would make a mistake big enough to discredit him.

"*Mother!*"

CHAPTER TWO

The *Destiny* had once been part of the daughter's fleet, preying on Imperial shipping and helping to defend Pacta Servanda when Syndar had attacked. In the intervening years the wooden three-masted sailing ship had been upgraded a bit, a new steam boiler installed for propulsion to assist the sails, and breech-loading deck guns mounted fore and aft to replace the ballistae that had formerly been the *Destiny*'s main armament. She was now part of the fleet of Tiae, on loan from Queen Sien for Mari and Alain's trip down to Tiaesun.

Kira leaned on the starboard rail, staring into the west. Somewhere out there was the Western Continent, a once-mythical place that had been visited by only a couple of expeditions since the fall of the Great Guilds.

Without her willing it, her Mage senses reached out, feeling for the amount of power available to cast spells. Like all other areas on the water, there was little power here. Surprised, Kira tamped down her Mage senses. The last thing she needed was for them to do something without her directing them to, especially if it was in a place where other Mages could tell she was the source. Fortunately, her father was the only Mage aboard this ship.

Her mother came to stand by her. "How are you doing, Kira?"

"I'm fine," Kira said. "I'm on my way to formal social events where

I'll have to make nice to the Imperials who are obsessed with forcing me to marry into the Imperial household. And my own parents and my queen…excuse me, my former queen, are painting a great big target on my boyfriend and hoping the Imperials try to kill him. And on top of that, I keep stumbling over my own name because it's a different name than I thought I had for seventeen years."

"You're doing pretty well, then."

"All things considered, yes."

"Dearest, there is going to be an awesome amount of security around Jason. Neither you nor he will be able to see most of it, but a fly won't be able to get through to hurt him. I promise."

Kira sighed. "You do keep promises."

"Have there been any more bad dreams since we left home?"

"If there had been you would have heard," Kira said. "I'm told that my screams would terrify even a Mage."

"Your father was not trying to make you feel bad when he said that," her mother said. "He, and I, were scared when our daughter let out with that shriek in the middle of the night."

"I'm sorry," Kira said. "It's only happened a couple of times. I think after what I went through six months ago a nightmare every now and then isn't all that strange." She looked out over the long, slow swells of the ocean, seeking a way to change the subject. "What was it like when you sailed these waters during the war?"

"Like this," Mari said, leaning on the railing next to her and letting Kira's change of topic slide. "As Captain Banda told me, the ocean changes her moods all of the time, but she's always the same under all that."

"The first time you captured another ship, what were you thinking?"

Her mother grinned. "I was thinking it shouldn't feel so exciting and almost fun, because I was also scared. That was the *Pride*, you know. The first ship we captured was the *Pride*. And now everyone talks about how my daughter fought the sea and beat it."

Kira shook her head, laughing at the idea. "I did not beat the sea. We barely survived it."

"Your father heard some of the sailors on this ship talking. The story going around is that any ship you're on will never sink in a storm."

"People are crazy," Kira said. "Did I ever tell you how rough and uncomfortable the sailor clothes were?"

"Tough, though, right?" her mother sympathized. "Sometimes you have to be practical. Oh, speaking of clothes, Sien told me she's having some special matching dresses made for you and me to wear to the big formal event."

"Really?"

"You do know if I had mentioned matching dresses a year ago that you'd have exploded, right?" Mari said, smiling at her.

"That was another Kira, who thought she would never be anything but a pale shadow of her mother."

"The only bad part is that we won't be able to wear any kind of coat with them, so we'll have to wear thigh holsters under the dresses. I brought mine, and Sien said she'd make sure one was ready for you."

"A thigh holster?" Kira asked. "You'll have to show me how to use that safely."

"What are mothers for?" Mari gave her a look. "You also need to warn Jason if you're wearing it."

Kira felt her face grow warm. "I don't need to warn Jason. He doesn't go pawing around down there. I set limits and he respects them."

"Good." Her mother paused, looking at the ocean as the swells made their endless progression. "What's going on with him, Kira? You know how it was with me and your father. I fell in love with him without realizing it, spent a while trying to talk myself out of it, then embraced the inevitable about the time he chose to stand by me against a charging dragon."

"Father still says that he's worried some day you'll realize you could do a lot better," Kira said, laughing. "Jason and I...it's hard to explain. He loves me. I know he does. And I feel like I'm caring for him more and more, but it's like there's something waiting, something that isn't there yet, and when it happens I'll know, but right now I don't."

Her mother didn't say anything else for a long moment, looking out over the water. "Kira, there's something I've noticed about you. When it comes to doing things, dealing with external matters, you're as impulsive and direct as I am. Get it done! But when it comes to your heart, to important things inside you...you're a lot more cautious and guarded."

"What if I am?" Kira replied, feeling defensive. "I've got plenty of reason to be that way. You know how guys have stalked me like I was prey, because they wanted to bag the daughter of the daughter of Jules so they could boast about it!"

"You don't think Jason is like that, do you?"

"No! It's just...I don't know. All right? Maybe I'm being overcautious, but don't I have a right to that?"

"You do," her mother agreed. "Absolutely. You shouldn't feel pressured. You know your father and I like Jason, but whether he's that special person for you is your decision and yours alone."

Kira paused, uncertain how to ask. "Mother, how are you?"

"I'm fine," Mari said. "Weight of the world on my shoulders, everyone counting on me to save the day, a daughter who's actually being pretty nice to me most of the time these days. The usual."

"I mean inside."

"Oh. The surgery? Doctor Sino did a follow-up. Didn't we tell you? She says everything looks great. I should be able to once again carry a child to term and have a safe delivery."

Kira grinned, hugging her mother. "I'm so glad. Um, are you and Father going to, uh, start...trying?"

Her mother smiled back. "We already are, dearest. We didn't think you wanted to hear about it, though."

"I don't! Thank you!" Kira laughed again. "Did I ever tell you that Jason says his parents used to talk about that in front of him? What they were doing with other people?"

"Ugh," Mari said with an exaggerated shudder of disgust. "How did two people with apparently no redeeming qualities produce a boy like Jason?"

"Well, you know how multiplying two negative numbers produces a positive number," Kira said.

"I don't think people work like that when they multiply. Interesting idea, though. Hey, want to see if they'll let us fire some test shots from the forward gun? I looked at it. It's one of your Aunt Alli's models."

"They'll let us do that?"

"I'm pretty sure if we ask they will. Do you think Jason would want to join in?"

"I'll get him!" Sometimes her mother could be really cool.

With sunset approaching, Kira raced Jason up the shrouds and the ratlines to the small platform high up on the foremast. They sat close, arms about each other. "I'm sorry Mother is using you as bait," Kira said.

"I thought it was your mother and your father and Queen Sien," Jason said.

"It is, but Mother had to buy off on it, or it wouldn't happen. And I think she's right. Enough people have seen us together that the Imperials must already be planning to deal with you somehow, and forcing their hand when we're most prepared is the safest thing for you."

"I never expected an Empire to be gunning for me," Jason remarked. "But as long as you're happy. You are happy, right?"

Kira sighed, looking toward the sun sinking through a rosy sky. "I guess. I'd be happier if the Empire just disappeared from the face of the world. And every time I say my name I start out 'Kira of Pacta—' and then remember and say 'Dematr,' so everybody is going to think I come from somewhere called Pacta Dematr. It feels so weird."

"What exactly is your status?" Jason asked.

"The same as Mother's. I'm a citizen of everywhere. I don't want to belong everywhere. I liked belonging in Pacta Servanda. I liked knowing I was a citizen of Tiae. I liked knowing that Sien was my queen, because she is awesome. Now I don't have that."

"If you're a citizen everywhere, aren't you still a citizen of Tiae?"

"Not like that. It's like 'citizen' in quotes. Sien cannot command me. I don't owe her allegiance. I swore that, did you know? When I joined the Queen's Own Lancers as an honorary officer I swore allegiance to Queen Sien. But Mother showed me a decree that Sien signed a long time ago releasing me from that oath. So it didn't really mean anything. It never did."

"I'm sorry."

"It was part of being somebody other than my mother," Kira said, resting her head on his shoulder. "It's hard to let it go. I talked to my commander…my former commander…before we left. I told him that I'd turn in my uniform and armor as soon as I could." She sighed again, remembering the conversation. "He told me to keep them, that as far as he and the rest of the Lancers were concerned I'd always be one of them."

"That was pretty cool of him," Jason said.

"Yes. He's a good commander. Only the very best get command of the Queen's Own. Even though he died before the unit was formed, Major Danel is considered the first commander, and everyone works very hard to live up to his example." Her arm tightened about Jason's waist. "I was so proud to be a Lancer. But I don't know if I can stand being an…imaginary honorary member of the unit. And knowing that if they went off to war I could never be part of them. It's not that I ever wanted to go to war, but I knew if we did I would be a Lancer and I would be side-by-side with them and we would fight together and never let each other down." She blinked away tears. "I'm sorry to be dumping all of this on you."

"I'm glad that I'm someone you can talk to," Jason said. "I wish your parents had told you a long time ago."

"I did, too. And then I realized that if they had, I never would have been a Lancer. And I'm glad that I was a Lancer, and proud of it." She wiped her eyes with her free hand, smiling. "Do you remember how impressed you were by that the first time you met me? That I was a cavalry Lancer?"

"I'm still impressed," Jason said. "I think your commander is right. You'll always be a Lancer."

"Thank you." She sighed once more. "Jason, there's something you're not saying that you want to say."

She felt Jason's body jerk in guilty reaction. "How do you do that?"

"It's kind of like a lie, Jason, because you're trying to hide something. And you know I can tell when someone is lying."

"Your dad's Mage teachings, yeah. All right," Jason said. "I'm scared."

Kira squeezed him again with the arm about his waist. "Don't be. I mean, use your head and be careful, but don't be scared. No assassin is going to get within a hundred lances of you."

"That's not what I'm worried about. It's the…the powers thing."

Kira closed her eyes, upset. "How many times do I have to say I'm fine?"

"But, Kira, when I talked to you about the Invictus drive right after you…did that thing, it wasn't just that you didn't understand." Jason moved his hands as if groping for the right words. "It was like…I was looking in your eyes and seeing someone else."

That was scary. Kira felt herself tensing up as she remembered those moments, soon after facing the dragon and knowing that the ship from Urth was probably closing in on them. Trying to do something she didn't even know she could do, but knowing that the fates of two worlds rested on her. She made an effort to relax. "I can see how that would bother you. You didn't say that at the time."

"There was a lot going on at the time."

"I know. Are you sure that's what you saw? Or is it maybe what your worries have convinced you that you thought you saw?"

Jason shook his head. "I don't know. Maybe it was the way you were looking at me and I couldn't figure out what it meant. You didn't feel different?"

Kira hesitated. "I'm not going to lie to you. I don't remember."

"The memories are too confusing?"

"No. I don't remember anything. I know I did the spell because you told me. But I don't remember anything about actually doing it. Just vaguely something about looking at a rock. Jason, stars above, relax! It feels like I have my arm around that steel cannon on deck!"

"Okay." He looked down, obviously more worried than ever.

"Remember when I wouldn't let you say okay?" Kira said, trying to lighten the mood. "Jason, I promise, if I experience anything that worries me, I will tell you."

He gave her a sidelong glance. "How about anything weird, even if it doesn't worry you?"

"All right. I promise. I will tell you and I will tell my parents. Let's try to talk for a while about things that won't upset either one of us. We have to eat dinner with the captain tonight and I'd prefer not to be an emotional wreck when we do." Kira paused, looking toward the east. "Smoke. There's a steamship there. No, two. Are there more columns of smoke?"

"Yeah. I think I see four," Jason said, standing up and holding onto the rigging to get a better look. "Maybe five, I can't be sure. When the sun finishes going down we'll lose sight of them."

Kira was about to yell down to the deck when she paused and looked back at the mainmast. The lookout there, a bit higher than Kira and Jason on the topsail platform, was gazing steadily ahead instead of looking around. She cupped her hands around her mouth. "Hey! Lookout!"

The sailor jerked to awareness, looking toward Kira. She pointed to the east and held up her hand with all five fingers spread.

The lookout stared at her, stared to the east, then shouted down to the deck. "Five steam ships to port, a point forward of amidships! On the horizon!"

As an officer ran up the rigging with a far-seer, the lookout gave Kira a wave of thanks and a smile. "You made a new friend," Jason said.

"I just did what I would want someone to do for me," Kira replied. "Uh-oh. Mother sees us. Let's get down on deck before it gets full dark." She went down the rigging, Jason following, finding Mari waiting as she reached the deck. "I'm sure it's the Imperial Squadron," Kira reported. "They're putting out a *lot* of black smoke. It looked to me like they aren't providing enough air to the boilers."

"That's my girl," Mari said. "Lukas told us the boilers on those ships were a good design, so the Imperial crews must not have the skills to operate them at best efficiency. That's useful to know."

The captain of the *Destiny* walked up, saluting Mari. "We're losing sight of them with night coming on, but they had a slow bearing drift forward. Unless they slow down, they'll reach Tiaesun several hours before we do."

"That's fine," Mari said. "I want those ships tied up and out of the way when we enter harbor."

The next morning, as the *Destiny* pulled into the harbor of Tiaesun, she flew from the highest mast a very large version of the daughter's banner, a gold sun on a blue background.

Kira, standing at the rail as the *Destiny* sailed past the pier where the Imperial ships were tied up, saw members of each ship's crew pausing to stare at the banner. "Prince Maxim is on that one," she told Jason, pointing to one of the Imperial ships. "That's his banner."

"Your mother's banner is bigger," Jason said looking up to compare.

"Yeah. She knew that would annoy Maxim." Kira felt a fierce smile on her face. "Mother's banner in particular. Prince Maxim's father was the Prince Maxim who commanded the attack on Dorcastle."

"Your mother beat his father?" Jason said.

"Beat him like a dirty rug," Kira said. "The legions broke before Mother's banner as it flew next to her on the last wall. Right where that statue is, remember? You can bet Prince Maxim is thinking about *that* right now. The Imperials are hoping that the visit of the Gray Squadron will overawe the people of this city, but Mother is doing her best to overawe the Gray Squadron instead."

"Um...so we're supposed to make Maxim so mad that he tries to kill me?"

"Yeah. Basically."

"Should we do that public affection thing while we're going past his ship?"

"Yeah," Kira said. "Why not?" Nervous, she turned, pulled his face to hers, and kissed Jason, holding it despite her growing embarrassment as she thought about not only Maxim but the other Imperials and everyone else on this ship and elsewhere in the harbor watching them.

"You're allowed to come up for air occasionally," her mother said from close by.

Kira broke the kiss and glared at Mari. "Please stop sneaking up on me while I'm kissing Jason."

"Maybe you ought to keep your eyes open while you're kissing."

"Mother, don't be disgusting!" Kira paused as a thought hit her. "Did you do that?"

"During the days when it seemed there was someone around every corner trying to kill us? You bet I did. Your father didn't mind. He actually thought it was kind of exciting."

"I really don't want to hear that," Kira told her mother. "Please don't make this harder than it has to be."

"Sorry," her mother apologized. She looked toward the ships. "Maxim either saw that or will hear about it. You two had better get ready to leave the ship. As soon as we tie up we're going to Queen Sien's palace."

"We're going to stay in a palace?" Jason asked.

"Yes. What's the matter, Kira?"

Kira looked out across the city, seeing frequent patches of trees and other greenery rising amid the white walls and red tiled roofs. "Nothing. Except the fact that I spent seventeen years thinking she was my queen, and she wasn't."

"You *will* be properly respectful, won't you?" Mari asked.

"Yes, Mother. I was raised right. I seem to recall you having something to do with that."

Her mother's grasp on Kira's shoulder was firm, comforting. "And

I recall how many times I was barely holding it together, and your father got us through it. And the times your father and I had to go away on...special missions. I know it was hard on you. You turned out so very well, though."

Kira put her arm about her mother and they stood there at the rail, watching the *Destiny* approach the pier. Jason stood nearby, part of the group, yet still separate.

Mari stood at a window looking out and down toward the harbor, remembering when it had been choked with silt and wrecks of ships. "I'm sorry Kira was so formal with you, Sien."

Queen Sien came to stand beside her. "She was hurt. I wish there had been a better way. And she is probably very worried about Jason, though like her mother she rarely speaks openly about her deepest worries."

"Are we doing the right thing?"

"Any attempt against Jason will be stopped. And exposing it will make Maxim look incompetent at best, and a fool at the worst. Undermining his position is our best chance to prevent a major war."

Mari shook her head, watching the people in the streets below, uncertainty gnawing at her. "What if we're wrong? What if Maxim decides to go after Kira?"

"Kira is being protected," Sien reminded her. "But would Maxim be such a fool? We would easily tie him to the act, and an attack on your daughter could precipitate a war the Empire is not ready to fight. You saw the latest reports from my embassy in Palandur. The Empire has not mobilized. They are not prepared for war."

"Maxim can't be an idiot," Mari said. "He wouldn't have gained his position as crown prince if he wasn't smart as well as ruthless. But smart people can mess up as badly as dumb people, especially if they come to think they're smarter than anyone else."

"If you or Kira are attacked, those Imperial ships will not leave this harbor," Sien promised.

"Any new word on what Syndar is doing?"

"Keeping their heads down. They've yet to recover from the losses of twenty years ago, and show no enthusiasm for risking a similar outcome. I never thought to see Syndar showing more wisdom than the Empire. I came up here to tell you that Jason and Kira are going out into the city. There is an army of agents and guards, including Mages, keeping watch on them."

"If anything happens to Kira or Jason I will never forgive myself, Sien. I will hang up this job and sail to the western continent and let this world go to blazes."

"We'll have to make sure that doesn't happen," Sien said. "I'd miss you."

Kira walked with Jason, her arm through his, occasionally smiling happily at him, feeling like a fool as she put on a show for the people looking to see, crowds which grew with every lance length they walked.

Tiaesun was called the Jewel of Tiae, sparkling with fountains and countless gardens large and small and groves of trees set amid the curves and arches common in architecture this far south. Bright white walls and red tiled roofs lined the wide streets of the city. During the decades of anarchy when Tiae was known as the Broken Kingdom the fountains had been dry and broken, the gardens overgrown masses of weeds or barren dirt, the walls cracked and stained from fires, the streets cluttered with trash and debris. In the years since Sien had reforged the Broken Kingdom with the help of Kira's mother and father, Tiaesun too had been reborn. But there were walls amid the rebuilt ones that still displayed scorch marks and the pits of neglect and battle, deliberately left as they had been as a reminder and memorial of what the city had once endured.

Horse-drawn carts and wagons and individual riders were being diverted to other streets by the city police, but the wide boulevard down which Kira and Jason were walking seemed to grow increasingly narrow as the number of people watching them kept growing. Kira thought the windows looking down on them felt like menacing eyes, potential places for snipers to lurk, while the gardens offered possible places for other attackers to hide in wait. What would it have been like to grow up not having to worry about assassins? Against that backdrop, the smiling faces of the people watching her felt unreal, especially since Kira couldn't really understand why so many people would care about her love life.

"This really is uncomfortable, isn't it?" Jason mumbled to her. He tried a return smile that didn't quite work.

"Try not to think about all of the people watching us," Kira said. She smiled again, this time waving to some of the spectators, who waved back excitedly. "When this walk is over and we get back to the palace I am going to go to my room and die of embarrassment," she said around her smile.

"I'm a bit worried about dying before I get back to the palace," Jason said, nodding to some of the spectators.

A voice called loudly from the crowd. "Are you two getting married here?"

Kira braced herself, locked a smile on her face, and called a reply. "We're still underage!"

Cheers and applause answered her.

"Why are they cheering?" Jason mumbled to her.

"I have no idea," Kira said, remembering what her mother had "suggested" she and Jason do to cause maximum distress to Prince Maxim. "Jason, we ought to…um…uh…blast it, just kiss me!"

"Now?"

"Now!"

They kissed, Kira trying not to flinch as a loud chorus of whoops sounded from many of those watching. "I'm going to die, Jason. Any minute now."

"Is that the jewelry stall we're supposed to notice and decide to visit?"

"Oh, blazes, not the jewelry stall."

Pretending to spot the stall and urge each other toward it, they walked that way, pausing to look over the rings, bracelets, and earrings on display. Kira realized that the watching crowd had grown silent with anticipation. Like any other girl, she had imagined the first time she went with someone to get jewelry. This wasn't how she had always dreamed that moment would be like.

"This would look good on you," Kira said, touching a ring with a bright blue stone in it. She picked it up, nerving herself, and took Jason's hand so she could slip the ring onto it.

The cheers and applause that filled the street startled her so much that she barely noticed Jason picking up a pin with an enameled dragon on it. "A red dragon. That's appropriate, right? For a dragon slayer?"

He tried to pin it on her, fumbling so badly with discomfort that Kira worried about the sharp pin sticking her. "Jason, I don't want to get blood on this nice shirt." She helped him fasten it, losing herself for a moment in the task, for just that instant getting a romantic vibe from the experience. But that vanished as a new round of cheers erupted and Kira wished the street would open up and swallow her.

Queen Sien had made a discreet offer to give them the money for the jewelry, but Kira was determined that her first purchase like that would be real even if the event was staged. The customary haggling over the cost didn't feel right, though, so Kira just offered the owner of the stand what she hoped was a fair price.

Having insisted that he would pay as well, Jason brought out some of the money he had earned in Danalee from tutoring students in math, offering the coins with pride that was, Kira thought, endearingly awkward rather than self-assured.

"We have to kiss each other again," she muttered to Jason.

It felt uncomfortable and forced, but none of the onlookers appeared to be disappointed.

"Can we go back to the palace?" Jason whispered.

"Yes. Please. Yes."

"You owe me!" Kira yelled as she stomped into the suite her parents occupied. "For the rest of my life! Which may not be that long, because I want to die!"

"All right, dearest," her mother said. She was seated at the desk. "You can take off that pin now."

"No! Jason bought it for me!" Kira paced back and forth. "Do you have any idea what that was like?"

"It could have been worse." Mari dropped a slim dagger onto the desk.

Kira paused in her pacing, walking over to examine it. "Is that poison on the blade?"

"That is poison on the blade. The owner of the blade was stopped as he worked his way through the crowd toward you two." Her mother dropped a small, concealable hand crossbow next to the dagger. "The bolt loaded onto this is also poisoned." She added a pistol. "No poison here, but the owner was in the act of aiming at Jason when she was taken down."

"That's everything?" Kira asked, puzzled.

"Pretty much. Two Mages tried to use invisibility spells to get through the crowd."

"I didn't sense them."

"They got stopped before they got anywhere near you. Both had those long Mage knives like your father carries."

Kira sat down on the bed. "Why is part of me saying, 'Is that all there is'?"

"Because it's not much. It's a pathetic level of effort to kill Jason. The Imperials must have known he'd have tight security around him. Why didn't they try harder?" Her mother pushed aside the pistol. "Not a single rifle. A sniper is an obvious threat. We were watching for multiple snipers. There weren't any. And no Mages capable of sending fire or lightning."

"Maybe they just weren't ready," Kira said. "We caught them off guard. Oh, stars above, will Jason and I have to do that again?"

Mari shook her head. "Whatever else you can say about the Imperials, they are not that sloppy. They should have done a better job. These attempts look like a feint, designed to throw us off or maybe make us complacent. We'll see what happens at the big diplomatic reception and dinner tonight. There will be delegations from all the embassies in Tiaesun, as well as a lot of notables from Tiae and Tiae's military, but also officers and officials from all the Imperial ships as well as from the Imperial embassy. Make sure Jason knows to keep his guard up."

"Yes, Mother. I know you and Father are concerned about Jason having a concealed knife tonight, but I really think Jason can be trusted with it. Aunt Bev has been teaching him how to use a knife. And he *ought* to have it if he's being used as bait."

Her mother frowned in thought, then nodded. "You're right."

Kira walked down the hallway beside Jason, her mother and father walking a short distance in front of them. Kira felt on display again, the unfamiliar weight and pressure of the thigh holster under her dress adding to her discomfort. At times like this her close resemblance to how her mother had looked at her age once again became a source of anxiety.

Her father was wearing his best Mage robes, of course. Jason was in a nice suit, looking to Kira's eyes like a dashing hero. The suit coat did a perfect job of hiding the knife in a sheath under Jason's arm. Kira and her mother were decked out in matching sleeveless dresses, draped over one shoulder and caught at the waist with jeweled belts which Sien had pressed upon them. Angled hems fell to the ankle on one side before rising to knee-length on the other. Discreet slits on the outer seams of the skirts seemed designed as wide pockets but were primarily to give easy access to the thigh holsters. Open sandals laced up to their calves completed the ensemble. Judging from the way Jason had stared when he'd first seen her in it, Kira looked pretty good in the outfit.

"Like a Greek goddess," Jason had whispered in awed tones.

"What's a Greek goddess?"

"Someone really special. I guess you'd be Athena."

"I'm Kira, Jason. They haven't taken that name away from me yet."

She didn't dress up very often, but it had felt good to see Jason's reaction. Now, with men of all ages gawking at her, Kira felt more self-conscious than beautiful.

"Lady Master Mechanic Mari of Dematr, the daughter of Jules. Sir Master of Mages Alain of Ihris. Lady Kira of Dematr. Jason of Urth." The functionary making the announcement of their entry had a nice voice that rang clearly across the great hall where the reception was taking place.

It was the first time she had heard herself called Kira of Dematr, and from the looks she was getting the name had surprised more than a few people.

"Don't leave my side," Kira whispered to Jason.

Like the streets of Tiaesun, the Great Hall in Queen Sien's palace had been almost perfectly restored except for places where the damage caused by the decades of anarchy had been left intact as a remembrance and a warning. The high ceiling was painted to mimic a night sky, golden stars shimmering as they reflected the light from chandeliers. The pillars supporting the ceilings were tinted to look like the trunks of huge trees, while the walls were white, aside from sections still marred by old scorch marks from fires, and where clever paintings in arched alcoves along the walls looked like doorways into real outdoor scenes set around the Kingdom of Tiae. "Trompe l'oeil," Jason said when he saw them.

"They're called eye tricks," Kira corrected him.

"That's what tromp l'oeil means."

"Then why didn't you just say eye trick instead of tromploy?"

"Because it sounds cooler in French," Jason said.

The hall was a riot of color, military uniforms from every country on Dematr standing out in shades of Imperial dark red, the Confederation's scarlet, the green and gold of Tiae, the various shades of blue from the Free Cities, the black and green of the Western Alliance, and the dusky purple of Syndar. The suits and dresses of the others present ran the gamut from white to black and every shade in between.

Kira stayed glued to her mother and father as they wandered through the hall chatting briefly with assorted diplomats, rulers, military officers and officials. Kira admired the way her parents without being obvious about it stayed clear of the white suits and dark red uniforms that marked groups of Imperials. As usual, Mari and Alain were the center of attention. The white shock through Mari's raven hair—what everyone called her Mage Mark, since it had appeared after Alain revived her at Dorcastle—drew gazes as it always did. But many eyes went to Kira and lingered as well. "I can't believe that I once wanted people to notice me," she said to Jason in a low voice.

"At least you belong here," Jason grumbled in reply.

"Why don't you belong here?" Kira asked.

"You're the daughter of Mari and Alain, and you've done some pretty great things, and I'm…not much."

"Jason, I am proud to be walking with you! Mother! Does Jason belong with us?"

Mari looked back for a moment and smiled. "Absolutely."

"See? You can't dispute the judgment of the daughter of Jules, you know. That would get you in all kinds of trouble."

"Kira…" Jason shrugged. "I can't help it. I keep thinking that any day now I'm going to wake up and find out I overdosed on some drug or something and have been hallucinating back on Earth. You're too wonderful."

Kira almost rolled her eyes in self-derision at that, but remembered in time how many people were watching them.

"What have I done to deserve any of this?" Jason continued.

"Saved millions, maybe billions of lives? Risked your own life doing that? Does that ring any bells?"

Jason shook his head. "I'll never really be one of your family. I don't belong."

Kira frowned, then gripped Jason's face firmly with both hands, gazing into his eyes. "Jason, are you saying that if I decided to propose to you that you'd turn me down?"

"No. But—"

"Because if you are sure that you'd never want to promise yourself to me just tell me so I can fall apart and then start trying to put myself back together again. I'm sorry I don't know for certain yet. But I do know that my misgivings have nothing to do with you and everything to do with me. And I know that I have never liked any boy as much as I like you. Not even close."

Jason finally smiled. "Okay."

Doctor Sino arrived at precisely the right moment. "Jason! How is my favorite patient?" she asked.

"Okay," Jason repeated, grinning. "How's life on an alien world?"

"So much fun," Sino said. "Making such a difference. The luckiest day of my life was when I got marooned along with you. Did you hear they told me to stop providing medical care?"

"Who did?" Kira asked.

"Earth. Over the Feynman transmitter. They said I am corrupting your planet's unique culture with disruptive technology."

"You're not listening to them, are you?"

"No," Sino said, grinning and shaking her head. "It's my job to save lives and help people. You should have heard what Earth said when they learned I'd been stranded with my med kit! I'm afraid someone is going to be in a lot of trouble when she gets back to Earth."

"Thanks for not saying my mother's name," Jason said.

"And thank you for what you did for my mother," Kira added. "It means so much to her and Father."

"I'm a doctor," Sino said, waving away the thanks. "Have you seen my horse? I've got a horse! I named her Twilight, because she's really smart. For a horse. Oh, there's Queen Sien. I have to talk to her. Excuse me!"

Kira, smiling, watched Sino walk away quickly, but her good humor faded as someone else spoke her name in rigidly formal tones.

"Lady Kira."

She turned to see an Imperial standing close by. He was a legionary, resplendent in the dark red uniform of the legions, a ceremonial short sword at his side. In his hand was an envelope sealed with golden wax.

"I have the honor of delivering this to you, Lady," the legionary said.

Kira's parents had turned. Her father spoke, his voice lacking all emotion as Mages had once been taught to speak, and sounding all the more intimidating for that. "Kira is underage. If that is an official communication, it should have come to Lady Mari. If it is personal, it should have come to her parents."

The legionary nodded, his face impassive. "I was ordered to deliver it directly to the hands of Lady Kira, sir."

"I don't want him punished for not doing as ordered," Kira said. She reached, took the envelope from the legionary, then immediately passed it to her mother.

"Thank you, Lady," the legionary said. He saluted Kira, then turned and vanished back into the crowd.

"That was a nice compromise, Kira," Mari said as she opened the envelope. "Maybe you will be able to take over my job someday and I can retire."

"Don't even joke about that, Mother."

"Hmmm. This is an invitation to a private meeting with Prince Maxim."

Kira shuddered at the idea. "No."

"Just you and him." Her mother passed the letter to Kira's father. "You'd have your pistol with you."

"No."

Alain folded up the letter and put it away in an inside pocket of his Mage robes. "Then you will not need this."

They reached Queen Sien, dressed in full cavalry uniform but wearing the formal crown of Tiae rather than a helm, who greeted them all warmly. Kira only nodded in reply, emotions warring within her, then defiantly saluted just as if she were still a Lancer and wearing the uniform.

Sien returned the salute gravely. "Thank you for coming, Lady Kira of Dematr. And for bringing Jason of Urth, who has done much for a world not his own."

"This is his world now, Your Majesty," Kira said. "He…doesn't belong anymore in the place that was once his."

"I hope he, and anyone else who feels so lost, realizes they will always have a home wherever their heart lies," Sien said. "A home where they will always be welcome."

Once through the line, her parents stopping to talk to some high officers in Tiae's army, Kira darted away, hauling Jason toward the bathrooms. "I need them even if you don't."

"I need them," Jason said.

It wasn't until Kira was inside the women's bath that she realized in her distress over the encounter with Sien she had not only walked away from her parents but also separated herself from Jason. She didn't even know if any bodyguards had followed them. Kira saw two women in stylish Imperial gowns looking at her and whispering to each other as she turned around and left.

Jason wasn't visible outside yet, so Kira went toward a refreshment table that was set near the door to wait for him.

Turning again with drink in hand, she froze, staring into the crowd. A young woman was just turning away, but Kira had the odd feeling that she resembled Kira herself so much that it was almost like looking into a mirror. Her hair and clothes were different, but the face had seemed eerily similar in the brief glimpse Kira had. She started to move away from the table, determined to catch that other girl and get a good look at her.

But before Kira could take more than one step she found herself confronting a semicircle of Imperial officers and officials who rapidly formed a solid barrier, penning Kira in next to the table. She stared at their impassive faces as her stomach knotted, her hand tightening on the glass she was holding.

CHAPTER THREE

What are you doing?" Kira said. "Let me by." Were the Imperials insane, pulling such a stunt in a room full of other people?

Instead of replying, the wall of Imperials turned their backs. Kira found herself facing a man in his late twenties in a legionary field marshal's uniform glittering with gold, silver, and jeweled medals. His smile was supposed to be winning but to Kira appeared arrogant and smug. "You have the honor to make the acquaintance of Prince Maxim, Crown Prince and heir to the throne of the Empire of Maran," he announced.

"So?" Kira said, her voice and expression both flat and unimpressed.

Maxim dropped his smile. "I had been told that you were schooled in court etiquette. Apparently I was misinformed."

"Apparently," Kira said, refusing to yield in the slightest.

"That can be remedied," Maxim said. "Once you are at the Imperial Court."

"I can't imagine anything I would want less."

"I will instruct you personally."

"I'd like to see you try," Kira said, mentally measuring the distance to Maxim's neck. Could she deliver a disabling blow with her free hand without leaving the side of the table? This dress wasn't suited for high kicks. "Excuse me?"

"I said," Maxim repeated in the manner of someone trying to control his temper, "that it is the wish of all the people of this world that our houses be joined to ensure peace."

"Oh, wow," Kira said. "Sorry. I'm actually really interested in a guy who came from another world."

"You are very confident of yourself, aren't you? Perhaps that is misplaced," Maxim said. "I am not to be taken lightly."

"See this scar?" Kira asked, pointing near her bare shoulder. "That came from a dragon's claw. While I was killing the dragon. Why would I be intimidated by *you*?"

Further conversation was halted as a wedge of officers from the Tiae army and fleet physically forced their way through the protective ring of Imperials, Kira's parents walking through the gap that had been opened. Kira saw the thundercloud riding on Mari's brow and smiled at Maxim.

"What is the meaning of this?" Mari demanded.

"I am simply attempting to make polite conversation," Maxim said.

"Then I suggest that you seek out other sources of conversation. Immediately," Mari snapped. "There had better not be a repetition of this kind of thing."

"You forget to whom you speak," Maxim said, glowering.

"I know exactly who I'm talking to," Mari said. "This isn't Imperial territory. A wise leader would know better than to try throwing his weight around when he's a guest in someone else's country. Kira?"

Kira followed her mother, getting the uncomfortable feeling that Maxim's gaze on her back was like that of someone aiming a weapon.

Jason joined them, looking anxious. "I tried to get through to you but some guys blocked me."

"You left Jason alone?" Mari demanded.

"I couldn't go into the bathroom with him!" Kira protested. "I didn't think—" She stopped herself, feeling awful. "I didn't think. I'm sorry, Jason."

"What did Maxim try?" her mother asked.

"I guess he thought I'd be impressed by meeting him. I'm pretty sure he could tell I wasn't."

Her mother laughed. "I've been the object of that treatment from you enough to imagine what went on. You burned him?"

"Like a welding torch," Kira said. "It's what I do to obnoxious men."

"I remember," Jason said.

"Oh, you got off lightly," Kira said. "I'm sorry, Mother. And I'm sorry again to you as well, Jason. I got so absorbed in my own…"

"Drama?" Mari suggested.

"Whatever. I promise I will be more careful."

A bell sounded, calling those invited to a special dinner. Kira held onto Jason as she followed her parents toward the large room where a long table was set, but as the line paused outside she suddenly remembered her brief glimpse of that other girl. "Jason, have you seen anybody else here who looks like me?"

"What?"

"Another girl who looks a lot like me. Not the same hair or dress, but about the same size and face."

"Ummm, no. Seriously?"

She gave him an aggravated look. "Seriously. It was almost like I saw myself in a mirror. I was going to catch her and take another look but then the Imperials blocked me and the whole Maxim thing drove it out of my mind until just now. You haven't seen her?"

"Someone who looks just like you?" Jason looked around. "I haven't seen anyone like that. Are you sure you it wasn't your mom?"

"Jason, I'd know if I saw my mother. This was a girl who looked about my age. But I'm sure I was mistaken. I mean, what are the odds?"

He grinned. "Maybe you saw a doppelganger."

"Maybe I saw a what?"

"It's a mythological creature, or a ghost thing," Jason explained. "Something that takes on your exact appearance and tries to replace you. Not an actual twin, but looks like it could be one."

"They have those on Urth?" Kira asked.

"No. Like I said, it's just a myth, though I guess sometimes people say that someone else who looks like them is sort of a doppelganger."

He paused, the smile replaced by a serious look. "You ought to mention it to your parents, though."

"Why?"

"Because you said you would?" Jason suggested. "Anything unusual?"

"All right," Kira said, putting on her best long-suffering expression. "I'll tell them. But if I worried about as many things as the people around me did I'd spend my life hiding under my bed!"

Once inside the banquet room, Kira searched for her place card. "Where's my place?" she asked, puzzled that it wasn't near her parents.

"Someone has moved the place cards," Sien said in a low voice that made it clear she was not amused.

"Here, Lady Kira," an Imperial official called from where she stood behind a chair at one end of the table.

Kira went there, finding her place card at one of the two seats on the end. The seat next to her was…Prince Maxim's.

She looked at her mother and father, seeing them signaling to play along for now.

Maxim took his place beside Kira, pausing to run his eyes over her. As happy as she had been when first putting on the new dress, Kira now wished that she was wearing trousers and a loose, long-sleeved shirt instead.

Partway down the table, Kira saw Jason standing uncomfortably between two Imperial women, one tall and thin in an elegant gown, and the other shorter but with a body that looked like a teenage boy's dream and a dress that showed off every curve and a lot of cleavage.

Kira was about to do something when Queen Sien paused on her way to the other end of the table, firmly taking Jason's arm to steer him along with her while directing a Tiae official to sit in that spot. The official was an old man from the House of the People's Senate, who beamed at his new dining companions.

Sien stopped at the other end of the table, directing Jason to sit beside her. "Tiae welcomes our visitors, in the hopes that the Peace of the Daughter will continue to bring prosperity and happiness to the world of Dematr." She sat down, everyone else doing the same.

"I had expected Tiaesun to be more impressive," Maxim remarked to Kira as if they had just met for the first time. "You will find Palandur to be greater in all respects."

"I'm not going to Palandur," Kira said, trying to keep her voice pleasant. Someone Kira recognized as one of Queen Sien's aides came by and without saying anything collected Kira's silverware, plates, and glasses, replacing them with fresh ones. She noticed the servers bringing the food to her, her parents, and Jason were men and women who had served as bodyguards. So were the stewards pouring her wine and water. At least she didn't have to worry about her food being tampered with.

It was a shame that the Imperials were here. Being dressed up, having a stylish dinner in the royal court, having Jason along, this could have been a lot of fun.

"I understand you have some instruction in the Mechanic arts," Maxim said.

"Yes," Kira replied, surprised that Maxim had shown any interest in her as a person. "In a variety of areas, including steam propulsion and electronics."

"I myself," Maxim continued as if Kira hadn't spoken, "have among my lesser titles that of Master Mechanic, having been personally instructed by none other than the Grand Master of the Mechanics Guild."

She barely refrained from rolling her eyes at him, thinking that Maxim's actual Mechanic knowledge was probably minimal. Of course he had been given the title Master Mechanic by the Grand Master of the Mechanics Guild, who had once ruled the world but was now reduced to tutoring imperial princes and princesses and handing out titles of skill to bolster royal egos. She would have to share that one with her mother.

Kira looked down the length of the table at Queen Sien, who was speaking to Jason. Sien's court was already well known for her sponsorship of scholars and the size of the library she was rebuilding from quite literally the ashes of the old Royal Library. The excesses of the

Imperial court were impossible to imagine in Tiae because Sien was determined to establish precedents that would prevent her kingdom from ever again suffering the decades of anarchy she had barely survived as a young girl. The contrast with Maxim couldn't be clearer.

Which made it all the harder to realize that Sien was not her queen, never really had been, and that Kira did not belong in Tiae any more than she belonged anywhere else. That felt far too much like not belonging anywhere.

"The Empire is the most advanced center of the Mechanic arts in the world," Maxim said.

Kira, still brooding over her new name, wasn't in any mood to play nice to Maxim's boasting. She gave him a regretful look. "I heard about the big industrial accident at Beldan. I hope the Empire has made some progress at cleaning that up. It's a shame someone tried to cut corners on the safety measures required for that level of technological manufacture."

Maxim didn't answer, giving Kira time to eat.

"You will enjoy Palandur," he finally said.

Did Maxim hear nothing except what he wanted to hear? "My parents have been to Palandur," Kira said. "They prefer Tiaesun. They've also been to Marandur," she added in an attempt to needle him. The once-forbidden city had been opened to the world, but Kira knew her mother and father's trips into and out of Marandur remained a sore spot for Imperial pride.

"There is little worth seeing in Marandur," Maxim said, frowning. "The sub-humans who once nested there have been cleaned out."

Kira's hand stopped partway to bringing her fork to her mouth. Sub-humans. That's what Maxim was calling the descendents of those men and women unfortunate enough to have been trapped in the ruined city when it was sealed off, people who under the extreme conditions of deprivation had over generations fallen into the lowest level of barbarism. Her mother and father had been hunted by those people, but they had never spoken of them as "sub-human."

She set down her fork, her temper rising. "I understand the carvings on Maran's tomb are of great interest," Kira said. "My mother found them well worth seeing."

A pool of silence spread along the table. Kira saw the Imperials either staring at her or making every effort not to stare at her. Her mother had heard and was giving Kira a look of disbelief.

The rumor still existed among the Imperials that Mari had visited that tomb during her trips to Marandur because she actually was Mara, the Dark One, and had wanted to compare her present looks to the carvings showing her beauty centuries before when Maran had ruled the Empire. The fact that Kira's mother didn't consider herself beautiful, and had nothing in common with the vain vampire of legend, only made Mari more upset at the supposed connection.

Her mother was going to have some words with her, Kira knew, but at least her comment had silenced Maxim again.

But not for long. "Your mother confessed to the world that she has no real link to the first consort Mara. That was part of the treaty ending the last conflict," Maxim added as if saying something she should have known.

And she had known. Kira shook her head. "Mother agreed not to discuss the matter publicly any more as part of the treaty." She lowered her voice to a loud whisper. "There's a difference."

From her mother's expression she was going to really catch it tonight.

But at the other end of table, where someone was whispering what was probably an account of the conversation to Queen Sien, the queen was smiling at her.

The meal finally over, wine glasses all filled for ceremonial toasts, Prince Maxim stood. "To the emperor."

The other Imperials stood and raised their glasses.

The rest of those at the table raised their glasses politely as well, but remained sitting.

The old man who was the leader of Tiae's House of the People's Senate stood as the Imperials sat down. "To the queen of Tiae!"

This time everyone but the Imperials stood up.

Maxim stood again. "To those who have died for the emperor at home and on foreign shores."

Kira hadn't been to a lot of state dinners, but she had been to enough to know how tactless and provocative that toast was. The toast, clearly phrased to include those legionaries who had died trying to capture Dorcastle, was almost a slap at Kira's mother and father.

The Imperials stood again to raise their glasses, but Sien kept her glass on the table and everyone else followed her example.

The old man rose again as the Imperials sat. He no longer looked happy at the dining companions he had ended up with, instead giving Maxim a glare. "To those like my niece who died defending Dorcastle and the west, who helped overthrow the Great Guilds and free this world from tyranny!"

The Imperials stayed in their seats as Sien rose to lead the toast.

Kira waited, wondering who would fire the next shot in what had turned into a duel between the Imperials and the rest of those present.

Sien did, staying standing and extending her glass toward Mari. "To the daughter, who has sacrificed so much for us all, and who held the last wall."

This time the toast was accompanied by shouts of approval from those from Tiae, the Bakre Confederation, and elsewhere in the west. Kira saw her mother looking down, uncomfortable with the praise and the attention, as Kira herself smiled at her and drank the toast.

Maxim gave Mari a hard look, shoving his glass away. "It is ill manners to mock the sacrifice of Imperial soldiers."

Mari looked back him, her own expression unyielding. "You. Weren't. There."

The three words silenced the room again.

"If I had been," Maxim finally said, "things would have turned out differently."

Kira could see her mother was about to explode. It wasn't about her, Kira knew, but rather about those who had died fighting alongside her. No one spoke a critical word of them or minimized their sacrifice in her mother's hearing.

But if her mother unleashed on Maxim, it would look bad. The daughter was supposed to be neutral. Someone would have to intervene.

Kira broke the tense silence by sighing so heavily it drew everyone's attention. "I suppose that someone could have asked the Imperial commanders about what they might have done differently, but they left Dorcastle so quickly that no one had the chance to catch them before they departed."

This time the Imperials sat as if turned to stone, but slow smiles appeared on the faces of the others present. Kira could almost feel the rage radiating from Prince Maxim, whose father had been the highest of those commanders.

Queen Sien stood up, her expression showing nothing but her eyes revealing anger as she looked at Maxim. "Tiae thanks those of the Empire who have visited this land, and wishes them a safe voyage home, as well as the wisdom to avoid repeating the mistakes of the past." She walked away from the table, signaling that the meal was over.

Kira got up and went quickly to her mother. "I'm sorry," she whispered.

Mari shook her head at Kira, then unexpectedly smiled. "We're supposed to prevent wars, Kira, not feed the flames. But you nailed him good."

"You're not mad about me mentioning..."

"You got in some good jabs," her mother said. "It's all right. By now I ought to be used to jokes about that conceited blood sucker. Though you'd think anyone who had seen me wouldn't confuse me with someone supposedly beautiful beyond compare."

"Father thinks you're beautiful beyond compare," Kira pointed out. "But remember, you and I are *exotic*."

"Oh, yes. I'd forgotten. You're still giving Jason a hard time about that? Let's collect him and your father and find Sien."

"Mother..." Kira looked down, biting her lip. "Is it all right if Jason and I go back to our rooms?"

Mari gazed at her sympathetically, touching her cheek with one hand. "It really hit you hard. I'm sorry. Sien cares for you a lot, Kira. I hope you can be comfortable with her again."

"I just need a little more time," Kira said. "And I really want to get out of this dress."

"You look lovely in it!" Mari looked around. "But I understand. You know how it was for Mage Asha when she was your age. All the wrong kinds of attention, and if she took notice of it she was told it was her fault. Go ahead and take a break from the eyes of the public. But make sure you and Jason don't run away from your bodyguards this time."

"I won't! Thank you, Mother." Kira paused and smiled. "I love you."

"Even though I made Jason a target?" Her mother scanned the crowd again. "Be careful. The imperials just tried to provoke us. There must have been a reason."

"Jason and I are going back to our rooms where we will be safe," Kira promised. "And since the bodyguards in the hallway will be watching us, you don't have to worry about either of us deciding to visit the other's room."

"Dearest, if you think I don't trust you to make the right decisions about that, you still don't know me very well."

Kira hesitated, looking around to ensure that no one was close enough to hear her. They were close to a wall, those passing them by leaving a courteous distance for Mari's privacy. Something about the dinner tonight, about Prince Maxim's pressure on her, had rattled her. Especially coming on top of the threats against Jason. "Mother, I know you married Father when you did because you two literally didn't know if you'd survive the next day. And I know you waited until then to sleep together."

"We had slept together many times," her mother said. "But that was all we did before then. Sleep. And talk."

"What if you'd waited and Father had died? Before you were married? Would you have always regretted that?"

Mari gazed back at her, solemn, her eyes sad in that way they often got when she thought about the past. "Regretted it? Kira, if your father had died I would've regretted losing him for all my life. He truly is the man I was meant for, which I don't think is fair to him, given what I can be like. Would I have regretted never having known him physically? Oh, yes. Stars above, yes. But that would have been only part of the regret, and a small part, for not having him with me."

Her mother looked down, running one hand through her hair. "Even after we were married, we knew we couldn't risk having a child. Not with so many trying to kill us, not with the war looming and then all around us. Your father or I could've died before you were conceived. You know what happened at Dorcastle. The idea of a world that never had you in it seems incredibly sad to me. But it could have happened. Many things could have happened. Don't make that decision based on fears. Or on hopes. It will be right when it feels right to you. Don't force it. Don't let anyone make you think you have to force it. You told me Jason isn't trying to do that."

"He's not. It's not that he's perfect or anything…I mean, he's really great…but Jason knows me well enough to know that if he pushed me I wouldn't give in. I'd push back."

"That's my girl." Mari smiled at her. "Trust yourself to know when the time is right and the person is right. Sleep well."

Kira and Jason made their way through the still-crowded main hall, Kira ensuring that she could see the bodyguards pacing them through the crowd. She breathed a sigh of relief when they left the hall. She knew that some people hoped that she would someday take over for her mother. And then she would face this kind of thing over and over again for the rest of her life. Kira wasn't sure she had the endurance for that. She was certain that she didn't have the wisdom for it.

At the door to her room she paused to smile at Jason. "Thanks for being there for me tonight."

"You had to sit next to that jerk," Jason said.

"And you got to sit next to Queen Sien," Kira said.

"She asked me how you were taking things and I told her you were sad."

"Oh, Jason! You shouldn't have told her!"

"Queen Sien said she already knew," Jason said. "So I didn't really tell her."

"All right," Kira said, too tired to fight about it. She leaned close and kissed him, trying not to think about the guards at each end of the hallway who were watching.

Jason smiled at her as he turned partway toward his room. "Uh, Kira? Are you ever going to wear that dress again?"

"I don't know. Why?"

"You look really good in it."

"Thanks," Kira said. "You're the man I wanted to know felt that way. All the others…not so much. I'm really lucky to have you in my life."

He smiled again. "I'd do anything for you."

"I know." She remembered him saving her life during a storm, and how he had looked when they talked about Prince Maxim. "Jason, there's a rule in our family that I haven't told you. You're not allowed to die for me. Even if it's the only way to save me."

He didn't answer.

"Jason, do you understand? I don't want you to die trying to save me."

"I heard you." His eyes met hers. "You already know my answer. I gave you that answer back on *The Son of Taris* during that storm."

She couldn't help smiling at him. "Father never listened to Mother about that, either. Jason, please be careful. For me."

"I will."

She went inside, closing and locking the door. The room had a single window, which was closed. Kira peeled off the dress, letting out a breath of relief, and then unstrapped the thigh holster, wondering what Jason would have said if he could have seen her wearing it.

Jason…

Kira flinched as her reverie was interrupted by a memory from this evening. She had promised Jason that she would tell her parents about the doppelganger thing. It was silly, but she had promised, and by morning she might have forgotten. Jason probably would have forgotten as well, but that was all the more reason to make sure she honored her promise. Kira had decided some time ago, probably because of the people willing to cut her too much slack because of who her mother was, that promises kept only because you didn't want to be caught breaking them weren't really anything to be proud of.

Kira groaned, not wanting to get back into the dress and have to parade in front of spectators again. Maybe it was late enough that she could get away with her usual clothes. She got dressed, feeling better to be in jeans, the nice shirt, and her boots. Remembering the behavior of the Imperials, she also took the time to put on her shoulder holster and put her pistol in it, then put on her jacket over it.

She paused, wondering why her Mage sense was suddenly active again. What had triggered that?

Kira went to the window, looking out cautiously.

A hand came around from behind her, clasping a wet cloth over her face. Startled, Kira inhaled without thinking.

Her mind fell into a black, bottomless pit.

Mari bolted awake as someone pounded on the door. She had her pistol in her hand as she called out a reply. "Yes?"

"Lady Mari," someone called through the door, "my apologies, but I was told to inform you that Lady Kira has left the palace."

Mari was on her feet as Alain also got out of bed, both of them rushing to the door. Mari took only enough time to ensure her bedclothes covered her decently before pulling the door open.

A major stood there, his face rigid with worry at having woken her. "Kira left the palace?" Mari asked, trying to avoid letting fear into her voice.

"Yes, Lady. Less than ten minutes ago, just before dawn. She asked the guards at the door she left by to, uh, 'not bother anyone,' but they informed the guard supervisor who informed me."

"They did well," Alain said. "Kira gave no indication of why she was leaving the palace?"

"No, Sir Mage. The guards said she appeared to be cheerful."

"Cheerful." Mari ran to the door to Kira's room and pulled it open. The bed was empty. She searched the room hastily. "Alain, I checked when we got back from the reception and Kira was in this bed. I didn't disturb her. There isn't any note. Why would Kira leave at this time of the day and not leave us a note?"

"Jason," Alain said.

"Make sure he's still here," Mari said.

She and the major searched Kira's room more thoroughly while waiting, still finding no clue to Kira's departure.

"Jason is here," Alain said, indicating the boy in hastily pulled on clothes who stood nervously by his side. "The guards at either end of the hall saw Kira leave her room a little while ago. She went past one pair of guards, saying she was just going to walk to the nearest east-facing window to watch the sun rise."

"The guards still should have notified someone," the major said, his tone promising harsh words later for those guards.

"Something happened to Kira?" Jason asked, his voice cracking with worry.

"She left the palace less than twenty minutes ago," Mari told him. "There isn't any note. Alain, her pistol is gone. Jason, did Kira say anything about leaving the palace? I don't care if she swore you to silence. Tell us."

"Kira didn't say anything about that! She didn't do anything to make me think she was planning to do that!"

Mari glanced at Alain, who nodded to show that Jason was telling the truth. Not that she had needed that confirmation. Jason was obviously upset.

Queen Sien arrived, trailed by two aides. "Kira has left?"

"Yes. But it doesn't make any sense. She didn't tell me, or her father, or Jason, anything. She didn't leave a note. Kira is not so irresponsible that she would just wander off into the city without telling someone first. She knows how dangerous it is. Something is wrong."

"I agree," Sien said. She turned to one of the aides. "Notify all police and military forces inside Tiaesun that they are to search for and find Lady Kira of Dematr. Get Colonel Jolu up here with a far-talker."

"Immediately, Your Majesty."

As the aide ran off, Sien looked at Jason. "Did you quarrel?"

"No!" Jason protested. "We…we kissed goodnight, and Kira smiled and told me she was glad I'd been there because the dinner and all had been sort of stressful, and…and…uh…"

"Say it," Mari ordered.

"Kira said she was…lucky to have me in her life. And…"

"What?"

"She tried to make me promise not ever to die trying to save her," Jason said, looking miserable. "I wouldn't. Then she closed the door and I went to my room."

"Why would she—?" Queen Sien began.

"It is a family thing," Alain said. "I would not make such a promise to Mari, either. But it could mean that Kira had a foreboding of danger, one she was perhaps not consciously aware of."

"That would make her departure alone even less understandable! I was notified that Prince Maxim's ships left at about midnight. Is that correct?" Sien asked the major.

"Yes, Your Majesty. I can get the exact time."

"But you are certain it was several hours before Lady Kira left the palace?"

"Yes, Your Majesty. I spoke with the late watch when I came on duty, and they reported that the Imperial ships had cleared the harbor and steamed out of sight within the hour of leaving their pier. They were last seen headed northwest."

Colonel Jolu arrived at a run, trailed by two soldiers. "These are the sentries who saw her leave the palace."

Queen Sien turned her eyes on the two, who quailed but stood at attention. "Why did you not stop Lady Kira from leaving?"

"Your Majesty," one of the sentries said, "our standing orders are not to hinder the movements of Lady Mari or any of her family."

"Those are their orders," the colonel confirmed. "There was no expectation that, uh…"

"I understand," Mari told him, trying to remain calm. "Are you certain that it was Kira?" she asked the sentries.

"Yes, Lady," the second answered. "We were on duty yesterday when she and her young man came back. We saw her and heard her then. The girl who left looked like her and sounded like her. She was also dressed the same as yesterday."

"This makes no sense," Sien said. "Kira is not an irresponsible child."

The colonel listened intently to a call on his far-talker. "What's that? The east gate?" He looked at Sien. "Lady Kira left by the east gate of the city several minutes before they received word to stop her. They can still see her."

"Stop her now," Sien ordered. "Tell them to follow and bring her back."

"Yes, Your Majesty." Colonel Jolu passed on the orders, frowning at the response. "Are you certain? Wait." He looked at his queen again, visibly nervous. "Your Majesty, the guards at the east gate report that just outside the gate a Mage was waiting with a Roc. As I was ordering them to pursue Lady Kira, they saw her climb onto the Roc. It has taken flight."

Mari stared at the colonel in disbelief. "She's flying off on a Roc? Alain!"

Her husband shook her head, his expression unusually grim. "I will check with all other Mages in the city."

"The Roc is headed straight east," the colonel added. "The guards will lose sight of it soon. What is that?" he added, listening. "You're certain that she said that? Stand by." The colonel shook his head at Mari. "Lady, as your daughter left the city, she told the guards at the gate that she was going to Palandur. They say she smiled as she said that."

"*Palandur?*"

"This cannot be right," Alain said. Mari barely heard him through the distress filling her mind. "Kira would not have done such a thing."

"Alain," Queen Sien said, "is there any possible way a Mage could have altered Kira's mind? Put some spell upon her that caused her to do this?"

"It is impossible," Alain replied. "No Mage has surpassed me in being able to directly affect another person, but nothing I can do can cause any change in the mind of another or bend their will."

"Drugs?" Sien asked herself. "No. We ate from the same trays as Kira, drank from the same pitchers and bottles. Did Lady Kira look in any way impaired?" she demanded of the sentries.

"No, Your Majesty. She looked bright and alert. I commented on it, saying I wished I felt that good, and Lady Kira laughed."

"Why would she have left me?" Jason asked, bewildered. "Am I really just dead weight to her?"

By an effort of sheer will, Mari yanked herself out of her own fears. Others needed her, not least Kira, but including those here. "Jason, whatever has happened, that was not the reason. Whenever Kira has talked about you to me she always speaks of the things you did, how much you contributed, and how you saved her life during that storm."

"Could someone have threatened Jason?" Sien asked. "Done so in such a way that Kira thought only by doing this could she ensure his safety?"

"I can't believe that she'd do that," Mari said. "Why wouldn't she have left a note if that was the case? If Jason was in that much danger, Kira would have let us know. The Imperials have to be behind this somehow. But how?"

"There was that time last night when I was away from her," Jason volunteered with a miserable expression.

"When Prince Maxim talked to her? But she said nothing to indicate that Maxim had said anything to sway her." Mari turned to Sien. "She has to be on one of those ships. Or Maxim must know something. Even if the Imperial ships are swinging wide of the coast and moving fast, one of your ships out of Minut would have a chance at intercepting them."

Sien gazed at her for a moment before answering. "Lady Mari, Sir Mage Alain, let us enter your room and discuss this. The rest of you wait out here."

Mari paused, seeing the look on Jason's face. "Queen Sien, may Jason of Urth come inside with us?"

Sien looked Jason over, then nodded. "Jason of Urth as well."

It wasn't until the door was closed behind the four of them that Sien spoke in a low voice. "What are you asking me to do, Mari?"

"Stop those ships and find out what's going on," Mari said.

"Each of those ships is legally Imperial territory," Sien said. "The Great Guilds once held themselves above such things, insisting on the right to go where they would and search what they would. You fought to stop that."

Mari bit back her first response, trying to control her temper. "That's not what I'm asking."

"It is. I can send a ship out to look for the Imperial squadron. If it finds them, I can request that they permit a search, and the captain of the ship can request an interview with Prince Maxim. But if they say no, I have no legal right to demand otherwise."

"They must know what's going on with Kira!" Mari insisted, knowing how desperate she looked. "You could threaten them!"

Sien bowed her head, then raised it again to meet Mari's eyes. "I have no dearer friends in the world than you and Alain, but I am the Queen of Tiae. I cannot act without thinking of my people and my country. Even under the laws I have championed to grant more power to my people, in an emergency I can order such an action as you suggest. But I have no grounds for doing so, Mari. There is no evidence tying those ships to Kira's departure. Eyewitnesses saw her leave this palace long after those ships left, and with apparent good spirits board a Roc! And on that basis you ask me to order an act of war against Imperial ships?"

Alain spoke, his voice heavy. "If Tiae commits an act of war with no evidence to support it, the world will see it as an unprovoked attack. Even the Bakre Confederation might not back Tiae in such a case, leaving Tiae alone exposed to Imperial retaliation."

Mari closed her eyes, trying to control herself. "Sien, this is Kira."

"I love Kira as much as if she were my own daughter," Sien said, her voice strained. "But she knows she is not a citizen of Tiae. I do not even have the justification of trying to protect one of my people. How many might die, Mari? And what would I tell their families?"

"What if Maxim wants this?" Alain asked. "What if the Imperials have arranged this to trigger an attack, knowing that it would leave Tiae alone?"

Mari opened her eyes again, seeing Jason looking at them, miserable. "Jason. Are you absolutely sure that Kira gave no clue as to why she would have left this morning?"

"I'm sure," Jason said, his voice barely able to be heard.

"Did any of the Imperials say anything to you last night? Did anyone?"

Jason clenched his teeth. "When I was in the bathroom, there were a few officers from different places there and one of them said to me… said to me…"

"What?" Mari pressed.

"That he hoped I knew I was the luckiest guy on Dematr," Jason said. "I do know. But if something has happened to Kira—"

"Calm," Alain said. "Maxim made numerous attempts to provoke us. This could be another."

Queen Sien nodded. "Meaning that Maxim hopes we will act without thinking."

"What would happen if your ships from Minut intercepted the Imperial squadron?" Alain asked. "And if they attempted to attack?"

"My forces at Minut cannot outgun the Imperial squadron," Sien said. "There would be a running fight, my forces would take the worst of it, and the blame for the battle would rest at the feet of my country."

"So it would accomplish nothing," Alain said.

"Nothing good. But it could accomplish much to further Imperial aims."

They waited, looking at Mari.

Mari turned away, not wanting to see them. For how many years had people been looking at her to save the day? *What do we do, Mari? Can you save us, Mari? We need the daughter. We need you.*

She was so tired of it. Tired of endless labor to save others who ended up needing her again. Tired of having to put her family second when duty called. Tired of having her family and friends exposed to danger because of her. Alain knew. He knew how she felt, and she knew how much he was hurting inside right now as well, but he was doing his best to think things through for her, to help her plan, just as they had always worked together.

Mari made a fist and hit the wall hard. She hit it again. And again. And a fourth time, each blow hurting her hand more. She stopped, her head lowered, eyes closed, trying to find inside herself the strength to do the right thing, to not scream in frustration and anger. "I'm supposed to be the most powerful person in the world," Mari finally whispered. "Something has happened to my daughter, my only living child, and I can't even find out what's going on, let alone protect her."

Alain came up behind her and put his arms about her, holding her. Mari breathed in and out, imagining a world without her daughter in it and rejecting the possibility. "We have to find her, Alain."

"We will," he said, making a promise of the two words.

Mari put her hands over his where they met over her heart. "How?"

"We must trust in Kira. Whatever has happened, our daughter will find a way to protect herself. We must not do whatever the Imperials hope we will do, acting in ways that would weaken the authority you have in this world, the authority that has kept the peace for so long."

"I have to be the daughter of Jules," Mari said, trying not to feel. "Not a mother. Even when my own daughter needs me, I have to be that other person."

Queen Sien's voice was low but firm. "Perhaps what Kira needs is the daughter of Jules, and the power the daughter of Jules can bring to bear to help her."

Mari sighed, turning to break Alain's hold and look at Sien. "I'm sorry. I shouldn't have pressed on you this. You're right. An act of war would only serve the interests of Prince Maxim. But if he harms Kira,

I will make him pay in ways that will cause the world to tremble." She saw Jason staring at her and wondered if she had ever shown that side of herself to him. "Queen Sien, may Alain and I impose on your hospitality for a while longer? I'd like to stay here while we try to learn what has happened. I'd also like to have the use of your long-distance far-talker so I can speak with President of State Jane in the Confederation."

"Of course," Sien said.

"What about me?" Jason asked. "I need to do something. Just tell me. Anything."

Mari looked from Alain to Sien, then back at Jason. "The attempts on your life here must have been deliberate diversions from whatever the Imperials were planning against Kira. But now that Kira is gone they might try to eliminate you. Jason, as hard as it is for you, I think the best thing you can do is go back to Danalee. We'll send you with enough guards to ensure your safety. Alli and Calu will make sure you're safe. And when we learn what the Imperials are up to, we will notify you and anything you can do—"

"Lady Mari," Jason begged. "Please. Don't just send me off."

"There is nothing you can do here," Alain said.

"Sure," Jason mumbled, his shoulders slumping. "This is adult stuff, and I'm just a kid."

Mari walked to him and took his chin so that he had to look into her eyes. "Jason, you have more adult in you than many twice your age. That's not what this is about. When we find Kira, when we know what needs to be done, we need you to be alive and well and able to help. And if— *When* we get Kira back, she will want you to be all right."

"There's nothing I can do?" Jason asked, plaintive.

"Not now. Jason, there's not a lot *I* can do," Mari said. "Do you think *you're* unhappy about this? But if we keep our heads, and trust in Kira as her father advised, then Kira will have a chance. Do you believe that?"

He nodded. "I know the last thing you need to worry about is me. Not when Kira needs help."

Queen Sien reached to squeeze Jason's shoulder. "I will speak with my people and arrange Jason's transport north by train. Mari, you can also call Alli on the palace far-talker to let her know what is happening."

"Strength, Jason," Mari murmured to him. "That's what Kira needs. For us to be strong."

Kira opened her eyes, blinking in confusion at her surroundings. This wasn't the room she had been staying at in Sien's palace. It wasn't anywhere she remembered. The furnishings looked—no certainly were—those of a ship, everything fastened down. The bed she was in, the whole room, was moving, rocking in a way Kira had no trouble recognizing.

She was on a ship, and one that was under way.

CHAPTER FOUR

How had she come to be on a ship, and why did her head hurt?

Sitting up carefully as her head spun with dizziness, Kira looked around for some clue as to what ship this was. The room wasn't that large and didn't contain much. The bunk she was on, fastened against one wall. A small desk with a single chair before it. A small alcove to one side, which Kira could see contained a wash basin and a chamber pot. Two sealed light fittings with electric lights in them. A ventilation grate about as long as her lower arm and as wide as the length of her palm, and with a tight metal mesh over it, was high up on one wall. Everything seemed luxurious for a ship, though.

She looked at the furnishings again, the designs of the light fixtures, the quality and style of the fabrics. They all reeked of Imperial opulence. Kira herself had never been to the Empire, but she had seen things from there, and the objects in this room reminded her unpleasantly of items she knew had originated in the Empire. And they all looked new, as if this ship had not been in service long.

Kira realized that she could feel and faintly hear the vibrations from a steam engine driving a propeller. This wasn't a sailing ship.

A new steam-driven ship with Imperial fittings inside. That added up to a very ugly answer as to where she was.

Kira paused to look down at herself, seeing that she was fully dressed in the shirt and trousers she last remembered wearing. What if she hadn't changed out of that dress? Nice to look at, but not the sort of thing she would have wanted to be wearing now.

Kira looked under her jacket and saw that her shoulder holster was gone, along with the pistol it had held. So was the sailor knife she usually wore at her belt.

Still a little dizzy, she carefully got to her feet, took a couple of shaky steps to the door, and tried to open it. Kira wasn't surprised to find it locked. She glanced at the door's hinges, which were inside the room but with plates fixed over them to prevent access.

That left the porthole on one wall, a cover in place over it. Kira went to it, and discovered that the metal cover of the porthole was also locked firmly in place.

This wasn't a room. It was a prison.

Kira leaned her head against the door, trying to think. She heard people on the other side. Footsteps on what sounded like a metal deck matching that under the fine carpets in her room. Muffled conversations.

She raised one fist and banged on the door.

No response, except that the closest conversations halted.

Kira rapped her fist against the door again. "Open up!" she called.

Still no answer.

She went back to the bunk and sat down, her head still spinning slightly. Whatever had knocked her out wasn't completely out of her system. What had it been? Something wet on that cloth. A chemical, most likely. Quicker-acting when inhaled than a drug.

How had they gotten into her room, and taken her out of the palace?

Kira inhaled deeply before exhaling slowly to calm herself, cautiously probing with her Mage senses. The ship was definitely well out to sea. She could tell by how little power was available around it. But there was something else….

A Mage was aboard this ship. She yanked back her senses, working to suppress them and hide her Mage presence again. Whoever that Mage was, he or she was probably employed by her kidnappers. The last thing she needed was for them to realize that she had any Mage powers.

Heavy footsteps sounded outside her door. Kira got up, standing with her arms crossed as she heard the sound of the lock opening. The door swung open.

Kira's heart sank as Prince Maxim strolled into the room, smiling victoriously at her. Coming right behind him, four powerful-looking bodyguards spread out, their eyes on Kira.

She wouldn't let him know she was frightened. Not even a little. "Release me immediately," Kira said, keeping her voice level.

"I told you that you were going to Palandur," Prince Maxim said.

"Are you that pathetic a man, that in order to get a woman you have your followers kidnap her?"

"Once in Palandur," Maxim continued, "you will become my primary wife."

"Your widow, you mean," Kira said. "Because you'll die if you try to touch me."

"This will be better than I thought," Maxim continued as if Kira hadn't spoken. "I require a compliant woman. You will fill that role, and ensure that your mother does not act against the rightful and proper actions of the Empire to establish its predominant place in this world."

"I know that men in love are delusional, but you've got something a whole lot worse and a whole lot uglier going on," Kira said. She was surprised how firm her voice sounded, not reflecting how worried she was inside. She knew this was a very bad situation, and she had no idea how she was going to get out of it.

"I was annoyed by your attitude," Maxim said. "But then I realized that breaking the will of a dragon slayer would be doubly rewarding. The day will come when you beg me to let you fulfill my every desire."

"Just out of curiosity," Kira said, hoping that she could get Maxim to reveal something by offering him the opportunity to brag, "how did you get me out of the palace and out of Tiaesun?"

He smiled again. "Our Mages have learned a few new tricks. Did you know that one Mage can block the presence of another Mage as well as the presence of themselves? Leaving the other Mage free to cast spells, whose presence is blocked from detection by yet a third Mage. We sent nine Mages into that palace. No other Mages spotted them or their spells. It required a lot of training and coordination, but the Empire excels at such things."

"Congratulations," Kira said, hoping that she would have a chance to warn her father about that new tactic. "Let me go. Now."

Maxim's smile this time held the cool arrogance of someone backed up by several strong guards. "Your attitude will make my victory all the sweeter." He turned to go.

"Maxim," Kira said, deliberately not using his title. "If you harm me, then if I don't kill you, one of my family or friends will. But I'll do my best to make sure I'm the one who pulls the trigger."

He walked out without acknowledging her words.

The door closed and locked again.

Kira sat down. She wanted to beat her fists bloody against that locked door, but she held herself quiet and thought.

The Imperials had managed to spirit her out of Tiaesun. That was bad. But why hadn't they been intercepted by ships of Tiae's fleet? She could see a bare sliver of light at the sealed porthole that told her it was daylight. Her mother and father would realize that she was gone, that she must be on Maxim's ships, and Queen Sien would send out her fleet. Because Kira might not be one of Sien's subjects anymore, but she was still Mari's daughter.

And if the Imperial ships got past Tiae's naval forces, which had grown slowly since the kingdom had been reborn, the Bakre Confederation would surely send out ships. Jane of Danalee would know that allowing the Empire to get away with kidnapping Kira would vastly increase the risk of further Imperial aggression. And Julan, the Confederation's President in Chief, was a tough old bird who had lost a son during the last war. He wouldn't hesitate. The Imperial ships would have to transit the Strait of Gulls, leaving them no room to evade a Confederation flotilla.

But what if somehow the Imperials made it past the Strait of Gulls?

They'd still have to get past Gullhaven and Dorcastle, but they'd have a lot of room to hide in the Sea of Bakre. And once past Dorcastle there would be nothing to block them from reaching the Empire.

Kira gazed at the sealed porthole. At this moment the Imperials were surely running north through the Umbari Ocean toward the Strait of Gulls, far out of sight of land. If she made it off this ship now, she'd find herself drifting in the Umbari with odds of survival that pretty much added up to zero. But the Strait of Gulls was another matter. The stretch of water between Larharbor and Cape Astra wasn't small, but there would be land visible on both sides, and either the Confederation or the Alliance would offer her protection if she made it ashore. Most likely, there would be friendly warships waiting that she could find refuge on.

But how to know when the ship reached the strait? The first mate of *The Son of Taris* had talked about the strait once. What had she said? Something about the waves of the sea and the waves of the ocean meeting to fight it out. Choppy waters.

Kira felt the sway of this ship on the long swells of the Umbari. She would know when they reached the strait and the waters changed. If the Imperials had gotten that far without being stopped, Kira would have to take a chance then.

She wasn't sure how much time had passed when the door was unlocked again. Four guards were visible outside as a tall, thin Imperial lady carried in a tray and set it on Kira's desk. "Your dinner, *Lady* Kira."

"You were at the dinner at Tiaesun," Kira said, mentally labeling the woman Lady Elegant.

"Yes. We were supposed to distract that boy you were walking around with." Lady Elegant smiled insincerely at Kira. "He looked so innocent. Do you like that sort? Teaching them how to please you before they learn any wrong lessons from other girls?"

"No," Kira said, not trusting herself to say more. She lowered her voice. "If you help me—"

"Don't bother," Lady Elegant interrupted. "Nothing you could promise would be worth it to me. My loyalty to Prince Maxim is unshakeable," she added, speaking loudly enough that all four guards could easily hear. "And, really, the idea of you becoming his ceremonial wife and learning your proper role appeals to me a great deal."

"Why?" Kira said. "You don't know me."

"I know you well enough. I look forward to the day when your proud little head is meekly bowed before Prince Maxim while you beg to do anything he asks of you. Instead of strutting about like an empress, you'll be crawling on your knees and liking it!"

Kira stared at her. "How could you wish such a fate on another woman? How could you wish such a fate on anyone?"

Lady Elegant's eyes flared with anger. "Listen, little girl, you know nothing of the world. While you were born in a palace and getting everything you wanted and having servants do everything for you, I was born on a farm, the fourth daughter in a family of six children! I was working the fields from dawn to dusk as soon as I could walk! My fate was to either do that all my life, or marry some other poor farmer and bear him a litter of young while still working myself to death!

"But I did not accept that! I left that farm, and I fought, and I used people and I let people use me, and I made it to the Imperial Court when I was about your age," Lady Elegant snarled at Kira. "Only I wasn't a princess born and raised. I used everything I had to get close to power and to get rid of anyone in my way. And here I am, almost too old to have a chance left, and you come in, all fresh and innocent, candy for the appetites of the Imperial Court. You'll probably destroy my last chance. I hope you suffer every moment of every day."

Kira flinched, part of her wanting to retreat before Lady Elegant's hostility. But that made her angry, stiffening her resolve. "How would me suffering make your life any better?"

"Only a fool would ask that question!"

"No," Kira said. "My father has talked about this, about what the Great Guilds used to teach their members. They thought that tearing other people down made them higher. It didn't. They stayed in the same place, because hurting other people never raises anyone. It just produces the illusion that you have gained stature when actually you're going nowhere."

Elegant's eyes sparked with renewed anger. "I'll remind you that you said that when you're crawling at Maxim's feet. We'll see who's higher then!"

"And I wasn't born a princess in a palace!" Kira shot back. "I never lacked for the necessities of life, but I have never had luxuries and never had servants. Mother and Father insisted that I work and earn anything I wanted! And I seriously doubt that you have spent your entire life worried about assassins and kidnappers such as your contemptible Prince Maxim!"

The older woman looked like she was about to hit Kira, but drew back when Kira glared a warning at her. Lady Elegant whirled about in an eddy of fine fabric and perfume and paraded majestically from the room, leaving the tray on Kira's desk.

The door shut firmly, the lock clicking into place.

Kira sighed, looking at the lock. Even if she had managed to hide her lock picks on her they wouldn't do any good, since the lock was only accessible from the outside. That wouldn't stop her Mage talents, if she could summon them again, but that was something to be saved as a last resort.

The food was decent enough, slightly spicy in the Imperial style, and watered wine in the glass served to quench Kira's thirst. She ate and drank cautiously at first, concerned about what might be in the food, but when no ill effects occurred Kira finished her meal.

Lady Elegant eventually returned to collect the tray. Kira just sat and looked at her, saying nothing, knowing that she had no friend in this woman.

But when Elegant had left, Maxim reappeared, once again backed by his extra guards and this time accompanied by a Mage. Kira would have had no trouble knowing what he was even without the robes he wore. Old enough to have been an Acolyte in the former Mage Guild, the man gazed at her with eyes that held no feeling in a face that showed no trace of life. It might as well have been the face of a dead man. She had seen that sort of face before in Mages, and once even from her own father, who had shown it after Kira begged. The experience had frightened her enough that she had sworn never to ask her father to look at her that way again.

She clamped down tightly on her own Mage presence, trying to look like she was only mildly curious at the arrival of the Mage.

"Well?" Maxim demanded of the Mage.

The Mage looked over Kira as if she were of no more interest than a lump of dirt. But Kira knew this Mage had even less regard for her than that. She would only be a shadow to this Mage, an illusion born of the Mage's own mind, worthy of no consideration or care. Those had been the teachings of the Mage Guild, supposedly required for any Mage to be able to wield his or her powers.

"It is nothing," the Mage said, his voice as dead as his expression, calling Kira "it" to further dehumanize her.

"No Mage powers? Nothing?" Maxim said.

"Nothing. A very tiny potential at best. The shadow is nothing."

"Good," Maxim said. "You said you had felt something earlier."

"It could not have been that one," the Mage said.

"My father knows wisdom," Kira said to the Mage. "Master of Mages Alain. You should seek out his followers and regain the life the Mage elders stole from you."

The Mage responded not in words but with another flat stare. Most people would have seen nothing in that stare, but thanks to her father's training Kira was able to perceive the anger hidden deep within it. This was one of the Mages who rejected the truths her father had learned, clinging to the past.

"That one has no wisdom," the Mage said in the same monotone.

"He can do what you cannot," Kira said, deliberately provoking the Mage to see if it would cause trouble for Maxim. "It is you who lack wisdom."

The Mage began to raise a hand but Maxim halted him. "She is mine. You have checked her and found nothing. Leave."

Just before the Mage turned away Kira saw the flash of a different anger, this aimed, she was certain, at Maxim. But under that anger was something else. Contempt and…confidence? As if Maxim was serving the Mage, rather than the other way around?

Who then was the Mage serving? Were the unrepentant Mages trying to use the Imperials just as their elders in the old Mage Guild once had?

Maxim, the Mage, and the bodyguards departed, the door was locked, and Kira sat down again. Whatever the Mage was up to, he definitely was no friend of hers.

As long as they didn't know that she had Mage powers, she had one small advantage that she might be able to use to escape. But she would have to wait. There was too little power to use out here on the open sea, and any attempt to form a spell would be spotted by that Mage.

Each time someone had entered this room there had been at least four guards outside. But Kira had watched them carefully, seeing that only two had been present each time the door had opened. When the door was locked, only two guards must be posted.

She could handle two guards. She had seen the way they looked at her, with the smug assurance of physically strong people. That would make it easier to surprise them when the right time came.

Kira heard footsteps that sounded like those of crewmembers on the deck over her head, telling her that she was only one level below decks. The footsteps died down over time, as did the sounds of people in the passageway outside her door. Before turning off the lights in her room she moved the chair, wedging it firmly under the door handle so that it blocked the opening of the door. At least she couldn't be surprised while sleeping. With the lights off the room was pitch black, no light coming in from outside. The door must have seals around it.

Feeling her way to her bunk, Kira stretched herself out and began relaxing, using the meditation routines her father had taught her. She needed to rest so she would be ready when the time came to act.

Her mother and father must be doing something. And Jason. He wouldn't just be sitting around.

"There was something odd," Asha said. The female Mage sat opposite Mari and Alain, betraying little emotion but to Alain's eyes looking very distressed.

"We were able to sense that ten Mages left the ships of the Imperials," Asha continued. "Four of them did not depart with the ships, but were seen leaving the city separately afterwards."

"That leaves one," Alain said.

"Perhaps the one who created the Roc that Kira met outside the east gate."

"But we still have no proof of anything," Mari said, her eyes shadowed by worry.

"No," Asha said. "But why nine other Mages? What was their purpose? Have you spoken to Mages who are frequently in Tiaesun, Alain?"

"Yes," Alain said. "They can offer nothing." He paused, thinking. "Nine Mages."

"Yes," she echoed him. "I have been to this palace enough to know the levels of power that are normally found here. They are much lower than usual. As if many spells were cast here recently."

"How could I not have sensed those spells being cast?"

"I do not know. My uncle Mage Dav has heard rumors, though. Rumors of attempts to use the work of one Mage to mask that of another."

"Nine Mages," Alain repeated.

"But what does that mean?" Mari demanded. "What could nine Mages, or a hundred Mages, have done to cause Kira to walk out of this palace and climb on that Roc to fly east?"

"I do not know," Asha said, her distress growing.

Mari looked at her, then got up and went to hug her, remembering the first time she had hugged Asha, ironically in Palandur, and how the female Mage had been stiff and uncomfortable then at human contact. "Asha, I know you're doing everything that you can. Thank you."

"I know you would do the same if Devi or Ashira were missing," Asha said, a small, grateful smile appearing.

"How is your husband?"

Asha's smile grew slightly. "Mechanic Dav is recovering well. He complains that his collection of walking sticks will soon be useless. How do I thank Doctor Sino for fixing the bones that once healed awry?"

Mari sat down next to Asha. "I already tried. Sino just waves it off and says that's her job."

"She is almost as good as a Mage at hiding her pleasure at the thanks she receives," Alain said.

"Queen Sien gives her anything she asks for," Mari added, "but the doctor hasn't asked for much aside from that horse she loves, a place to live, and an office to work out of. Sino laughed when she told me that while Maxim was here the Imperials offered her a palace and all the treasure she wanted if she'd move to the Empire. Her main worry is that some of the components in her med bag will run out before much longer, and we don't have the means in Dematr to replace them. But Sino can keep teaching our healers as long as she is alive."

"If only one of her skills could help us find Kira," Asha said. "How is Jason?"

"About as unhappy as a teenage boy can be, and that's extremely unhappy," Mari said. "We almost had to tie him up to get him on the train for Danalee. But he'll be better off there." She looked out the window at the sun's position. "Kira's been gone for a day and a half. It feels like so much longer."

Another day nearly ended, and nothing had happened except for two visits by Lady Elegant to bring her meals, during which someone else emptied the room's chamber pot. Kira had waited for some sign that the Imperial ships had been intercepted—sudden changes in courses, signs that speed had been increased, shouts of alarm and rushing feet on the deck overhead—but there had been nothing. The swells on the surface of the Umbari must be slightly longer now, altering the slow roll and recovery of the ship, but that had been the only change Kira was aware of.

The lock turned.

Kira stood up, alert, tensing her body to be ready for anything. Had Prince Maxim returned to gloat? Had the Mage detected a trace of her presence again?

But the two people who entered the room were a woman and a man in familiar dark jackets. The jackets that had once advertised their owners as full members of the Mechanics Guild that had ruled the world, men and women qualified in the Mechanic arts and able to operate, build, and repair the limited technology allowed by the Guild. Kira had grown up seeing that kind of jacket on her mother and many of her mother's friends, because since the fall of the Guild many Mechanics still wore the jacket as a mark of professional skill.

But the gazes of the two Mechanics held no trace of friendship. The woman, who looked to be about Kira's mother's age, had a wooden expression, trying to hide feelings that Kira's Mage training could still spot. Hate. Contempt. Disdain.

The male Mechanic, younger, openly displayed a contemptuous smile as he looked at her.

Neither said anything. Kira had spent most of her life dressing like her mother, without really being aware of it until recently, so her own clothes almost matched those of the Mechanics. Even her jacket, while not that of a Mechanic, still resembled one. She finally broke the silence. "Why are you here?"

The woman spoke, her accent revealing that she had been raised in the Sharr Isles. "We wanted to see with our own eyes what the daughter of a traitor looked like. I wanted to see the face of a girl whose mother killed my brother."

"She doesn't look like much," the young man said. "Though she does like to dress like she's playing Mechanic."

"How does Mari sleep, girl? Does she have pleasant dreams, remembering all the people she killed, all the families she destroyed?"

The woman was using the old Mechanics Guild tactic of deliberately avoiding the use of Mari's proper title. Kira shook her head, determined to correct that. "My mother, Master Mechanic Mari of Dematr, regrets every death. Memories of the war haunt her. But she hurt far fewer people than the Mechanics Guild did. The old Senior Mechanics killed far more Mechanics than she ever did."

"She doesn't know anything except the garbage she's been fed on a silver spoon," the young man commented.

Kira didn't reply, not wanting to let the accusation that she had been raised in luxury get to her again. She knew a lot of people believed that, even those who admired the daughter of Jules but mistakenly thought her mother had accepted riches after the war.

"How many friends of hers did Mari betray?" the woman asked Kira.

"None," Kira said. "Her friends are with her still. Master Mechanic Alli, Mechanics Calu and Bev and Dav, Master Mechanic Lukas—"

"Those are the survivors," the female Mechanic interrupted. "Did she ever tell you the name of Hors of Caer Lyn and his sister Jil?"

"No," Kira said.

"Hors was my brother. Did she ever tell you how we tried to be her friends when we were all apprentices at the Mechanics Guild Hall in Caer Lyn? Did she ever tell you that she shot Mechanic Hors at Dorcastle? Put a bullet in him while he was trying to shield his friends? Murdered him in cold blood?"

"Dorcastle was a battle! It was war!"

"A war she started!" Jil hurled the accusation at Kira. "So she could rule everything."

"Mother rules nothing," Kira said. "The Guild tried to kill her. Over and over again. To keep her from learning the truth, and then to keep her from saving this world from the tyranny of the Great Guilds."

"There was only one great guild," the young man said. "You even believe that nonsense about Mages, don't you?"

"Professor S'san and Master Mechanic Lukas believe it. Why shouldn't I?"

"They're both old, their minds failing, and they lost their integrity when they joined Mari." The female Mechanic took a step closer, gazing at Kira's eyes. "I was your mother's friend once. I tried to be. But Mari only cared about people who would follow her without question, who could help her in her ambitions. When I refused, she cast me aside."

"I don't need to know your history with my mother to know that's a lie," Kira said. "That's not who my mother is." But she could tell the woman believed what she was saying.

"Watch your mouth around your betters, girl!" the woman warned.

"You're not better than me or anyone else," Kira said. "I'm very sorry you lost your brother. I know a lot of people who lost family members defending Dorcastle. I know how much those memories still pain them. But the Great Guilds had no right to continue ruling this world. The Mechanics Guild was a fraud to begin with, created by the crew of the great ship!"

"She believes that drivel about the ship bringing people to our world, too," the young man said.

"Look up at the Twins," Kira said. "They are parts of that ship. Another ship came from Urth about six months ago! How could you not know about that?"

"And you have proof of that event?" the younger Mechanic mocked.

"Of course I do! Doctor Sino lives in Tiaesun. And my boyfriend… my man," she corrected, openly claiming him as her close partner, "is Jason of Urth."

"Your man?" Mechanic Jil mocked. "Are you dreaming of a happy life with some boy? Maxim will show you what a man is."

"Maxim has no idea what a man is," Kira said.

"Maybe she's planning on keeping the boy on the side," the young man said. "An extra lover for when Maxim is out of town or busy with another."

Kira gave him a withering glare. "Were you born being a creep or did you have to study for it?" She shifted her gaze to the woman. "And you. Defending the old Guild. Were you an apprentice at Emdin in those days? Did you know any? My Aunt Bev was one of them." Kira saw that shot had gone home. "Is that what you're defending? A Guild that could treat boys and girls like that and not punish those responsible?"

"I don't know anything about Emdin," Mechanic Jil denied.

"You're lying."

Jil's face tightened with anger. "I might help you. If you help us. Just tell us how Mari did it."

"Did what?"

"Convinced so many Mechanics to turn traitor. What was her secret? What hold did she have over them?" the woman demanded.

Watching Jil of Caer Lyn closely, Kira could tell there was something lurking under the hostility of the question. Something calculating. Why were these two here? To help Maxim and the Empire? Or to help the humiliated remnants of the Mechanics Guild inside the Empire, whose members still dreamed of regaining past power?

"Master Mechanic Mari didn't have any hold over anyone," Kira said. "She just did what she thought was right, treating others with respect, being honest with them—"

"Like she did at Caer Lyn?" Jil scoffed. "I wasn't surprised when Alli and Calu joined her. Calu was always her lap dog, and Alli tried to hide her incompetence by sleeping with any—"

"Do not speak of her that way!" Kira interrupted, trying to control her rage at the woman's words. "Master Mechanic Alli is the most respected weapons designer in the entire world! And the most talented! She taught me to shoot! What is your problem? Do you think that hating other people is going to make your life even one tiny bit better?"

"My brother's life ended because of your mother and her friends!" Mechanic Jil yelled back. "Return him to me, you spoiled little brat, and maybe I'd listen to your self-righteous rants! Can't your father do that? Raise the dead?" she mocked Kira.

Kira tried again to control herself, noticing that the young man appeared amused by the harsh words that she and Jil were exchanging.

"He doesn't claim that ability. He never has. If he could raise the dead, my own brother would still be in this world."

"All lies. Mages can do nothing. Admit it!"

"I have seen countless demonstrations of the Mage arts. I—" Kira caught herself. Had she been about to blurt out her own minor Mage skills, goaded into admitting to them? "I don't have to prove anything to you," she finished, speaking calmly. "I regret your bother's death. I know my mother does, too. But he was fighting for the wrong cause, fighting to ensure that this world remained in chains."

The young Mechanic yawned as if bored by Kira's words. "She'll never admit to it. Her mother wanted to sleep with a Mage. Slept with a lot of them, from what I hear. I wonder if she knows who her real father is?"

Kira didn't get mad, knowing that was what they wanted, channeling her anger this time into a look of icy contempt. "Come a little closer to me and say that again, little boy," she said, raising one first toward him. "If you dare."

He tried to maintain his own cool disdain of her, but Kira saw the heat in his eyes. "I thought you liked little boys who you could order around and feel superior to."

"No," Kira said. "I love a man who is my equal. If you two don't have anything to say that's worth listening to, you should leave."

"You can't give us orders," Mechanic Jil said, mocking Kira. "You're the one in a prison."

"I'll leave this room," Kira said. "But unless you two abandon what remains of the Mechanics Guild you will never leave the prisons that you've made of your own minds and your own lives. I feel sorry for you."

Those words went home. "Feel sorry for how your mother will react when she sees you sitting at Prince Maxim's feet, bound to him for life," Jil spat.

"And feel sorry for your little brother, who that man you think is your father let die for his Mage purposes," the young man said.

Kira's vision hazed red with fury. Before she knew what she was doing she had taken two steps, thrown a punch as a feint that the young Mechanic hastily tried to block, then followed up with a knee strike that left the man doubled over in pain. Kira grabbed his throat, pushing him against the door, her free hand menacing Mechanic Jil of Caer Lyn.

"Never come near me again or I'll rip that tongue from your mouth," Kira whispered in a voice she didn't recognize as her own. "My brother's body was harmed when he was breech born. It was the fault of no one that he died soon after birth. My father would have died to save my brother. He and my mother mourn my brother to this day. I pity you. But I will hurt you if you ever speak to me again."

The door was shoved open as some of the guards outside forced their way in, responding to the sound of fighting. Kira stepped back, seeing that at least five guards were present, too many to take on even if she had been able to surprise them. She watched wordlessly as the two Mechanics retreated and the door shut, the lock clicking firmly into place once more.

Kira sat down on her bunk, crossing her legs and berating herself. *Angry people make mistakes*, Aunt Bev had told her time and time again during her self-defense lessons. *Don't let anyone else make you angry and make you do something without thinking.*

She had certainly failed that test. She had let those Mechanics and their Imperial masters know that mocking her little brother's death was a path through Kira's inner armor. She would have to be very careful not to let that work again.

Kira breathed in and out slowly, rehearsing in her mind the conversation.

"I love a man who is my equal."

She had said that, not realizing the importance of it at the time. *"I love a man."* Jason. Kira looked up, staring at the steel plates overhead blocking her view of the sky. *I love him. I do. Why did it take me so long to realize that?*

She felt an odd sensation and looked down at herself, spotting what looked like a single strand of spider web running from her body to one wall of her room. Startled, Kira batted at it, expecting to sweep it away, but her hand went through the strand as if it wasn't there. She squinted down at it. She could definitely see something there, not drifting in the air currents of the room but running straight from her to that point on the wall.

No, not on the wall. Through it. And onward.

A thread that was there but wasn't there.

Her breath caught as she realized what it was. Like the thread that connected her father to her mother, and the one that Mage Asha had told her she could see leading to her husband, Mechanic Dav. The Mage presence inside her must be strong enough to show the same thing.

Because she knew it did lead to Jason. She could feel that, though she couldn't explain how she knew. He was there, even though the thread was so thin and stretched by distance that it might not hold much longer.

Kira smiled down at the thread, blinking back tears.

She sensed something else, a feeling of movement. Not here. Where Jason was. He was moving fairly quickly. Was he on a train? Where was he going?

She tried to learn more, tried to gain a better understanding of where he was, what he was feeling…

Worry. Fear. For her.

She tried to send back reassurance and some sense of where she was, but had no idea if that was working. As far as Kira could remember, her mother had never felt or experienced anything as a result of the thread her father could sense.

Kira realized that the distance between her and Jason was growing as they moved away from each other.

She felt the thread grow too thin to be sensed or seen.

But Kira also felt a certainty that it would never completely go away.

★

"We lost him."

"You *lost him*?" Mari almost yelled, struggling to control herself. "How could you have lost Jason?"

The voice of the supervisor of the guards who had accompanied Jason north toward Danalee sounded unhappy over the long-distance far-talker. "He suddenly got all excited. He'd just been sitting there, but when the train was slowing down to go through Minut he jerked as though someone had said something to him. A moment later he started yelling at us. And then he pulled himself out the window next to him and jumped before we could stop him! By the time we got the train stopped and ran back to check he had disappeared."

"What did he yell?" Mari demanded.

"He said, 'It's the dobblegongeh. Tell them it was the dobble-gongeh.' And he insisted that Lady Kira was on the Imperial ships."

"What did you say?"

"I told him we would inform Lady Master Mechanic Alli and Sir Mechanic Calu as soon as we got to Danalee. And that was when he jumped out."

Alain nodded to Mari. "The response of the guard supervisor was reasonable."

Mari nodded as well before hitting the transmit button on the large, long-distance far-talker again. "I can't fault that. Obviously it wasn't enough for Jason, though."

"No, Lady, it wasn't. He kept saying it would take too long, that Lady Kira needed help now."

Mari lowered her face into her hands, collecting herself before answering again. "Make sure all the Minut authorities know that Jason is out there, and make sure every form of transportation out of the city is under the closest watch possible."

"Yes, Lady. I deeply regret failing you."

"Let's just try to fix it now," Mari said.

She turned to Alain. "We've lost both of them again."

"What does dobblegongeh mean?" he asked.

"I have no idea. Why would Jason say that?"

"It seemed that he expected us to know what it meant."

"Kira never told us anything about that. Was she supposed to have?" Mari paced restlessly. "It's not a Mechanic term. As far as I can recall it's nowhere in the tech manuals that survive from the great ship. But maybe I forgot it. I skimmed most of those texts twenty years ago in pretty tense circumstances."

"We should ask the keepers of the tech manuals at the library in Minut to look for the word."

"Good idea. What else can we do?"

"It is time to head north," he replied.

"Foresight?" Mari asked hopefully. But those hopes were immediately dashed as her husband shook his head.

"A…feeling," Alain said. "Nothing more."

"That's good enough for me. The one thing I feel certain of is that Kira is getting farther from Tiae with every hour. Going east toward the Empire would dead-end us against the Waste and the lands around Ringhmon. If Kira really did fly on a Roc in that direction, she's out of reach already. But if she's on those Imperial ships, going north into the Confederation will bring us closer to her."

"Jason acted as if he felt something," Alain added. "As if for a moment he knew what Kira was experiencing."

Mari paused, looking intently at her husband. "What are you thinking?"

"I am remembering when we were in Ringhmon, and I felt your pain as you were struck from behind."

"But that was because you already had that weird thread thing that isn't there leading from me to you," Mari began. "Because you were already in love with me even though you didn't—" Her breath caught. "Asha feels the same thing linking her to Dav. Kira has some Mage powers. Do you think she could be experiencing that? And somehow reaching through it to Jason?"

"It is possible," he said. "How else to explain his sudden urge to act?"

"That would certainly answer the question of whether or not she's in love with Jason! And it would mean she does need our help! How long will take to get Rocs lined up?"

"They await us now," Alain said.

"I love you." It took only a short time to say their farewells to Queen Sien, assemble some packs small enough to bring with them on the Rocs, and head for a nearby courtyard, where the population of Tiae was giving very wide berth to two immense Rocs.

Mage Alera turned to look at Mari, which among Mages counted as an effusive greeting. "Kira is in trouble?"

"Yes," Mari said. "We need to get to Dorcastle. If Swift can get us to Danalee, we can find other Rocs there to take us the rest of the way."

She had never before seen Mage Alera actually look offended. "Kira needs us. Swift will take you all the way to Dorcastle, but stop in Danalee if that is needed."

Mage Saburo, standing by his Roc, spoke in the same dispassionate tones as Alera. "Hunter will carry Mage Alain all the way to Dorcastle."

"That is a very long trip," Mari said. She smiled at both Mages. "Swift and Hunter are mighty Rocs."

Minutes later she and Alain were lying on the backs of Swift and Hunter, respectively, the Mages seated before them, as the Rocs leapt upward, their mighty wings driving the impossible and magnificent birds upward and to the north.

CHAPTER FIVE

Kira sat up in her bunk. The feel of the ship had changed. Instead of a repetitive roll along the ocean swells, the ship had begun twisting, the bow rising and falling in quick, irregular pitches and heaves.

They were in the Strait of Gulls.

Why hadn't anyone intercepted these ships yet?

She couldn't wait any longer. This would be her best chance to escape.

Kira breathed deeply, readying herself. The guards outside must have orders to do something if Kira seemed to be in trouble.

She stood up, going to one of the ornamental curtains hanging beside the sealed porthole and yanking down the curtain with as much noise as possible. She dragged the chair under one of the light fixtures and made noises as if tying the curtain to it. Another inhale, then Kira kicked the chair loudly to one side, and as she ran to stand by one side of the door let out a brief shriek of pain and terror that ended with the best choking sound she could manage.

The lock clicked and the door slammed open, a guard stepping inside quickly.

She hit him hard, a disabling blow that would take out even a large man. Without pausing, Kira leaped past the falling guard and hit the one still outside the door, a flurry of blows rocking the surprised man against the side of the passageway, dazed.

Kira ran, seeing a ladder going up, a shaft of light beckoning her with the promise of freedom. The light was grayish, filtered through haze, so it was either much earlier in the day than she had thought or the weather was bad outside.

She passed one, then two, startled sailors, who didn't react in time to stop her. Up the ladder, taking the steps two at a time, past a shocked Lady Elegant whom Kira shoved aside.

She was on the deck, the side of the ship only a few lance lengths distant. Fog enshrouded the ship, allowing vision out only a few hundred lances before the world was swallowed in gray gloom. The lands on either side of the Strait of Gulls were invisible, giving her no clue as to which way to swim for safety. That didn't matter. She had to get off this ship.

Kira headed for the rail, aware of the sailors turning to see her, shouted orders, men and women beginning to move to cut off her escape.

The fog had condensed on parts of the ship, dripping down to form pools. Her foot slipped as it hit one such puddle, slowing her movement and requiring a moment to right herself.

Kira recovered almost immediately, launching herself for the rail, but the instant lost was fatal. Hands grabbed at her, slowing her further.

She fought her way through, her hand almost on the rail to pull her the rest of the way over the side, but now there were several members of the crew on her, seizing her arms and her body, holding her back.

They pulled her away from the railing, two holding each of Kira's arms and two more holding her body from behind. She made a convulsive attempt to break free, almost getting one arm loose, then subsided as the grips on her tightened. Kira almost growled with frustration, breathing heavily after her effort, her hair drifting across her face.

Prince Maxim appeared before her, his expression angry. "Who—"

Kira snarled and swung a kick at him, narrowly missing as the crewmembers jerked her backwards and Maxim hastily took a step away.

Maxim glared, not at Kira, but at those standing near him. "Who let this happen?"

The two guards she had gotten past were shoved forward, their eyes enraged as they looked at Kira and fearful as they turned back to Maxim.

Maxim shook his head. "Which one of you unlocked her door?"

One guard instantly pointed to the other, who stared at Maxim.

"You will spend the next day shoveling coal for one of the boilers," Maxim said. "Until this time tomorrow you will work constantly, no breaks, and if you fall or cease to work you will be cast over the side. If you survive, you might be permitted to serve me again. I do not tolerate failure. The next person who fails me," he said, looking around the deck at everyone, "will not receive any second chance."

"Coward," Kira spat. "Hiding behind thugs with less honor and feelings than the worst Dark Mage."

"Take her below," Maxim ordered. "I will deal with her later."

"You'd better have a lot more people holding me the next time you get within reach of me!" Kira yelled, furious as she was dragged back down the ladder.

"Careful," she heard the crewmembers holding her advise each other. "Don't let her bite you!"

"I know who her mother is!" the man who had been warned snapped in reply.

She got a last glimpse of the weak daylight coming down through the hatch as she was carried through the passageway to her prison and tossed inside. Before Kira could get back to her feet, the door shut and locked.

She walked to it and kicked the door as hard as she could, the sound echoing in her room and the passageway outside.

Why had they thought she would bite them?

"You're evil, Kira." It was that Mara nonsense again. The crewmembers were the sort of Imperials who believed that her mother, and Kira, were tied to the old legend. *I know who her mother is.* Apparently the Imperials, seeing her with Mari, had decided that Kira must be the

daughter of the vampire rather than Mara herself. They had feared she was after their blood, and Kira reflected that she had probably looked angry enough to drink someone's blood when she was carried back down here. Maybe she could use those Imperial fears to help herself. If she got the chance.

Some time later she felt the motion of the ship change, and knew they had cleared the Strait of Gulls and were steaming eastward through the Sea of Bakre.

Where was the Confederation fleet? How had the Imperial ships gotten through the Strait of Gulls, even during fog, without some Confederation ships engaging them?

Alli and Calu met them as the Rocs landed at Danalee. "Have you heard anything about Kira or Jason?" Mari asked as she slid off of Swift's back to stand on the paving of a large courtyard that had rapidly cleared as the huge birds came in to land.

"Only Jason. He got out of Minut," Alli said.

"How?"

"I can only guess," Alli said. "And that guess would be that your daughter taught him a few things."

"Blazes. Is there any idea where he went?"

"Fast freight to Larharbor."

"Then—"

"Which he wasn't on when it got there," Alli said. "Best bet is that at the new railyard north of Lake Annan, Jason jumped to an express passenger train for Gullhaven."

Mari slapped her forehead. "Are the authorities at Gullhaven looking for him? How hard is it to catch a single teenager?"

"You know how hard it was six months ago," Calu said, depressed. "Jason's a quick learner, and he's been listening to Kira. And we know who taught Kira how to not get caught."

"This is not my fault," Mari said.

"What made Jason suddenly run off? Any ideas?"

"Kira's in love with him, whether she realizes it yet or not."

Both Calu and Alli frowned at her in confusion. "How could that—?" Alli began.

"It's a Mage thing. Alain? Did you have any visions on the way here?"

"No," he said.

"Why does your foresight only work when I don't want it to? Yes?" Mari added as an official ran up to them.

"We've just received a report from Gullhaven which may be related to the search for Jason of Urth," the official reported breathlessly. Mari's momentary leap of hope vanished as he continued. "A boat was stolen from the harbor this morning."

"A boat?" Alli asked sharply. "What kind of boat?"

"A small craft, single sail, suitable for short jaunts out to sea. Something one person could handle alone."

"Blazes." Mari looked helplessly at Alli and Calu. "Have either of you ever heard the word dobblegongeh?"

"No," Calu said. "Alli and I have been wracking our brains. Maybe it's a word from Urth."

"What can we do if it is?" Mari asked.

"Maybe Doctor Sino would know what it means."

Mari hit the side of her own head hard enough to sting. "Gah! I'm an idiot! Doctor Sino! I didn't even think about her because she only does healer things. Where's the nearest long-distance far-talker?"

"In my offices," Alli said.

It took a frustratingly long time before they heard Doctor Sino's voice coming over the far-talker. "This is a cool radio. Really retro. Voice only? Amazing."

"Doctor," Mari said, trying to sound patient and calm, "have you ever heard the word dobblegongeh?"

"Dobble-what?"

"Something like dobblegongeh," Mari repeated.

"Huh. That's a new one on me. It's not one of your words?" Before

Mari could say anything else, her heart sinking, Sino continued. "I brought my med bag. Let me do a search. My med bag's database isn't nearly as exhaustive as the one on the ship that left, but it might find something. Hold on. You know, it's a good thing my gear can recharge using solar or it'd be cold dead by now. Hmmm. Are you sure the word wasn't doppelganger?"

"What is doppelganger?" Mari asked, hope blossoming again.

"It's an old term on Earth. I've got it in my database because sometimes people get a little off-balance mentally and think a duplicate of themselves is causing trouble for them or scheming to replace them. It's rare, but it happens. And then there's the related Capgras delusion, where someone thinks one of their friends or family members has been replaced by an imposter who's an exact double."

"A double?" Mari asked. "You mean like a twin?"

"Right," Sino answered. "Only not a twin. Someone malevolent who isn't actually related but looks identical."

Alain's sudden grip on Mari's arm surprised her. "A double. Someone who looked like Kira. She did not leave Sien's palace at dawn that day. It was a double you saw in her bed, and a double the guards saw at the palace and at the east gate to Tiaesun."

Mari stared at him. "That's why she smiled as she mentioned going to Palandur? Of course. Why didn't we think of that? But if Kira didn't leave the palace at dawn—"

"She could have been abducted much earlier. Early enough to be brought to the Imperial ships before they left at midnight. We suspected this had been done, but did not know how. Now we know."

Mari nodded, weak from relief at the first solid clue since Kira had left. "Doctor? Thank you. That's exactly what we needed to know."

"Is Kira going to be okay?"

"I hope so." The call ended, Mari looked at the others in the office, which now included the local militia commander. "Kira is on one of those Imperial ships. We can do something now."

"Can we?" Calu asked. "We don't have proof. This dopple..."

"Doppelganger," Mari said.

"Explains the actions of the person who looked like Kira, but there's no evidence to support it. We have only Jason's word for it."

The militia commander had the expression of someone knowing she was delivering bad news. "I had a message sent to Gullhaven while we waited to hear from Doctor Sino. They replied that if the Imperial squadron has maintained the speed they are capable of, they have probably just cleared the Strait of Gulls."

"The ships were not seen?" Alain asked.

"No, Sir Mage. Bad weather. Fog. That's not unusual for the Strait."

"If the Bakre Confederation sends out ships now from Gullhaven and Dorcastle," Alli said, "they might be able catch the Imperial ships. But the Sea of Bakre is wide past the Strait. And what will the Confederation do when we have nothing but the word of a seventeen-year-old boy that Kira is on one of those ships? I believe Jason. But would the Confederation be willing to commit an act of war on his word alone?"

"If the daughter demanded it..." the militia commander began with clear reluctance.

"I could force a war to start," Mari finished, feeling sick. "I could use some advice, people."

"Talk to President of State Jane," Calu urged. "See what the Bakre Confederation is willing to do. They know the daughter wouldn't ask something of them without very strong grounds for it."

"What if this what the Empire wants?" Alli asked. She clenched her fists in frustration. "I'm sorry! I *like* Jason. And he may be dying somewhere out there now! But we've been out-maneuvered."

"I'll call Jane, and then Alain and I will go on to Dorcastle."

"Lady," the militia commander said. "I have some experience with naval matters. Even if the Bakre Confederation orders ships to sail from Dorcastle and intercept the Imperials, they may not be able to get up steam and sortie quickly enough to catch them before they are past. If it's a stern chase toward the Empire, and those new Imperial ships are in the lead, we won't be able to catch them."

"I understand," Mari said. "But if it comes to that, maybe the arrival of Confederation warships off of Landfall will make it clear to the Empire that they had better cough up Kira fast."

The call to President of State Jane was short and frustrating. "I'll do what I can, Mari. But the lack of proof will make it hard to get immediate action ordered, and it sounds like we are already too late."

As Mari and Alain walked back toward the waiting Rocs and Mages Alera and Saburo, Alli and Calu accompanied them.

Mari noticed Alli blinking away tears. "Is that for Kira or Jason?"

"Both."

"I didn't know you were that fond of Jason."

"We are," Alli said. "The kid never had decent parents. He...he was talking to Gari once, and said that if Kira ever decided she wanted to marry him, he wondered if Calu and I would act as his mother and father at the ceremony. Can you believe that? Mari, we've got to find him, help him and Kira."

"I'm doing all I can, Alli."

"As am I," Alain said.

"We can't ask better than that," Calu said.

"And the big guns you built for those new Confederation ships should ensure the Empire knows they had better return Kira," Mari answered. "Yes, I'm scared for her and Jason, too. But if there is one thing I know, it is that Kira is not going to accept being a prisoner. She's going to fight them."

Expecting to be punished for her attempted escape, Kira was surprised when Lady Elegant showed up with dinner. The Imperial woman said nothing, sitting down the plate and glass, then leaving. The guards outside the door glared at Kira the entire time it was open, plainly hoping she would try something while they were prepared for her.

She sat down to eat, not hungry because of the tension riding inside her, but knowing that she had to keep her strength up. The food was spicier than usual, which normally wouldn't have been a problem for

Kira, but on top of the stress of the day it was too much. After only a few bites she shoved the plate away.

She took only one sip from the glass before realizing the wine in it wasn't watered at all. Kira looked down at the liquid suspiciously. Why would the Imperials give her unwatered wine after the events earlier today?

Shoving away the wine glass as well, Kira glared at the locked door, trying to think of a new plan. She tried to remember everything she had ever heard about Landfall. If she could get away as the ship entered the harbor, there should be a lot of places to hide in the old city. Even the Imperials might not be able to...

Kira blinked, feeling dizzy.

She shook her head, but the dizziness worsened. Standing up took an effort. Kira kept a firm grip on the chair as she stumbled to the bunk and fell onto it, rolling onto her back and staring upwards. Inexplicable tiredness warred with nausea inside her as her vision distorted more, rendering familiar objects hard to recognize.

How much time passed as she lay on her bunk, trying to stop the world from swirling around her? Kira couldn't tell as she fought the unnatural weariness that begged her to fall into sleep.

They must have drugged her. As punishment for the escape attempt, or as part of a predetermined plan to start breaking her spirit before the ship even reached Imperial territory? As she fought to stay aware and awake, Kira realized that if she had eaten her full meal and drunk all of the wine she would certainly be unconscious by now.

She heard the door to her room opening and closing, but could not muster the strength or the concentration to look toward it. A figure came into her frame of vision. Distorted and blurry though her eyesight was, Kira made out the face of Prince Maxim. What did he intend?

That became obvious as Maxim leaned over, his hands reaching. Kira felt pressure on her chest. Maxim's hands moved again, and she realized that he was pulling at her shirt.

More than ten years of self-defense training kicked in without conscious thought, overcoming the effects of the drugs. Kira's leg snapped up, driving her knee against the side of Maxim's head as he bent over her from the side. He staggered backwards as Kira made an immense effort fueled by her rage, managing to roll to her side and up, lunging to plant a fist in the center of Maxim's body.

Maxim kept backpedaling as Kira stayed on her feet by sheer will, forcing her feet into motion toward him, hands poised for another strike.

He reached the door, yanked it open and dodged out, pulling it shut behind him.

Kira hit the door with her full body as it slammed shut. Unable to remain on her feet, she slid down to the deck, trying desperately to keep from passing out. "I'll kill you if you come in here again!" she shouted through the door. "Do you hear me, Maxim?"

Sitting on the deck, she slumped against the door as the room seemed to spin about her. The urge to surrender to sleep was almost overpowering. But she didn't dare pass out, senseless, prey to whatever the Imperials might do.

Kira fought one of her toughest battles that night, minute by minute, doing everything she could to stay awake. She had never known a night could be so long. But whenever the effort seemed too hard, she remembered Maxim pawing at her and enough anger came to fight off the drowsiness.

She knew when morning had arrived by the sounds of the ship. The feet on the deck above her and in the passageway outside of her room, the conversations she could hear only murmurs of, and the rattle of equipment in use.

Kira sat on her bed, cross-legged. The effects of the drugs had worn off and her mind was as alert as that of someone who had stayed up all night could be. She thought she probably looked like someone who had been buried a week before and just recently dug up again. But that was all right. That matched her mood.

The Imperials thought that mother might be Mara, the Dark One, and Kira her unnatural offspring?

She'd give them the Dark One's daughter.

The lock clicked open, the door opened, and Lady Elegant came in with the breakfast tray as if nothing had happened the night before.

"Get out of here and take your drugged food with you," Kira told her, pitching her voice into a deep growl. "The same goes for you as what I told Maxim. Come in here again and I'll kill you."

Elegant hesitated, then gave Kira a smug smile. "You're going to be very hungry, and very, very thirsty, by the time we reach the Empire."

"You're not listening," Kira said, getting to her feet. "Maybe I should satisfy my thirst by drinking *your* blood."

She only took one step toward Lady Elegant before the woman fled the room so fast that she hit the opposite side of the passageway. Kira's last glimpse before the door hastily closed again showed Lady Elegant and the breakfast tray tumbling to the deck.

Kira walked over to the tiny sink, hefting the small pitcher of washing water next to it. Fortunately she hadn't washed her hands, so the pitcher was full, but there wasn't very much of it, and she didn't dare try to ration it because the Imperials might remember it was a source of water for her.

She went back to the bunk with the pitcher, drinking the water, and sat down again. There were running feet over her head on the main deck. Had Lady Elegant told others of Kira's threat?

Were the crewmembers and other Imperials aboard engaged in an anxious debate on whether or not Mara's offspring would prey on women as well as Mara's traditional quarry of young men? Were the young men anxiously fingering the talismans that many surreptitiously wore to protect them against Mara?

The thought shouldn't have been funny. Nothing should have been funny. But she laughed a little anyway. Because laughter was the only way to keep darkness at bay.

She wished she could feel the thread to Jason.

★

Captain Hagen, commander of the police forces of Dorcastle, met Mari and Alain as they dismounted from their exhausted Rocs. "I have bad news, Mari. The decision was made to send out warships to shadow the Imperials, but our search line hasn't spotted them. Either they are swinging very far north, or they got past Dorcastle before our ships went out."

Alain looked out to sea, trying not to let despair enter into him. "President Jane is here?"

"Yes, Alain. And I have been told that President in Chief Julan is on the way to Dorcastle. A message has gone out for Bakre Confederation forces to mobilize, though it is being characterized as a drill so far, not preparations for actual war. If the Imperials are going so far as to attack the family of the daughter, and word of that gets out, as it will, our hands may be forced even if the government doesn't want war. The people will demand it."

"I don't want war either," Mari said, looking around. Alain knew that she was remembering the last time war had come to Dorcastle. "But the Empire seems determined to force the hands of everyone." Mari rubbed her mouth, looking north. "I need to talk to the ambassador for the Western Alliance, as well as the one representing the Free Cities. Can you get them here, Hagen?"

"I'll see to it."

Mari turned to Alain. "Should we fly to Landfall? Try to meet Maxim at the pier as he tries to sneak Kira onto Imperial soil?"

He shook his head, fearing only darkness lay ahead for the world. "You know how badly certain persons in the Empire would like to have a clear opportunity to ensure you had a fatal accident. We would be putting you into serious danger, with no certainty that we could save Kira."

"Alain, there is nothing between those Imperial ships and the coast of the Empire."

"I know."

She heard the pain he kept hidden, and held him. They stood looking out to sea, together, yet thinking only of the one who was not with them.

Kira sat on her bunk. She had spent the last few days doing that or lying down, sleeping with her nerves still alert to wake her if the door opened, or meditating to slow her metabolism, conserving energy and minimizing the amount of fluids leaving her body. *I knew a fella stranded on a rock in the sea who lasted almost a week without water*, the first mate of *The Son of Taris* had reminisced. *He was in awful shape when we picked him up, but he'd spent the time lying in the shade of the rock instead of running around in the sun. Knew another sailor who'd been in a lifeboat with some others, under the sun down south. Her companions started dying after a day.*

"Thirsty" wasn't an adequate word for how Kira felt. Her throat was painfully dry. Her tongue felt too large in her mouth. She moved slowly when she had to, wanting to avoid expending strength. But so far her heart seemed to be fine, and she didn't feel dizzy or disoriented. She felt certain that in an emergency she could still summon enough speed and strength to deal with any immediate threat.

She hadn't been disturbed for days, not even to empty the chamber pot. Since her need for that had diminished with dehydration, Kira hadn't minded. The Imperials were obviously waiting for her to give in so they could safely enter the cabin. Kira had no doubt that any water given her would be drugged.

The hardest part had been the first few hours, as she had struggled with the sense of isolation. The loneliness of her imprisonment was finally taking a toll. But as Kira sat staring at the door that blocked her path to freedom, she had remembered being told to go to her room at home. Usually because of mouthing off to her mother. How many times had that happened?

She began thinking about her mother, and her father, and Jason entered the mental picture, too. They were out there, somewhere. They wouldn't abandon her. She might look alone, but she was not. Her parents and Jason were with her. The thread to Jason was too weak to see, but she was sure it was still there. Kira called up memories, reliving her life. What was that poem that Jason had quoted to her once? She hadn't understood it, so Jason had tried to explain what it meant. But now Kira did grasp the meaning of those words. *Stone walls do not a prison make, nor iron bars a cage...*

As long as her mind was free, she was not alone.

But she would also free her body, or die trying.

And so Kira remained calm, and quiet, through the days and the nights, waiting for a chance that she hoped would come.

The motion of the ship had been monotonously regular as it plowed through the waters of the Sea of Bakre, though the vibrations had diminished over a day ago, meaning the ship had slowed, probably to conserve fuel since the Imperials weren't running the boilers at their best efficiency. Now Kira felt the motion finally change even more, the ship slowing, turning, feet running on the deck over her head, the feel of the water altering. They were out of the swells of the sea, into somewhere with smoother, protected waters. A harbor, Kira thought. They couldn't possibly have reached the Empire yet. There were no decent ports along the south coast of the sea between Dorcastle and Landfall, and surely Maxim wouldn't have veered so far north as to be able to stop in a port of the Western Alliance or the Free Cities.

The Sharr Isles. They had to be there. The best port in the Sharr Isles was Caer Lyn, and if she knew anything about Maxim it was that he would insist on stopping in the best port.

Why had they stopped here? Kira heard the rumble of the anchor chain going out.

A while later the ship rocked to the thump of another ship coming alongside. Kira waited, hearing a lot of noise as orders were called. A low, irregular thunder began resonating through the ship. It sounded familiar, like an avalanche of small stones that went on and on.

Coal. The ship was taking on coal.

This would be her last chance to escape before the ship reached the Empire, an unexpected opportunity, what Jason bafflingly referred to as an "eastern egg." Kira looked toward the sealed porthole. She couldn't escape in clear sight during the day because getting ashore would offer no refuge. Technically neutral, the Sharr Isles had once again been under growing pressure from the Empire, which had gradually increased the number of "embassy guards" and other forces on the Isles until they outnumbered the Isles' own small militia. Her mother, trying to eject the Imperial forces with pressure short of war, had yet to succeed as the Empire kept pushing against the limits put on it by the treaty that had ended the war twenty years before. To all intents and purposes, the Sharr Isles were no more friendly to her than the Empire itself would be.

Would the ship leave as soon as coaling was completed? If that happened, Kira knew she would have to try to escape as the ship was leaving the harbor, hoping to make it ashore and hide inland. That would be a very slim hope with the Imperials in active pursuit, though.

But the other ships must need coal as well. And coaling took a long time, hours of backbreaking labor by the crew. Each ship would have to take on coal in an operation that would take all day, and even if this ship finished first it would wait on the others. Kira felt sure that Maxim would not want to arrive home in a single ship rather than leading the whole squadron in a triumphant entrance to Landfall.

She would know when night fell by the sounds of the ship. The crew would be tired. If she could get out and off the ship, she might have time to find a hiding place. That would mean taking out the guards outside her door, but Kira was desperate enough and determined enough that surprise should enable her to quickly overcome them.

Kira relaxed her control of her Mage powers very slightly, probing for the presence of Maxim's Mage. There he was, close enough to be still on the ship, but betraying no trace that he had noticed her. She felt for the power around her. Water was never a good place for power, but harbors were better than open water. There should be enough. She wouldn't need much for the small spell needed to get out of this room. That might alert the Mage as well. She would have to be prepared to silence him if he came to investigate.

Wait. Wait. Stay calm. Kira heard the work of coaling eventually end, but the anchor wasn't brought in and the ship remained gently rocking in the harbor. She had guessed right. Night would come, and she would escape this time. Because the alternative was too horrible to contemplate.

Kira waited, mentally walking through her escape time and again.

There had been more noise that Kira couldn't identify. What was going on? Following that the sounds of many people on deck, diminishing and then ceasing.

She heard an occasional noise as her guards shifted position outside her room. Still two of them. After so much time with nothing happening, they would be complacent, bored, unprepared for a surprise.

It was time.

Kira got down off the bunk and quietly, carefully, slowly, stretched her muscles, preparing them for an explosion of effort when she got through the door. When ready, she went to one knee in front of the door, her eyes on the lock. The illusion of a lock in the illusion of a door on the illusion of a ship floating in the illusion of a sea. That was how Mages saw the world, how they had to see the world in order to work a spell. Kira would have to set aside her Mechanic view of the world and, for a brief time, fully accept that of a Mage if she was going to succeed.

She had done it once before. She could do it again.

Kira focused on the lock, reaching out to the power in the area. Waiting for a reaction from Maxim's Mage, she was surprised not to be able to sense him nearby. He had left the ship. Her spirits buoyed by that unexpected windfall, Kira set her mind fully to her task. The illusion of a lock. But if part of that illusion was overlaid by another, an illusion that made part of the lock not there, then it would not hold. The door would be open for her.

Kira knelt before the lock and concentrated, trying to recall how she had done the same thing six months before. The illusion of a lock. The smaller illusion that part of the lock was missing. That—

CHAPTER SIX

Breathing heavily as if after sudden exertion, Kira looked around, totally disoriented.

She was standing in the passageway. This was still the Imperial ship.

The bodies of the two guards were lying on the deck outside her door. Both were breathing, but one was bleeding and neither one was conscious.

Kira had an Imperial dagger in her hand. She must have taken it from one of the guards. There was blood on the blade.

Her nose hurt. Something was trickling down from it past the corner of her mouth and over her chin. She reached up to wipe under her nose and saw blood on her fingers. Without really thinking about it she pinched her nose to help stop the flow of blood.

A door close to her sagged partly open. Still stunned, Kira opened it slightly more to see that it led into the room where she had been held prisoner.

The spell must have worked. She must have gotten out of the room, and then…

Kira stared down at the Imperial guards. She must have surprised them, suddenly coming through a door they knew was locked.

Why couldn't she remember anything?

Aside from her and the out-cold bodies of the guards, the passageway was empty. Kira had grown used to hearing people walking past her door, so she knew that was an often-used walkway. She had hoped there would be little traffic during this evening, but she couldn't hear anyone else or any activity at all. The ship felt oddly deserted.

A bucket of drinking water rested in a wall-mounted holder nearby. Kira grabbed it and drank greedily, pausing to catch her breath, then drank again, feeling strength flow back into her. She had never known that tepid, flat water could taste that good.

A single pair of footsteps sounded. Coming closer.

Kira sat down the bucket and spun to face them, gripping the dagger tightly, determined not to be taken again. She felt a final trickle of blood from her nose wander down her chin and wiped at the distraction with her free hand.

A woman came around the corner and stopped at the sight of Kira. She studied the scene, taking in every detail. Perhaps thirty years old, she wore a fine suit, carrying the aura of power and confidence.

"Interesting," the woman said. "No one helped you?"

"No," Kira said, bringing the dagger into a position in front of her which could both defend and be used for attack.

Kira realized the woman was looking at the blood around her mouth with horrified fascination. "Who are you?" the woman asked.

"Kira of Dematr," she answered, wiping at her lower face again with her free hand, wishing she had taken a moment to wash her face instead of drinking all the water. "Pardon my appearance. I was thirsty."

The woman's eyes widened and went to the pool of blood on the deck. "You...have no other name?"

Why would she ask such a thing? Just because of...Kira remembered the blood around her mouth. Oh, blazes. She thought Kira had been drinking blood. And the guards at her feet were young enough to be the traditional prey of the Dark One. Or the Dark One's daughter.

Maybe it wasn't a bad thing at the moment for the woman to be scared about that, though.

"I'd rather not say," Kira replied. "Are you a friend or an enemy?"

"That depends. Do you intend killing me?" the woman asked.

"Only if I have to."

The woman smiled, the expression disconcerting to Kira. "I don't think that will be necessary. I would prefer to be a friend to such a… person as you. We haven't been introduced. I am Sabrin."

The name rang a bell with Kira. "Princess Sabrin? Of the Imperial household?"

"The same." Sabrin walked closer to Kira, still studying her. "You were about to die in an unfortunate accident for which Prince Maxim would be blamed."

"As much as I'd like to cause trouble for Prince Maxim," Kira said, "I don't like that plan."

"I see that it would have been a mistake." Sabrin stopped, barely out of reach of Kira's dagger. "If it could have been done at all. I have been told that the stories of your exploits were greatly exaggerated, that you were simply a spoiled child, weak and incapable. Yet you withstood the attempts to break you during this voyage. And clearly you are neither weak nor incapable, despite what my source among Maxim's followers reported. The door to your former prison is still locked, but hangs open. I am not a believer in fairy tales, and yet—"

"All you have to know," Kira said, "is that I can defend myself."

"That is obvious. What else have you inherited from your mother? Time will tell. The mistake of underestimating her cost the Empire dearly. Would you accept my assistance?"

"Yes," Kira said, watching Sabrin to be sure she was making a good-faith offer to help.

"Unfortunately," Sabrin said, "my options are limited. I do not have sufficient forces on hand to deal with Maxim should he dispute ownership of you."

"What if you were my hostage?" Kira asked.

Sabrin shook her head. "Maxim would like nothing better than for me to 'accidentally' die during an attempt to rescue me from you. Your best option is to flee, having slain all the guards aboard this ship."

"I haven't—" Kira began.

"The others are dead. Never mind how. You'll be given the credit. And I do think you could have done it, couldn't you? If you are finished with these two, I have people who will deal with them." Princess Sabrin studied Kira again. "Like Maxim, I had seen you as an obstacle. But you would make a good ally, wouldn't you? And I do wonder to what lengths Maxim would go to try to recover you. He doesn't like failing."

"An ally?" Kira asked, her mind having fastened on that unexpected word.

"Unfortunately, because of the balance of forces in this harbor, I can be only a passive ally of yours once I leave this ship," Sabrin said. "Time is short. If you will accompany me?"

Kira followed warily as Princess Sabrin walked to the end of the passageway and opened a door. "Your pistol and holster are in the top drawer there. You will find additional ammunition in the next drawer down. I recommend that you take it. I will go on deck and await you."

"Wait," Kira said. "All the rest of the crew is dead?"

"There were only about twenty left aboard," Sabrin said. "Scattered about the ship. Some of Prince Maxim's personal staff and followers are still ashore. Another, who was actually my follower and hidden among Maxim's, will leave with me. The rest of the crew are in longboats from this ship and others in the Gray Squadron. Maxim's Mage foresaw the arrival of a boat in this harbor late this evening carrying a certain young man whose very existence enrages Maxim. Maxim can't stand the idea that you would prefer someone else to him."

"Jason?" Kira said. She looked down at herself. There it was again. The intangible thread, leading off into the darkness. Jason must be close enough for it to be visible once more. "How did he—?"

"You'll have to ask him. Maxim waits with his crew to ensure the boy's death. They are just inside the harbor, wanting to be certain that he cannot escape." Sabrin looked Kira over. "It's quite a compliment to your man that Maxim thought he needed such a strong force to deal with him."

"I'll let him know you said so."

"Is he…like you?"

"Maybe," Kira said. The legends about Mara varied, but most painted her as almost unstoppable, her undead body nearly impervious to harm and unnaturally swift as well as strong.

"I see. I nonetheless advise that you move quickly. I assume you are wise enough to know that trying to hide in Caer Lyn would be folly? Of course you know that. If we meet again, remember that I am not your enemy. And if you should meet your mother again, you might inform her that Princess Sabrin aided you at a time when it mattered. We could do much together, don't you think?"

"Why?" Kira demanded. "Why are you different from Maxim? Are you different from him, or am I just a weapon for you to use against him?"

Sabrin eyed Kira for a moment before answering. "I do what I must, but unlike Maxim, I know the value of people. People who can think. Who can be counted on. Who deserve some loyalty in return. Some think that a weakness. If you are like your mother, I know that you do not." Her gaze on Kira grew defiant. "You *are* like your mother and your father, are you not? Loyal to that man of yours and no other? I saw it in you when I mentioned him. I have one husband, Lady Kira. And no other lovers. You understand? I'm the odd one at the Imperial court because of that. But the court has not always been as it is, and it will not remain as it is. The court is weak, because its culture rewards betrayal in every form. I will change that."

"I understand." Kira had heard enough about the Imperial court to know what Sabrin was referring to. The debauchery that had become common in the decades since the massive Imperial defeat at Dorcastle and as the old emperor aged might have been exaggerated in the telling, but her mother had told Kira there was a sordid truth behind the lurid stories. And Kira could see that Sabrin was telling her the truth about her own intentions. "You'll make a good empress."

Sabrin smiled. "If you became Maxim's consort, I think I'd have some serious competition. You have no…historical desire in that direction?"

"No. I'm happy in the west. You can have the Empire."

"I will have it. If I live." She turned and walked away, going up a ladder and out of Kira's sight.

Kira hesitated for only a moment, yanking open the drawer and finding her pistol just as promised. Kira hurriedly strapped on the shoulder holster and examined the weapon, making sure it was ready for use. The extra magazine was also there. She found a couple of boxes of ammunition in the next drawer down and stuffed them into the pockets of her jacket. In the same drawer she saw her sailor knife and returned it to the sheath on her belt.

Holding the Imperial dagger in one hand and her pistol in the other, Kira went cautiously up the ladder and found herself on the main deck, enshrouded in the darkness of late night. Only a few clouds obscured the stars above Caer Lyn, but the moon wasn't up. After the light below deck, the night felt ominously dark.

As Kira's eyes adjusted to the darkness, she saw Sabrin speaking with a half dozen other men and women, who gave her a wide berth as they walked past Kira and went down the ladder. Naked blades glittered in their hands as they went by her. "Where are they going?"

"I told you my people would take care of those two," Sabrin said. "Those guards have more blood on their hands than you can imagine, and their deaths will be far more quick and merciful than the murders they have carried out at the orders of Prince Maxim. Two of those sent to kill them have personal reasons for vengeance."

"They're unconscious. Unable to defend themselves."

"So was the boy one of those men slew to help clear Maxim's path to being declared crown prince."

The six came back up on deck, their leader nodding to Princess Sabrin. "I am leaving," she told Kira. "When I do, you will be the only…person left on this ship. Farewell until we meet again."

Sabrin went down the ladder on the side of the ship, her six followers coming behind. Running to look over the railing, Kira saw Sabrin getting into a boat. One more empty boat bobbed in the water next to it.

As Sabrin sat down and her followers began working the oars, Kira spotted another figure huddled in the boat. Despite the cloak muffling the figure's shape, Kira thought she could identify Lady Elegant. Elegant had been Sabrin's agent among Maxim's staff? She must have told Sabrin that Kira was aboard this ship. But Lady Elegant had done nothing else to help Kira, either to protect her secret role or because she had disliked Kira as much as she appeared to.

Kira looked across the water in the direction that Sabrin's boat was heading, seeing the barely visible shape of another Imperial craft. Not a warship like this one, but a much smaller yacht-like craft. If that was all the force Sabrin had available to her in Caer Lyn, it was little wonder she said she couldn't withstand an attack by the ships and sailors available to Maxim. That yacht, sail-driven, couldn't have outrun the warships either, if Sabrin had tried fleeing with Kira.

Kira looked to her left and right. A little ways forward of her, several shapes huddled unmoving on the deck. She had no desire to examine those bodies more closely. Sabrin's followers must have surprised Maxim's guards, probably with the help of Elegant.

Maxim's guards. Like the ones outside her prison. Kira took a deep breath, looking at the dagger she still held in one hand. What had happened? Why couldn't she remember? What if she had returned to awareness to discover that she had killed both of those guards, without even being conscious she was doing it? She'd have to tell Jason—

Jason.

Kira jerked around, staring toward the entrance to the harbor. How far off was Jason? Could the thread tell her? Almost as if answering her unspoken question, Kira gained a sense that Jason was still a ways from the harbor. She had a little time.

She felt anger rising at the memory of Maxim's assault on her. He had kidnapped her, drugged her, tried to hurt her, to "break" her.

A distraction would help her get out of the harbor and ensure Jason's safety at the same time. If that distraction also covered her tracks and caused a world of hurt to Maxim, all for the better.

And this ship had just filled its coal bunkers.

Despite having spent most of her life denying any similarity to her mother except in appearance, Kira was at her core her mother's daughter. People who attacked them paid a price.

Kira turned and ran for the ladder. She didn't know her way around this ship, but she knew the general layout of steam ships, knew well enough where the large engine room had to be to find it quickly. The wide hatch that should have sealed it hung open. Inside that room, two massive boilers sat gently glowing with heat, their fires low but ready to be built up when the ship had need of steam to drive its screw. Whoever was supposed to be watching the boilers had apparently suffered the same fate as the rest of those left aboard the ship.

What had happened to the two Mechanics? They had probably gone ashore, secure in their status to enjoy the night while the rest of the crew worked.

Kira knew boilers. She knew how to work them properly, and she knew what to avoid. Fire. A wonderful tool when harnessed. A deadly foe when out of control. Holstering her pistol and shoving the dagger into one pocket of her jacket, Kira braced herself and used both hands to push over the coal scuttle holding a supply of fuel ready to be added to one of the boilers, the dark, angular rocks of coal spreading across the deck. Walking to the other scuttle, she dumped it on the deck as well. Grabbing a metal tool hanging nearby, Kira hooked a handle and yanked open the door to the fire box of one of the boilers. Picking up one of the nearby shovels and wincing from the heat, she scooped out a pile of glowing coals. Turning, she tossed the live coals onto the layer of coal from the scuttles. Another shovel of burning coals added to the first, and Kira could see the coal from the scuttles beginning to catch fire.

She pulled open the heavy fireproof access door to one of the large fuel storage bunkers beyond, full of newly loaded coal waiting to feed the boiler. She pushed the shovel into it, pulling out coal and scattering it in a chain leading to the now-burning pile on the deck. She kept at it until a thick column of coal led from the burning pile into the bunker. Panting from the burst of heavy work, Kira paused to catch her breath, then yanked open the second coal bunker servicing the boiler room and spread coals from it as well, running these out the hatch and into the passageway beyond.

A water bucket rested near one bulkhead. Suddenly aware of how very thirsty she once more was, Kira seized the ladle and drank repeatedly, emptying the bucket.

How long had her sabotage taken? Kira brushed coal dust off of herself, pistol in hand once more, and vaulted up the ladders until she reached the main deck again, making sure every hatch along the way hung open. She found the second small boat still tied up. Princess Sabrin's boat was nowhere in sight.

Kira started down the ladder on the side of the ship, seeing wisps of smoke beginning to stream out of a hatch on the upper deck. She dropped the last steps into the waiting boat, worried that she had taken too much time ensuring that Prince Maxim's flagship would not be leaving this harbor.

The small utility boat/life boat wasn't anything big or fancy, an open craft which might comfortably have held ten people at the most, a single collapsible mast fastened to the floorboards just forward of amidships. Two oars were fastened on the floor boards. Just before the mast a wooden chest rested, doubtless carrying survival supplies. Otherwise, the boat was empty.

She moved quickly, releasing the lines holding the boat to the ship, bringing up the mast and shoving in the heavy pin to lock it upright and raising the sail. Shoving the boat away from the side of the ship, Kira swung the tiller as the sail caught the breeze. The boat slowly gathered speed through the calm waters of the harbor.

The winds, blocked by the hills surrounding Caer Lyn, were too light. She wouldn't be moving fast within the confines of the harbor. As her boat cleared the side of Maxim's ship, Kira stared forward into the dark, looking for the entrance to the harbor. She racked her memory for anything she could recall from the visit of *The Son of Taris* to Caer Lyn. Over there. The entrance should be that way.

The thread that wasn't there angled almost in that direction. Kira adjusted course and the sail, trying to gain speed, sweating out the slow progress of the boat. Maxim's boats had a lot of rowers. They could easily catch her in a sprint if she was spotted.

In contrast to the turmoil inside of her, the harbor felt too peaceful, too calm. Ships rode at anchor, dark but for the single lantern burning on each one. The waterfront showed little in the way of lights or activity, so it must be late enough that even most sailors had called it a night. The moon still wasn't up, the only illumination coming from the stars looking down at her with cold, distant indifference. Kira strained to hear any sounds that might warn of Prince Maxim's boats or any other danger. She couldn't hear anything. *It's quiet. Too quiet.* One of Jason's weird jokes from Urth. Was this what it meant?

She looked back, seeing a spreading cloud of smoke rising from Prince Maxim's ship, visible as a greater darkness against the night that obscured the stars. She caught a flicker of light on the underside of the smoke cloud. The fire she had set must be close to reaching the deck, unhindered by hatches that hung open, racing along the open passageways and up the ladders in search of fuel and air to feed its insatiable appetite. The metal of the ship wouldn't burn, but all of the freshly loaded coal, the oil and lubricants, the paint, the wooden decks laid over the steel structure, the many wood fittings, and the many fabrics and other cloth would feed the fire. Kira wondered how hot the fire was in the boiler room by now. Probably hot enough to melt and warp metal.

How long would it be until someone noticed that fire, sounded alarms, and the harbor erupted into activity?

Kira looked ahead again, willing her boat to move faster, grateful when a gust of stronger wind came to fill the sail. She could make out the darkness of the seawall to one side and the high ground marking Meg's Point on the other. The lighthouse on Meg's Point came into sight, giving her a clear mark to steer by. The wind picked up again as sheltering headlands around the harbor fell behind her.

Where should she aim for? Anyone lurking in ambush would be on one side or the other. She had no idea on which side Prince Maxim's boats were lying in wait. With no better option, Kira aimed for the center of the entrance, trying to remain equally distant from both sides.

A bell began clanging loudly behind her, breaking the calm of the night. Distant shouts carried faintly across the water. Kira risked a look back and saw that flames were now shooting up from the deck of Prince Maxim's ship, illuminating the harbor around it. Setting her face forward again, Kira drew her pistol and held her course.

She slid down low as the boat neared the entrance to the harbor, hoping that no one would be able to see her in the light from the stars and from the rapidly growing fire on the ship behind her. A blind man couldn't miss the sail, of course, but Kira had to hope that no one would pay attention to a boat leaving the harbor while they were scrambling to deal with a burning ship. The fire was now lighting up boats from the other Imperial ships pulling alongside Prince Maxim's ship and figures clambering aboard to try to fight the fire. Kira didn't think they'd have much luck at that.

More shouts, coming from a different direction as the roar of alarms and excitement grew around the burning ship. Kira risked a glance to port and saw several longboats leaping out of concealment near the breakwater just inside the harbor entrance. She held her pistol ready, barely breathing as the boats swung away from the breakwater, oars flashing in the night as they sent white spray flying. The sight made Kira remember the "white-winged ships" of Jason's favorite story from Urth.

No one on the longboats seemed to notice Kira's little craft as they raced into the harbor toward the floating bonfire that Prince Maxim's ship was rapidly becoming. Lying low, Kira thought she caught a glimpse of the robes of Maxim's Mage in one of the longboats. She redoubled her efforts to hide her Mage presence.

The wind freshened some more, pushing her boat along faster. Maxim's longboats were well past, so Kira risked raising herself to see better as her boat sailed through the broad channel between the breakwater and Meg's Point. The light from the burning ship had become so strong that it shone on Kira's sail. She took another look back and saw the ship fully engulfed in flames. Squinting against the brightness of the fire, Kira saw Maxim's longboats still a little ways from the ship.

The harbor rocked to the blast of a detonation as the aft ammunition magazine exploded, the combined force of all the shells tearing apart the stern and hurling debris in all directions. Kira felt the force of the concussion on her back and saw it ironically offer an extra push to her sail.

Another look back as her boat cleared the harbor. She couldn't see Maxim's longboats. How badly had they been hit by the force of the explosion? It was too much to hope that a flying piece of shrapnel had hit Maxim, but Kira wished for it anyway. The burning ship's bow rose upward as the shattered stern sank to rest on the bottom of the harbor, fire engulfing what was left of the ship.

"I hope you're enjoying the show," Kira said, imagining that Princess Sabrin could hear her.

The swells of the sea began rocking the boat in an oddly gentle rhythm. Where in the expanse of waters was Jason? Instead of relaxing as Caer Lyn fell behind, Kira's anxiety spiked again as she searched the night for any sign of Jason's boat.

The thread. It wasn't there. Kira's heart sank. If the thread connecting her to Jason had vanished, did that mean…?

She got a grip on herself. This was a Mage thing. What would her father advise? Search inside yourself. But she was concentrating so hard on blocking her Mage presence that—

Of course. She was suppressing the thread along with everything else related to her Mage powers.

Kira cautiously relaxed her efforts, hoping that Maxim's Mage was too far off to spot anything.

There it was! Visible as a slightly luminous gleam like glowing spider silk leading off to starboard. Kira gasped with relief and adjusted her course, the thread acting as a compass aimed at Jason.

Kira caught her breath. A patch of white had briefly appeared to one side as she swept her gaze across the sea. Looking back that way full on revealed nothing. Blast it! Just her imagination at work.

Wait. One of the sailors on *The Son of Taris* had told her a trick for when acting as lookout at night. A faint image, a faint light, would be invisible when looked at directly, but if you turned and looked from the corners of your eyes it would appear.

She tried, aiming her sidelong gaze with the help of the faintly visible thread. There it was. A small white object, barely illuminated by the light of the stars. Kira tacked the boat, swinging the tiller as she aimed to intercept the sail.

She could see it clearly now, the thread leading straight to it and strengthening as the distance grew less. Kira adjusted her course again, aiming ahead of the other boat's track to intercept it.

Closer and closer. Now she could see the hull, then the faint outline of one person at the tiller of the other boat. Was he looking her way? She couldn't tell. The figure looked like it was slumped over, not sitting straight. But the thread was like a cable now, pointing unerringly toward the other boat. Kira damped it, clamping down on her Mage powers to avoid the chance of being sensed.

Closing rapidly now, and still the huddled figure at the tiller of the other boat hadn't moved. Unable to restrain herself any longer, Kira yelled as loudly as she could. "Jason! Jason, it's me!"

No response. Closer. "*Jason!*"

He must have been pushing himself hard. Too hard? Had the exertion and exposure been too much for him? Had she gotten this far only to find Jason had perished? No, impossible. The thread would've broken if Jason died. But he could be on the edge of death, too far gone to save. Fear drove another shout. "Jason! Answer me this instant or I'll never speak to you again!"

"Kira?" the hail came back in a raspy, weak voice that was nonetheless clearly Jason's. "It's really you?"

She didn't know whether to laugh with relief or yell again. "Yes, it's me! Heave to so I can bring this boat alongside you."

His sail dropped. Kira, nervous, swung the tiller too late and her boat slammed against the other, but Jason grabbed it before it could bounce away and looped a line over a cleat to hold the boats together.

And Kira was reaching across and Jason was doing the same and they were holding each other and she was kissing him and sobbing with relief and joy.

They weren't safe. Not by a long shot. But they were together.

"I'm a little delirious, I think," Jason said. "I'd been imagining finding you, and thinking I had. So when I heard you calling I thought it was that again, my mind playing tricks. But that last time, you sounded so worried. And I said to myself, 'She's worried about me. That's really Kira.'"

"Of course I was worried about you! I'm so glad to see you again and you're all right!"

Another tremendous explosion sounded from the direction of the harbor. Kira looked that way, seeing a fountain of fire blossoming into the sky, dots of black amid the inferno marking large metal fragments that had once been part of the doomed ship. The forward ammunition magazine must have finally blown.

"Did you do that?" Jason asked, staring.

"Why do you think I did it?"

"Did you?"

"Yes. I had a good reason! It's Prince Maxim's ship."

"Great! Was he aboard it?"

"No."

"Too bad," Jason said.

"Yeah. Can't have everything. With any luck, by the time the fires die down whatever remains of that ship will be so messed up they won't realize I escaped before it caught on fire." Kira laughed. "Actually, I left the ship right after it caught on fire. That'll teach them to pay attention when a girl says 'leave me alone'!"

"Kira," Jason said, "I love you, but sometimes you're a little scary."

"I get it from my mother. Jason, your boat is in awful shape!"

"Yeah," he said. "I sailed it from, uh, Gullhaven."

"Gullhaven? In this? Jason, this is a short-haul sailboat. It's not even supposed to be sailed out of sight of land."

"I know. But it was all I could get and I knew I needed to get to the Sharr Isles."

"You did?" Kira looked around Jason's boat, which had water sloshing in the bottom. The hull was leaking. The lines holding the sail were badly worn and looked ready to break. "You came all that way in this. You're amazing! But this thing is not going to stay afloat much longer. What have you got that you need to transfer to this boat?"

"Just a…a couple of empty bottles."

"Empty bottles? You don't have any food left? What about water?"

"It gave out a while back," Jason said, blinking at her like he was having trouble focusing.

"What gave out? The water or the food?"

"Both."

"You poor thing! You went through that for me! Give me the bottles and then get in this boat." Kira helped Jason clamber into her boat. She carefully got into Jason's battered craft. Should she sink it? If the Imperials found out they'd guess it was Jason's.

Maybe that wasn't a bad thing. Kira looked toward the coastline not far off.

She got both craft onto a heading for the rocks off Meg's point, putting a loose loop of line around the tiller of Jason's craft to hold it on course without making it obvious that the tiller had been tied in place. Raising the sail on Jason's boat again, she got back into her boat from Jason's empty craft, untying the line that held the two boats together. Leaving Jason's boat to be pushed by its sail and the surf toward the rocks, Kira swung her boat about and away, heading out to sea again.

The uproar from the harbor faded behind her as they got farther away.

But Kira felt something, like someone looking for her, and once again clamped down very tightly on her Mage senses. Maxim's Mage was trying to find out if she had escaped.

Everything began catching up with her. The days without food, the exertions of the evening, the tension since she had been kidnapped. She wanted nothing more than to curl up on the bottom of the boat and sleep after stuffing herself with whatever provisions the lifeboat had aboard. But Jason was obviously in even worse shape, having sailed in an open boat this far. She would have to hang on a little longer, but that didn't mean she couldn't get something into her stomach. "Jason, can you open that chest? There should be emergency supplies of food and water in it."

"Yeah," Jason said as he pulled out a brass pin and opened the chest. "Looks like bottles of water. And crackers. Hardtack, I guess."

"Hardtack would last a long time. Give me one bottle and some crackers. Can you break a cracker for me? There's a knife fastened to the inside top of the chest. Take some of the water and cracker pieces for yourself, too."

Having literally broken the bread for their meal, Jason sprawled on the bottom of the boat, looking at Kira. "I can't believe I made it."

She took another look back to gauge their distance from the harbor. "I can't believe you tried. Did I tell you that you're amazing? How did you know to come here?" she asked around the piece of hard cracker softening in her mouth.

"That guy Lukas told us."

"Master Mechanic Lukas? When did he say that the ships would stop here?"

"At that talk after the dinner at your parents' house," said Jason, as if the answer was obvious. "He said those ships could get from the Sharr Isles to Tiaesun but it would be as far as they could go without refueling. So it's obvious that if they left Tiaesun with full coal loads they would have to stop at the Sharr Isles on their way back."

Kira felt like slapping herself, but she had a water bottle in one hand and the tiller in the other. "I completely forgot about that. I wonder if Mother and Father remembered? Do you have any idea why the Imperial ships weren't intercepted while they were heading up the coast of Tiae and the Bakre Confederation?"

Jason nodded. "The Imperials were real smart, Kira. Do you remember at that party, when you thought you saw yourself?"

"I'd forgotten. Do you mean that was real?"

"Yeah. Not something supernatural. Someone the Imperials had found who looked a lot like you. I bet she was at that party to hear you talk and see how you walked and stuff like that. Then later they probably made her up to look like your double. You know, the hair and the clothing."

"She couldn't have fooled Mother and Father!" Kira protested.

"She didn't. She left the palace at dawn before your parents got up, in full view of everybody long after Maxim's ships had left. It didn't seem possible that you could be aboard those ships."

"Couldn't they catch her and figure out she wasn't me?"

"She flew off on a Roc! Headed east!"

"Blazes," Kira sighed. "They were smart."

"It took me a while to figure it out, too. But I sent a message to your parents. I told them it was the doppelganger. So they know."

"The doppelganger?" Kira repeated, feeling a little sick inside.

"Yeah. You said you'd tell them."

"I was on my way to do that when the Imperials knocked me out! I never got the chance!"

"Oh," Jason said.

"It's my fault. I forgot to tell them earlier. Is that why you had to come in this boat? Why aren't you on a Confederation warship?"

"They wouldn't listen to me!" Jason said, his voice breaking. "They thought I was losing it. And maybe I was. I just suddenly got this feeling that you really needed me, right then, and I couldn't wait."

"You got that feeling suddenly?" Kira asked, shocked. "Were you on a train?"

"Yeah. How did you know?"

"Um…I'll tell you later. Why didn't you explain to Mother and Father what the doppelganger was? Weren't you with them?"

"No," Jason said, shaking his head. "I got sent back to Danalee while your mom and dad stayed in Tiaesun, but before I got there, when the train was going through Minut, I got that feeling and no one escorting me would listen, so I, um, left the train."

"While it was moving?" Kira asked.

"Yeah. And then I jumped off another train and onto a third train somewhere north of that, because I knew I needed to get to Gullhaven."

"You jumped off of a train all on your own?" Kira said, feeling an absurd desire to laugh.

"Two trains," Jason said. "Because this crazy girl taught me that no one is allowed to go anywhere by train without jumping off along the way."

"I'm so proud of you! Someday, Jason, you and I will ride a train to wherever it is going and not jump off. How'd you get that boat?"

"I…borrowed it."

"Stars above, Jason, I just sent it onto the rocks! Why didn't you tell me that you'd stolen it?"

"I was going to," Jason said, "but that ship blew up!"

"So it's *my* fault?"

"Um…wow…so tired…about to pass out…"

"You're not fooling anybody, Jason. But it's all right. Sorry. I'm still sort of tense." Kira felt tears of relief finally starting. "I can't believe we're together, and I escaped from that awful ship, and you were coming to get me, and now we have a chance, Jason. Did I tell you that I love you?"

"What?" Jason's eyes were wide in the night.

"I realized it. On the ship. Maybe it was my feelings finally reaching that point or maybe I finally realized what my feelings meant. And then I saw the thread. The thread was proof, Jason. I love you."

"I…I love you, too," Jason stammered. "Thread?"

"It connects us!" Even with her Mage powers damped, when she and Jason were this close the thread glowed between them. "It's there now! Only it isn't."

"Are you okay, Kira?"

"Yes! Ask my father! It's a Mage thing! Aren't you going to say anything?"

"I did! I love you, too! I feel awful, I can barely think, but I can't believe how wonderful I felt when I heard you say that."

"Good." Kira smiled at him. "Because it felt so wonderful when I realized I loved you. Get some sleep, Jason. I need you to rest so you can take over from me. No, wait. Before you sleep, there's something we have to decide."

She waved her hand toward the east. "At this time of year, the prevailing winds come out of the west and head that way. You made really good time from Gullhaven, didn't you? Home is to the west, but if we try to beat against those winds we'll make such slow headway that we'd be sitting ducks. But we can't go east because there's nothing east of us but the Empire, and I am not going there."

"Where's the closest land from here?" Jason asked.

"South," Kira said. "But that would take us to the salt marshes north of the city of Ringhmon, and anywhere near Ringhmon is at least as bad a place for us as the Empire."

"That leaves north."

"Yeah. The Free Cities. But coming out of Caer Lyn means we're already east of Marida. We'll have to steer as close to northwest as we can and still make good speed. If we hit the coast east of Marida it'll be a long, tough walk to the city, but still better than any other option we have. We'd be safe in the Free Cities. They'd protect us."

Jason nodded. "I remember the coast around Kelsi, those mountains coming right down to the sea."

"Yes," Kira said. "Pretty much the same thing until you go far enough east to reach the end of the Northern Ramparts, but then you're in the plains west of Umburan, which are Imperial territory."

"North is still our best bet, right?"

"Absolutely. We go north?"

"Yes, Lady Kira, let's go north."

"There should be a compass in the chest. Yes. Thanks. Did I tell you that I love you?"

"A couple of times," Jason said. "Are you all right?"

"Not really, but I can hold it together until you get some sleep."

"I'd better sleep, then." He was only silent for a moment, though. "Kira? I was so scared. Seeing you again, safe, is…"

"I know," Kira said. "The worst is over."

She didn't believe that. But she could always hope.

CHAPTER SEVEN

Kira spent the rest of the night fighting off tiredness as she tried to hold the sailboat on a northerly course. She kept waking up to find that the boat had swung under the push of the wind toward the northeast. Finally she lashed the tiller, forcing herself awake at intervals to make sure she didn't need to tack the boat or adjust course. The stars looked down at her as swell after swell rolled the boat, the motion making it even harder to stay awake.

A larger than usual passing swell slapped the boat as dawn was brightening the sky to the east, splashing spray that woke Jason. He stared around, disoriented, finally focusing on Kira. "You're really here."

"I think so," Kira said, barely able to keep her eyes open.

"I thought it must have been a dream."

"Yeah. That's me. A dream."

"Kira, did you really…?"

"What, Jason? Set that ship on fire and make it explode? Yes. If you're going to be with me, you'll just have to accept that sometimes I'll do things like that."

"What I meant was, I thought you'd said something to me."

"Oh," Kira said, trying to focus on Jason. "You mean when I said I love you? Yes. I love you. I love you. I really mean that, but Jason, if you don't take over at the tiller I am going to pass out in another minute."

He scrambled back to the stern, sitting down next to her. "I've got it. I'm sorry. You said you were in bad shape, but I didn't realize—"

"You were in worse shape," Kira mumbled. "Compass. Here. Steer as much to the north as you can without losing too much speed. We have to reach the coast as fast as we can without going too far farther east."

"I got it."

"Wake me up if you need me."

"I got it, Kira."

"And if..." She concentrated, trying to remember what she had been going to say. "Never mind."

Kira crawled enough forward to have room to curl up in the bottom of the boat and let sleep finally fill her.

She opened her eyes to see the side of the boat. The sight made her smile. As bad as things were, Jason was in this boat with her, and the boat represented freedom from the prison she had escaped, and a chance to reach safety. Looking up, Kira saw a bright blue sky flecked with clouds and realized how much she had missed being able to see the sky. "How long did I sleep?" she said, grimacing as she felt the taste in her mouth. What was that?

"It's about noon," Jason said, still seated at the tiller. He looked tired, but all right otherwise. "Some hero I am."

"What do you mean?" Kira sat up, sticking out her tongue as she tried to clear her mouth. "What the blazes did I eat last night?"

"Hardtack," Jason said. "But there's something around your mouth."

"Around my mouth?" she asked, wiping her hand roughly across it and looking. "Oh, yeah, the blood. And some coal dust."

"That's blood?" Jason asked, suddenly alert and staring at her.

"It's my blood," Kira reassured him.

"That's supposed to make me feel better?"

"It'd be a lot worse if it was someone else's blood around my mouth. How bad do I look?"

Jason hesitated.

"That bad?" She pulled a water bottle from the survival chest and took a drink. The water cleared out some of the muck from her mouth. "That's better. What was that about not being a hero?"

"I was going to rescue you. Instead you rescued me."

Kira made a derisive snort. "Jason, I thought we weren't keeping score. Besides, knowing that you were out there somewhere kept me going. Having you here now is…you don't know how good that feels. And if you hadn't been here to take over steering I probably would have passed out and this boat would be running aground on an Imperial beach east of here about now. And also besides, if you hadn't been coming, Maxim wouldn't have almost stripped that ship I was on of crew so he could sure of killing you."

"Wait. What?" Jason asked, looking worried and baffled.

"He had a Mage who had a vision that you were coming to Caer Lyn. Maxim wanted you dead. Which gave Princess Sabrin a chance to kill those of the crew he left behind and for me to escape from the room I was imprisoned in," Kira finished.

"Did you use your Mage powers to do that?"

"Yeah. I guess."

"You guess?" Jason's gaze on her sharpened again. "You don't remember?"

Kira sighed, looking over the side at the water. "No. I was in the room, getting ready to do the spell to open the lock, and then I was outside the room with two unconscious guards at my feet and a bloody nose."

Jason looked at her, his gaze troubled. "You can knock out guards and not even remember it?"

"Lots of girls have special talents," Kira said, picking up a small broken-off piece of hardtack the consistency of slate rock and putting it into her mouth to soften.

"Kira—"

"Look, there's nothing we can do about it now. All right? Anyway, after I got out of the room, I met Princess Sabrin, who told me where to find my pistol...I've got it, see?...and left me this boat."

"She's an Imperial princess and she boarded Maxim's ship to save you?"

"Actually," Kira said, "I think she was coming to kill me so she could blame it on Maxim. Because Lady Elegant hates me. But Sabrin changed her mind and now she and I are best buds if she doesn't change her mind a second time and try to kill me again which she isn't sure she can do anyway because she thinks I drink blood and am the daughter of Mara."

"I must still be really tired," Jason said. "I'm having trouble following this."

"The important thing is, the fact that you were coming to Caer Lyn enabled me to escape," Kira said. "Which makes you really important, and once again my hero, and the guy I love. This thread is so amazing."

"What thread?"

"The one running between you and me! The one that's not there! With us so close it's strong enough for me to see in full daylight. How cool is that?"

"Kira, please drink some more water."

She obliged him, knowing that she would have to inventory their remaining supplies to see how much they would have to be rationed. "So, um, where was I? I love you. I was so worried that I'd never get to tell you that because I was afraid I'd never see you again, but now no matter what else happens, we're together."

"Right." Jason pointed behind them. "The smoke from the burning ship was still visible for a while, but I lost sight of it some time ago. The fire must have burned out."

"Once the ship sank to the bottom of the harbor only the parts still above water could keep burning."

"Oh, yeah. I haven't seen any stacksmoke that would mean they were after us."

"I hope they think I was killed in the fire. If they can access the room I was imprisoned in they might be able to figure out there isn't any body in there, but the bodies of the two guards—"

"You killed those guards?"

"No!" Kira looked down. "Princess Sabrin's people killed them. Anyway, they'll have to figure out whether one of those bodies belongs to me. If they're in really bad shape that might not be too easy."

"It's pretty easy to tell a female skeleton from a male skeleton," Jason said.

She stared at him. "Can you do that?"

"I think so. I mean, health and science and medicine and stuff. The pelvis is the easiest place to spot the difference."

"Just like when people are alive, huh?" She noticed that Jason had fallen silent and looked his way. "What?"

"Kira," Jason said, his expression strained, "did they—"

"No."

He sighed. "I'm glad you weren't hurt."

"Me, too." Kira dug in the emergency chest so she could find an excuse to change the subject. "We've got a fishing line and a hook. We can try using hardtack for bait after we soften up a piece enough to stick the hook through it. We've also got some more hardtack crackers. Some more bottles of water. A chart of the Imperial coast that we hopefully won't have need for. And the knife. I've already got two. Do you want this one or the Imperial dagger?"

"I'll take the survival knife," Jason said.

"You still have the knife you were wearing at the banquet, right?"

"Wrong. I was asked to surrender that knife when I packed to go back to Danalee."

"Seriously? I'm going to give my parents a hard time about that when we see them again!" She looked in the chest once more, hoping to find anything else that might help. "I guess putting a blanket in here would have strained the Imperial budget," Kira complained. "We could have used that to make a tent during the day and...hey, why isn't your skin damaged? You spent all those days in that open boat and you don't look like the sun hurt you at all."

"Damage from the sun? Oh, you mean skin injury from solar radiation? The standard Universal Life Systems gene pac protects against that. No skin cancer and no burns."

"Exposure to the sun can't hurt you?"

"No," Jason said. "I mean, if I spend enough time in it I'll get dehydrated and maybe suffer heat stroke, but—"

"Let's not talk about dehydration," Kira said. "So, if you and I had kids—"

"Huh?" Jason stared at her. "Kids? You and me?"

"It could happen. Jason? Jason! Stars above, snap out of it! You look like every circuit breaker in your brain tripped at the same time!"

"I'm sorry, I just, um…" He gestured vaguely, looking confused. "You told me last night for the first time that you love me, and this morning you're already talking about having kids!"

She shook her head at him, exasperated. "Do you think I want to start trying to have kids right now? No, you're a guy, so you're probably *hoping* I'll want to do that. I know that when guys look at girls they're just thinking about what they'd be like in bed, but believe it or not when girls look at guys they're also thinking about what might come along nine months after the fun and whether they'd be happy that particular guy had been part of making that happen. Girls are weird that way."

"Oh." Jason nodded, looking down, his mouth tight. "That's why you had to take a while with me. I understand."

"Understand what? What did I say that made you unhappy?"

"It's okay. You know what my parents are like, and you know that I'm the product of them, mostly anyway. I understand why you were worried about what kind of parent I'd be and—"

"No," Kira said, giving the word force. "That never played a role in how long it took for me to decide. You have nothing in common with your parents."

"People inherit stuff, Kira."

"People are more than what they inherit! Each one is unique and able to be whoever they are, not who their parents were or who everyone else is! My father showed me that, my mother fought to break a

Guild that claimed some people were born better than others, and I've seen it in the people around me. Look at me! I'm not my mother. Or my father. I'm me! And you're you! Why don't you know that, Jason from the wonderful world of Urth?"

He looked at her for several moments before smiling. "Maybe we've spent so much time looking at the trees that we've forgotten to pay attention to the forest."

"Is that another strange Urth saying?"

"Yes. What it means is, you're right."

"So we could have saved a lot of time if you'd just conceded I was right from the start?" Kira said.

"I ought to start doing that," Jason said, grinning.

"Yes, you should. I can tell you're joking, but you really should. How about we talk about something less stressful, like what we're going to do if those Imperial ships show up behind us and heading our way?"

"That would be less stressful," Jason agreed, turning to look back to the south. "What are our chances?"

"If we see them coming? Depends what time it is and how close we've managed to get to the coast," Kira said. "If they spot us during daylight and we're too far off from land, they'll run us down easily, even if we turned and ran straight with the wind. If it's night, each of those ships has a searchlight, but we might have a chance of not being spotted if we lower the sail and stay low." Kira also looked south. "The biggest advantage you and I have right now is that Maxim doesn't know I escaped in a boat. I ran your boat aground so he'd think you'd made it to Caer Lyn. If Maxim spends enough time searching the island for you we'll be safe."

Jason looked at Kira. "Something is worrying you, though."

Kira made a face. "There is the problem of no body in my former room on the ship. And I'm pretty sure Lady Elegant was Princess Sabrin's agent among Maxim's people. Elegant did not like me. She also knows I escaped Maxim's ship by boat. If she feeds that information back to Maxim, we're in trouble."

"It might take her a little while to pass that information in a way that Sabrin won't know about," Jason suggested.

"It might. And every hour makes a difference." Kira sagged back against the mast, suddenly aware of how tired she still was.

"How bad was it?" Jason asked.

She hadn't even realized that was what had hit her again. But Jason had seen it. That allowed her to smile slightly at him. "Pretty bad. I kept remembering the dinner, and how wonderful my parents looked, and how handsome you were. It had all been so beautiful, but when I got kidnapped I was surrounded by ugliness. On the outside, most of it looked nice. Like Prince Maxim. But on the inside, it was all ugly. I knew I couldn't let the ugliness win, so I kept remembering you and Mother and Father to remind me that beauty did exist."

"I'm glad I could help," Jason said, smiling.

"It got harder when I wasn't eating or drinking anything for the last few days, but even then I told myself that I was a Lancer, and no matter what I would not embarrass my fellow Lancers. I would win. Or die."

Jason's smile vanished. "You thought it might come to that?"

Kira shrugged, trying to pretend that it wasn't a big deal. "I knew that if I had to risk death to escape, I would. Aunt Bev told me about that. People who want to make you weak, their captive, try to break you down, try to make you doubt yourself and fear them. And even someone as strong as Aunt Bev had trouble breaking free of that. I knew I had to get away before they did that to me."

"That kind of mental conditioning is really hard to resist," Jason said. "Even the strongest people can be worn down. It sounds like you were scared of that."

"I wasn't scared, Jason, I was—" She looked down, laughing softly at herself at the same time as she tried to fight off tears. "Yeah. I was scared. I couldn't admit it to myself, though. Still can't. If I stop to think about what could still happen, what could happen to you, it's…it's hard."

"You can tell me," Jason said. "I know all about keeping things inside and letting them hurt."

"I know. I just…" Kira looked at him, trying not to hide anything. "It's hard being the daughter of the daughter, you know? Still is. I have to be someone that she would be proud of, and someone who people expect me to be because of who my mother is. I can't be weak. I can't fail. Because that would make Mother, and my father, look bad."

Jason gazed back at her, his eyes sad. "Kira, how can you not know how proud they are of you? You're supposed to be able to tell when someone lies to you. Can't you see the truth in your mother when she tells you how great she thinks you are? And look what you've already done, dragon slayer!"

"That was almost an accident," Kira said. "You know how terrified I was and just acting by instinct, and everybody is all 'Wow, she slew a dragon in hand-to-claw fighting' when all I was doing was trying to keep from having my arms bitten off."

"It still counts," Jason said.

She found herself smiling at him again. "It does, huh? Says who?"

"The rules say anyone who kills a dragon is a dragon slayer. Right? The rules don't specify how. They don't say you have to slay the dragon while making witty jokes and pausing to drink tea. So it counts."

Kira smiled wider. "Have you heard my mother talk about her first dragon? In that warehouse in Dorcastle? How she was so scared, but my father, who wasn't even her boyfriend then, stood with her and how much that helped her?"

"Yeah," Jason said.

"You'd do the same thing, wouldn't you?"

"I…hope I would."

"I know you would." She got up, wincing as stiff muscles protested and carefully made her way back to sit beside Jason at the stern as the boat rocked beneath them. "Maybe I'm not my mother, but I've got a man as good as the one she found."

He stared back at her in disbelief. "Me?"

"You're the only man I've got," Kira said. She kissed him, keeping it quick since she suspected her breath was as bad as that of the dragon she had killed in Ihris. "And I couldn't be prouder of him."

Jason laughed, shaking his head. "We are both mental cases. Do you know that? But as long as we're both happy I guess that's all right. I sure wish I'd had a father like yours."

"I'm willing to share, Jason. Uncle Calu thinks a lot of you, too."

"Do you realize that we're all at sea but finding ourselves at the same time?"

"Is that another Urth thing? Jason, sometimes I wish you'd just talk like a normal person." Kira flinched. "Oh no. That's what Mother says to Father sometimes when he's going all Mage on her. I'm turning into my mother. It's like a curse I can't fight."

"I'm okay with that as long as you don't turn into *my* mother."

She hit him. But not very hard.

Kira took over steering the boat so that Jason could sleep some more. He resumed steering again a little before sunset. Unhappy with the amount of food and water available to them, Kira baited the hook with hardtack and managed to catch a decent-sized fish before night fell.

She looked at the fish, then at Jason. "You're the guy who eats raw fish. Do you want to do this?"

"No," Jason said, shaking his head quickly. "On Earth, I'd get a plate of sushi or sashimi that someone else had prepared. I have no idea how to do it myself."

"I don't enjoy gutting fish," Kira told him. "You owe me."

The Imperial dagger wasn't made for this kind of work, but Kira's sailor knife was. Knowing that unpleasant tasks didn't get any easier with delay, she closed the wooden chest, laid the fish flat on it, and slit open the belly from gills to tail. "We really ought to eat the guts, too."

"No, thank you," Jason said.

"How about the eyes? Good source of liquid."

"*No.*"

"We may not have a choice next time if our water gives out." Scooping out the innards with her bare hand, Kira tossed them overboard, quickly rinsing off her hand and the fish in the sea beside the boat.

She brought the fish back to the chest, scaled it, then pulled the fish apart to separate the flesh from the bones. "My Aunt Bev loves fishing. She loves doing this. There are a lot of things I admire about Aunt Bev, but she can have cleaning fish."

Kira offered Jason a chunk of raw fish on the knife blade. "Here. I made dinner, so you can wash the dishes."

"There aren't any dishes," Jason said, reluctantly putting the fish in his mouth and chewing slowly.

"Somebody is going to have to clean off the top of that chest."

When they had haggled off all the flesh they could, Kira set aside the fish head and tail to use as bait the next day. She settled back, resting. The sailboat cut steadily through the sea, its sail billowed out on the boom, rolling gently as it rode the broad swells marching across the Sea of Bakre. She gazed at Jason as he steered the boat, seeing the wind ruffle his hair, the small movements as he adjusted course to steer as close to north as the wind made possible. It was enormously comforting to see Jason like that, to know she wasn't alone, to know that his skills complemented hers, to know how much he would do for her.

It was almost possible to pretend they were sailing off of Tiae, that in a little while they'd come around and head for the dock, that her mother and father would be waiting, they'd have a nice meal, they'd talk about what they'd all done today and maybe get her parents to reminisce about their adventures in the old days, and when the sun set she'd kiss Jason good night and go to bed, knowing he was in the guest room. There had been weeks like that in the last six months, when Jason had visited from Danalee, and Kira wondered if she would always look back on those days as a special, golden time.

Of course there had always been worries, because her parents had a world to keep an eye on and too many people wanted to hurt them, or their child. And when it became widely known that Jason of Urth was spending a lot of time with Kira he got added to the list of those in danger. She had felt guilty about that, and about not being able to know that she returned his feelings. Jason, wisely, hadn't pressed it, but Kira had wondered what she was waiting for.

That time was past. The thread that was there and wasn't there glowed in the dark between them. It was strange to think that Jason couldn't see it or sense it at all. *"Every person sees the world differently,"* her father had told Kira. *"Each may view the same thing, yet what they see is not the same, if only in very small ways. And what each of us sees may change. Something familiar may take on new meaning. Is it not amazing to live in such a dream as this?"*

It was amazing, Kira thought as she looked at Jason, recalling her first impressions of the sullen, unhappy boy from Urth. Amazing and wonderful, despite the ugliness that some people tried to use to paint the world. They were far from safe, the Imperials might already be searching for them, but for the moment she was surrounded by beauty again. "Hey, Jason."

"What?"

"Did I tell you that I love you?"

His smile was all the answer she needed.

"Sir Mage, we have word of your daughter." The ambassador from the Free Cities, Beran of Palla, radiated eagerness as he stood at the door to the suite of rooms that Dorcastle had made available to Alain and Mari.

"Come in," Alain urged as he led Beran to the main room, where one wall was adorned by an ornate map of the world. "Mari!"

She came immediately at the unusual urgency in his voice. "What is it?"

Beran crossed the room to point at the map. "There was an accident in the Sharr Isles a few days ago. In the harbor of Caer Lyn. The Imperial Gray Squadron had stopped there to take on coal. That evening, Prince Maxim's flagship caught fire."

"It was damaged?" Mari asked.

"It was destroyed, Lady," Beran said. "The Imperials have tried to keep any information from leaving the Sharr Isles, but the Free Cities embassy finally got a message out. Their report says that *fire* is a small word for the conflagration that overcame Maxim's flagship, which caused the ship's ammunition to explode. By morning only a burned-out wreck remained of that Imperial warship."

"That sounds like Kira could have been involved," Mari said, her face lit with hope.

Beran smiled. "We know that she was involved. A confidential source, someone we believe is highly placed in the Imperial court, sent word to the embassy of the Free Cities in Caer Lyn that Lady Kira of Dematr was aboard that ship before the fires began and escaped before they engulfed the ship."

"Where is she?" Alain said.

"I cannot tell you with certainty. You know the degree of Imperial control of the Sharr Isles," Beran said. "Your daughter must have known that even if she had reached one of the friendly embassies the Imperials would come after her. We were told she had a sailboat. It has not been found. She must have left the harbor."

Mari took quick steps to gaze at the map. "The winds are from the west at this time of year, right? Kira must have gone north toward the Free Cities. That's the only path that would have offered her any hope."

"That is the bad news," Beran said. "Prince Maxim must have somehow learned that your daughter was still alive and had escaped in a boat. Well after the accident, the remaining four ships of the Gray Squadron hastily departed Caer Lyn and were last seen turning north and spreading out in a search line."

"Are the Free Cities sending ships to search for Kira?" Alain asked.

"Orders have gone out, Sir Mage. But our information is days old. By the time our ships leave Marida and Kelsi and reach the coast to the east, your daughter will very likely have already reached the coast herself. And, if our estimates are right, Prince Maxim's ships have a decent chance of catching her before she can do so. It depends on the winds and how well she uses them."

"She's alone?" Mari said, despairing. "Kira can't stay awake for days making sure she's making best use of the wind."

"She may not be alone, Lady," Beran added. "There was something else in the report. The morning after Lady Kira escaped and Prince Maxim's flagship burned, a wrecked sailboat was found on the rocks outside the harbor. Our embassy was able to discover that the boat had registry information indicating it had come from Gullhaven."

"Jason's with her?" Mari grabbed Alain's hand, smiling. "Jason's with her!"

He nodded to her, feeling himself smiling as well.

"Lady Mari, Sir Mage," Beran said, "I feel obligated to point out that Jason of Urth may have reached Caer Lyn but failed to meet up with your daughter. The Imperials have searched the island for him without result, but that does not mean—"

Alain held out one hand. "We understand. Some time ago, my foresight showed them together, in what now seems a situation soon to take place. They were being pursued through mountainous terrain. Kira is surely sailing for the Free Cities, but will most likely come ashore at some place where the Northern Ramparts meet the Sea of Bakre."

"That is reassuring, as well as grounds for us acting as quickly as possible. There is one thing more," Beran added. "An unarmed Imperial yacht with Princess Sabrin and a few of her followers aboard was also in the harbor of Caer Lyn. The sailors under Maxim's command forcibly searched the yacht after his flagship was destroyed, apparently seeking your daughter. Sabrin's yacht stayed at Caer Lyn until Maxim's ships had departed, then left, last seen steering east toward Landfall."

"What's Sabrin up to?" Mari wondered. "She's no friend of Maxim's. I know that much. Could Sabrin be the source of the Free Cities' information, Beran?"

"We suspect so," Beran said. "Maxim clearly thought that she might have aided your daughter's escape. He may have been right."

"If Sabrin helped Kira, she would have done it knowing not only how much that would hurt Maxim but also how much it would indebt me to her. Alain, we should go to Marida," Mari added, then paused, staring at the map. "If your vision six months ago showed what will happen soon, what might already be happening, Kira and Jason will come ashore in the territory of the Free Cities."

"I must point out," Alain said, "that more recent visions other Mages have had contradict the one I had six months ago. Conditions may have changed. Kira and Jason may not make it ashore."

Mari gazed at him, then nodded once. "Fine. You've told me that foresight often requires some stake in the outcome, some emotional tie to who or what is shown. I intend working from the vision that came to Master of Mages Alain, the father of Kira, who has the strongest ties and, I believe, the clearest vision of Kira's possible futures. I believe that she and Jason will get ashore in the Northern Ramparts. What will Prince Maxim do?"

"Prince Maxim," Beran said, "is known for his temper and his refusal to ever admit defeat. He carries inside him always the knowledge that you defeated his father at Dorcastle, and has clawed his way to the position of crown prince of the Empire by promising to avenge that failure."

"My vision showed Kira and Jason being pursued," Alain said again.

"Which means Maxim *will* land forces in the territory of the Free Cities," Mari said. "An invasion. How many forces would he employ? How far would Maxim go?"

"There are two Imperial legions facing the Northern Ramparts," Beran said. His face reflected sudden worry. "The last I heard they were conducting training in the plains west of Umburan. If ordered into action, they could respond immediately. Would Maxim go that far?"

"From what we saw of him in Tiaesun," Alain said, "Maxim would."

Beran faced Mari, his voice and bearing taking on a grim formality. "If the Empire invades lands of the Free Cities, will the daughter stand with us?"

"Of course she will," Mari said. "The Free Cities will not be alone if it comes to that. I will work to marshal every state in the West to stand with you. Syndar probably won't answer, and Ringhmon can't be counted on for anything except double-dealing, but I'm sure the rest will support you against the Empire."

"Thank you," Beran said, bowing toward her. "In truth, I believe that when the people learn that the Empire has attacked your family directly, they will rally to you and demand war."

Mari exhaled slowly. "The people…yes. The Empire against every state in the West. If Kira stays out of Maxim's reach and he calls in those legions, this could explode into a major war within days. We can't go to Marida, Alain," she said, her voice full of pain.

"Kira needs us," Alain objected, surprised at Mari's words.

"The world needs us. President in Chief Julan is coming here. President of State Jane is already here. The ambassadors of the Western Alliance and Tiae should arrive tomorrow. Beran, if the Free Cities want my opinion, I would recommend that they begin mobilizing their full military strength immediately. I think it is very likely that Imperial forces will enter their territory soon, if they haven't already." Mari looked at Alain. He could read the pleading in them. Pleading for understanding. "I'll handle things here. You go to Marida, Alain."

"My place is with you," Alain said. "We are a team. That is what the daughter of Jules has always told me."

"The mother of Kira wants you in Marida." Mari looked away, her mouth tight.

"Lady," Beran said, "I promise you that if your daughter is on her way to the territory of the Free Cities, we will ensure her safety. I know that patrols were already being prepared to be sent out in search of her. And I will recommend to the Free Cities that they do as you advise and begin immediate preparations for war."

"I will stay here," Alain said, the four words among the hardest he had ever spoken. "By the time I could reach Marida it would be too late to make a difference. I will send word to the Mages in the Free

Cities who can be counted on, and to our friends. They will search for Kira, and aid her."

"Her mother and father should be in the forefront of that," Mari said, "instead of being stuck in Dorcastle trying to keep this situation from turning into a bloodbath. What did Jason call those big wars on Urth? A World War?"

Alain nodded, reluctantly accepting the truth of what Mari had said earlier. "It could dwarf the losses at Dorcastle twenty years ago. Yet what could we do in Marida that those already there cannot?"

"Not a thing," Mari whispered. "Not a blasted thing. But we might be able to save a lot of lives by staying here. Thank you, Beran. May I share your information with the Bakre Confederation?"

"Of course, Lady."

"Then if you will excuse me," Mari said, turning and walking into the next room, closing the door securely behind her.

Beran nodded to Alain. "I should go as well. I must pass on the daughter's advice to the Free Cities."

The ambassador from the Free Cities had barely closed the door when Alain heard Mari's scream of rage and frustration, not completely muffled by the closed door and the pillow she must be screaming into. After that came the sound of her fist striking a wall, over and over.

Alain looked at the wall nearest him, pulled out his long knife, and with all of his strength half buried the blade in the wood with the fury of his own sense of helplessness, the sound of the blow filling the air about him as if mocking his own powerlessness. Then he went in to Mari to offer what comfort he could to his wife and a mother who had to place the needs of countless others over the fate of her own daughter.

That was their hope, he realized as Mari came into his arms. "It is Kira," he murmured. "She will rise to any challenge. She is your daughter."

"And yours," Mari whispered.

"We have taught her to be strong. To never give up. And she

believes in herself now. She knows she is our daughter in spirit as well as name."

"Can she handle this kind of thing, Alain? Can anyone?"

"She is not alone. Just as you and I survived because we had each other, my vision showed that she has Jason. You are right. It *must* happen as I saw it." He did not want to even consider the possibility that it would not, that Kira and Jason's boat might be caught before they could reach the coast to the north that offered their only chance of refuge.

With the right winds and a large ship, the journey from the Sharr Isles to the northern edge of the Sea of Bakre could be done in three or four days. In a small sailboat, tacking with a wind from the east, Kira guessed that it would take them six days. After the tension of the first day, the next four days passed without incident except for occasional sightings of masts and sails in the distance. In every case, those sailing ships went onward and below the horizon without taking notice of the small boat. Kira and Jason had alternated time on the tiller, and he had hooked another fish during one of his off times, allowing them to choke down more raw fish. Kira had eyed their dwindling supply of water grimly, then closed her eyes and popped one of the fish eyes into her mouth, trying to swallow it whole.

Jason, shuddering, did the same with the second eye.

The fifth night had been clear, both a blessing in ensuring the seas stayed calm enough not to menace a small boat among big waves, and a source of worry since clear nights would aid any search for them by the Imperials. Kira had looked up at the stars as she steered through the last of the night before dawn, thinking about the other worlds where humanity had placed colonies. She knew the names. Places like Brahma and Osiris and Amaterasu. But that was all anyone on Dematr knew. Earth had refused to tell them anything else, "protecting" her world from "cultural disruption." And none of the other colonized worlds had been willing to break that embargo of knowledge. "We're not children," she said to the stars, whispering to make sure she didn't awaken Jason. "And we're not animals in a zoo. We defeated the Great Guilds and can finally make our own decisions. And we will, no matter what you do to try to fence us in."

The stars didn't answer, but then they never did.

She lowered her gaze and let the feel of the sea run through her. Had she always felt this way about the great waters of the world, or had she gotten sea water into her blood during her and Jason's time as members of the crew of *The Son of Taris*? The sea rolled by beneath Kira's boat, immensely powerful and cloaked in mystery, yet somehow comforting and familiar. Kira breathed deep the salt-scented air, feeling as if she had always belonged here on the water like this, her boat moving with the endless rhythm of the restless seas.

She had grown up knowing that her mother was the daughter of Jules, descended from the legendary pirate and explorer, founder of Julesport and hero of the Bakre Confederation. Kira's mother had never been comfortable in the role, admitting that Mages could see it in her but insisting that no one really knew who the descendents of Jules were. At times like this, with her body feeling at one with the sea, Kira could feel a connection to the old pirate who was very likely her many-times-removed grandmother and had once sailed these same waters.

The timeless seas made her wonder what Jules would think of Kira if somehow those waters could for a few moments close the gap between now and then. Suppose Jules' ship loomed out of the dark and challenged this boat? Heave to and be boarded! And Kira would be brought before the pirate queen and look her in the eyes and see if she recognized what was in them. And the pirate queen would look at Kira and see who her daughters would be. They would yell at each other, because that was what women in her family did, and then they would embrace and promise to fight side by side forever, because that was also what her family did. And then time would heal itself and Kira's boat would be alone on the sea again, Jason sleeping unaware of the adventure he had missed, Jules once more only a legend of the past but one that still lived in Kira and her mother.

The last part of the night wore away, Kira letting daydreams and the sea's glamour fill her for a while and drive away fears of what the day might bring.

As dawn began to lighten the sky to the east on the sixth day, Kira gazed intently ahead to the north. Was she imagining things?

Jason yawned and sat up, smacking his mouth and grimacing. "It tastes like I've eaten two raw fish and an eyeball."

"Me, too," Kira said. "Maybe we should put off our morning kiss. Look." She pointed ahead.

Jason stood up, steadying himself by holding onto the mast as the boat rolled over another swell. "Are those mountains?"

"Yes," Kira said, grinning. "I'm sure of it now. It's the Northern Ramparts. The dawn sun is lighting up their peaks. Safety is in sight, Jason."

He turned toward her, grinning as well, then his smile went away as Jason stared past Kira. "So is something else."

She turned to look south, her heart sinking. Four columns of smoke rose into the air, no longer masked by night but instead illuminated by the growing light, each column widely separated from the next. "They'll be sailing just far enough apart to see the top of the mast of the next closest ship. That way they can cover as much of the sea as possible while looking for us."

Jason swung his gaze from one column of smoke to the next. "If we turned and ran straight east we might get past the farthest ship on that side. But then we'd be so far east we wouldn't have a chance of landing in Free Cities territory, right?"

"Right. It would just be another way of getting caught." Kira looked ahead, where the peaks of the Northern Ramparts glowed golden in the light of the new day, then back again at the columns of smoke. "I wonder how far off the ships are? They're still under the horizon, but that might mean they're just under it or a long ways from it."

"Do you think we can make it?" Jason asked, still standing and holding onto the mast as he looked south.

"I don't know. It depends on how far off those Imperial ships still are, and how close the coast is. We're seeing the highest peaks of the Ramparts, which are a ways inland. I just don't know, Jason. What do you think?"

"The same," he said. "I was hoping that you'd have a more optimistic assessment than I did."

"We'll have to make the best time we can," Kira said. "If we can stay away from them until night falls, it'll give us a chance."

Jason shook his head. "Can they be that far off? I'd think they'll be on us by sometime this afternoon at least."

"Probably," Kira said.

He stayed silent for a while, and so did she, not knowing what to say.

"Kira, that thing you said about escaping or dying," Jason finally said in an unnaturally calm voice, "is that still true?"

She gazed back at him, not trying to hide her unease. "Yes."

"Then here's what we'll do. We'll swap jackets. They know what yours looks like. We'll stay huddled down in the boat, and if the Imperial ships are going to overtake us before we reach the coast I'll jump out and they'll stop to pick me up thinking I'm you and you'll have enough time to—"

"No," Kira said. "They'd kill you, Jason. They'd kill you and then come on after me."

"Kira, it's the only chance you have."

"I'll tell you what we're going to do, Jason," Kira said, trying to keep her own voice calm. "They want me alive a lot more than they want you dead. If I jump out of the boat, they will stop to pick me up. I have my pistol. I'll be able to fight them off for a little while. That'll give you more time." She had to swallow before continuing. "Don't worry. I'll be fine."

"How could you be fine?" Jason demanded. "You said you'd die rather than be taken to the Empire."

"I can fight to the death," Kira said, hearing the quaver in her voice on the last word. "With my pistol and my knives I can keep fighting until—"

"*No!*" He stared at her in disbelief and denial.

"Jason—"

"No!"

"Jason, they want *me!*" Kira cried. "Me! If they overtake us before we're near the coast there is only one way that one of us could possibly survive!"

"Then it's going to be you!"

"I will not let you die to save me! I won't be the cause of your death!"

"I don't care!" Jason shouted. "I won't let you die!"

"How can you be so selfish?" Kira demanded, wondering why Jason had to make something this hard even harder.

"*Selfish?* Because I won't let you kill yourself to save me?"

"*Yes!* They want me! If you have any real feelings for me, you will let me do this!" She stopped to catch her breath, knowing how strained her voice sounded. "So I wouldn't have the guilt of living knowing that it was my fault you died. And because wherever I end up after I leave this life, I will know that you are all right. That you have found an…another…girl, and she's…she's…made you happy…and…"

"You don't get it, do you?" Jason shouted. "You still don't get it! How can you be so smart and not get it?"

"Get *what?*" she yelled back.

"There is no other girl! Not anywhere! Not in the entire universe! There's only *you!*"

"Jason, this is no time for your delusions!"

"This is the perfect time for my delusions! Because I will not accept a reality without you in it!"

"Well, I won't accept a reality in which you die to save me!" Kira shouted at him.

"You're not going to die to save me!" Jason yelled.

"Fine! Then I guess we'll both have to live!" Kira glared at him. "Promise."

"I promise I'll live," Jason said. "You, too."

"I promise. Now take over steering. You're a lot better than I am at getting the best speed out of this boat. I'll see if I can adjust the sail to eke out a little more push with this wind."

"Okay," Jason said.

"And kiss me. My breath is probably beyond awful, though, so keep it quick."

As Kira worked on the sail, she paused to look at him. "Jason? That time at Dorcastle, my parents thought they were going to die."

"Which time at Dorcastle?"

"The first time. And I guess the second time. And there have been other times since then. Dorcastle is kind of a place of mixed emotions for my parents. Anyway, my point is, Mother told me they were standing on that barge, a dragon charging them, and my father wouldn't leave her even though she told him to. She told me she had never thought that she'd find someone like that, who would face death beside her and not waver." Kira paused again, looking over the stern at the four columns of smoke. "And then she thought she had to give him up, to keep him safe. She thought she'd never find another guy like that. And she didn't. She found Father again, and they never separated after that."

Kira looked at Jason once more. "I never thought I could find a guy like that, who would stand with me in the face of that kind of danger. I was wrong. I have found him."

Jason smiled at her, embarrassed by her words. "I never thought I'd find a girl like that, who would stand by me with death coming at us. We were both wrong. See, you're not always right."

She smiled back at him but her eyes remained solemn. "You promised, Jason. You can't die."

"So did you."

Behind them, the four columns of smoke rose into the sky like fingers of a far-off hand.

CHAPTER EIGHT

They had drunk the last of their water, stowed in their pockets what little hardtack remained, and made sure the knife from the boat's survival chest was secured in Jason's belt. There wasn't much else to do but wait as the sun climbed toward noon, and the coastline to the north drew closer at a rate that felt far too slow, and the smoke columns to the south approached at a rate that felt far too fast.

"Can you think of anything to talk about that isn't whether or not they'll catch us before we reach the coast?" Jason asked as he adjusted course slightly again to try to catch a little more wind in the sail.

Kira leaned against the mast, gazing south where the Imperial ships still hadn't come over the horizon. She had checked her pistol, readied it, and left her jacket open so she could draw the weapon quickly. "You don't talk much about the people you knew on Urth. You had classmates, right? Because you got to go to a normal school? And teachers?"

"Sort of," Jason said. "A normal school on Earth has a lot of virtual components. But, yeah."

"And?"

Jason shrugged. "Um, well, first of all, it's funny but I always have to remember that because of the relativistic effects of the trip out here, they've all aged almost ten years from when I knew them. What seemed like two months to me was ten years to them."

"That's strange to think about," Kira said, watching the columns of smoke behind them, which had grown steadily thicker as the Imperial ships drew closer. "Imagine going away and then coming back and everyone you knew was ten years older."

"So, everybody who knew me probably doesn't even really remember me, and if they do they're remembering the jerk that I was back then."

"What's our agreement about the jerk thing, Jason?"

"I'm talking about before I met you! I didn't know the thing about not calling myself a jerk was retroactive." Jason smiled slightly in memory. "There were a couple of teachers I really liked, and who I thought liked me. If they remember me now it's probably just because I was the kid who got pulled out of school to go on an interstellar flight. Same for the guys and girls I used to do games with."

"Did you know the librarians at Altis have reported back to Urth on you, using the Feynman unit?" Kira asked.

He bent a worried look her way. "What have they said?"

"Mother showed me a transcript. Stuff about what you were doing, and you being healthy and all, and Mother and Father being your legal guardians here. That got Urth pretty interested. Didn't anybody ever tell you? Urth was all like, he's the adopted son of Lady Master Mechanic Mari and Sir Master of Mages Alain? Because like you told me, Urth is all excited about the daughter of Jules and what Mother did to free our world and all. And the librarians said my parents hadn't exactly adopted you, and…" She rolled her eyes. "The librarians told Urth that you and I were dating."

"People on Earth know that Lady Kira is my girlfriend?" Jason said, staring at her.

"Oh, do not do that," Kira warned him. "Dating me does not make you look special."

"You do realize that you're the only person on at least two worlds who thinks that, right?"

She gave him another eye roll. "If I thought that was why you were dating me I'd probably toss you over the side right now and let the

Imperials get you. Anyway, what do you think those old friends of yours would say if they could see you now? In a boat, being chased by ships, a knife at your belt, me standing at the mast..."

"They'd think it must be the best virtual reality game ever," Jason said. "No way would they think it could be real."

"Why not?"

"Because the me they knew wouldn't be doing this. Not for real. And not with someone like you!"

"I guess they didn't know you, then," Kira said, her eyes on the horizon. Was there something appearing at the base of one of the columns of smoke?

"I didn't know me then," Jason said. "Or I was a different me. You didn't exactly like me the first time you met me, remember? Are you seeing something?"

"I think so. That smoke column closest to being right behind us. There's a darker dot where it meets the horizon." Kira breathed in slowly. "It must be the highest part of the ship's mast. It won't be much longer before enough of the ship is over the horizon for the lookouts to spot us."

She turned to look ahead. The mountains rose into the sky, lit by the sun high overhead so that every detail stood out clearly, but down toward the water details were lost in a grayish-white mist. "I'm still not sure how close we are to the coast. That haze could be mist off the water or surf hitting rocks. We'll have to get nearer before we can see."

"We'd be able to see Marida by now if we were anywhere near it, right?" Jason asked, raising himself a little to look at the mountains visible off the bow.

Kira nodded reluctantly. "If we were anywhere close, we'd have seen Marida. And all of the shipping near Marida, ships and fishing boats and everything else. I didn't think we had much chance of bearing far enough northwest to reach Marida, but hopefully we're not a long ways east of the city."

"Okay. Are we sure that the land ahead of us belongs to the Free Cities?"

"It's definitely Free Cities territory. Their lands start at the edge of the Northern Ramparts, which end abruptly on their eastern side. That's why they're called the Ramparts. Father fought here, and says they're like a mighty wall across the northern part of the continent. If we were off of Imperial territory, we'd see rocky beaches and the high plains around Umburan where my parents almost died in a blizzard."

"Do you or your family ever go places just to sightsee?" Jason asked. "You know, on vacations rather than to fight battles or duel with Imperial kidnappers and assassins and stuff?"

"Go somewhere to relax?" Kira asked. "What a weird idea."

"Is there any water left?"

"No," Kira said, tasting the salt on her lips from the sea spray, "sorry. 'What need have I for food and water when I have you beside me to feed my soul and quench my sorrow?'"

"Is that a quote?" Jason asked.

"It's from a pretty famous poem," she explained. " 'A Sailor's Home-coming.' A sailor gets shipwrecked, and while he's adrift at sea without food and water he has these hallucinations about the girl he loves, and the last lines are about him seeing her again in his mind as he dies. See, he believes that he's home with her when he dies, so he's happy."

"As uplifting and inspiring as that poem sounds," Jason remarked, "I'm not sure I wanted to hear about it under these circumstances."

Kira smiled at him. "Captain Banda explained it to me. Part of it is that sailors go to so many places but always hold home in their hearts even if they never get back there. And part of it is about how people can find comfort under the worst of circumstances. And another part is about how love can transcend death and distance. The sailor died at home, in his girl's arms, because he believed he did. They were together."

Jason frowned at the coastline still too far ahead of them. "Girls think that stories about people dying are romantic, don't they? I mean, as long as they die because they're in love. See, I like the stories where the people in love have some adventures that they survive and then they live long and happy lives."

Kira nodded to him. "If you like that kind of story, that's the story you and I will have to live. It won't be as romantic, of course, because a love story requires somebody to die, but I'm willing to accept that for you."

He grinned at her. "Maybe Maxim could be the one who dies."

"That's a good idea." The top portions of all of the Imperial ships were visible by now, the one most directly astern showing parts of the upper superstructure. But at least being able to see the ships directly gave her a much better feel for how fast they were overtaking their own boat.

Kira turned to look forward, seeing details of the coast finally beginning to emerge amid a welter of spray from the waves crashing against the rocky coast, then gazed back at the oncoming Imperial ships. "Jason, I think we'll make it. Not by much, but I think we've got enough of a lead."

After so long with only a vague sense of how close they were to the coast and how far behind the ships were trailing, the situation was now easily visible. Kira kept swiveling her head, switching her gaze from the looming shoreline ahead to the growing shapes of the ships behind. The entire superstructure of the nearest Imperial ship was now above the horizon. "Keep it up, Jason. If we can maintain this speed we'll get to the coast before they catch us. I'm sure of it."

"The wind isn't steady," Jason said, licking his lips nervously.

"Do the best you can. Oh, blazes. The closest ship just gave off a big cloud of stack smoke. They're feeding the boiler to increase speed." She looked at the other three Imperial ships. "So are the others. We've definitely been seen."

"Kira, is that coastline as ugly as it looks from here?"

She nodded, trying to keep her breathing calm and steady as the boat rocked more in the rougher waters as they drew closer to the coast. "Yeah. I told you it was bad. It's all broken cliffs with a carpet of fallen boulders and rocks in front of them."

"There isn't any hidden but convenient sheltered cove for me to run this boat into?" Jason demanded. "There's always something like that in a game. What kind of lousy story is this?"

"The one we're stuck with," Kira said. "There's a good part. The Imperials can't keep charging at us or they'll hit the rocks. They'll need to slow down as they get closer to the coast."

"So will we." Jason gave her a worried look. "Won't we? You have a plan, don't you? This is like that jumping-off-the-train stuff where you don't tell me until the last moment so I won't freak out, isn't it?"

"Jason, you're good at steering and the feel of the boat. Better than I am. Aim for a place where we can ram this boat onto the rocks. We need it to hang on at least a little so we'll have time to jump off onto the rocks before the boat sinks or gets battered to pieces by the waves."

"You're kidding."

"No." Kira looked ahead at the coastline, where it was now easy to see white spray being flung high as waves pounded into the boulders littering the sea in front of the broken cliffs. "The rocks are wet, so make sure you don't slip off, especially when more waves hit while we're trying to get up onto drier ground."

"Make sure I don't slip off," Jason repeated. "This time we're jumping off a boat onto rocks." He stole a glance back at the Imperial ships, the hull of the closest one now visible, a bone in its teeth as the ship sliced through the water kicking up a wide, white bow wave . "Okay. Let's do it."

She grinned at him, her face and hair getting wetter as the rougher waters and ever-closer spray flung water into the air. "That's my hero." Kira studied the approaching coast again. The cliffs on shore rose up like unyielding walls, but the sea had been pounding away at them for countless years. There were numerous breaks near the water, where channels and canyons and rifts and crevices ran jagged tracks through the rock. The boulders torn from the cliffs as the sea waged endless war on them ranged from monsters the size of buildings to smaller ones not much bigger than their sailboat. Another wave thundered in as she watched, smashing into the rocks and hurling out great gouts of spray. "Jason, you won't be able to tie the tiller before we hit," she said, her smile fading.

Jason nodded, his expression grim and determined. "No. It's too turbulent close in. If we want to hit a good spot instead of crashing into a big rock head-on, I'll have to steer us in all the way. Not that there actually are any good spots. But some are a lot worse."

"All right. If you don't make it off the boat, if you get stuck back there when the boat wrecks, I'll come back for you."

"No, you won't," Jason objected. "If I'm stuck back here the boat's going to be getting pounded to pieces against the rocks and—"

She shook her head. "Jules would never forgive me if I left my man behind."

"I'm your man?" Jason asked, grinning despite the worry in his eyes as he scanned the coast ahead.

"Sure are. That tells others how close we are, even more than buying jewelry for each other. So you just hang on if you get stuck when we hit. I'll come for you." She paused to snap her holster shut, then closed her jacket. Getting off of those rocks might require some serious physical work. Kneeling by the survival chest, she pulled out some of the empty water bottles and stuffed them inside her jacket, where hopefully they would stay through whatever happened next.

Kira went forward, crouching in the bow. The Imperial ship just behind them was growing in size rapidly now, charging to intercept the sailboat before it could reach the coast. The wind was pummeling them, carrying salt spray with it, and the boat rocked heavily in the backwash from the waves crashing against the coast.

The sound of a rifle shot echoed from the cliffs ahead. Then another and another. Kira looked back and saw figures lining the rail at the bow of the closest Imperial ship, steadying rifles and firing. Had Prince Maxim decided that he preferred her dead to having her escape yet again?

Kira looked at Jason in the stern, realizing that he was likely the one the Imperials were aiming at. "Keep your head down!" she yelled.

Jason shook his head stubbornly, both hands on the tiller now as he fought the turbulent waters. "I have to see where to aim for!"

Most of the rifle shots seemed to be going wide, but Kira heard a few thunks and felt the boat vibrate in time to hits. Small holes appeared in the sail.

A loud roar sounded behind them as one of the forward gun mounts on the Imperial ship fired. Kira heard the shell tear past overhead, seeing it explode before her just short of the nearest rocks, sending a geyser fountaining skyward. Were they trying to sink the boat, or just trying to scare her and Jason into turning?

Kira looked back again. Jason's face was frozen into a mask of concentration, focused on the violent surf ahead. The Imperial ship dead astern seemed practically on top of them, looming high against the sky, the big white bow wave in its teeth hurling spray to either side. Imperial rifles cracked again and again, bullets raining down close alongside, hurling up small spurts of water. But the sailboat was bouncing around so unpredictably in the surf that most of the shots were clean misses.

Not all of them, though. Kira saw splinters fly up not far from where her hand gripped the bow as a bullet struck there.

"Hold on!" Jason yelled over the crash of the rifles and the thunder of the surf. "We're going in!"

The sailboat rocked upward as it caught a swell rising to hammer the rocks. Kira grabbed on tighter, rapidly switching her gaze between the jagged rocks ahead and the sharp bow of the Imperial ship behind. The Imperials would have to turn soon.

Jason swung the tiller one way, then back, the sailboat weaving across the top of the swell and down the other side, the force of the building wave now at its back, pushing the sailboat ahead faster and faster, Kira's heart pounding so hard that her pulse filled her ears in a counterpart to the rumble of the surf.

The Imperial ship behind them had finally begun turning away, but now it shuddered and jerked to one side, heeling hard to starboard. Kira caught a brief glimpse of a large gash below the waterline to port where an underwater rock had ripped through the ship's hull. The ship wallowed as it swung parallel to the surf, trying to turn away even as its own momentum and the force of the waves combined to try to push it onto the rocks before it could get its head around.

"Kira!" Jason shouted.

She swung her attention forward again, just in time. The massive salt-sprayed rocks were close, the sailboat rushing toward them with terrifying speed as it rode the wave. Kira could see the spot Jason must be aiming for, a small gap where the sailboat might be able to wedge itself, and braced herself to jump onto the lower of the two rocks framing the gap as chill seawater flung upwards by the pounding waves splashed back on her. The gap was right before them and then it was there and the sailboat screamed as its sides rammed into the space between the rocks.

The collision broke her hold but Kira had already launched herself up. She hit the rock she'd aimed for and scrabbled for a grip, blessing her experience with hanging on in the rigging of a sailing ship as she slid on the wet, slick surface, and grateful that none of the empty bottles in her jacket had broken. As one of her hands seized an out-cropping and held, Kira twisted back to check on Jason.

The mast had snapped and fallen forward when they hit. Jason was scrambling over the sail while the boat wrenched and jolted beneath him as more waves came in and broke over the boat's stern. Kira reached out and down as Jason got to the bow and jumped without pausing, hitting heavily and sliding on the slippery rock, but Kira seized his arm and hung on even though his weight momentarily threatened to pull her other hand loose from its grip.

Everything seemed to pause for a moment like that, Kira gritting her teeth with the effort of holding on to the rock despite the weight of Jason tugging at her other arm, another big wave coming behind as the last retreated. Kira pulled at Jason as he tried to get a hold on the rock, yanking him upwards with a strength she hadn't known she had.

He was beside her, he had a grip on the rock, and Kira looked back and stared with horror at the sight of the side of the Imperial ship hurtling toward them, a wall of metal rising above her and to either side, out of control under the enormous force of the surf, sailors on the deck racing around in panic.

"Run!" Kira screamed at Jason, and without wasting time to ask why, Jason followed as she pulled herself to her feet and leaped recklessly to the next rock and onward faster than anyone not fleeing certain death would have risked on the slippery boulders.

A tremendous grinding roar marked the collision of the Imperial ship with the rocks. Kira felt the shock of the impact through her hands and her boots, heard screams and shouts, and came to a stop to look back, seeing the tall side of the ship rearing over the coast, rocking under the impacts of waves as it hit the rocks, bounced off, then was hurled onto them again. Sailors were falling off from the force of the blows or making futile efforts to launch boats that would never survive the surf this close in. Kira and Jason's sailboat had disappeared, crushed to splinters by the impact of the Imperial ship.

"Come on!" Jason yelled at her, and she followed his tug as they jumped and grabbed and slipped and pulled their way over the broken rocks toward a cleft leading upward through the cliff before them.

Reaching that place of relative safety, though still lashed by spray, Kira paused to catch her breath and look back again. "Our boat is gone!" she yelled to Jason.

"That's what you're worried about?" Jason yelled back, incredulous.

"It was a good, faithful boat!" Kira stared at the Imperial sailors struggling in the water, the waves smashing them against the rocks as their ship continued to be battered helplessly.

Jason put his face, dripping with spray, close to hers. "This break in the cliff seems to lead all the way to the top. Come on! We can't help them! Even if we didn't die trying, they'd just kill us or take us prisoner!"

"I know." Kira turned her back on the doomed sailors, feeling sick, and followed Jason up the cleft.

Despite her experience in climbing rigging, it was a difficult ascent, especially since they didn't dare take it slowly and carefully. Kira paused again about halfway up the cleft to catch her breath and look back. Some of the sailors had made it onto the relative safety of the rocks. Their ship had dropped lower in the water having sunk onto the rocks offshore, but the part remaining was still shuddering in time to the pounding of the waves which would eventually reduce it to a pile of debris. Behind the wreck, far enough out to avoid the fate of their sister ship, Kira could see the other three Imperial ships lowering boats.

"At least they're going to rescue the survivors," Jason gasped where he hung in the cleft beside her, also breathing heavily from their exertions.

Kira shook her head. "The sailors going down into those boats have rifles slung on their backs. They wouldn't need those for a rescue."

Jason shook his head, laughing in short, pained gusts. "They're not giving up."

"No," Kira said. "They're not giving up. They're going to come ashore and keep chasing us." She felt her muscles quivering from tiredness, her stomach knotted with tension. Looking upward, Kira could see the wandering path of the cleft ending in a notch in the face of the cliff where it met the top. That notch still seemed way too high above them. "Let's see if we can get to the top of this cleft before I throw up."

"If we do," Jason said, "I'm going to throw up when we get there."

They started climbing again.

By the time Kira painfully pulled herself out of the cleft to sprawl on her back on the top of the cliff, her vision was hazing from exhaustion. Jason crawled next to her and fell onto his stomach, breathing so loudly it almost masked the sound of the surf below.

After a few minutes, Kira rolled her head enough to look about them. The edge of the cliff was still too close for her comfort. From that edge a long, steep slope covered in tough grass and a few bushes led upward toward the nearest mountains. She tried to measure the effort it would take to scale that slope and shuddered.

"Are we having fun yet?" Jason gasped.

"Don't look up," Kira wheezed in reply.

He did, wincing at the sight of the long slope. "I should have listened to you."

"You'll learn someday." Kira grimaced with effort as she forced herself to her hands and knees and cautiously looked back down the cleft and outward.

She could see the stranded ship, even lower in the water now, waves washing across the deck as the wreck rocked under each successive blow from the sea. Some sailors were moving around on the ship, clambering through the superstructure, acting with purpose instead of panic. Others had gathered on the rocks, where some lay and others stood on the uncertain footing. Kira tried to judge their numbers and wondered how many had drowned or been smashed against the rocks. She felt guilt strike her again, wondering why people had to die because of her.

"It's not your fault," Jason said from where he lay looking at her.

Kira looked back at him. "How did you know what I was seeing?"

"I didn't. But I know the expression you get when you're thinking you're responsible for someone getting hurt or in trouble. Kira, all you were trying to do was escape from being kidnapped. They were trying to stop you, to kidnap you again, and they were trying to shoot us. All of which means it's not your fault."

"Why does it have to happen?"

"What does your father say?" Jason asked.

She looked back at the wreck and the survivors. "He says that destiny gives us choices. The options we have may be predetermined by someone or something, but we have the choice of which one to take. And each choice we make impacts on the next set of choices. Because each person is responsible for the choices they make and whatever results from those choices."

"Could you have made any choices other than the ones you did?"

"No," Kira said. She edged over a little to see more. "The longboats are still offshore. I think they're looking for places to land their people that won't destroy the boats."

"They definitely have rifles?"

"Yeah. I can see the barrels sticking up and the sun glinting on the metal. They all seem to be crew from the ships though. I don't see any legion uniforms."

"That's good?" Jason asked.

"That's good," Kira said, crawling back to drop down beside him. "We don't want to have to mess with legionaries. The legions are tough." She stared up at the sky. "Should we stand and fight here?"

"Is that a serious question?"

"Yes. They have to scale the cliffs. I have my pistol, but even your knife would be effective as they try to climb up over the edge. They'll be tired from the climb. We could take them out as they came up until they stopped trying."

Jason didn't answer for a long moment. "You're talking about a last stand, Kira. There are other ways up these cliffs and a lot more Imperial sailors than the two of us. Sooner or later some of them would get up here, probably on both sides of us, and we'd be trapped."

"I'm tired of running."

"Is that a good reason to trap ourselves?"

She glared at the sky. "You sound like my father."

"Is that good or bad?" Jason asked.

Kira sighed, closing her eyes to think. "It's good. What I really am is mad, Jason, as well as tired, mad that they've chased us this far and mad that they're still chasing us. Everybody I ever knew has told me not to make decisions when I'm mad. Why aren't you mad?"

"I'm too tired to be mad."

"Thanks for not being too tired to think." She raised herself up a little and looked to the west, toward where Marida lay somewhere along the coast. A few hundred lances in that direction, the open slope they were on was riven by a wide fissure that narrowed as it ran upward to merge with the flank of a mountain. Beyond it, more mountains sloped directly into the sea, merging with the cliffs. "We can't walk west along the coast. It's impassable. We'll have to go inland a ways, then cut west when we can."

"Inland." Jason looked up the slope behind them. "Kira? Have you ever noticed that whenever we're being chased, it's always uphill?"

She frowned as she thought. "Yeah. It is always uphill. Why is that?"

"Did that happen to your parents?"

"I don't think so. They've never mentioned it. I need to ask Mother about that," Kira said. "The next time I see her. Don't let me forget."

"I won't. I hope this isn't one those family things that your dad is always warning me about," Jason said.

"I don't think so," Kira repeated. "Wait. What exactly has my father been warning you about?"

"Huh? Oh…uh…nothing. Nothing…important."

"Yeah. I was going to let us rest another few minutes, but if you have enough breath to make bad jokes, you have breath to walk. Let's go." She and Jason got to their feet, looking up the slope.

"One step at a time?" Jason said.

"One step at a time. Let's hold on to each other. And if we fall, let's make sure we fall forward so we don't lose even a little ground."

"Got it."

They moved up the slope, their eyes on the grass at their feet, trying to maintain a slow, steady pace. The sound of their heavy breathing as they labored upwards masked most of the noise around them, but one time when they stopped to rest Kira heard a faint trickling noise off to their right. "This way."

They angled right, still going upwards, until they stumbled across a small trench wandering down the slope, a stream of water in the bottom splashing its way toward the sea, singing on the rocks with a sound like fairy harps.

Kira, abruptly aware of just how dry her throat was, dropped down beside the stream, lying full length to bury her face in the wonderful, cold, bright splendor of fresh water. She drank, gasped in air, drank, gasped some more, then drank some more. Her mouth numb with the coldness of the water, she splashed it on her face, washing off salt and blood and all the other leavings that had accumulated. "Oh, that's good."

"Yeah," Jason agreed, lying beside her. "How long has it been since you drank your fill of fresh water?"

"It's been a while," Kira said. "I guess you haven't done that since you left Gullhaven. Did I ever thank you for that?"

"Let's see, you keep telling me that you love me, so I think that covers it," Jason said, grinning at her.

"I think I finally washed the taste of things I don't want to taste any more out my mouth," Kira sighed. She leaned over and drank again, then splashed water over her neck to clean the salt off it as well. "I want to take a bath. Just pull off all my clothes right now and wash every part of my body and— What is that look on your face, Jason? Are you really thinking about that? Now?"

"I'm a guy," Jason said.

"You also said you were tired! Sorry to disappoint you, but you won't be seeing anything of me today that you haven't already seen!" She hesitated, then leaned forward and dunked her head as far as she could into the frigid water, scrubbing her hair furiously. She hadn't been able to clean it since being kidnapped. The cold was briefly excruciating, then she pulled her head out, combing her hair with her hands and feeling better than she had for a long time.

Jason was eyeing her. "How bad did that hurt?"

"Not too much. You get numb pretty quick. It's like scrubbing yourself with ice."

"You make it sound like fun." Jason bent down, flinching as he ducked his own head in water. He stayed that way for several seconds, hands rubbing over his head and neck, then pulled out and stared around, shivering with cold. "That's a real wake-up."

Kira smiled and helped him comb his hair into shape. She pulled the bottles from the front of her jacket, finding that one had cracked sometime since the boat had hit the rocks. But three more were intact. She filled them from the stream, jamming the corks back into place.

"I'll carry two of them," Jason said.

"Thanks," Kira said, passing them to him, realizing now that her thirst was slaked just how hungry she was. "It's too bad this little rill is too small and fast for any fish to live in it."

"Yeah. Right now I could eat one scales and guts and all." He shoved the bottles into the deep pockets of his coat, looking around. "We've gotten pretty high up. I didn't realize how much we'd climbed, which is kind of funny considering how much I hurt from climbing."

"Tell me about it." Kira came to her feet cautiously, looking back the way they had come. The cliff blocked her view of the coastline, but she could see one of the Imperial ships moving offshore. Which meant that ship could see her and Jason. "They're watching us. They know where we are. We have to get to the top of this slope, and then move out of sight of the sea."

"What's inland like?" Jason asked. "Have you been near here before?"

"I've been in the Northern Ramparts," Kira said, "but only in the parts west of here, around Alexdria. I think we went to Cristane once when I was little, but I don't remember much about that. There are trails and roads through the Ramparts, so we just have to head north inland until we're out of sight of the sea and then bear west, watching for any paths we can use. Even the best places are going to be pretty rough going, though."

"I sure wish that Mage Alera was nearby with her Roc. What are our odds of finding food?" Jason asked.

"Not good," Kira admitted. "Anything in these parts of the mountains is going to be small and fast, and we can't set snares and wait around for something to get caught. Even if we stumble across a mountain lake I don't know if we'll find fish in it."

Jason struggled to his feet. "Do we have to go to Marida? What if we find a road to Alexdria?"

"Alexdria is farther off, but any of the Free Cities would protect us." Kira rubbed her face, not wanting to think about how much farther they had to go up the slope. "Our problem is that we're too close to the border with the Empire, and none of the Free Cities are anywhere near the border with the Empire. Any city too close to that border would have become part of the Empire whether it wanted to or not."

"So we got a schlep," Jason said, looking up the slope.

"A what?"

"A long hike."

"Why didn't you just say…? Never mind," Kira said. "It's my own fault for falling in love with a guy from another world. Mother warned me about this!"

"She did?" Jason asked as they began trudging up the slope again. "Your mother warned you to not get involved with a guy from another world?"

"Yeah, she's been telling me that for years."

"For *years*? Aren't I the only guy in your age range from another world that's ever been here? I only got here about six months ago!"

"Yes," Kira said, "but what Mother meant was that some people might as well be in their own worlds, and if you end up wanting a guy like that, you'll get his world along with him. She meant like my father, who lives a lot in Mage world, which is this world but an illusion."

"Speaking of Mages," Jason began.

"Not feeling anything," Kira said. "Maybe because I'm worn out. I might be able to use my Mage powers again in an emergency. Mountains aren't as good for finding power as lowlands are, but they're a lot better than oceans and seas."

They headed upwards again, not trying to push themselves any harder because each step already required an effort. Kira kept them near the small stream so they could take occasional breaks to get quick drinks.

Her eyes on the ground at her feet, Kira was surprised when they finally came up against a sheer rock face down which the stream cascaded in ribbons of clear and white foam and silver. She stumbled to a halt, breathing heavily, looking to the right and the left. This cliff face was only about three lances high, but still looked daunting.

"I think we can get up it over there," Jason said, pointing to their left. "See where part of the cliff has given way? There's a fall of rock we can climb."

"Yeah. Let's rest a little first. We should be way ahead of the Imperials, and I'm worried about trying those rocks when we're this tired."

Kira turned to study the way back towards the coast. The slope they had come up seemed to fall away at a dizzying rate, ending at the cliff edge with nothing beyond it but the sea. She grabbed Jason to steady herself, grateful that her experience climbing the masts of sailing ships had helped her learn to cope with heights.

The three surviving Imperial ships were all visible from here, steaming slowly back and forth. Kira squinted, wishing that she had a far-seer. "Can you tell if the longboats are back with any of those ships? I think I see one or two."

"Maybe," Jason said, shielding his eyes with his flat hand. "Yeah. At least one."

"Blast. That means they probably got the people in them landed."

"Unless they gave up," Jason suggested.

"Weren't you the guy who reminded me that these guys aren't giving up? If they've gotten more people ashore, they definitely haven't gotten up the cliffs yet."

"Do you see that?" Jason said, pointing to the west. Kira followed his gesture and saw a tiny, vague shape almost lost in the haze. "Is that a ship?" he asked.

"It might be. I wonder whose ship it is? And whether it's coming this way?"

"It's coming from the west. Wouldn't that make it a Free Cities ship?"

"Not necessarily," Kira said. She jogged her chin toward the east. "The Empire's northern flotilla is based at Sandurin. They routinely patrol out past the mid-point of the Sea of Bakre because the Empire has never renounced its claim to rule the entire sea."

Jason grimaced. "I guess it doesn't matter. We can't wait around to find out. And even if it is a Free City ship, the Imperials have three ships to its one."

Still bothered a bit by the dizzying view, Kira sat down, breathing slowly and deeply. "Let me know when you're ready to tackle that cliff fall."

"I think we'd better rest some more before we try it."

He sat down next to her, their shoulders touching in reassuring contact that she welcomed. "Do you remember when I threatened to hurt you if you touched me?" Kira asked.

"I don't recall thinking of that as a threat," Jason said. "More like a sure thing. I wasn't tempted to find out. Did you ever…?"

"Did I ever what? If it involves boys, the answer is probably not."

"No," Jason said. "Foresight. About you and me. Didn't your mother say that your father saw them in the future, being married and all, soon after they'd first met?"

"He did," Kira said. "But he didn't realize they were married until Mother explained what the promise rings they were both wearing in the vision meant. She was…unhappy when she learned about that."

"Why? She didn't like him?"

"She liked him fine. Mother was already in love with him. But it's that destiny thing. Who wants to be told 'you're going to marry this guy' as if you don't really have a choice in the matter? Although," Kira added, "Father saw himself in that vision, too, which meant it was a possibility, not something sure to happen. So Mother had the choice. I'm sort of glad she decided to go ahead and marry him."

"Me, too. I like a world with you in it." Jason leaned his back against the rock. "Being able to see the future, possible futures anyway, should be a big help to this world, but I get the impression it isn't."

"Sometimes it is. Usually Mage visions don't help at all because you can't put them in any context," Kira explained. "Mother says the visions Father had during the war didn't help them, because they couldn't understand what they were doing in the visions or why until they actually reached that point in time. Oh, yeah, like that vision Father had six months ago of you and me being chased through mountains? How much good did that do us?"

Jason looked around, shaking his head. "We didn't know where we'd be, or when, or why, or…anything that would have helped. Anything that could have told us what we should do to keep it from happening."

"Keep it from happening? You can't." Kira fell silent, depressed.

"What?" Jason asked. "You've got that sad look."

"Father had another vision before Dorcastle, of Mother looking like she was dying," Kira finally said. "He told me he did everything he could to avoid that, and it happened anyway."

"But you haven't— Have you?"

"No. What if I did? What if I saw a vision of you dying? I couldn't save you the way Father did Mother. I don't have that ability. Only a handful of Mages, the most powerful and skillful, have been able to do similar things. I don't want to see something like that and know it's coming."

"Yeah, that'd be an awful thing to see coming," Jason said. "But, did you ever have a good vision of me?"

"No. Sorry. Remember, my foresight abilities didn't appear until the day your ship arrived from Urth."

"What if it had started earlier than that? Maybe a year ago? And you'd had a vision of us sitting here right now?"

She laughed. "I would have said, Who is that guy? Why is he touching me? Why do I look like I've spent a few weeks being bounced around in the back of a wagon full of rocks and dirt? What's happened to my hair? Why am I laughing? Am I going to go crazy? The only thing I would have been sure of was that if anything was wrong it would be my mother's fault!"

"So it wouldn't have been too helpful." Jason looked toward the sea. "Suppose a couple of years ago somebody had shown me a picture of you and said 'If you get to know this girl, a lot of people are really, seriously going to be trying to kill you someday.' That would have bothered me a little when I first saw you. It probably would have messed things up a lot. Hey, that story I tell about the Trojan War? The Iliad?"

"Yeah? Hey, that's where I heard about those Greek people!"

"The ones with goddesses," Jason said. "Yeah. Wow, you looked good in that dress. Anyway, remember the Greeks had been trying to capture the city and built the big wooden horse? There was this one Trojan woman named Cassandra who could see the future."

"Cassandra was a Mage?"

"No, she was cursed by the gods. They made it so she could see the future, but no one would ever believe her. She knew the horse would be big trouble, but no one listened to her."

Kira snorted. "I bet they made up the part about the gods cursing her so no one would believe her. They just didn't listen to her and then wanted to blame her for them not listening."

Jason stared at her. "I wish I'd thought of that when I did a report on the Iliad. You know this world is named after a Greek goddess, right? Demeter."

"How many times have we been over this? This world is named Dematr," Kira said. "Day-mat-er."

"The Greek goddess of the earth was Demeter—"

"Dematr."

"And she—" He suddenly stopped talking.

"And she?" Kira prompted.

"She had a daughter, and the lord of the underworld kidnapped her to be his wife," Jason said as quickly as possible.

Kira exhaled slowly. "What happened? Did the daughter escape? Did her mother rescue her?"

"Sort of. She finally convinced the other gods to make the lord of the underworld give her daughter back, but because the daughter had eaten some food while in the underworld, she forever after had to spend part of the year with the lord of the underworld as his wife. That's what winter supposedly was, the time when her daughter was in the underworld and Demeter was too sad for anything to grow."

Kira stared into the distance. "The Imperials tried to feed me food with drugs in it. If I'd eaten it, I wouldn't have been able to escape."

"This isn't that story."

"No. My story won't end like that." Kira spotted something near the cliff edge. "Here they come." She saw the figures, tiny with distance, struggling up over the edge of the cliff. "See? They're exhausted. We could've—" More figures came up, spread out for dozens of lances on either side. "—been trapped," Kira finished. "It's a good thing I listened to you."

"At least we've got a big lead," Jason said.

"Not nearly big enough." Kira stood up. "Look at all of them. Maxim must have stripped most of the crews off at least a couple of those ships. And they're going to have food to keep them going, which we don't. Let's get up that rockfall and out of their sight."

"It's getting dark," Jason said as they approached the fall of rock that offered a path up this cliff. "How well can we move when it gets dark?"

"I don't know. We can't afford to walk off a cliff. We'll improvise, Jason."

"I'm with you," he said.

She looked out to sea for a moment, the three Imperial ships still visible just off the coast. "I wonder if Mother and Father have heard anything about what happened in Caer Lyn? If the Imperials tried to keep anyone from sending the information, people elsewhere might just be hearing about it, days later. My parents might not be able to come themselves if the Imperials are stirring up trouble elsewhere, but they'll figure things out and send help, Jason. I know they will. We just have to stay ahead of the Imperials until the help gets to us."

They clambered up the rocks, already tired, more and more Imperial pursuers coming up onto the top of the sea-facing cliffs behind them.

CHAPTER NINE

The rockfall was helpful but also treacherous. "Like a minor character in an action movie," Jason commented.

Kira paused in her climb to glare at him. "Jason, if we die out here, please do me the favor of ensuring that your last words are something I can understand!"

By the time they made it up the last segment of the cliff the sun was low in the west, their path already shadowed by the bulk of mountains blocking the light. Kira felt the sweat on her grow unpleasantly chill as the warmth of the sun gave way rapidly to the cold of the breezes whipping among the crags.

From the top of the small cliff, she looked back one last time at the now-distant cliffs fronting the sea. The Imperials who had come up the cliffs were forming into groups, some of them just starting up the slope, their paths still illuminated by the last rays of the sun, their shadows stretching out beside them in long patches that created the illusion of vastly more pursuers.

Kira turned to look around. To the west, a sheer wall of rock reared toward the darkening sky. Even in full daylight that might be too steep for them to attempt. East offered a series of ledges heading upward. North was another slope, covered with scree and larger stones.

"That's going to be treacherous to walk through at night," Jason said. He looked haggard, sweat forming small streaks down his face, his chest heaving with deep breaths.

"It's better than the alternatives," Kira said. "Just don't fall."

"Have you noticed that you say things like that, as if I need to be told not to fall if I can help it?" Jason said. "And that you usually tell me something like that while you're doing something like shoving me off a moving train?"

She shook her head at him, catching her breath. "Are you going to complain about the train thing again? I've only pushed you off of moving trains twice. It's not like I do it all the time."

"That's true. I should count my blessings."

"And don't fall."

They started walking up the latest slope as darkness deepened about them, stars beginning to appear overhead. The heights on either side loomed like the walls of silent fortresses. Their feet kept slipping as the treacherous footing of small rocks and other detritus slid beneath nearly every step.

Both of them stumbled to a halt as they reached a ridge that marked the crest of the slope, night shrouding the areas behind and before them. Kira stood unsteadily, her legs two pillars of agony, feeling dizzy from exertion as cold winds buffeted her and Jason. "Wait here," she gasped.

Kira staggered forward, looking around. On the other side of the crest the land dipped down slightly before climbing a little, forming a small saddle at the top, and then dropping down. Higher peaks rose on either side of the saddle, their tops vaguely visible against the stars, the land between littered with rocks of various sizes which had fallen from above.

Kira forced her reluctant legs to carry her to the other side of the saddle. She looked down a slope that seemed slightly less steep than the one they'd climbed but much shorter. Though it was hard to tell in the dark, the slope seemed to end fairly quickly in another upward rise of land to the north and east and another peak to the west. The areas she could make out were covered with loose patches of soil and gravel, small, stunted plants, and occasional larger boulders.

She stumbled back to where Jason was sitting. He'd come off the crest and down into the saddle a little ways, propping himself against a stone the size of a carriage that offered some protection from the wind. Kira fell down near him, wishing the fire in her legs would go away. "The other side looks a little treacherous. I don't think we should tackle the next stretch for a while."

"Kira," Jason replied in a voice slack with fatigue, "it doesn't matter how rough the terrain is. If we don't rest we'll collapse. We have to take a break. A long break."

Despite wanting to deny that, Kira knew the truth of it. She could feel the truth in her rubbery, pain-filled legs, and in the raw feel of her throat as she tried to pull in deep breaths of air that had grown thinner and drier as they climbed. The wind gusted, bringing a renewed sense of chill.

Kira got to her hands and knees, crawled close to Jason, and pressed herself next to him, grateful for the warmth and the sense of safety he offered. "Okay. We'll rest."

"I love it when you say okay."

"Sure. Whatever. We'll rest and maybe sleep for just a little while. Who gets the first watch?"

"I'll take it," Jason answered immediately.

She wanted to argue, but she was incredibly tired. Kira forced herself to get out the bottle she was carrying and drank half the water in it. She had been snacking on the small remaining pieces of hardtack throughout the day, holding them in her mouth to soften as they climbed. Only crumbs were left in her pockets. Her belly complained of the emptiness, loudly enough for Jason to hear.

"Take this," he said, offering her a small piece of hardtack.

"You need it," Kira said.

He laboriously laid the hardtack on a flat rock next to him, using his knife blade to split it. "Here," Jason told her, giving her the bigger piece, which was about as long and wide as her thumb. "I made dinner."

"I'll do the dishes," Kira said, picking up a crumb from the rock.

She put the hardtack into a pocket to serve as breakfast. "I love you. Wake me in a little while," she ordered before surrendering to exhaustion.

She woke up to the noise of something scurrying along the rock they were leaning against. Whatever it was ran off to the north to the fading sound of little paws. Kira blinked up at the stars, guessing that it was well after midnight. Jason had passed out, too, sleeping with the slack jaw and slow breathing of exhaustion. Despite knowing how dangerous it had been for both of them to be asleep, Kira didn't feel any anger toward him. It was amazing that he had been able to stay awake at all for any longer than she did.

Shivering with cold, she snuggled closer to Jason, trying to stay alert. How long could they keep going like they had yesterday? Without any more food than the two fragments of hardtack they still had? Over terrain that still seemed to be all uphill, just as Jason had pointed out?

And, most importantly, how much longer could they rest here? She and Jason both needed more sleep, and this terrain was nothing to tackle in the dark, but the Imperials surely hadn't given up their pursuit. Worse, the wind was moaning through the mountains loudly enough that she couldn't be sure of hearing them approach.

Kira reluctantly woke Jason. "We shouldn't have stayed here so long. We need to find a better place to rest where we're not so exposed."

"Right," Jason mumbled, taking a drink of water and popping his last piece of hardtack into his mouth. "Can I finish breakfast first?"

"Sure. I need to take care of some business, anyway, before we start walking again. You do yours, too. I've got dibs on the backside of this boulder."

Kira struggled to her feet, cold and stiff, wincing at the pain in her legs as overstressed muscles protested working again so soon. The first steps were agony, but her muscles started loosening a little as she went behind the rock.

Yawning, Kira headed back toward Jason. He was just coming out from behind a second large rock, moving as if every step hurt. She winced again, this time in sympathy for how hard it was for Jason to move. "You're amazing," Kira said in a whisper.

She came close and kissed him, something causing her to remember her mother's advice and kiss with her eyes open. It felt weird, but also sort of interesting, to be looking partly past Jason as their lips met.

Which was why she saw the Imperial with a rifle in his hands struggling over the crest only a few lances away from them.

Kira used one hand to shove Jason aside while her other hand went for her pistol, drawing it as her thumb clicked off the safety. Jason, surprised, swung to one side, drawing his knife as she leveled her weapon at the Imperial.

The sound of the shot echoed deafeningly from the rock walls around them, shattering the silence. Her bullet caught the Imperial in the chest. He fell back at the impact, tumbling into another Imperial who had been close behind and knocking her down as well.

Kira spotted the head of another Imperial rising over the crest, a rifle barrel swinging their way, and snapped a shot at him. As the Imperial ducked, Jason grabbed her. "There might be a hundred just out of sight! Run!"

She nodded and ran with him, hearing a babble of shouts from the Imperials who were out of sight below the crest, commands being called and warnings being passed and at least one demand that she give up. Kira felt an inner chill that matched the outer cold as she heard the words "kill the boy" among the commands.

It was amazing how their tiredness and stiff muscles were forgotten as she and Jason took off, racing down across the saddle and up the other side. Kira risked a glance back and saw the dark silhouettes of easily a dozen Imperials over the top of the slope, some of them pausing to aim rifles. She and Jason went over the north side of the saddle and down the slope on the other side as rifles barked behind them, the sounds of the shots echoing and reechoing from the heights as if a war had broken out, the crack of the bullets passing close overhead lending speed to her feet.

Despite the darkness, they took the slope recklessly, sliding and slipping on loose patches, dodging among the larger rocks. Kira had to shift her view from the immediate area ahead to the bottom of the slope in order to figure out where to go next. Even at night, trying to climb the rising terrain to the east would be suicide with rifle-carrying Imperials on the top of the ridge behind them. Up ahead the slope ended in a welter of fallen rock that lay at the base of a mountain whose side offered no cover. But to the west the peak that rose on that side still blocked them.

She was about to despair when a patch of darker shadow grew into the mouth of a small canyon to the west of them, as if a giant had dug a trench in the side of the mountain with an immense sword. Kira jerked Jason to the left.

He followed without hesitating as more shots rang out and bullets whined as they ricocheted from boulders. "Get in front of me!" Kira yelled, shoving Jason before her so that she was between him and the rifles. The fire from the Imperials faltered for only a moment, then resumed. With the echoes crashing continually around them, Kira had no idea how many rifles were firing, but it sounded like more and more every moment.

Darting between boulders and trying not to slip on patches of gravel, Kira followed Jason into the canyon, where more rocks littered its bottom and a deeper darkness fought against the radiance of the stars above them. "Watch your step!" Jason yelled as he swerved. "Hole!" Jason swerved again. "Another hole!"

Kira narrowly missed planting her foot in one of the holes as she followed him through the canyon whose sides were getting lower. The gully curved slightly, then ended in an abrupt, steep slope that fortunately wasn't very high. Kira took it at a run even though every breath of the chill mountain air was burning in her lungs, Jason even with her again, each helping the other whenever they started to slip.

They rolled over the top of that slope, taking a moment to lie there and stare back the way they'd come, gasping for breath. Kira still had her pistol in one hand, while Jason gripped the survival knife from the boat. With the sound of the rifle shots having ceased, Kira tried to listen for the Imperials over the sound of her own labored breathing.

"Those guys looked too worn out to have chased us very fast," Jason got out between breaths.

"We have to keep moving," Kira told him.

"They shot at you," he said as they got to their feet again.

"Yeah," Kira admitted. "Maybe they're hoping to wound me enough to stop me but not kill me."

"Or maybe Prince Maxim has decided that if he can't have control of you to stop your mother, killing you will at least get you out of the picture."

"Maybe," Kira said. "From now on, we'll have to assume we're both targets."

"So you don't put yourself between me and Imperial rifles again," Jason said, giving her a look that said he wouldn't give in on this one.

"All right." She looked around. "That way. Which is downhill."

"It looks uphill to me," Jason grumbled.

Kira led Jason along another, higher but still narrow cleft, this one almost choked with rocks and boulders. Rounding a boulder big enough to have hidden their sailboat, Kira saw a long, shallow channel leading down and toward their right. No longer worrying about compass directions, but only at putting distance between them and the Imperials, she took it, her feet sliding on the small loose rocks covering the slope. Jason cursed as he fell but came up again quickly, waving her onward.

The channel split, one side dropping fast down the side of a mountain and the other curving slightly upward. As Kira hesitated Jason tugged her in his direction and she yielded as they ran up a short stretch that gave way to a deeper cleft beyond. Jason led the way as they slid down the near side of the cleft, then climbed up the other side. This time Kira chose the path, pointing back east where a narrow pass cut between a pair of cliffs. They scrambled up the scree-covered slope to the pass, then between the cliffs, finally sliding to a halt.

Exhausted, Kira and Jason leaned against the near-vertical wall of rock at their backs and against each other, breathing hard.

It was at least several minutes before either could speak. "No way they followed us through that," Jason wheezed.

"There are a lot of them," Kira gasped in reply. "They can split up to search every route and still badly outnumber us. But it's going to take them a while, because I don't think they're as motivated to catch us as we were to run."

She realized she was still holding her pistol. Resetting the safety, she reloaded to top off her magazine and holstered it.

"Was it your Aunt Bev or your Aunt Alli who told you to reload at the first chance?" Jason asked, staring out at the tortured terrain about them.

"Aunt Alli." Kira paused. "And Aunt Bev. And Mother. And Uncle Calu. And Queen Sien."

"You have the coolest aunts and uncles." Jason managed a grin. "I have one aunt, but she volunteered for the research habitat just outside the Oort Cloud, so I never heard much from her. My dad always claimed it was so she could get away from my mom. That may be the only thing he ever told me that was true."

"What's the Oort Cloud?"

"It's this huge mass of rocks and ice and stuff a long ways from the sun. My aunt's research station was about seven and a half light hours from Earth." Jason pointed at the starlit sky. "Your star has an Oort Cloud, too. You just can't see any of it because it's too far from your star and too cold."

"Does it matter?" Kira asked.

"Depends what you're talking about," he said. "Does it have any effect on you? Only in terms of the impact that mass has on the structure of local space-time. Long term, like life-of-the-universe long term, it adds up. Umm…speaking of life, you saved mine back there, didn't you? Shooting that guy?"

"We're not keeping score, Jason," she reminded him. "You saved mine by breaking my focus on shooting and telling me to run! It's a good thing I kept my eyes open while I was kissing you."

"You had your eyes open?" Jason stared at her. "Have you always done that?"

"No! You heard my mother's advice back in Tiaesun. You were there!"

"Yeah, but…"

"Because she said it could save your life," Kira reminded him. "And it did, didn't it?"

He nodded, then gave her a sidelong look. "What was it like?"

She shrugged. "Different."

"What else has your mother told you about that kind of thing?"

This time Kira smiled knowingly at Jason. "If you're really lucky, someday you might find out." She smothered a laugh. "Did I say that without looking like an idiot? Because I was trying not to laugh."

"I don't know. My mind just kind of blanked out when I realized what you were saying." He half smiled at her. "When I first got to Alli and Calu's place, it was pretty clear they were worried about what I might have done with you while we were off alone together. I was like, she said she'd hurt me if I touched her and that was all there was to it. Except when she kissed me."

"And when you caught me to keep me from going overboard in that storm. Which you never mention to anybody."

"I just don't want to seem like I'm bragging or something." His smile went away, replaced by an earnest look. "Alli and Calu have been so great to me. I wonder how I'd have turned out if I'd had them as parents?"

"You'd still be Jason," Kira said. "And I might have grown up thinking of you as a big brother like I did with Gari. In which case I would *not* be kissing you." She looked up, seeing the edges of the peaks to the east growing sharper as the sky began brightening behind them.

Jason laughed. "What light through yonder mountains breaks? It is the east, and Kira is the sun."

She shoved him back into motion. "You're obviously not too tired to make weird statements, so let's start moving again. I have no idea which direction we went while running."

"We took the easiest paths," Jason said, then paused. "We took the easiest paths," he repeated, sudden worry on his face.

"Oh, yeah, we did." Kira grimaced. "That is so obvious a trail. We'll need to take a route that follows some of the tougher options." Jason groaned. "I'm sorry. But you know I'm right."

"I'm the one who pointed it out," he reminded her. "Which I'm kind of regretting at the moment."

"I'm not. You think of things I don't. But maybe I can help you feel better. We didn't finish that morning kiss," Kira told him, leaning in to do that.

And keeping her eyes open again.

A narrow canyon framed by two heights, its bottom littered with rocks, offered the only reasonable way onward from where they had ended up. Kira and Jason walked through it, trying to keep to a pace they could maintain for a while. As Kira neared the end of the canyon, she looked ahead and almost missed the stone that turned under her foot.

She caught herself against the nearest large rock, angry at her own carelessness, and at the mountains, and at the Imperials chasing her. "I am so tired of every—" Kira growled, using a string of obscenities she had learned while a sailor on *The Son of Taris*.

"I haven't heard some of those words for a while," Jason said. "Are you okay?"

"I think so. But I almost turned my ankle. We'd be dead if that happened, Jason." Kira cautiously pushed herself to her feet. "I'm all right. You know, I did accidentally use one of those words around Mother a couple of months ago. She gave me this clinical and detailed description of what it meant and I've never been tempted to use another in her presence. There are some things that you do not want to know your mother knows about."

"Maybe some of those guys chasing us will turn their ankles," Jason said as they moved on to the end of the canyon. "They have got to be totally worn out. They must have climbed through most of the night to catch up with us."

"From what I've heard of Imperial military discipline, I should have expected them to keep going," Kira said. "I shouldn't have let us stop for so long."

"We had to rest, Kira. I think we both passed out. Sorry. And if we'd gone on in the dark you or I probably would have sprained an ankle at some point. Or broken a leg."

She paused, grimacing. "Yeah. Moving in the dark is too dangerous. Not nearly as dangerous as running through the dark while the Imperials shoot at us, but still bad. Wherever we stop tonight, it needs to be a place off any possible path, somewhere where even if they catch up, they won't spot us."

Jason looked around. "I'll let you know if I see anything like that. Hey, Kira, thanks."

Kira gave him a baffled look. "For getting you into this mess? You know, if you'd gotten involved with a regular girl you probably wouldn't be constantly running for your life."

"What kind of fun would that be?" Jason asked. "Boring, right? No, thanks for listening to me, and taking what I say seriously. You know so much more about this world and this stuff, but when I say something, you think about it."

"You're welcome. It's part of respecting somebody. I couldn't love you unless I respected you." They cleared the canyon, Kira studying the surrounding terrain again. "The easiest-looking path looks like the one to the north, along the flank of that mountain. They'll expect us to go that way. If we go southwest, we'll have to climb up that slope, but it looks like it leads to easier terrain farther on."

"That's a cliff, Kira, not a slope," Jason said.

"Jason, I'm too worn out to climb another cliff right away, but I can get up a slope. That's a slope."

He looked at her, puzzled, then nodded. "Got it. Let's cli— I mean, let's get up that slope."

The sun finally cleared the mountains to the east as they struggled up the nearly vertical "slope." Kira had to pause twice to rest and plan the rest of her path upwards, but she made it as the sun warmed her back, she and Jason helping each other up over the edge at the top.

The morning sun highlighted every detail of the angled path along the top, where dirt mottled by patches of tough grass had settled against the mountain behind and inclined quickly down toward the edge. The width of the top varied from a fairly comfortable almost-a-lance to a nerve-wracking half-a-lance or less, the "slope" dropping away almost straight down beyond. Kira led the way, watching her feet, worried that the Imperials might reach the area behind them in time to spot her and Jason up here.

"Whup!"

She spun about at Jason's exclamation, already reaching, and caught his arm as he slid toward the edge. "Was that some Urth way of saying help?" Kira asked as Jason carefully regained his footing.

"No," he said. "That's an Earth way of saying 'I'm slipping and I'm too scared to remember how to say the word help so I hope someone understands this.' "

"Got it. Ready?"

"Yeah." Jason looked ahead. "We've got a ways to go."

"One step at a time, my love, just like up that slope."

He grinned through a sheen of sweat on his face. "I'll follow you anywhere if you keep calling me that."

She felt an urge to rush that kept growing, but Kira kept her speed down, knowing that moving too fast might cause either one of them, or both, to slip again. The sun had quickly become hot enough to be a distraction. She wanted to remove her jacket, but that would be too dangerous with so little room to move and such treacherous footing.

After a seeming eternity, the ledge finally widened. She looked ahead, seeing it lead to where two mountains met, the area between forming a narrow dell whose sides curved up to meet the peaks flanking it. "It's downhill. There's grass."

Jason came up beside her as Kira pulled off her jacket. "Maybe there's water," he said, taking off his coat.

"How much do you have left?"

"One bottle."

"Let's save it until we know if there's more water down there," Kira decided. "If you see anything move, and it looks edible, let me know."

"Okay." He peered down at the dell. "What's our criteria for edible?"

"Probably anything that moves."

They made rapid time, heading down through the smooth footing of the dell. Kira glanced back to see that they were out of sight of anyone following their prior route and breathed a sigh of relief.

The grass was thick enough to cushion their steps, but Kira saw no trace of water as they followed the dell part way around one of the peaks. They walked for a while in silence, the sun rising higher and gradually casting its rays into the more sheltered depths of the Northern Ramparts. Coming to a branching of possible routes, Kira paused. "What do you think?"

Jason looked one way, then the other. "They both look painful."

"Pick a number."

"Five trillion—"

"Jason!"

"Sorry. Six."

"Even. We go that way," Kira said, pointing. They had to walk carefully along a fairly steep slope, watching out for loose spots that might send them sprawling in a long, tumbling fall.

Reaching a ledge that was almost a lance wide and offered fairly level footing, Kira sat down, looking up at the sun. "It's about noon."

Jason sat down next to her, took out their last water bottle, and offered it to Kira. "You first."

"Thanks, my love." She drank about a quarter, passing it back to him. "What do you want to have for dinner when we get home?"

Jason fixed a startled glance on her as he finished drinking, leaving half a bottle remaining. "What?"

"Dinner. Mother says we can have anything we want. I'll go first. I want roasted chicken and fried potatoes. With all the water and wine I can drink. And for dessert I want Ihris cake with sweet syrup. What do you want?"

"Uh…the same as you. Only shave ice for dessert. Nice, cool, wet shave ice."

"I've never heard of shave ice."

"I guess I need to introduce it to your world. You'll thank me. How come you're torturing yourself with that?" Jason asked. "Imagining food we can't have?"

"It's fun, isn't it? Girls like to dream of food we can't have. Don't guys do things like that?"

He made a noncommittal face. "Sort of. Only we don't dream about food we can't have. We have fantasies about girls we can't have."

"Oh?" Kira looked a question at him. "And just which girls have you been having fantasies about, Jason of Urth?"

"Me? None. I was talking about other guys. I haven't thought of any girl but you since the moment I first saw you."

"I'm sure. What about Devi?"

"Devi?"

"Yeah," Kira asked. "Do you ever think about Devi?" Her Aunt Asha's eldest daughter had inherited her mother's beauty and attracted guys the way a magnet drew metal.

Jason shook his head in feigned bafflement. "Devi who?"

"Liar. You are such a liar."

"I'm still not going to answer that question."

"I'm sorry." Kira leaned her head back against the rock behind them, closing her eyes, the sun warm on her face and bright even through her eyelids. "I wonder how long we can keep going without food? It wouldn't be so bad if we could just hole up somewhere and rest all day, but this work requires fuel for our bodies, and we haven't got any fuel."

"We can get by for a while on our bodies' stored fat reserves, but, yeah, at the rate we're having to burn it those won't last very long."

Kira giggled. "The Imperial diet. They chase you through the mountains with no food until you lose all that fat."

"And if you slow down, they shoot you," Jason said. "I thought you didn't giggle."

"I don't. That was—" Kira tensed as the sound of a shot echoed among the peaks. With little room to move on the ledge she dropped down as best she could, Jason beside her. "Where did that come from?"

"No idea," Jason said. "The sound is bouncing off every rock within hearing distance."

"I didn't hear a bullet or an impact," Kira said, gazing around carefully. "Maybe the shot was fired as a signal."

"They could be trying to herd us," Jason said. "Making noise to drive us in the direction they want us to go."

"That's brilliant, Jason. Just like hunters." She came to one knee, gazing outward. "And we're the prey."

Another shot sounded. Kira tilted her head, trying to sort out the echoes from the original. "That was a little west of here, I think, but a ways behind us. More than a thousand lances."

"Two kilometers?" Jason shook his head. "I can't tell. But I agree that it's behind us. They're definitely trying to send a message."

Kira looked at the pair of peaks rising to the west of them, the two mountains joined far above where she and Jason now were. "I wish we could head straight that way, but that's not a passable route. And, if we tried, once we got that high the Imperials might be able to spot us easier." She pointed closer to north. "If we continue around this high ground we might find something easier beyond. Or we could double back to the east."

"Those steps were hard enough the first time," Jason said. "I don't want to go over them again."

"Then we go north. Careful. If we start sliding we'll have a lot of trouble stopping ourselves."

Kira took a deep breath and started along the side of the slope again, trying to set her feet on any rock bulges or outcroppings that would offer better footing. As she put her foot on one outcropping, it proved to be a rock barely embedded in the slope that gave way almost immediately. Kira managed to jerk herself backwards to better footing, breathing heavily, Jason grabbing her arm to help steady her.

She heard the rock bouncing and clattering for what felt like a long time before it reached the bottom.

Ironically, the near-deadly rock left behind a pit that offered a decent foothold as Kira edged farther along the slope. She was getting increasingly worried that this perilous route would simply wend its way around the mountain, bringing them back to heading east, but finally a flatter area came into view. Her legs tired, she had to keep her progress slow to avoid more missteps, but eventually reached a spot where a gentle slope covered by rock fragments led down to a flatter area that gradually widened as it descended.

Getting down the slope over the treacherous rocks proved almost as difficult as walking along the side of the mountain, but Kira finally found herself on level ground covered by grass and a scattering of bushes twisted by the harsh environment. She stood, breathing slowly and deeply, grateful for a safe place to stand.

Jason stood nearby, his eyes closed as he caught his breath. But he suddenly looked at her. "Do I hear water?"

"Water?" Kira listened, catching a sound like crystals striking lightly against each other. "It's down there."

Her legs found new strength as they walked quickly down the vale that was widening out before them. Dirt had gathered here over the ages, providing a welcome place for vegetation tough enough to withstand the winters. "There it is. Jason, wait."

"What?" he stared at her, impatient and upset.

"If the Imperials get to any source of water before we do, they'll plant an ambush. We go slowly, and carefully, and watch for trouble," Kira said.

"Oh. But they shouldn't be—" He caught himself. "Unless they found an easier route. Okay. Slow and careful and all that."

Kira went to one side of the dale, gesturing to Jason to go to the other. They moved along the edges with their eyes on the heights on the opposite sides. The sound of the water grew agonizing as it teased them, but Kira kept her attention focused on sweeping her gaze across any spot where trouble might lurk. But she saw nothing, and if her Mage foresight was still present it offered no warning.

They finally reached the source of the water with no danger apparent. A stream burst from a fissure in the mountain to wander away along the narrow valley they were now in. Where the water splashed down to the dirt, a small pool had formed.

Kira drank gratefully, scooping up handfuls of water and letting them satisfy a thirst that had once again gotten agonizing, then filled her bottle. As Jason filled his two bottles, she sat back to enjoy the break and spotted something where the small pool spilled out into a shallow stream. "Hey. I wonder if that's what it looks like?" Scrambling to her feet, Kira walked carefully to where tall green shoots rose among the scrub grass. She pulled out the Imperial dagger and dug carefully until she was able to unearth a white root the size of her thumb.

Jason knelt next to her as she washed it off. "What is it?"

Kira rinsed off the root in the stream and took an experimental nibble. "Wild onion. I don't believe it. Wild onion. We can eat the bulbs and the green stalks."

Shoving the first one into Jason's hands despite his protests that she should eat first, Kira dug up another, washed it off and wolfed down the bulb, then chewed and swallowed the green stems. The bulb itself was sharp, but that didn't bother Kira enough to slow her down. Jason had brought out his knife from the ship and was digging up more.

They didn't stop until the patch of wild onion was gone, loose soil marking where each onion plant had been. She and Jason ate most, but left a small amount to carry with them. "I guess that goddess was looking out for us," Kira said as she stowed away half of the remaining onions in one of her jacket pockets.

"Demeter?"

"Dematr. If you're going to live here, you should say it right."

"But— Never mind." Jason studied the dug-up ground as they got ready to leave and shook his head. "I guess they'll know we came this way."

"It is pretty obvious, isn't it?" Kira said. "And look at our footprints in the moist soil around the pool. But there's no way to cover it. We have to hope they don't find this particular spot, or don't find it for a while. Hey, let's walk in the mud on the edge and leave footprints in the grass heading back the way we came. Maybe that'll confuse them on which way we went when we left here."

It took a little while to carry out that plan, while Kira eyed the sun. "We've got maybe an hour left before the sun sinks enough to put low areas in shadow. I want to keep going as long as possible, but we need to watch for a good place to hide for the night."

As if triggered by her words, three shots sounded, one right after the next. Jason pointed to the south. "One was there, I think."

Kira nodded. "And another was almost due west of us. How did they get that far? Maybe it was farther south than that."

"The third was between those two. Why aren't we hearing any shots to the east?"

"Because you were right. They're trying to herd us. Groups to the east aren't firing shots so we won't know they are there."

Half an hour later as they walked up a slight rise headed north out of the vale, Kira stopped and pointed. "A trail."

Jason stooped to examine it. "Not much of one. Is this even a trail humans use? It's pretty narrow."

"It could be larger animals use it. There are goats in these mountains."

"Where? I could eat a goat."

"Raw?" Kira shrugged. "Me, too. But people from the Free Cities hunt the goats, so they stay away from people, and those gunshots probably spooked every goat within hearing distance. Odds are we won't see any. This trail leads a little west of north, I think. Let's take it."

They walked in and out of shadow as the sun sank lower in the west and the trail wended among the peaks and up and down along ridges. Reaching a place where the trail split, Kira paused to look down each possible path.

"Hey, Kira!" Jason gestured upwards.

She followed his gaze, seeing a series of ledges above the trail. "One of those looks big enough to lie down on, doesn't it?"

"Yeah. One of us could lie down and the other one sit up to keep watch and make sure the sleeping one doesn't roll off."

"There's a route up, I think." She bit her lip, looking around again. "We could keep going for maybe another hour before it got too dark."

"Are we going to find any place better than this to sleep?" Jason asked.

"I don't…" Kira remembered the Imperials coming up over the ridge last night, imagining what might have happened if she had been dozing at the moment, or if she had waited even a few minutes longer to wake Jason. "You're right. It's better to have a safe place. Let's get up there and try not to leave obvious signs we climbed along here."

Kira had taken the first watch this time, watching the light fade to be replaced by the dark of night before waking Jason and lying down to instantly fall asleep.

At some point her dreams found her back on the street in Ihris, people moving around her with the vague features of those in dreams. Kira saw two police officers walking her way and felt her heart begin to race, afraid to turn and look across the street. Turning with painful slowness, she—

Awoke to Jason's fingers across her lips. She stared at him in the dark while he gestured down to the trail about two lances below their perch. She lay silent and listened, hearing the rattle of a rock and a soft exclamation. Vague noises resolved into the tramp of boots along the path. Jason already had his knife out and was leaning back against the rock behind them so that his seated figure was as concealed as possible from whoever was below. Kira slowly and silently drew her pistol, making sure the safety was still on before rolling a little to be able to look down on the trail from her prone position.

As she waited, Kira wondered what might have happened if Jason hadn't woken her, if that all-too-familiar nightmare had reached its usual end. She should have warned him before now. She had to tell him before another night fell.

"Watch your feet!" someone growled.

Kira recognized the accent. Whoever had spoken was from the Empire.

Dark shapes became visible, moving along the trail with the weary shuffle of very tired men and women. It wasn't easy to see individuals in the darkness shrouding the trail, but she thought there were about fifteen. Even in the night, though, she could see the straight lines of rifle barrels jutting up.

The column stumbled to a halt. "It splits here," someone said. "Which way do we go?"

"Keep it down. Let me check the map."

Kira saw a light appear below, silhouetting the shapes of two Imperial officers crouching over a map. Handheld electric lights had once been available only to Mechanics, but in the years since the fall of the Great Guilds several workshops had begun turning them out in larger numbers and selling them to anyone who wanted one and could afford it. A rustle of movement marked the rest of the weary column dropping down to sit, their backs against the same rock wall that held the ledge Kira and Jason were on. She couldn't see them without leaning out, but could hear their labored breathing. The Imperials must be pushing their people very hard.

"This trail isn't on the map," one of the officers said in a low voice to the other as she pointed to the paper. "We must be about here. This path looks like after it splits one way goes northeast and the other northwest."

"Orders are if we can't kill them we need to make sure they don't make it west," the other replied. "We'll take the path to the northwest. The other groups to the east should catch them if they're east of here, and if they try to go west we should catch them."

"What about leaving some people here to watch this trail in case they come down it from that eastern side?"

"Good idea. Make it five, and pick somebody good to be in charge. You know what Prince Maxim will do to anyone who screws this up."

"How many people are we supposed to lose chasing that demon spawn?"

"As many people as Prince Maxim wants."

"We don't have to try to capture her alive any more, right? As long as she's dead, *really* dead, the prince will be happy?"

"He still wants her alive if possible, but accidents happen. We'll wait another ten minutes for everybody to rest and then move on."

Kira saw one of the officers, who seemed to be far too close below her, move to face the Imperials seated beneath her ledge. If the officer looked up and shined a light, she would be able to see Kira. She would be the last thing that Imperial officer saw, Kira resolved, gripping her pistol, but that would leave fourteen Imperials right beneath her and who knew how many others who might be nearby and come running in response to a gun battle.

"You five are staying here to guard this spot," the officer said, pointing. "Pul, you're in charge. Make sure you keep an eye on the trail from the east. Everybody else, ten minutes."

Barely audible grumbles came from the Imperials. "Can't we wait until dawn?" an Imperial sailor asked. "It's treacherous footing, the trail's really narrow—"

"Do you want to personally explain to Prince Maxim why you let that girl get away?" the officer asked, her voice hardening.

"It's night," another Imperial mumbled. "I don't want to catch *her* at night."

"She doesn't like girls. Your blood's safe," a third responded.

"That's not what the sailors from the *Drusa* say. She went after women, too, when they had her aboard. I heard she had her teeth in one's neck before they pried her off. Maybe when she gets thirsty enough she doesn't care."

The Imperial officer's voice grew harsher. "You know your orders. Anyone caught spreading rumors about *her* is going to regret it. This girl is the daughter of Master Mechanic Mari, who the emperor says is not *her*."

"But Prince Maxim said—"

"Prince Maxim isn't emperor yet."

"What about the guy with her? He's from Urth, they say? Somebody told me those people from Urth came here because *she* told them to. To bring that guy. For *her* daughter."

Another sailor spoke up. "Yeah, 'cause no regular man could survive being with that girl. They needed some kind of demon from Urth."

"Prince Maxim can handle the girl," the officer said, her voice even more stern. "If you all have enough breath to gossip like old fools maybe you don't need any more rest time."

That quieted the sailors. Kira watched the Imperial officer go back to talk to the other officer, the two keeping their voices low enough that even this close Kira couldn't be sure what they were saying. She only caught a few words as she strained to listen. "Report...*Drusa*...blood...darkness..."

If she had been alone Kira would have been pounding her head against the nearest rock. *"I heard she had her teeth in one's neck before they pried her off."* If the Imperials didn't kill her, her mother would, when she found out how much Kira had reinforced the Mara story.

Although Jason had now been incorporated into it as well. A demon from Urth, brought to Dematr to be Kira's companion. She wondered whether Jason was also supposed to be dangerous to others, or if his special power was simply the ability to endure being Kira's boyfriend.

That thought, on top of her tiredness and overstrained nerves, brought her perilously close to laughing.

After what felt like an extremely long ten minutes, the two officers headed out with eight of the sailors, leaving five to guard the area. "If anything happens, signal. One shot to alert. Two shots close together if you see her. And you'd better be sure it's her before you fire those two shots!"

Jason pantomimed frustration to Kira, who responded with a gesture urging patience. These Imperials were worn out, their officers gone. It seemed likely there would be slacking off that she and Jason could take advantage of.

Sure enough, after the sound of the others had faded into the night, a sailor who must have been Pul spoke up. "One of us can watch that trail while the others get some rest. Right? You take the first watch, Nik."

"Why do I have to take the first watch?" Nik complained. He sounded young to Kira.

"Because you're the most junior of us, and because I said so," Pul replied. "I'm in charge here, remember? It's easy. Just stay awake and keep an eye on that path from the east and if you hear anyone coming, you wake the rest of us up."

Kira gave Jason a nod as they heard four of the sailors settling a short distance down the trail, where the path was wider and they could lie down.

She looked up at the stars, trying to gauge the time. It was well after midnight, maybe only an hour or two until dawn.

It wasn't long before she heard deep breathing and snoring from where four of the Imperial sailors were sleeping the sleep of the exhausted. Nik, grumbling under his breath, walked slowly back and forth for a little while before sitting down beneath the ledge. Kira listened intently until his breathing slowed and deepened. She brought her lips to Jason's ear. "I'll jump down. If he wakes, I'll distract him while you jump down behind him. Use a rock to knock him out."

Jason nodded, reaching to grasp a fist-sized rock as he put away his knife.

Kira moved very cautiously, trying not to make a sound as she slid to the edge of the ledge. She needed both hands free to do this, so she holstered her pistol. Lowering herself until she hung by her hands, she dropped as lightly as she could to the ground near Nik.

—Who was still awake and stood up, turning to look at the sound of Kira's boots hitting the trail.

"Adel?" Nik whispered as he stared at Kira. His head turned toward the four sleeping sailors, and Nik jerked in surprise as he saw them all still asleep. "W-who are—?"

Kira, her pistol still holstered, remembered the earlier conversation of the sailors as well as the stories she had heard about Mara. She whispered a reply in a very friendly voice. "Hi. Are you lonely?"

"W-what?"

"Are you lonely?" Where was Jason?

Nik flicked on a hand light, pinning Kira with it. "W-who?" he gasped again in a very faint voice.

She didn't have much experience with this, but she had heard the sailors on *The Son of Taris* laughing about pick-up lines they had heard, and remembered some of them. "Would you like to have a night you'll never forget?" Kira whispered, smiling. "Come here."

The light on her began twitching around. Kira realized that the young sailor's hand was shaking so badly he couldn't hold the light steady.

Jason finally jumped down, landing behind Nik, who was so focused on Kira that he didn't notice. A moment later, Jason swung the rock in his hand against the back of Nik's head, the impact of the rock making enough noise for Kira to flinch. Nik fell forward, unconscious, as Kira dashed in to catch his body before it hit the ground.

She barely managed to grab Nik in time, the sailor's limp body falling against her. "Go," she whispered to Jason, using her head to indicate the trail to the northwest. As he backed away, Kira carefully lowered Nik to the surface of the trail, trying to ensure that his equipment didn't rattle loudly enough to wake any of his companions.

Nik's rifle would make a very useful weapon for Jason. But the strap was over Nik's shoulder. Could she get the weapon off without—?

Kira heard a gasp behind her and twisted her upper body to see that one of the sleeping sailors had awoken and was staring at her with eyes so wide the whites were easily visible in the night. Kira realized that Nik's hand light, still on, was illuminating her crouched over his body. The female sailor had grabbed her rifle and was already raising it.

CHAPTER TEN

Kira's pistol was still in her holster. Aunt Bev had acted out moments like this for Kira, demonstrating that if someone already had a weapon pointed in your general direction, they could get off a few shots at you before you had a chance to draw your own. And even if Kira avoided getting shot before she had her own weapon out, she'd be facing three more sailors awakened by the noise, and forced to fire multiple times herself. Even if she escaped getting hit, everyone in earshot would know what the sound of a gun battle meant.

Her thoughts took only a fraction of a second before Kira bolted over Nik's body and along the trail to the northwest, shoving Jason into motion before her. She heard a babble of noise behind them as the other sailors awoke, but between the twists and turns of the trail and the darkness, Kira knew that she and Jason were already out of sight.

"The others went this way!" Jason whispered fiercely to Kira as they ran. A shot sounded behind them, closely followed by a second shot. "And they're going to be coming back!"

"I know!" Kira said. "They left over half an hour ago. Keep running for another several minutes and keep your eyes out for somewhere to hide!"

"What if the ones behind us chase us?"

"I don't think they'll do that, especially if they wake up Nik and ask him who knocked him out."

"What do you mean? He saw you! And what was that stuff about the night of his life?"

"I was pretending to be Mara's daughter! A blood-sucking young male-seducing monster! That's why he was too scared to shout a warning. And you are never to tell anyone about it! Aside from it having been *extremely* embarrassing, my mother will kill me if she hears I did that! Mother would never have pretended to be Mara, no matter how bad things were. Not in a million years would she have done that!"

Kira saw a place where the land fell off steeply into a series of small ridges beside the trail. "Here. Down here."

They dropped down to one of the ridges, standing on it with their heads about half a lance beneath the edge of the trail, hugging the rock before them. Kira hoped they would be almost invisible in the darkness even if someone looked down this way. Jason had his knife out again. She drew her pistol, clicked off the safety, and waited.

The sound of pounding feet came from the northwest, followed by a rush of movement on the trail above them. Kira tried to count, deciding that it was the entire group that had gone on ahead.

Once they were past, she set the safety and holstered her weapon again, and she and Jason helped each other back up onto the trail. They set off at a trot, trying to maintain a pace that they could sustain. "We're ahead of them again," Jason said.

"We hope," Kira said. "Those guys were already really tired. Running back all that way should make them unable to chase us for a while."

After covering what must have been several hundred lances they slowed to a walk out of necessity. Throats dry and stomachs empty, they took drinks from their bottles and chewed on the remaining onions as they walked. "Doc Sino is always telling me to eat more vegetables," Jason commented. "And she likes me getting exercise. So at least one person should be happy about what we're doing right now."

"Are onions vegetables?" Kira asked. "Remember to keep your voice down. We don't want any of them hearing us."

"They should have caught us back there," Jason said in a whisper. "We're toast, aren't we?" He sounded tired and discouraged.

"Don't give up, Jason."

"I'm just trying to accept reality."

"Don't! Look, I'm tired and scared, just like you are. Which is why I need you to believe we can make it. Do you understand? I need you to believe along with me! If we give up, if we decide it's hopeless, we *are* toasted."

"Toast," Jason corrected.

"Whatever! As long as we keep believing we can survive this, then we still have a fighting chance."

He looked at her in the growing light as dawn approached, a smile slowly forming. "Yeah. Okay. We'll make it."

She grinned back at him. "See? Doesn't that feel better?"

"I guess it does. Thanks for telling me that you needed me to help you that way." He laughed once. "After all, I am a special demon brought here for you. Am I dangerous?"

"You're a teenage boy, Jason. I'm sure a lot of mothers and fathers would consider you to be dangerous around their daughters."

He laughed again. "Yeah. I was such a threat to girls back on Earth. Why are the Imperials so superstitious and ready to believe stuff like that?"

Kira sighed, remembering talks that seemed to have happened an eternity ago. "Father told me it's because of the bargain the Imperials make. They give up a lot of freedom, a lot of control over the own lives, because in exchange the emperor will protect them and their families. That's the deal, see? But sometimes bad things happen anyway. The Imperials could admit that meant that their deal was messed up, that giving up their freedom hadn't actually made them much safer. But they don't want to do that. So instead they created the myth of Mara, someone with supernatural powers who is always trying to do evil things. Since she's so powerful, the emperor can't stop her. But the emperor is the only one who can fight Mara. So the Imperials can rationalize bad things happening and the need for an emperor to control their lives even though having that emperor is supposed to prevent bad things from happening."

Jason nodded, frowning as he thought. "They're not the first people to make that kind of bargain. It's self-reinforcing, isn't it? The more bad stuff that happens, the more powerful someone like Mara has to be, which makes it all the more important for them to back the emperor."

"Exactly," Kira said. "And now, with lots of bad stuff happening because the old emperor doesn't have a firm grip on things any more and the various princes and princesses are fighting for influence and power, it must mean that I'm not just your average dangerous teenage girl but a teenage monster who's a mortal danger to every young man."

"And woman," Jason said. "You had your teeth in the neck of one, remember?"

"Which is another thing my mother will kill me for if she hears about it," Kira said, unhappy with the turn the conversation had taken. "Bad enough that young men from the Empire get the shakes when she looks at them. If the young women start doing it, too…"

"Chemically, there's not much difference between the blood of young adults and older adults. The lymphocyte levels decline, but that's about it," Jason said. "Why do you only crave blood from young people?"

She glared at him. "I don't know, Jason! Maybe I think it's inappropriate to date and drink the blood of people outside my age group! Hey, I've got an idea. You know how much my mother *loves* talking about her supposed association with Mara. Why don't you save up all these questions and when we get home you can ask her!"

He jerked backwards, surprised by her reaction. "That wouldn't be very smart. I know how your mom feels about…"

"Is there a light going in there, Jason? Are you starting to realize something important?"

"You don't like to talk about people thinking you're a vampire either," Jason said slowly.

"And there it is!"

"I'm sorry," Jason said. "I was thinking of it like something in a game. You know, role playing."

Kira shook her head. "I've never really understood that whole role-playing thing, Jason. But it is a game, and this isn't. This is me, and other people thinking I am literally a monster. Not just a freak, a monster."

"I really am sorry," Jason said, his face twisted with emotion. "I should have known that. My mom and dad sort of treated me that way, always finding new ways to tell me how awful I was. And I hated that. I won't bring that stuff up again, Kira. But…can we make a deal? I can't call myself a jerk. That's good. Can we also have a deal against you calling yourself a freak?"

She frowned down at the trail. "Do I do that a lot?"

"Even once is a lot, isn't it? Because you're not. Not any more than you're a monster."

"All right, Jason. It's a deal." She relented and leaned close to kiss his cheek. "You're not a bad person, so I know when you say or do something wrong it's not on purpose. Sorry I got mad. How are you doing?"

"Um, I believe we can still do this but I'm really tired, my whole body hurts, my stomach is really empty, it's still cold, and I've got one bottle of water left."

"Same here, except I don't have any water left. Once the sun rises high enough we should get warmer, at least. And we'll be able to see anyone coming from farther off." Someone coming toward her. Kira suddenly remembered the dream she had been having when Jason woke her. "Jason, there's something I haven't told you, and you need to know about it because it could endanger both of us. If you see me sleeping and it looks like I'm having a bad dream you need to wake me up right away, because if I screamed, like when that group of Imperials was close, it would give us away."

He gave her a worried look as they kept walking. "Why would you scream?"

Kira struggled with something inside that tried to freeze the words within her. It took all she had to force them out. "I'm dreaming that…I'm…back in Ihris. And…and…the dragon…is charging…and…I don't pick up the club…and…when the dragon bites down…on…my arms…it…"

"When your arms were in its mouth? You have a nightmare that it bites down?" Jason shook his head, more upset than ever. "No wonder you wake up screaming. Do your parents know?"

That was easier to speak about. "Well, yeah, duh, they hear their daughter screaming in the middle of the night and they come really fast." Kira inhaled convulsively. "I've only had that nightmare twice. I mean, where it gets to the point where it…bites. But it was starting when you woke me up tonight." She looked into his eyes. "Do you? Have nightmares about that?"

He nodded. "A few times. Only, I'm standing there, and I can see the dragon charging you, and I can't move. My feet won't move. And I try so hard but I can't get to you."

Kira smiled at him even as she had to blink away tears. "You've always gotten to me when I really needed you. I'm sorry I didn't tell you before about the nightmares."

"I don't imagine you like thinking about it," Jason said.

"Not thinking about it doesn't make it go away," Kira said. "That's not something I figured out. Mother told me. And she's sort of an expert on that."

The slight trail they had been using became even less easy to follow as the now-faint trace bent up along another ridge, then along the side of another mountain. Somewhere along the way they had gained more height. Kira tried not to look down too much since she was finding the views dizzying. That probably had as much to do with lack of enough food and water as it did with the heights. Uncertain where the Imperials might be, they kept quiet for long stretches to avoid alerting any groups that might be nearby but out of sight.

The deceptively peaceful mid-morning was shattered when the distant sound of gunfire echoed from the west. Kira and Jason stopped to listen, trying to guess what the rattle of shots meant and where they were located.

The battle, if that was what it was, lasted for about twenty minutes before tailing off into a few, scattered shots whose noise faded to leave the mountains quiet again. "I think some of the Imperials ran into some Free Cities' people," Kira finally said.

"Who won?" Jason asked.

"The shots sounded like they faded toward the west, which would mean the Free Cities' patrol retreated back toward Marida," Kira said.

"So they'll call for help."

"They might not have a far-talker, and even if they do, getting hand-held far-talker signals through in mountains like this is nearly impossible," Kira said.

Jason shook his head. "The mountains shouldn't make any difference. The uplink to the nearest sats—" He caught himself. "Oh, yeah. No satellites."

"Hand-held far-talkers are pretty much line-of-sight," Kira said. "It might take a while for anyone to learn that Imperials hit that patrol. And if the Imperials wiped them out," she began, then had to stop as she thought about those men and women dying and the words stuck in her throat.

"It's not your fault," Jason said. "The Imperials are the ones driving this."

"Keep reminding me of that," Kira whispered. "Let's keep going. We have to find a good path west or even northwest so we're not having to crawl through this awful terrain."

They'd just reached the end of a route along a succession of stony ridges when Kira heard the sound of a shot, followed a moment later by the crack of the bullet impacting a boulder behind Jason. The shot broke off fragments of rock that pelted Jason as he and Kira threw themselves to the ground.

Rifles crashed, and more projectiles slammed into the rocks near them. Kira stared upward, seeing figures silhouetted against the sky along high ground to the west. "They've got this way west blocked! Back the way we came!"

Jason, ducking under the barrage aimed at them, didn't need any encouragement to do as Kira said. They ran back along the slope, Kira risking a quick glance back to see figures pelting down the mountain toward her and Jason.

They hit the next ridge and ran full out along the top, gaining ground on the Imperials. But as they rounded another height Jason gave a cry of despair. "They're coming from this direction, too! At least a dozen!"

Kira skidded to a halt, looking frantically around. Exposed on the ridge, they could neither run nor fight. Trying to make a stand here was hopeless.

"Any ideas?" Jason asked urgently, looking ahead and then behind.

"We can't stay here," Kira said, looking around again. "We can't go back. We can't go ahead. That way is…south. Shallow ravine that leads into another bare mountainside. We'd be sitting ducks on that exposed mountain. That leaves north."

"North?" Jason looked down that side of the ridge. "That's a cliff."

"It's a slope," Kira said. "We can slide down a slope."

"What about the vertical parts of that slope?" Jason demanded, looking frantically ahead and behind. "We're trapped."

"We're not trapped. Mother says there's always an option. It's just a matter of being willing to take that option." She holstered her pistol and closed her jacket. "Sheath your knife. We're going down."

Jason put away the knife, closing his coat. then followed Kira's gaze down the cliff. "You're serious?"

"It's our only option that doesn't guarantee death, Jason," Kira replied, sitting down on the edge of the cliff, her feet dangling over.

"You know, all of the sudden being shoved off of trains doesn't seem so bad," Jason said as he sat down next to her, his words quick and tense.

"We're making this jump together. Try not to fall too fast," Kira ordered.

"Huh?" Jason gave her a disbelieving look.

"Try to stay upright and check your fall by grabbing at anything in reach!"

"Oh, right."

She smiled at him despite the fear filling her. "I love you. See you at the bottom." Kira pushed off as gently as she could, fearful of losing contact with the surface of the slope/cliff that was her only hope of slowing her fall. As she went off the edge, a brief glimpse of the distance to the bottom almost froze her with fear as gravity grabbed her and pulled her down with voracious force.

Kira hoped Jason had pushed off as well, hadn't been paralyzed with terror as she almost had, but didn't dare turn to look as she dropped, trying to check her fall with her heels without catching them and flipping herself into what could well be a fatal tumble down the cliff. Her hands caught at bushes and tufts of grass as she dropped, scrabbling at rocks and projections, getting bruised and slashed and cut as she fell. Her back slammed and skittered over the rough surface of the cliff, picking up a new assortment of bruises.

Kira could feel sharp projections ripping through her trousers. Abrupt jerks told her of rock edges snagging on the back of her jacket and tearing short gashes before breaking free. She didn't mind, in fact felt grateful in the midst of her fear that each snag and rip slowed her fall a bit.

A projection of stone punched her left leg, drawing a cry from Kira. Her right arm jerked painfully as her hand gained a momentary hold on a sturdy bush growing out the cliff, only to have the bush slide through her grip with agonizing friction and a few more lacerations of her palm.

She couldn't afford to look down to see how close she was to the bottom for fear of overbalancing. She couldn't look over to see how Jason was doing. She couldn't look up to see if the Imperials had reached the point from which Kira and Jason had pushed off. All Kira could do was keep trying to slow her fall down the steep slope and wonder how many pieces she would be in when she reached the bottom.

Her right boot caught on something and she let the leg collapse to keep it from breaking. That tossed Kira into a sideways roll down the cliff. She desperately hoped she was almost to the bottom.

She bounced off another rock, then through a daze of confusion felt her fall being checked rapidly as she slid out onto a sloping pile of dirt, pebbles and rocks which had accumulated at the base of the cliff. Kira glided to a halt, coughing in the dust raised by her descent, more gravel and dirt dislodged by her fall showering down on her, trying to gather her scattered thoughts and wondering just how badly she'd been banged up in the plummet down the cliff.

A moment later Jason came down nearby, spinning on his back as he slid past her a little ways in his own cloud of dust.

Kira pressed her hands to her head as if physically forcing her thoughts into place and staggered to her feet, limping as what felt like a nasty bruise on one hip made her leg protest, then came to her knees next to Jason. "Are you okay?"

He looked up at her, plainly dazed as well, then grinned. "You said okay."

"*Are you?*"

"No bones are sticking out." Jason struggled to his feet, himself favoring one leg. "We really survived that?"

A shot followed his words, the bullet slamming into the dirt between them.

"Not yet," Kira said. "I think we've got two good legs between us." She put her arm over Jason's shoulder as he did the same with her, and supporting each other they ran as fast as they could manage down the slope before them.

More shots followed them, bullets sending up puffs of dirt or sprays of rock as they hit to either side and ahead. "In vids, bullets are always just behind running people," Jason gasped.

"They're shooting downhill," Kira replied between her own ragged breaths. "People have to remember to aim low when they do that or their shot will go high, but they usually forget."

"Alli told you that?"

"Yeah. Good thing she didn't teach these guys to shoot."

Kira stole a glance back, seeing Imperials clustered near the place where she and Jason had pushed off. Most were aiming and firing rifles at them, but a few were looking down the cliff. None had tried to follow them down, though.

"They're all bigger and heavier than us," Jason gasped again. "They wouldn't actually fall any faster. Because physics. But they'd have a harder time braking their falls enough to keep from being badly hurt when they reach the bottom."

"They're also probably not as desperate as we were," Kira said.

A ravine opened up ahead, bending to the right so that they passed out of sight of the Imperials and the rifle fire stopped. But they were heading east again. Kira let go of Jason, cautiously testing her muscles and wincing as various pains told of bruises and other minor injuries. "I think I can walk now. How about you?"

Jason nodded, grimacing. "Yeah. I'd say we should take it easy for a while but I can look around me and tell that's not going to happen."

The ravine they were in led to a series of ravines and passes between mountains now rising high enough to boast white caps of snow that shone and glittered in the sunlight. "Uphill all the way," Jason grumbled as they climbed, their route leading steadily higher.

As they gained altitude the air kept thinning and kept getting colder as well, the icy breezes coming off the snow-laden slopes above them lashing their exposed skin and penetrating the rips in their clothing. They finished the last of their water, their insides aching from the lack of any other food since the wild onions. Kira knew her body was a mass of bruises from the way most movement hurt, and her hands were stiff from cuts and scrapes on the fingers, backs and palms.

Jason moved as stiffly as she did, but they both kept going, determined not to be trapped again.

As they climbed to the top of yet another ridge, Kira came to a sudden stop, the spectacular view momentarily driving away thoughts of their peril. They'd been climbing a broad mountain with a shallowly sloping side, and now they stood on a flattened peak that offered awe-inspiring views for a considerable distance in all directions before being blocked by the higher mountains hemming them in.

Jason stopped beside her, looking around, breathing deeply from the climb and the thin air. "Cool. If I wasn't exhausted, half-starved, hurting all over, and freezing to death I could really enjoy this. Do you think we finally outran the Imperials?"

"I think there's a chance, yeah," Kira agreed.

"Maybe there's also a chance we can get to Marida or another Free City."

"Maybe. We have to be a good ways north. We may be getting closer to Alexdria by now." Kira looked around again, spotting what she thought might be movement to the south. The Imperials chasing them, no doubt. If that was them, they were way behind Kira and Jason.

Kira let her eyes sweep across the mountains and passes to the east, where the rays of the late-afternoon sun were slanting down into the canyons and other low areas as well as lighting up the mountain slopes facing them.

She stopped moving, feeling a vast pit opening inside her, a pit that threatened to swallow every trace of hope. Light moved in the passes and along the slopes of the mountains to the east, reflections off of metal. Columns of people, moving into the Northern Ramparts from the east, filling every road and path and trail. People with metal weapons and metal armor. Nothing else could be producing those kinds of reflections. "Oh, blazes. That's all we needed." Weariness and hunger suddenly weighed more heavily on her than ever.

"What?" Jason came to stand beside her, looking in the same direction. "What is it?"

"Imperial legionaries." Kira shaded her eyes with a flat palm and scanned slowly across the vista before them. "It has to be. Look there. They seem to be spreading out onto every trail and possible route through the mountains. What I'm seeing is at least a legion. An entire legion, Jason. Chasing us. Do you feel important?"

Jason followed her gestures, rubbing the back of his hand across his mouth. "You're certain that it's a legion coming into the mountains after us? They can't be Free Cities soldiers?"

"They're coming from the east, Jason. The Free Cities never keep many troops on the border. Just scouts whose orders are to report any Imperial incursions and fall back." Kira sighed. Tired, cold, hungry, thirsty, already being pursued by Imperials from the ships, and now this. "At least once this is over I'll be able to trade stories with Mother about dealing with Imperial legions. They never caught her, you know."

"And you're definitely your mother's daughter," Jason said.

"Am I?" Kira asked, gazing at the oncoming legions. "I thought maybe I could be in some ways. But this... Mother started a war, Jason. The War of the Great Guilds. She didn't want to, but if not for her it wouldn't have happened. And she knows if not for that war, the Storm would have come and civilization would have fallen and nearly every person on Dematr would have died, but she still feels the guilt of it. Why am I starting a war, Jason? Because some conceited, idiotic, foolhardy Imperial prince wanted me in his bed? Could there possibly be a stupider reason for a *war*?"

"Kira," Jason said, his tone as harsh as Kira had ever heard it when he spoke to her. "Stop it. You're not the reason. Maxim is one of those idiots who wants a war because he thinks it'll be easy. Because he thinks he's so smart he'll out-think everybody else. Because he likes playing with soldiers and sailors because he's not going to risk getting hurt himself. Because he thinks the lives entrusted to him are less important than his pride. Because he wants to strut around and call himself a hero because of the sacrifices of others. It's not about you, Kira. You just happen to be what's making him move now. It's about him. This is *his* war, not yours. There have been people like him all through history. But there have also been people like you, people who fought and stopped people like him."

She looked at Jason, feeling a smile on her lips. "Have there also been people like you? To keep people like me fighting when it seems hopeless?"

"I guess," Jason said. "I shouldn't have given a stupid speech—"

"Oh, shut up." Kira grabbed Jason and kissed him with all the fervor of love, hope, and despair mingled. Then she looked him in the eyes. "It was a great speech. If you won't let me give up or blame myself, we'll just have to keep fighting until we win."

He grinned. "And you're a Lancer, right?"

"I'm a Lancer," Kira agreed. "But even Lancers don't take on a legion without a lot of help."

"Won't the Free Cities help? This is an invasion, right?"

"Yeah," Kira said. "It's definitely an invasion. But the Free Cities will have to mobilize their forces. The standing armies of the individual cities can't handle at least a legion on their own. I don't know exactly how long mobilization takes but we're talking maybe a week. That's just to get the Free Cities soldiers gathered and ready to go. Then they have to get from their cities to where the legions are."

"There's no chance the Free Cities had any kind of advance warning the legions were going to invade?" Jason asked.

"Before they saw the legions coming?" Kira shook her head. "It's possible, but we can't count on it. We have to assume we're still on our own for a while, Jason."

Jason shrugged. "At least we have a head start on them."

"The legions make the sailors we've dealt with look like amateurs," Kira said. "The legionaries are going to be rested, with food and water, and they're coming into the mountains along passes and paths while we're still moving overland. They'll travel a lot faster than we can. We can't afford to go north or east any more or they'll overrun us." She pivoted to look south. "And the Imperials chasing us from the shore are all somewhere in that area and we know they're trying to push west to block our way to Marida. We'll have to aim north of west to try to thread the needle between the advancing forces, go as fast as we can, and hope." She shivered as another gust of cold wind howled past them.

Jason made a face. "If this was a game, I'd definitely decide I was too far behind to have a chance and hit the restart button. I'd go back to, uh, a saved game. In Tiaesun. Before the meal started. And this time before we went into that meal I'd drag you over to your parents and I'd say, 'Kira has seen someone who looks like her double, so the Imperials obviously have plans already underway to kidnap her and try to take her back to the Empire against her will on the prince's ship. We need to get her out of this palace right now!'"

Kira couldn't help laughing, imagining the scene. "And my poor parents, hearing you say all that, would decide that their daughter had finally succeeded in driving you crazy."

"You can't drive me crazy," Jason said. "My special demon powers, remember?"

"Oh, yeah." Kira stopped laughing as she looked at Jason and saw the weariness in him, the gauntness from their lack of food, and the way he was looking at her. "I'm going to say this because it's an option. I can wait here or head east to meet the legions. Once they have me, they won't keep chasing after only you."

"You know my answer already, right?" Jason said. "Didn't we already both promise that neither one would die for the other?"

"We did," Kira agreed.

"So if you head east, I'm going with you. I'm not leaving you."

"Just like my father stood with my mother," Kira said. She looked around again at the magnificent and forbidding scenery, then back at Jason. The cold wind whipped at her hair, so she had to brush it back, thinking about the choices she had. The choice she could make now. There were moments when truth seemed very clear, when the right path was easy to see, and as Kira looked at Jason she realized this was such a moment for her. "Hey, Jason."

"What?"

"Will you promise yourself to me someday? Will you accept my promise on that day?"

He stared at her without speaking for a long moment while Kira waited nervously. "That's a marriage proposal, right?" Jason finally said. "You just proposed to me?"

"Are girls not allowed to do that on Urth?"

"Sure they are." Jason blinked, breathing fast. "I've got to be crazy. This couldn't happen to me."

"Is that a yes or a no? I think I deserve a clear answer, Jason."

He opened his mouth, closed it, swallowed, then nodded. "Sure it's a yes. How could I not say yes? You want to marry me? Me? Really?"

"Yes," Kira said, smiling. "Somebody has to keep on eye on you. It might as well be me. And you're usually fun to have around, and you're also pretty handy when I get attacked by a dragon or kidnapped or chased by an Imperial legion."

"But you only said you loved me a little over a week ago!"

"It's been a pretty eventful week, Jason. Yes, I spent a long time deciding how I felt," Kira said. "Trying to understand how I felt. Maybe I've been in love with you for months. I don't know. But when I decided, I knew. And I know now. Just like I know that you really love me. Love me enough to face death with me. The thread doesn't lie, Jason. It's right there!"

"Except the thread isn't there," Jason said.

"It's intangible! What's so strange about that? Can you see love, Jason?"

He smiled back at her. "Right now I can. I'm allowed to ask you, too, right?"

"If you want to," Kira said. "Yes."

"Will you, um, promise yourself to me?" Jason asked.

"I just said yes," she pointed out. "But I'll say it again, because it's important. Yes." Kira took a deep breath. "So…we're engaged. We don't have to get married as soon as we turn eighteen. We can wait. I'm fine with that."

"What about your parents?" Jason asked, visibly nervous.

She eyed him. "Are you scared of my parents? I thought you were prepared to stand by me against anything and anyone."

"They are the daughter of Jules and the Master of Mages," Jason pointed out.

"So?"

Jason looked around at the mountains surrounding them. He

shrugged. "So. I'll stand by you. This all has to be an elaborate hallucination, anyway. I'm sure I'm really under deep sedation somewhere back on Earth."

"Are you saying I'm an hallucination?"

"No one as amazing as you could be real," Jason said, grinning.

"Oh, you are so delusional. Maybe I'm one of those goddesses."

"That's it! And I'm the mortal champion who you've selected to fight for you! Best game ever! What happens next?"

"We walk again," Kira said, smiling at him, wondering how she could feel so elated when they both appeared to be doomed. She pointed to the northwest. "That way. Down the slope until it meets that ridge, which I think leads to some low areas. I will have you note, Jason of Urth, that our path from here is downhill."

"See? That's a good omen!"

"What's an omen?"

"It's like foresight," Jason explained. "Omens are sort of ambiguous signs of what the future holds. They're usually hard to interpret."

"So they are just like foresight," Kira said.

"Kira, we're going to make it."

"Yeah," she said. "We're going to make it." For this moment, she could believe that.

Kira and Jason headed down off the peak, the chill winds biting into them, their bodies sore, their stomachs hollow, and the Imperial legionaries continuing to fill the mountains behind them as the sun sank lower in the west.

CHAPTER ELEVEN

The Peace of the Daughter has ended," announced Beran of Palla, his expression that of a man attending the funeral of a loved one. Mari and Alain, and the other officials in the conference room, gazed somberly at the ambassador from the Free Cities as he gestured to the map on the wall behind him. "The two Imperial legions in the north have entered the Northern Ramparts and are moving rapidly westward."

The moment of silence that followed was profound. "Where are they striking for?" Olav of Ulrick, the ambassador from the Western Alliance, finally asked. "Merida? Alexdria? Cristane?"

"None of them, as far as we can tell." Beran moved his finger across the map. "All of the reports we are receiving from scouts are that the legions have broken up into numerous small columns which are sweeping through every low spot and path in the Ramparts."

"That's insane."

Tiae's ambassador to the Bakre Confederation, Tresa of Tiaesun, leaned forward, intent on the map. "That doesn't sound like an attack aimed at taking one of the Free Cities. It sounds like a search."

Beran nodded in reply. "We believe the same."

"What are they searching for that would be worth that kind of risk and provoking war?" Ambassador Olav wondered.

"The daughter of the daughter," Beran said, gesturing toward Mari.

"So the Imperials did kidnap your daughter Kira?" asked President in Chief Julan of the Bakre Confederation.

"Yes," Mari said. "It's now certain that she was taken from Tiae aboard the flagship of the Gray Squadron after being kidnapped on orders of Prince Maxim. The girl who was seen leaving Queen Sien's palace at dawn was a double, left there to deceive us about the time when Kira was kidnapped."

"The Bakre Confederation failed to act in time to intercept that squadron," Julan said, his voice heavy. "We let our doubts delay us. We owed you better, daughter. You did not delay in coming to Dorcastle in our hour of need. We should have not have delayed in acting as you asked."

"I do not blame you, sir," Mari said, her stomach knotting at the idea of Kira trying to outrun and outfight two entire legions. "I know what it's like not to be able to do what you want to do. You're not the only one who sometimes finds their hands tied."

"Maxim has actually sent legions into the Northern Ramparts in pursuit of Lady Kira?" Olav asked incredulously. "Who would start a major war in pursuit of a girl? Or a boy? Lady Kira isn't the daughter of Jules. There are no prophecies concerning her. Am I right?"

"You are right," Alain said. "There are no prophecies. Maxim appears driven by a refusal to accept the failure of his original kidnapping plan."

"Failure at the hands of the daughter of the woman who humiliated his father!" Beran said. "No one else could have driven him to this. He sought to avenge his father's failure by not only defeating you, Lady Mari, but also by humiliating your daughter."

"Bad idea," President of State Jane remarked.

"Yes. Instead, she is humiliating him." Beran pointed to the map again, this time along the coast well east of Marida. "On the advice of the daughter, the Free Cities began mobilizing our forces four days ago. One of our coastal patrols encountered three Imperial warships here in our waters and was driven off. Marida responded by sending out two warships. They discovered that two of the Imperial vessels were carrying only skeleton crews and unable to put up a fight. One of those was sunk and one captured. The third managed to escape."

He paused. "The captain of the captured ship confirmed that the Imperial ships were the remnants of the Gray Squadron. Prince Maxim received information that Lady Kira had gotten away alive from Caer Lyn after destroying his flagship, and sent the remaining ships of the Gray Squadron in pursuit. They caught up with her sailboat just off the coast but not in time to stop her from making it ashore."

"Was she alone?" Mari asked.

"No. As you and your husband guessed, the boy from Urth had managed to find her. Maxim ordered such an unrelenting pursuit that another Imperial ship was lost on the rocks while trying to catch them. Our ships saw the wreckage on the coast."

Jane leaned forward, disbelieving. "Kira set afire one Imperial ship, and caused another to run aground and be destroyed? She accounted for two-fifths of the Gray Squadron?"

"It's tempting to see what she could accomplish against those two legions," Olav of Ulrick commented, then looked an apology at Mari and Alain. "I would not seriously suggest such a thing, of course."

"We understand," Mari said, unable to resist a brief smile. "Alain and I do have quite a little girl, don't we?"

Beran of Palla cleared his throat. "The captured Imperial captain said that most of the crews of his ship and the one we sank were sent ashore in pursuit of Lady Kira and Jason of Urth. The ship that escaped had Prince Maxim aboard." He paused. "There is something I should mention, but I know the subject is a delicate one."

Mari looked steadily at him, all humor fled. "Was Kira assaulted?"

"Not to our knowledge!" Beran hastily assured her. "No, this concerns the Dark One. The captain we captured insisted on repeatedly warning us that the 'daughter of darkness' is a great danger to the west."

"The Imperials are calling me the daughter of darkness?" Mari said. "I suppose that's—"

"Not you, Lady. The captain used that term for your daughter."

"Daughter of the Dark One," Alain said.

"Exactly." Beran grimaced, plainly uncomfortable. "He said that Lady Kira had been discovered one evening crouched over the unconscious body of a young sailor, preparing to...pardon me, Lady, but this is the term the captain used...preparing to feed. The sailor's companions drove her off, and when he regained his senses the young sailor claimed that Lady Kira had appeared out of nowhere to seduce him."

"Mara can be invisible?" Mari asked.

"The legends vary on that point, Lady. Usually it's described as being able to blind the senses of men. The officer said that in addition to some sailors having witnessed her supernatural abilities and, um, unnatural appetites, the total destruction of Maxim's former flagship is also being attributed to Lady Kira's malign powers."

President Jane shook her head in disbelief. "The captain of an imperial warship said that? Not one of the crew?"

"That is correct," Beran said. "The belief that Lady Mari is a cover for Mara the Dark One is a longstanding one within the Empire, but it has been confined to the lower levels of society there. For a high-ranking official to express it is highly unusual."

"No one has actually seen Kira drinking blood, have they?" Julan asked.

Beran nodded. "Yes. A very highly placed someone. The captain said that Princess Sabrin claimed to have confronted the daughter of darkness while alone, encountering her in the act of drinking the blood of a young man, and to have walked away from the encounter unharmed. Sabrin commented in the hearing of some of Maxim's officers and sailors sent to search her ship that she had required no guards to protect *her* from Mara's daughter, and had ordered Kira not to harm her. Apparently Prince Maxim never encountered Kira without several guards present."

"Why would anyone high in the Imperial household stoke fears of Mara by claiming she had a daughter that was loose in the world?" President Julan asked.

"Maxim has been claiming that like Emperor Maran he could control Mara," Ambassador Olav said. "But if instead he has loosed Mara's daughter on the world and has proven unable to control her…"

"Then," Alain said, "Maxim will be proven both unable to match his boasts, and responsible for unleashing a peril against the Empire. A peril that Princess Sabrin is claiming to be able to confront and control."

"Yes," Beran said. "And the proof exists, in the eyes of that captain at least, in the fact that the daughter of darkness destroyed Maxim's flagship but spared Sabrin's yacht."

"Wonderful," Mari said, letting her unhappiness show. "Sabrin is trying to discredit Maxim and build up her prospects by portraying Kira as a blood-sucking monster, which also reinforces the Mara claim against me."

"But how could Mara even have a daughter?" Olav wondered. "Why would the Imperials believe that? Don't the stories all say that she traded away her ability to have children along with many other human attributes in exchange for unfading beauty and eternal unlife?"

Beran spread his hands, speaking apologetically. "The Imperial captain told us that Mara's alliance with the most powerful of Mages is responsible. Mara required such a potent Mage to cast the necessary spell to call an offspring of hers into being."

Mari surprised herself and everyone else with a brief laugh. "I have to admit that my husband played a vital role in the creation of our daughter. I couldn't have done it without him." She paused, thinking. "As unhappy as I have always been about the Mara thing, if Kira is aided by the rumor that she is the, uh, daughter of darkness, and that same rumor creates problems for Maxim, any embarrassment to me is a small price to pay."

"It is indeed aiding her," Beran said. "The captured captain told us that the group of sailors who witnessed your daughter's, um, assault on a young sailor were badly rattled by the experience. Word of that was passed around quickly, and on top of the extreme fatigue that all the Imperial search parties were suffering from, discipline was disintegrating. Prince Maxim was told that the search parties from the ships were rapidly losing any semblance of an organized military force."

"So he ordered the legions to go in," Jane said. "Faced with failure, he more than doubled down on his bet."

Beran visibly hesitated again. "I feel obligated to mention that both the male and female sailors in the search parties were frightened of encountering your daughter, Lady. According to every captured sailor we spoke with, Kira is believed to be a threat to young women as well as young men."

Mari stared at him. "Why?"

"The sailors claimed she had attacked women with a clear aim of... satisfying her thirst."

Mari covered her face with one hand. "What has your daughter done, Alain?"

"I am more concerned that by escaping and evading Maxim she has triggered the war we feared," Alain said.

She dropped her hand and gave him a glare. "Kira did not start this war. She bears no responsibility for refusing to be a victim!"

"I am sorry. I did not mean to imply otherwise," her husband replied.

"I think," said President of State Jane, "that the kidnapping of Kira and the Imperial hunt for her has set things into motion, but these are all things that would have happened eventually. For them to happen now, when the Empire is not prepared for the war it has been edging toward, may be to our immense benefit. Does the information available to the others here agree with ours, that the Empire has not mobilized?"

"Yes," Beran of Palla said. "By moving the two legions in the north into the Ramparts, Maxim has left the northern Empire effectively undefended."

"That matches our information as well," Ambassador Olav said. "The Empire has been caught flat-footed by Maxim's impulsive actions."

Mari inhaled deeply before speaking. For the moment, she would have to stop thinking of her daughter and instead guide what had become a planning session for war. Guide it in ways that would produce the least damage and the most viable peace afterward. "That gives us an opportunity. If we act together. What are the intentions of the Free Cities?"

"We have been invaded, Lady," Beran said. "As our forces continue to mobilize, they will move east to meet with and destroy the legions that have entered the Ramparts. Those legions would have been extremely dangerous if concentrated into large units, but with them spread out we should be able to defeat the individual small forces one by one."

Ambassador Tresa from Tiae nodded. "Maxim isn't an idiot. He must have thought he could get the legions into the Ramparts, catch Kira, and establish strong defensive positions before the Free Cities could mobilize and hit back."

"If we hadn't begun mobilizing days ago, that might have worked," Beran agreed. "Lady Mari, Sir Mage, the forces of the Free Cities also have orders to search for your daughter and the boy."

"I am extremely grateful for that," Mari said. "Kira has spent time in the Free Cities. If she sees soldiers from any of them she will know she can trust them."

"Lady, what exactly is the status of the boy?" Beran asked. "Is he a citizen of Tiae? How does he stand in relation to you?"

Mari spoke slowly and carefully. "Jason of Urth is not a citizen of any country on Dematr. As of yet. But my family is in debt to him. He saved Kira's life. And she is very...fond of Jason."

"How does that guide us in how to regard him?" Olav asked.

"Regard Jason as one of my family," Mari said. She saw Alain stare at her, so surprised that he momentarily let it show. "Regard him as my son." She didn't know exactly where those words came from, but she felt a truth in them.

"And mine," Alain added, just as if this was something they had discussed many times.

Jane raised her eyebrows at them. "I thought Kira was still deciding on her feelings for Jason."

"Master of Mages Alain and I have decided on our feelings for the boy," Mari said. "You have your answer. Regard the boy as our son. Now, tell me, Beran. The Free Cities will very likely be able to annihilate the two legions which have invaded the Northern Ramparts. What then?"

Beran nodded. "Lady, the Free Cities know of your concerns and have taken your advice of twenty years ago to heart. I have been officially authorized to tell you, as well as the Bakre Confederation, the Western Alliance, and the Kingdom of Tiae, that the forces of the Free Cities will stop at the edge of the Northern Ramparts. Conquering Umburan in a lightning strike would likely be easy, and a rich prize. But occupying it, controlling its hostile populace, and maintaining control of the lands around it would be a bleeding wound that would suck endless treasure and lives from the Free Cities. Our goal is to destroy and expel the invaders, trusting in the daughter of Jules to arrange a new peace in which the Empire will *respect* the borders of surrounding states."

"Thank you," Mari said.

"But I should add that is the goal of the government. The people of the Free Cities have longstanding grievances and may demand Umburan. The leaders of the Free Cities would be very grateful if the daughter of Jules were to issue a statement that she believed the people were best served but not trying to conquer Imperial territory."

Mari nodded, exchanging a glance with Alain. "You'll get that statement."

Olav nodded as well. "The Alliance would not be willing to assist a war of conquest. My government will be happy to hear that the Free Cities do not intend that."

"Will the Confederation and the Western Alliance aid the Free Cities in defending their territory?" Mari asked.

President Julan leaned forward, his eyes studying the map. "The Empire has not mobilized. Even if it has already begun the process, mobilization will be done with all of the bureaucratic deliberation and ponderous momentum the Empire has mastered. It will be a month before all of the reserve legions have been fully assembled and ready for battle."

"Imperial warships are another matter," Olav of Ulrick commented. "And we have no desire to leave the Empire free to attack any other place once those legions are assembled."

"Agreed." Julan pointed at the map. "The Imperials have enough naval strength to meet either the Confederation or the Alliance on equal terms. But if we strike them together, the Imperials will be badly out-numbered."

"The Alliance recognizes the truth of your statement, sir."

"Suppose," Julan continued, "the Bakre Confederation sent naval forces to blockade Landfall and destroy any Imperial warships they encounter, and the Western Alliance sent its warships to do the same for Sandurin? The Empire would be bottled up. Not only its fleet, but also most of its trade."

Beran of Palla spoke up. "This is exactly the aid the Free Cities most need. We ask that you do this. It will ensure that Marida and Kelsi remain safe from Imperial invasion from the sea."

"Are you in need of soldiers for defensive purposes?" Ambassador Olav asked. "If the Free Cities are throwing all of their forces at those legions, your own cities will be left lightly defended."

"In accordance with our agreements of self-defense, Ihris has already committed to send forces to aid the Free Cities," Beran said. "And they have told the Free Cities that if the Western Alliance also agrees to send soldiers, Ihris will grant them free passage through its city and lands."

"Ihris is famous for the skill of its traders. What price has Ihris asked for such cooperation?" Olav asked.

Beran smiled. "Ihris lies between the Free Cities and the Western Alliance. It is always in Ihris's interest to maintain good relationships with both. They are wise enough to know that having both indebted to Ihris will be to their benefit."

"Ihris is wise," Alain said.

"So speaks its wisest son," Beran said, nodding to Alain.

"Then what of the Sharr Isles?" Olav asked. "We are tired of trying to halt Imperial encroachments on the Isles, and the Imperial forces there will pose a threat to our blockades of Landfall and Sandurin."

"Who would deal with that?" Jane asked. "Would the Alliance be willing to allow the Confederation to expel the Empire from the Sharr Isles and destroy their forces there?"

"That will be a hard sell at Cape Astra," Olav of Ulrick said. "Control of the Sharr Isles would be a major coup for the Confederation and give it a large trade advantage in the Sea of Bakre. I assume the Confederation would feel the same about the Alliance gaining control of those islands."

"The Free Cities cannot spare forces," Beran said. "Nor would we want either the Confederation or the Alliance to gain the Sharr Isles."

"If no one state is acceptable, what if more than one took on the task. What of a combined expedition?" Mari asked. She paused, surprised that she was trying to make this happen—an invasion of the islands where she had been born. If it didn't happen, if the west didn't act because of mutual suspicion, the Empire would end up still in control of the Sharr Isles and ready to use them as a springboard for more aggression. But if the west did act, the people of the islands would be caught in the middle.

Mari hid the pain her next words caused her. "The Empire must be evicted from those islands. What if half the ships and soldiers for that task come from the Confederation, and half from the Alliance? The forces remaining to occupy the Isles and maintain their security would also be from both."

"If a garrison is to be left there following hostilities, the Free Cities would contribute as well," Beran said.

President of State Jane exchanged glances with President in Chief Julan. "The Bakre Confederation would agree to such an arrangement," Julan said. "I will commit to that now. A combined force, with ships and soldiers from both powers, to destroy Imperial forces on the Sharr Isles and lay the groundwork for a force that would ensure the long-term safety and neutrality of the Sharr Isles."

"I think the Alliance would also agree," Olav said. "But a major question remains open. Who would command? The daughter?"

"Yes," Beran declared. "That would make it clear to all that this is not an occupation aimed at benefiting the Alliance or the Confederation, but an action by the daughter to free those islands."

"I'm not qualified," Mari objected.

"You commanded at Dorcastle," Julan reminded her.

"In name, yes, but Field Marshall Klaus handled most of the military details."

"Then we need a similar commander working for you," Jane said.

"What of Commodore Banda?" Alain asked. "He is one of those who has sworn to serve the daughter again if she calls."

"Banda?" Jane sat back, thinking. "He's been part of Tiae's forces for a long time, but I know he is respected in the Confederation fleet."

"The same in the Alliance," Olav agreed. "It would be difficult to win agreement to place Alliance forces under the command of an officer from Tiae, but if he is serving the daughter, just as he did twenty years ago, that would be another matter."

"I have no doubt that Queen Sien would agree to loan Commodore Banda to the daughter for the duration of these hostilities," Tresa of Tiaesun said.

"Then let's proceed on that basis," President Julan said. "The expedition to free the Sharr Isles will be led by the daughter, under her commander Commodore Banda. Confederation forces taking part will be under the daughter's command."

"Is that acceptable to the daughter?" Olav asked, looking at Mari.

She sighed, thinking of how many had died at Dorcastle twenty years before. Deaths she still felt responsibility for. Mari glanced at Alain, who looked back with an impassive expression. Only his eyes betrayed that he knew how difficult this decision was for her.

But if she didn't agree, if she didn't lead a joint action, then the suffering could easily be far worse. How many times had she told Kira that there was always an option, if you were willing to take it? "Yes," Mari said, wondering how many lives that one word might end up costing.

"Then I am certain that the Alliance will agree as well," Olav said. "We must also think of Syndar, though. If the Alliance and the Confederation send the great majority of their forces east to engage the imperials, that will leave the west unguarded. Syndar claims to be totally neutral, but…"

"That is all too good a point," Julan agreed. "Offering Syndar that sort of temptation could be a mistake."

"Tiae's naval forces cannot match those of the Confederation and the Alliance," Tresa said, "and they have much farther to go to engage the Imperials. What if Tiae committed to using her ships to screen the coasts of the Confederation and the Alliance as well as that of Tiae? Syndar has learned to fear Tiae."

Julan nodded. "Tiae sent us aid twenty years ago, and our ties have been close ever since. We would trust Tiae's ships to defend the coast of the Confederation from Syndar."

"The Alliance's ties with Tiae are far less well established," Olav said dubiously. "To entrust them with defense of our coasts might be difficult to accept."

"What better time is there to create such ties?" Mari asked. "I will personally guarantee that Tiae's ships will not infringe on the Alliance in any way and act only in mutual defense."

"If the daughter offers that guarantee, the Alliance will very likely accept," Olav said.

"I must ask of you all what I asked of the Free Cities," Mari said. "What will you seek beyond supporting the Free Cities, blockading the Imperial forces, and freeing the Sharr Isles?"

Ambassador Olav answered first. "The focus of our government is westward. There will be little enthusiasm for war on Imperial territory when the Western Alliance is preparing to colonize the western continent. That's where we want to send our resources rather than see them eaten up in a death match over Sandurin or some other piece of Imperial territory. We also don't want the Empire biting us in the back, so there will be support for acting with the Free Cities. But not, I think, for expanding the war to Imperial lands. Our people, though, like those of the Free Cities, may need to be reminded by the daughter that she is looking out for their best interests in endorsing these limited actions."

President Julan nodded. "The people of the Bakre Confederation won't be as enthusiastic for war. The Confederation hasn't forgotten the cost we paid at Dorcastle. No one wants to refight that battle, and no one wants to spend Confederation lives trying to take Landfall knowing that we'd be the attackers. Victory's price would be too dear. Beat the Imperial fleet, free the Sharr Isles and leave enough forces there, jointly with the Western Alliance and the Free Cities, to ensure that the Imperials don't come back again, and the Confederation will be well content with the outcome. *If* the Empire's fangs have been drawn."

"Something must be done about Prince Maxim," Tresa of Tiaesun said.

"Agreed," Ambassador Olav said. "If he remains crown prince, and becomes emperor, imperial aggression will occur again. It would just be a matter of time."

"I understand," Mari said. "Maxim will be dealt with." Her last words came out with a finality that rang through the room.

A moment's silence followed that statement.

"What about the alternatives to Maxim?" Julan finally asked. "Who takes over after Maxim has been…dealt with?"

"Princess Sabrin is positioning herself as the strongest possibility," President Jane said. "She's as ruthless as Maxim, but far more disciplined and pragmatic. It's no secret in the Imperial household that Sabrin thinks the Empire would be better off focusing inward, developing their technology and industry, instead of trying to refight the battles lost twenty years ago. Maxim has been able to out-maneuver Sabrin by using arguments about Imperial pride and honor, but if those result in major military disasters, Sabrin will be in just the right place to pick up the pieces."

"Camber doesn't favor her," Mari said. "He hasn't ever directly said so, but my impression is that he thinks she wouldn't be aggressive enough in advancing Imperial interests. I think she'd be plenty aggressive, just in nontraditional ways that didn't involve military risk."

"We can beat the Empire in peaceful competition," Julan said. "That's one 'war' I'd look forward to."

After the others had left, Mari turned to Alain. "Tell me the truth. Has it become easier over time for me to give the orders that will result in men and women dying? The Mari who you first met in the wastes outside of Ringhmon couldn't have done it."

He looked at her with the same perfect solemnity that he had shown as a Mage, but with emotion now clearly visible behind it. "Yes, she could have. Even then, you did what you thought must be done to protect others. It has not become easier for you. Do you think I cannot see the pain it causes you?"

"Am I doing it because Maxim kidnapped Kira? Am I letting my personal desire to hurt him driving my decisions?"

"No." He shook his head at her. "You always ask the same questions, whether you are letting personal feelings decide you, and I always give the same answers."

"I need to hear them," Mari said.

"Why did you say what you did about Jason?"

"Why did you agree with me?" she asked in return.

"Because I felt a truth in your words," Alain said. "I, like you, have seen what is inside him. And, like Kira, we find much to admire there. I wonder that Urth could regard someone like him so lightly."

"Maybe he was in the wrong place," Mari said. "Maybe, on Urth, Jason would never have found what was inside him. He would have remained that sullen, unhappy man all his life, wondering what was missing, never finding it. But he came here, and he found what he needed. We needed each other to find the best inside us. Perhaps Kira and Jason are the same, two who together can bring out the best in each. They have to live, Alain. I've already sent a message to General Flyn, asking that he do what he can to aid in the search for them."

"There is something else," Alain said.

"Oh, you finally see that, Master of Mages?" Mari took a slow breath, then smiled at him. "I wasn't sure for a while, Alain, but now I'm certain. Another child is on the way." The look of joy and surprise on Alain's often impassive face made Mari smile wider. "My feelings exactly. But when I realized that another child would be coming to us, I realized something else. We've always been proud and happy to have Kira, even when she was at her most difficult, and we could never forget her brother Danel who died. But destiny also brought us Jason."

Alain studied her, questioning. "What do you mean?"

"I mean that while we've been hoping for another child, we never realized that destiny had already given us one six months ago, one who needed real parents. There are children of the body and children of the heart, Alain. Kira has been both, and if destiny wills a safe birth this time so will be this new child. But by his deeds, by being who he is, by his love for our daughter, Jason has won a place in our hearts, too. And our home. Whether or not Kira and he ever promise themselves to each other, he *will* be our son."

Alain nodded to Mari. "And the new little one? The one now beginning within you?"

"Stars above, Alain, do you think I can't love three children?" Mari paused, gazing at the map upon which war had just been decided. "We need to give them the kind of world they ought to have. We need to give every child that world. I hope the price is not too high."

She walked to a window that looked out in the harbor. Always busy, it now surged with furious activity around the Confederation warships. War had not come to Dorcastle again. Dorcastle was going to war.

And once again the daughter of Jules was at the center of it.

As was her own daughter.

The long slope down off the peak had gradually steepened into a perilously angled descent. Kira, her heart pounding from exertion and fear, finally found her feet resting on a narrow ledge running at an angle across the side of the mountain. Below that ledge, the slope turned into a cliff whose vertical drop was too far and too sheer to offer any hope of successful descent. "Are you all right, Jason?" she asked in between rapid breaths.

He spoke from beside her, the strain clear in his voice. "So far."

"I'm going to move along this ledge at a safe pace," Kira said, her face to the rock of the mountainside. "Don't look down and don't look out. Keep your eyes on the rock in front of us."

"Okay." The single word held not only fear but also trust in her decisions.

Kira hoped that her earlier choices hadn't already doomed them. She looked only far enough down to see where her feet would go next, needing every bit of her willpower to keep her eyes from straying toward the precipice beneath them. It already felt as if the empty space was tugging at her, trying to pull her into the void. Kira feared that if she looked into those depths they would seize her and yank her off the ledge.

She lost track of time as she slid sideways step after step, barely able to look more than a few steps ahead to ensure the ledge continued to offer a perilous but traversable path. What if the ledge ended, leaving her with nothing but the unforgiving cliff face? Could she and Jason back up if that happened, get far enough to retrace their path?

"Kira," Jason said in a thin voice. "I'm pretty scared."

"Me, too. Just stay with me." She realized that having Jason with her helped. Alone, the fear of the fall down that cliff might have overcome her. But Kira knew that if she failed, Jason would die. So she had to succeed, had to keep taking step by step along this ledge. Not just for herself, but for him. Because she could not fail him, not when he had never failed her.

How long had it been? She didn't dare look around for the position of the sun. The winds that swept through these mountains were gusting again, pushing at her and Jason, numbing their hands with cold. They continued to creep along the side of the peak. In a few spots the ledge grew so narrow that only part of their feet rested on it, but each time it expanded again to offer still-perilous but slightly wider footing.

What was that at the corner of her eyesight? Kira, her eyes locked on the side of the mountain so that she could see the ledge and nothing of the abyss beyond it, thought that something was there just beyond the ledge. What? How far down was it? It felt like they had been moving along that ledge for hours, though it was certainly far less time than that. What was beneath them now?

Kira paused in her movement, her breaths coming fast and shallow. "Jason, put your hand nearest me over my hand nearest to you."

"Are you okay?"

"No. I thought that was obvious." She tried to breathe deeply. "I need to look down. I can't do that unless I can feel you holding me to the side of this mountain. If you're holding me, I'll know I'm safe."

"Okay." Jason's voice quavered with both fear and tiredness, but Kira heard the rustle of movement and then his hand pinned hers to its frail hold on the face of the mountain.

She closed her eyes, calling on every lesson her father had taught her about maintaining calm, about remaining centered when the world tried to tear at you. Another deep breath, and Kira opened her eyes and swung her gaze far enough over to see down the side of the cliff beneath the ledge.

Tree tops?

No. Bushes.

Ahead of them, beneath the ledge, sparse, scrubby grass pocking rock-flecked dirt. Kira looked a little farther, directly below, and shivered at the chasm still looming.

Kira breathed out, then in again, and looked farther ahead. She had to wet her mouth before she could speak. "Jason, we're four or five lances from being above a wide area that has a slope but vegetation on it. I can't be sure, but I think the ledge merges with it maybe fifty lances ahead. We only have to go about a dozen more lances to be sure we're well over that slope."

"You're not telling me that so I'll keep going, are you?" Jason asked in a strained voice. "I can keep going."

"It's true, Jason. Just stay with me a little longer and we'll be able to rest."

She moved onward again, her feet sliding sideways on the ledge faster now that she knew that the drop beneath them was no longer so far and that a place to rest was close. The ledge was getting thinner as they went, but still offered just enough room for their feet.

Kira wasn't sure how far she had gone when the narrow remnant of the ledge under her feet gave way completely, her hands found no purchase on the wall of rock before her, and she dropped with a gasp of fear.

Jason grabbed for her, catching her hand, only to be yanked down as well.

She barely had time for a moment of horrifying guilt before her boots hit solid ground and she went tumbling down the slope.

How far was she from the edge that dropped off into the chasm?

Kira grabbed at everything within reach, sliding to a halt on her stomach.

Jason came sliding past her.

She shifted her grip on a patch of touch grass, flinging out her hand just in time to grab Jason. The grass gave a little as Jason jolted to a halt, but held.

She lowered her face to the ground, breathing heavily. "Can you get a grip on something?"

"Yeah." She felt Jason moving at the end of her arm. "Okay." The weight of him eased. "I got a good grip. Rock. You can let go of me."

Kira raised her gaze again and reached for a hold where a loose rock had left a divot in the soil. Pulling herself up, she finally let go of the grass and managed to grip a bush that felt firmly rooted.

Jason kept pace with her as they crawled up the slope.

Finally looking up, Kira saw that they had only fallen about a lance when the ledge gave way beneath her.

She crawled another lance up the slope before daring to look back.

The grass patch she had held onto was easily visible, some of the roots pulled partway from the ground.

The end of the slope, where it gave way to nothingness, was less than two lances beyond that. She had to look away, terrified by how close they had come to falling.

"Kira?" Jason lay nearby, gazing anxiously at her.

"Don't look behind us yet."

"You know what? This time I'm going to listen to you."

Kira raised herself enough to view the slope ahead. "Another few lances and it looks like it levels off a bit. Slow and steady. Test every hold before you put weight on it."

She covered more than a few lances at a cautious crawl low to the ground before feeling safe enough to get to her hands and knees. The slope crested, dipping for a short distance before gradually continuing to rise to a rounded ridge some ways ahead.

They tumbled into the sheltered groove in the landscape, shaking with relief.

Jason, breathing heavily, grasped her hand. "That wasn't fun."

"Yeah," Kira agreed. "Let's try to look ahead better next time."

"It was a great trap," Jason said, staring up and back at the thin line of the ledge as it ran along the mountainside in the direction they had come from. "In a game, I'd be saying that was awesome. It just gradually got worse and worse, and it always seemed harder to go back than keep going forward, until we found ourselves on that. Awesome trap," he repeated. "I can't believe I thought games like that were fun."

"Is there any water left?" Kira asked, her throat painfully dry.

"A little." Jason passed her one of his bottles. She worked out the cork and swallowed half of the remaining water, which was too little to even fill her mouth once. Kira passed the bottle back and Jason drank the rest.

"How are you holding up?" Kira asked.

"Still here. Really hungry," Jason added. "We have to get into lower spots, don't we, Kira? We're not going to find water or anything to eat this high up."

"The legions will be moving faster on the lower spots," Kira said. "But you're right. If we don't get more water and find some food we won't be moving at all. We'll have to risk going lower and following any paths or roads we find."

Wincing, she stood up. "Nothing broken or sprained, I think."

"Same here." Jason got to his feet, following as Kira staggered up to where the slope crested and looked down the other side, where the land fell away not too steeply into a gulch winding between peaks.

Eventually, the gulch widened, opening into a meadow choked with what were either tall bushes or stunted trees. Kira's eyes widened as she saw a path leading through the brush, the first clearly human route they had found.

Kira paused before entering the vegetation, drawing her pistol. Jason saw her and pulled out his knife.

She started along the winding path, listening intently for either sounds of water, the movement of animals, or any sign of Imperials who might have made it here.

She had heard nothing when the path turned a corner and Kira was shocked to find herself face to face with an equally surprised man in the lightweight leather armor of an Imperial scout.

CHAPTER TWELVE

Kira and the scout grappled, the scout grabbing her gun hand while swinging a dagger toward Kira.

She threw herself sideways, pulling the scout into the brush alongside the path, branches raking both of their faces, and locked her free hand on the wrist of the scout's knife hand. Both of them rolled to the ground, straining to keep the other's weapon away. The scout slammed his forehead toward Kira, who twisted her head to avoid a direct blow, grunting with effort as she suddenly let go of the scout's knife hand and drove her stiffened palm against the side of his head. During the instant that the scout was dazed, Kira rolled on top, using her knee to pin his knife hand while she pulled out her own dagger and thrust it into the scout's unprotected neck without pausing.

And stopped to stare, appalled, as the scout convulsed beneath her, shuddering before dying.

Kira got up, staggering backward. "Jason! Imperial scouts usually travel in pairs!"

She finally saw him, standing and looking down with a dazed expression. A second scout lay at Jason's feet, Jason's knife driven at a slightly upward angle through the scout's leather armor, between his ribs and into the heart in what must have been a perfect strike.

Jason looked over at her, unable to accept what had happened.

"I...I was rushing to help you, and the other one suddenly jumped out at me, and..."

Kira knelt to check Jason's knife, then pulled it clear, wiping the blade on the dead scout's trousers. "It's a good thing Bev has been drilling you on knife fighting."

"I didn't think! I did what she'd showed me and I...just... Dead?"

"Yeah," Kira said, lowering her head and trying to breathe calmly. "So's mine. Jason, don't feel. Just think. We don't have time to feel."

"Who—?"

"They're Imperial scouts. Forward reconnaissance, ranging ahead of the regular legionaries. Which means regular legionaries are somewhere behind these." She yanked the canteen from the belt of the scout that Jason had killed and tossed it to him. "Water."

He caught it without thinking, staring at the canteen as if it were a deadly snake. "I...I can't..."

"*Water*, Jason!" Kira rolled the scout's body enough to pull off his light pack, tossing that to Jason also. "There should be iron rations in there." She ran the few steps to the scout she had killed, picking up the dagger the scout had dropped instead of retrieving her own from his throat. Grabbing his canteen and pack took only a few moments.

She stood up. Jason stared back at her, the canteen and pack of the scout he had killed seemingly forgotten in his hands. Kira met his eyes, knowing that he was looking at her with bafflement and horror at her looting of the dead. "Jason, I was taught my whole life to defend myself, and that sometimes it would require me to do things I would not want to do. Things that I would never do if given a choice. But I will do them, Jason. I can't just be a victim. It's not in me. I will fight. If that means you want to reconsider your future promise, if you can't handle the idea of being with me anymore once this is over, I will understand."

He shook his head, looking down at the dead scout, then back at her. "I don't want to leave you. But...games don't feel like this."

"It's not a game," Kira said. "They lied to you, Jason. The people who said those games you've told me about were just like something real. Because in your gut you know they are just games. You know someone you 'kill' hasn't really died, and you know that you can't die. This is real, and real *hurts*. Listen, we don't have the luxury of standing around. We have to get moving, and head northwest or west again. Are you with me, Jason?"

"I'm with you." He grimaced, unscrewing the top of the canteen and taking a drink. "It's not just water."

Kira finished taking a long drink from the other canteen, coughing before she could speak. "Water and brandy. We'll have to be careful how much we drink." She looked at the bodies of the scouts, thinking they should try to conceal them off the path, but blood had pooled on the ground around both. There was no way to hide that, so time spent dragging the bodies any distance would be time wasted. Come on."

She moved as fast as she dared through the brush, finding the path forked not much farther on, and taking the westward fork without pausing. Her pistol was in both hands, questing ahead of her, Jason following with both packs and canteens.

"Food," Jason called in a low voice.

She paused long enough to reach back and grasp a strip of dried meat with dried fruit pounded into it. Most of the taste had gone out of the meat and fruit but it was food and it was energy. Kira chewed without really paying attention to the task as she and Jason made time through the brush.

Taken on a very empty stomach, the brandy in the canteen water was going to her head, making her slightly dizzy. Kira mumbled a curse at Imperial taskmasters who thought brandy made a fine stimulant.

They reached a cleft leading out of the meadow, the path continuing along it. Kira swallowed her bite of tasteless iron ration, took another, shook her head in a futile attempt to clear it, and led Jason onward at the fastest pace she could manage.

"Have the people in the Free Cities eaten every animal in these mountains?" Jason grumbled as he chewed on another piece of Imperial iron ration. "We see birds at a distance, we get insects swarming us, but nothing edible shows up. Why didn't the scouts have more food and water on them?"

"Because they're supposed to move fast for a few days, then get relieved by another pair of scouts when they've hit their endurance limit," Kira said, eyeing the last chunk of iron ration from the pack she had, trying to decide whether to eat it now or in the morning.

"I saw something that looked like rabbit tracks. I don't know much about real hunting. What do you think your chances are of getting something?"

"Slim to none. But if I kill it, you have to clean it," Kira told him. "I suppose I should drink its blood first, though." She laughed quietly.

"Have you been drinking from your canteen again?" Jason asked.

"Yes, I have." Kira raised herself up just enough to see off to one side the path they had been following. Near sunset they had found a welter of boulders near the path which offered cover as long as they kept low. In the growing murk as evening twilight turned into night, the path was visible only as a lighter strip amid the dark ground. "I'm getting a headache. Oh, wait."

She dug in the scout pack and found a leather pouch that proved to be a field medical kit. Among its contents were several white pills. "I'm saved."

"How do you know what those pills are?" Jason asked.

"They're embossed with a hammer. See? That's the universal sign for aspirin."

"It's not exactly universal," Jason said as Kira took two of the pills washed down with another swig from her canteen. "Kira, why am I alive?"

She settled back again, sighing. "You haven't had that much to drink, Jason. Did you take some of the blue pills?"

"No," Jason said, his expression serious. "I've been thinking."

"I like that in a man." Kira sighed again as the brandy in her latest drink hit. "As long as he doesn't think when he should be doing something. When's the last time you kissed me?"

"Kira, I'm not joking. Maxim told you his Mages got into the palace in Tiaesun and got you out without being detected."

"Right," Kira said, eyeing him. "What does that have to do with you being alive?"

"If the Imperials wanted me dead, why didn't they kill me then? They could have, right? Like, smothered me or something so no one could tell I'd been murdered." Jason shook his head. "I don't understand."

Kira rubbed her temples with her fingertips, trying to decide what to say. She had spent a lot of time when imprisoned on the ship thinking about that same question, and had come to some unpleasant conclusions. "I can tell you exactly why I think you weren't killed at that time, Jason. But you won't like it." He waited, obviously wanting to hear. "Fine. You asked for it. Maxim wanted you to suffer."

"How?"

"Let's see," Kira said. "I disappear, having apparently flown to Palandur on a Roc. You are left, without me, apparently abandoned even after buying me that nice piece of jewelry. Public humiliation and private agony. Word comes back that I am in Palandur and married to Maxim. How are you feeling right about then?"

"Pretty awful," Jason said.

"Then maybe you hear that I'm carrying Maxim's child. Huge public announcement about the future heir to the Imperial throne and the 'happy mother.' How do you feel then?"

"Kira, that's not funny," Jason said, staring at her, his voice as strained as it had been on the ledge over the precipice.

"It's not meant to be," she said. "I'll bet you that was Maxim's plan. Steal me from you, because to him a woman he wants has to be a thing to be owned, and then rub in your face what he's doing to me. What would you do, Jason?"

He stared past her at the rock that Kira was leaning against. "I'd have tried to get to you. Get you out of there."

"And gotten caught," Kira said. "Doing your lone-hero thing into the heart of the Empire, where they'd be waiting for you. Caught and tortured at Maxim's leisure and for his amusement. Probably while I'm forced to watch, because that would avenge my putdowns of Maxim at the reception. I suffer, I get to watch you eventually die in great pain, and of course you suffer and die. That's why Maxim didn't have you killed in Tiaesun. Do you feel better now?"

Jason looked at her, perplexed. "Shouldn't you be more upset?"

"I'm screaming inside, Jason," she told him. "I do that every time I think about how it could have happened just the way Maxim planned. Remember those Mage visions we were told about at my parents' house? Me as an Imperial consort and you dead? Those were possibilities. The idea scared me then. Now, what might have happened terrifies me. But Jason, I think between us we've messed up all of those possibilities and have created a whole new set of possible futures."

Kira leaned back, looking up at the stars that had sprung to life as the sky darkened above them. "Besides, Maxim's plans never would have worked. If he had drugged me and forced himself on me I'd have killed him. Somehow. Maybe I actually would have ripped his throat out with my teeth if I couldn't find any other way of doing it. Which really would have upset Mother, because it would have made the whole Mara thing look real. And then I would probably have been killed, which would have upset Mother a lot worse, and she and Father would have personally destroyed the Imperial palace and every living thing in it. This is much better, right?"

"Yeah," Jason said. "Before I got to know you, and your parents, I would have thought what you just said was an exaggeration. But that's exactly what you and your parents would have done, wouldn't you?"

"Probably," Kira said.

"Are you certain that I belong in your family?"

"Oh, Jason, I'm sure you could destroy lots of things if you put your mind to it," Kira said. "You helped me destroy that second Imperial ship. And you know how to build stuff. We do that. Remember, Pacta Servanda is the city my mother built."

"The Peace of the Daughter," Jason said. "That's the biggest thing she built." He paused. "Those legions coming into these mountains. Does the Peace still exist?"

"If it's broken," Kira said, "Mother will build it again."

"Can even she do that?"

"She won't be doing it alone," Kira said, looking up at the stars again. "Father will be with her. And so will I." She turned her head toward him. "How about you?"

"Me?" Jason asked.

"You. Are you going to be part of the family, or not?"

He smiled at her. "Yes. Right beside you." Jason's smile faded into a look of understanding. "I finally get it. People kept asking me if I knew what I was getting into when I was dating you."

Kira frowned at him. "They did?"

Jason nodded. "Your father, and Alli and Calu's son Gari, and Alli and Calu, and, uh—"

"I have so many friends in this world," Kira commented sarcastically.

"I didn't realize what they meant," Jason explained. "I thought it was just about you being, um…"

"Mother says the polite word for us is 'difficult,' " Kira said.

"Or about people looking at me differently because I was dating the daughter of the daughter," Jason said. "No, what they meant was, I'd have to take on a lot if I joined your family. Not…fame. Responsibility."

"Mother hates it," Kira said, remembering late-night talks with her mother. "The daughter thing. She can't just be herself. She has to be that person. And I have to be the daughter of the daughter, even though I used to hide from it. So how do you feel about all that?"

"Being with you is worth it," Jason said.

"Is it?" She gave him her most serious look. "I meant what I said after we killed those scouts. You can back out of the engagement at any time. Up until the moment that you actually give your promise. You'd better mean it, and it had better last. If you can't do that, do us both a favor and walk away before then."

"Nah." Jason grinned. "You know what they say. Pacta sunt servanda."

Kira sat up, staring at him. "What?"

"It's words from an old language," Jason said. "Latin. It means 'agreements must be honored.' "

"That's what Pacta Servanda means?" Kira asked. "The name of the city actually means something?"

"Yeah. On the way to this world I looked at the information that Earth had been sent by you guys and saw that town name and it looked like Latin so I looked it up and it was. You guys didn't know that?"

"How would we know that? Why would a town, because that's all Pacta was until Mother came along, be named Agreements Must Be Honored?"

"I don't know," Jason said. He turned his head to look south and west as if Tiae would actually be visible from here. "How old is the town?"

"A lot older than it ought to be, given where it's located," Kira said. "Some of the buildings seem to be as old as the oldest structures in Landfall."

"Huh. So that town was named by the crew, and dates back as far as the earliest cities on the planet. But there doesn't seem to be anything special about it." Jason frowned at her. "That's weird."

"Your mother's ship was looking for something around there," Kira said. "Mother and Father commented on it. Before you stole that drive and they started looking for you, those drones were flying over Pacta."

"They must have been picking up trace signals of something," Jason said. "Maybe...maybe that's where the crew hid the shuttles from the ship. They had to hide them somewhere if they didn't actually destroy or dismantle them. An underground hangar would have done that."

"When we get home," Kira said. "You tell my parents what Pacta Servanda means. Don't forget."

After Jason had promised and taken on the first watch for danger, Kira settled down to sleep for a few hours, so tired that she could barely wonder about the 'agreement' that must have been the foundation for the name of the city she had lived near all of her life.

The only thing she could be sure of was that if the original crew of the great ship had been involved, it was probably an agreement that had helped them maintain control of this world in the past. She hoped whatever it was wouldn't pose problems now or in the future.

"Coleen?" Mari stared at the head of the librarians of Altis.

"May I come in?"

"Of course. But I'm a little busy with a war at the moment." Mari watched Coleen enter and then stop in the center of the room as if uncertain. "What brings you to Dorcastle?"

Coleen looked down, then at Mari. "I have to ask a very large favor of you."

"Did I mention there's a war in progress?"

The librarian began to speak again, but paused as Alain entered the room. Mari didn't have a Mage's skill at spotting hidden feelings, but it was obvious to her that Coleen wasn't happy to have Alain watching her.

"You're going to hear from Tiae," Coleen said, her words abrupt. "You must tell them not to proceed. They must forget what they have found."

Mari leaned back against the wall, crossing her arms as she studied Coleen. "We've known each other a long time. I've never lied to you. Why do I get the feeling you're leaving out a lot of important details?"

"It doesn't matter! The consequences could be a disaster for our world!"

Before Mari could say anything else, a discreet knock announced the arrival of another guest. She opened the door to ask the new arrival to depart, put paused when she saw it was Tresa of Tiaesun. "What's this about?"

Tresa looked from Mari to Coleen. "I don't mean to interrupt, but

Queen Sien wanted you to know as soon as possible about…something I am to discuss only with you."

"Something that was found in Tiae?" Mari asked. "Come in."

"Yes. At Pacta Servanda," Tresa said as soon as Mari shut the door.

"Nothing has been found at Pacta Servanda," Coleen insisted, looking genuinely frightened.

"What exactly has been found?" Mari asked Tresa. "I think Coleen of Altis needs to hear this."

"We don't know exactly what it is," Tresa said. "The report I received under a seal of secrecy says that while excavating to repair a basement, the workers stumbled across a strange gray material. At first they thought it was rock, but it was smooth and uniform and so hard they couldn't dent it. After consulting just about everyone else, one of the librarians in Minut was called in and identified it as the same material the tower of the librarians at Altis is made of."

"It must be something made by the crew of the great ship," Alain said.

"Something underground," Mari said. "All they've found is a layer of that stuff?"

"Excavations are ongoing around it," Tresa said. "Whatever it is, it is large. Test shafts dug for hundreds of lances around that spot encountered the same material, as if something as big as the librarian's tower was buried there. I am sorry to bring you news like this when the focus of the daughter must be on preparations to counter Imperial aggression, and on your daughter, but Queen Sien ordered that I inform you."

"Does Queen Sien believe it is related to that ancient requirement that the rulers of Tiae must keep Pacta Servanda from falling to an enemy?"

"Queen Sien does not know, but is concerned that it may be." Tresa gazed with worry at Mari. "The queen wonders what secret might hide in the heart of her kingdom."

"A secret which must be left undisturbed!" Coleen said.

Mari turned to Coleen, her temper flaring. "Twenty years ago you told Alain and I that you knew nothing about Pacta Servanda!"

"No," Coleen said. "I told you there was nothing else I *could* tell you. I had taken the most solemn oath not to reveal what was known. Not until there was no alternative."

Alain nodded. "If I had not been so weakened and distracted, you would not have gotten that deceit past me."

"You must not tamper with what has been found," Coleen insisted. "You must bury it again and forget it is there. Queen Sien might not listen to me. But she will listen to the daughter of Jules."

"What's in there?" Mari demanded. "Why should I tell Queen Sien to forget what has been found? What's hidden beneath Pacta Servanda? Tell me the truth this time!"

"What lies beneath Pacta Servanda?" Coleen said. "I don't know. There may be some documents that speak of it, lost and forgotten in the files of the Mechanics Guild headquarters in Palandur, or in a long-abandoned safe, but if not no one knows."

"This time she speaks the truth," Alain told Mari. "But something has not yet been said."

Mari glared at Coleen. "You have no idea what's there, but you want it buried and left alone. What is it you're still not telling us?"

Coleen glanced at Tresa.

"I'm going to tell Queen Sien whatever you tell me," Mari said. "Which is exactly what Tresa of Tiaesun will do. So you might as well tell us both."

"There is a warning," Coleen finally said, her voice resigned. "Do not tamper with what lies beneath Pacta Servanda. Do not try to break in, or the consequences would be terrible."

"Why?"

"We don't know! The leaders of the crew of the great ship made some sort of agreement about what is buried at Pacta Servanda. All that is known to the librarians, and that only to the highest among us, is that whatever is there must not be disturbed or the results would include the total destruction of the tower of the librarians as well as cities such as Landfall."

"The crew might have threatened that kind of destruction," Mari said, "when they had the power to enforce it. But the power they passed down to their descendents in the Mechanics Guild is gone."

Coleen sighed. "We know only of the warning. You sent the boy Jason to our tower a few months ago so that he could see if certain devices the great ship should have had were among our collection. We showed him everything we had. He did not find those devices among our holdings."

"You think those might be buried at Pacta?" Mari asked. "The, um, beta field generators?"

"Yes. And perhaps other weapons."

"I can see why the crew wouldn't have wanted anyone messing with them. That would account for the warning. But any device buried there so long ago might have deteriorated into uselessness." Mari paused as a thought struck. "Or deteriorated to the point where it is dangerously unstable."

"The Mechanic devices in the keeping of the librarians have not posed any danger—"

"They were all deactivated before you were given them! And their batteries have long since lost power. But a weapon could be active, all this time, and whatever power supply it uses could still be functioning." Mari stopped to think, appalled. "Jason said a beta field generator could make objects for a radius of thousands of lances simply disappear. Something about canceling out the bonds holding atoms themselves together. That's what could be under Pacta?"

Pacta Servanda. A town that had grown into a city teeming with people.

"You see why it must not be disturbed," Coleen said.

"No! I see why we have to check on it! Coleen, you know that devices like far-talkers can catch fire if the circuits short out. If there is something immensely dangerous under Pacta, or something that used to be dangerous and no longer is, we have to find out. Those weapons could go off at any time!"

"But the warning," Coleen pleaded.

"Is the suppression of knowledge ever a good thing?" Alain asked her.

"Sometimes," Coleen said. "Even librarians acknowledge that some things are better not widely known. We kept secret the existence of our tower for centuries, and by doing that ensured the survival of it and everything in it."

"You don't leave weapons unattended!" Mari insisted. "If they're buried under Pacta, we need to do something to ensure they aren't a danger."

Coleen paused, glancing at Tresa of Tiaesun, who was listening with growing alarm. "Anyone in possession of such weapons might be tempted to use them."

Tresa spoke up before Mari could. "Not Queen Sien! She would never employ such weapons!"

"Tresa is right," Mari said. "I know Sien better than anyone else alive. Her sole concern is going to be making sure those weapons, if they are buried under Pacta, are disarmed and disassembled, the parts destroyed." She paused, rubbing her forehead. "Jason told me that he doesn't know many details of such weapons. Those are kept secret. Coleen, you need to return to the tower and use the Feynman unit to tell Urth what we might have found. Tell them it might contain beta field generators and other weapons left by the original crew of the ship. We need to have whatever information they can give us to allow us to safely deal with and deactivate those weapons."

"Urth tells us nothing," Coleen said, despairing.

"Even Urth must realize this is different! Tell them we need that information to save countless lives on this world!"

"What should I tell Queen Sien?" Tresa asked, looking fearful.

Mari paused to think again. "Tell Queen Sien what we've talked about here. I think she should stop all work on the site for now, to avoid the chance of disturbing anything. Once we've dealt with this war, we can decide how to proceed in the safest way."

"Jason will have some ideas," Alain said. "We need him there."

"If he's still alive," Mari said, the words catching in her throat.

"Queen Sien must not let anyone know there is anything of importance under Pacta," Alain told Tresa. "Queen Sien must ensure that no one thinks that artifacts of the past rest under their city. Such knowledge might lead greedy treasure hunters to act foolishly."

"Or cause panic," Mari agreed.

"Can we not let it rest as it has rested for centuries?" Coleen asked.

"That may be what we conclude we need to do," Mari said. "Once we know more about it. Jason told us there was a lot of equipment on the great ship that must have been either destroyed or hidden. Perhaps some of it is down there. Coleen, no decent Mechanic would leave old equipment unexamined, and the ancient tech manuals are full of warnings about the toxic nature of some of the inner workings of their most advanced technology. At this point, neglect could be far more dangerous than trying to learn more."

"Since I have no choice, I will return to Altis and speak to Urth," Coleen said.

"Why didn't you tell me the truth twenty years ago?" Mari asked.

Coleen looked down again, refusing to meet Mari's eyes. "You were the leader of a war. If you had known extremely powerful weapons existed at Pacta Servanda, you might have employed them."

Mari gazed at the librarian, realizing that her foremost feeling was disappointment. "You really thought I would do that?"

"I'm sorry. The more someone knows of history, the harder it is to believe in the good nature of human leaders," Coleen said. "Such knowledge breeds…caution."

"What if your suspicions are correct," Alain said, "that references to what exists under Pacta might still exist in the headquarters of the Mechanics Guild in Palandur? What would the Empire do with such knowledge?"

"The Empire has been going through those records," Mari said. "They might already have seen something. And that might mean that the remnants of the Mechanics Guild will learn of it. They might already be planning to try to get into whatever is down there."

Coleen stared at her and then Alain. "Can you do anything?"

And there it was, the plea for the daughter to save the day. Mari sighed and nodded. "I'll do what I can. Once this war is ended. Tresa, don't speak of this to anyone else. Tell only Queen Sien. I'm sure she can come up with some innocent-sounding but plausible reason why the excavations should be temporarily halted. Coleen, try to get Urth to realize they must tell us something about those weapons."

"Could Doctor Sino help?" Alain asked.

"No," Mari said, shaking her head. "Sino has told me she knows how to use her devices, but she doesn't know how they work. That's not her training."

"Isn't there anything else we can do?" Tresa asked.

"Hope with all your might that, in addition to Kira, Jason of Urth also survives and comes back to us."

Kira got to her feet, yawning, trusting to the dark night to keep her hidden. She was having too much trouble staying awake while sitting down. Her gaze moved slowly across the landscape as Kira searched for any sign of pursuers. But she saw nothing and heard nothing. That wasn't entirely reassuring. There should be noises. Animals moving in the night. But the animals had gone to ground, as if sensing the approach of many, many people. The legionaries often marched in step, hundreds of feet hitting the ground as one, creating rhythmic vibrations that could be felt for hundreds of lances. How far off could animals feel those waves of human movement?

Should she wake Jason and get them moving right now? Kira looked upward at the stars, judging that it was barely past midnight. Jason had hardly slept at all. He needed some rest or he wouldn't be able to keep going. But if the legions caught up with them…

Maybe it was foolish guilt at the idea of denying Jason the rest that she had already taken, but she decided to let Jason sleep a while longer.

Kira closed her eyes, letting loose the bonds she used to suppress her Mage powers. She quested silently, without moving, those Mage senses reaching across distances in search of any sign of other Mages. Mages in the hire of the Empire who would be accompanying the legions searching for Kira and Jason, or Mages aiding her mother and father, trying to locate Kira before the Imperials could seize her again. But she felt nothing and drew back her senses, locking them behind the strongest barriers she could create within herself.

She wished her lack of contact meant that no other Mages were close. But the same methods she used to hide herself could by used by any Mage. They could be close but still undetectable by her Mage powers.

Her Mage powers.

Kira shivered, but it had nothing to do with the cold breeze that swept among the rocks. She kept remembering the moment that wasn't there. The moment between the time when she had been staring at the lock of her prison's door, and when she was standing over the unconscious bodies of the guards outside that prison. The outcome had been what she had wanted, but what if it hadn't been? She couldn't recall anything of the fight. The idea that she had been doing something so complicated without being aware of it was deeply disturbing. So disturbing that she had made light of Jason's worries so that he wouldn't press her on it. What might she do next time, if there was a next time?

The only thing she could be fairly sure of was that the blackout was tied in with the use of her Mage powers. Which meant she had to reserve them for the worst emergencies. And keep them as tightly under control as possible the rest of the time. Jason was already worried about her Mage powers. So was everyone else who knew of them, but Jason was more concerned than others. Maybe that was because his knowledge from Urth, so useful when it came to the Mechanic arts, offered him no guidance when it came to the Mage arts he often called "magic." But what Jason called magic had no rules, allowing whatever anyone wanted, whereas the Mage arts had very restrictive rules.

Including the apparently ironclad rule that anyone capable of viewing the world from the perspective of a Mage could not also work as a Mechanic. A rule that had never been broken until Kira had displayed both abilities.

Had the blackout been somehow related to that?

Kira stood, looking out across the Northern Ramparts. The mountains loomed dark and featureless against the night sky. The moon was sinking toward them, chased by the Twins which most people of Kira's world had long believed to be tiny versions of the moon. Instead, they were two parts of the great ship that had brought people to this world along with animals and fish and birds and every kind of vegetation. Jason had told her that he had yet to see anything on Dematr that didn't appear to have originated on Urth.

But he also said that the coal used to fuel boilers had come from vast amounts of ancient vegetation, buried and compressed over ages of time. Which meant Dematr had once been a thriving world. What had happened? And had anything more than plants existed before that disaster? Had there been people of some kind? "The clues are here," Jason had told her. "Buried in ancient sediments. When you develop the right technology, you'll be able to figure out what happened."

And then he had paused, and smiled at her, and said, "I mean, when *we* develop the right technology, *we'll* be able to figure out what happened."

Kira looked down at Jason where he slept, brushing errant strands of hair from her eyes to see him clearly. He was here, he was part of Dematr now, in great part because of her. There were times when she felt guilty about that, especially times like this when Jason's life was in danger. But he had never expressed a single word of regret for not returning to Urth on the ship that had brought him here. Once she worked her way through all of Jason's odd references and sayings, they all came down to a sense of wonder that he had been given the opportunity to be here.

With her.

Kira knelt beside Jason. "Don't worry," she barely whispered, not wanting to disturb his sleep, "we'll get out of this."

Kira finally woke Jason when she thought he had slept as long as she had. She still had not detected any sign of Imperial presence nearby, but a feeling that danger was getting closer and closer had grown in her as the night wore on.

They set off down the path once more, drinking the dregs of water and brandy from their canteens and chewing on the last pieces of iron rations. "Maybe we should try to ambush a couple more Imperial scouts," Kira commented after swallowing her last bite.

"Was that a serious suggestion?" Jason asked.

"Yes. That seems to be our only chance to get our hands on high-energy food," Kira said. "Though if I never have to drink watered brandy again it will still be too soon." She studied the landscape as pre-dawn twilight began to brighten the sky. "But it would be a bad idea. The scouts could be using other paths to get ahead of us. Some might already be ahead of us. Some Imperial columns might be moving a lot faster than others and trap us while we're waiting to hit the scouts ahead of another column. It's just too risky."

Kira paused, staring to the northwest, where some of the highest peaks were already catching the first light of the rising sun. "I saw a glint. I'm sure I did."

Jason followed her gaze, anxious. "A glint? Like, off armor?"

"Maybe. But it looked more like glass reflecting light. Someone with a far-seer on that peak, looking this way." She rubbed her eyes, thinking. "They won't be able to see us yet. Not at this distance with us still in the dark. The morning sun will make it hard to look this way for a while. But who are they? If they are Free Cities scouts we want them to see us. If they're Imperials, we want to hide."

"How could the Imperials have gotten so far ahead of us?" Jason protested.

"A flying column, sent forward as fast as possible along the best routes with spare horses for each rider," Kira explained. "Leave the horses at the base of the height and send a scout team up with far-seers and a far-talker. It's the sort of thing I might have been ordered to do as a Lancer."

"Do we keep trying to head northwest?" Jason asked.

Kira shook her head, feeling tired. "I don't know. What do you think?"

"If there's a chance the Imperials are already northwest of us, why not head as close to straight west as the terrain allows?"

She thought about that, then nodded. "Why not? Let's see how close to west we can stick to. Keep an eye out for ambushes, Jason."

It was probably inevitable that soon after reaching that decision they ran into a series of knife-edged ridges running almost north to south, forcing Kira and Jason to climb up one side of each ridge, then down the other. By the time they cleared the last of those the sun was high overhead, they were both once more exhausted, and Kira's throat felt like the desert wastes around Ringhmon. "We need to climb," she rasped to Jason.

"Huh? I thought—"

"We have to be able to see where we're going! And that means getting high enough to have a decent view of the terrain ahead!" Kira pointed to a nearby slope. They struggled up it until able to see a decent distance to the southwest, west, and northwest.

"There," Kira said, trying to catch her breath. "See? Over that high area and beyond is a valley that looks like it leads into another valley." She stopped to look toward the peak where she had caught the flash of light, wondering if whoever was up there was looking at her and Jason at this moment. "All right?"

"Sure," Jason said, bent over, hands on his upper legs as he rested. "Whatever you say. It's downhill."

The valley proved to be the largest open, and sort of flat, area they had encountered. Kira paused where it began, her pistol in her hand, scanning the valley and the heights around it. "See that big patch of green? There may be water. We're going to approach it slowly and carefully." Kira had to stop speaking for a moment, trying to generate enough saliva to wet her throat so she could speak again. "Watch for ambushes."

"And don't fall," Jason muttered, his face haggard.

"If you have a better idea-!"

"Just trying to make a joke."

"Sorry," Kira mumbled.

"S'okay."

As they neared the area where green grass and a few trees grew, the sound of water trickling along rock made their slow pace agonizing, but Kira held herself to a cautious walk, her pistol ready. Jason did the same, his eyes studying everything around them, one hand holding his knife ready for use.

Finally they reached the first of the trees. Kira stopped them there, carefully looking up into the branches of the small trees for anyone hiding among them. "Go ahead through the grass," she breathed to Jason. "I'll cover you."

"I'm bait again?" he said, nodding.

"You're our scout," Kira corrected him.

Jason grinned. "That sounds a lot better."

He moved through the grass, looking ahead and from side to side. Kira held her pistol in both hands, aiming to one side of Jason and then the other.

Jason paused, looking to one side.

The hand holding his knife came around just before two Imperial scouts who had been concealed in the grass leaped to their feet on either side of Jason. Kira saw Jason continuing to turn to his right and swung her sights onto the scout to his left, firing, lining up her sights again, firing, then swinging her aim back to the right as the scout she had targeted fell.

Jason was grappling with the second scout, making it too dangerous to fire. Kira ran forward as the echoes from her two shots reverberated off the sides of the heights around the valley. She pulled out her dagger while the second scout tried to break free of Jason to face her. But Jason hung on until Kira got behind the scout and rammed the dagger into the scout's back, the lightweight leather armor offering little protection against a powerful thrust.

As the scout jerked with pain, Jason got his hand free and plunged his knife into the scout's chest.

Kira paused only for a moment to ensure the scout was falling, then ran to the one she had shot, slowing to take the last couple of steps slowly, her pistol ready.

That scout was already dead, though. One of Kira's shots had caught her in the side of the head.

Kira's hand shook as she holstered her pistol, then cleaned her dagger blade on the grass.

"Their canteens are empty," Jason said. He was kneeling beside the scout who had been stabbed. "There's just one piece of iron ration in this backpack."

"They must have been expecting to be relieved by another set of scouts soon," Kira said, checking the pack on the scout she had shot. "No food here at all. Get to the water. We have to fill our bottles and canteens fast and get out of here. The sound of my shots will draw every Imperial who heard them."

She led the way through mud to where water welled from a cliff face, running down the rock to form a decent-sized pool. She hesitated before burying her face in the water, not knowing exactly what was bothering her.

Jason stopped beside her, looking down at the water. "Why didn't they have full canteens?" he wondered.

Kira frowned as his question crystallized her own concerns. "Yeah. Why not?"

"Maybe they poisoned the water. That's what would happen in a game."

"Maybe they did," Kira agreed. "Imperials love poison. Let's fill our stuff using what's coming down the cliff."

She discovered that her bottle had cracked at some point, as had one of Jason's. They filled their one remaining bottle and all four canteens, taking drinks from the canteens as they filled at what felt like a far too slow rate. "Why didn't they have guns?" Jason asked Kira. "The scouts, I mean. The other two also only had knives."

"Because their job is to remain unseen," Kira said. "The Imperials only issue knives to their scouts because they're afraid that if the scouts had guns, they'd use them when they didn't have to and tip off anyone within earshot that a legion was near."

"How do the scouts feel about that?"

"From what I've heard, they're proud of it," Kira said. "Silent death or something like that. There, our last canteen is full. Let's go, Jason. As fast as we dare."

"Along the low ground or up higher?" Jason asked.

"With more scouts likely close by we'd be too exposed on that high ground. We stay low." As they trotted through the grass, Kira looked over at Jason. "Good job spotting them."

"I only spotted one of them," Jason said.

"That was enough. They were hoping both of us would pass by so they could get me and then hit you from behind."

"I wish they'd had more food. How close do you think the two scouts coming to relieve them are?"

"Too close," Kira said.

After a while she dropped their pace to a walk, afterwards alternating one hundred steps trotting with one hundred steps walking. The valley they were in gave way to another, then a third, linked like pearls on a string, the land tending downward, wild grass growing higher. Kira looked back and saw their path through the grass marked by trampled stalks, the route as clear as if it had been painted with bright colors.

At the end of the third valley, Kira began leading them through a tangle of gullies between two mountains. As they were working their way through one gully, out of the corner of her eye Kira saw Jason drop to his knees, then to all fours, his breathing heavy, his head down.

Kira stumbled to a halt, her legs shaking with tiredness, and collapsed to a sitting position beside Jason. "You should have said something."

"Just give me a minute," Jason got out.

She pulled the cork from their remaining bottle, took a long drink, then passed it to Jason. "We need food, but at least we've got water."

He raised his head enough to drink. "We can't keep this up unless we find food."

"I know. Can you walk over this way? See? I want to get us behind those rocks in case someone comes along." Kira helped Jason get to his feet. They supported each other off to one side, where Jason fell to lie on his back. She retraced their steps, looking for any signs that had left. The terrain in the gully was mostly rocks and hard dirt which didn't pick up many footprints or scuffs, but Kira tried to rub out a couple of places that might have offered clues to their passage before she went back behind the rocks to fall down next to Jason.

Her mind kept telling her that they needed to get moving again, but her body kept saying that rest was a necessity. Jason was clearly exhausted, so even if she had been able to get to her feet again, he probably wouldn't be able to move for a while. And there was no way she would leave him.

Neither one of them talked, too worn out to fashion thoughts or words.

Kira wasn't sure how much time had passed when she heard the soft tread of a foot and brought out her pistol, aiming back toward the main route through the gulley. It wasn't much more than a lance away from where Kira and Jason lay, but invisible to them behind the tumbled rocks.

She put her finger to her lips to warn Jason to silence.

More slight sounds could be heard on the other side of the rocks. Kira eased her finger to rest just above her trigger.

"They came through here," someone whispered. It sounded like the accent of someone from the northern Empire, perhaps from around Pandin or Fornadin. "See that mark?"

"Yeah," another replied in the same accent. "Heading west. They must not have drunk from that pool. If they had, they wouldn't have made it this far."

"Somebody fell here. The boy, I'm thinking."

"Yeah," the second Imperial scout repeated. "He's getting tired."

"How much farther do you think she'll drag him?"

"Until he gives out or she gets hungry enough. I wonder if he even knows he's just emergency rations for her?"

"Probably not. They say she can take control of a man, make him happy while she drains him. I'd bet that's why he fell. She's likely been taking a drink now and then from him."

"My dagger has a silvered blade. If she comes at me, she'll get it in the heart."

"Char had a dagger with a silvered blade. Didn't do him much good back in that vale."

"We'll come up behind them. She'll never see me. Let's go. We should catch them soon."

Kira heard the faint sounds of the scouts rising to their feet and heading on up the gulley. She finally looked down at Jason again, surprised to see him smiling crookedly at her.

He mouthed words without sound. "Emergency rations?"

She curled her upper lip to bare her canines at him.

Nothing should have been funny at the moment, but it was in a darkly humorous way.

Kira felt her head and body slump as she considered their situation. Imperial scouts were ahead of them. The legions would be coming on behind. And when a legion column went through this gully on a search mission, they would check behind every rock, because that was what legionaries did. Thorough, methodical, and relentless. Hiding wouldn't be an option.

She raised herself up carefully, ensuring that the scouts had indeed moved on, then lowered herself next to Jason again. Putting her mouth near his ear, she spoke as quietly as she could. "How long until you can move?"

"I can move now," Jason whispered in reply.

"For how long?"

"I don't know." He turned his head to look into her eyes. "As long as you need me to."

"Next time you're approaching your limit, you tell me," Kira ordered. "Don't keep going until you drop. I don't need hero-Jason. I need smart-Jason."

"I'll try to be both. How are you?"

"Pretty tired. Hungry."

Jason twisted his head away, exposing his neck to her. "Do you need a drink?"

She wondered if the intensity of her glare would actually burn him. "You are going to pay for that when we get home, Sir Demon of Urth. But for now, we can't lie around making very bad attempts at jokes. We can't keep going up this gully or we might run into those scouts ahead of us. We'll climb up that north side and see what we can of what's ahead." Kira rolled to her feet, using her grip on the nearest rock to help her up. She held out one hand. "Come on, Sir Demon. The fight isn't over."

Jason grasped the offered hand as he pulled himself to his feet. "Lead on, Lady Lancer."

"Everyone thought it would be impossible to hold that last wall at Dorcastle," her mother had said during a rare sharing of memories about that battle. *"But sometimes, Kira, you have to ignore the odds and just keep fighting. Even when it seems hopeless. Just keep fighting."*

Kira started up the north side of the gully, determined to keep fighting.

CHAPTER THIRTEEN

The north side of the gully offered a view of a labyrinth of gulches and ravines and gorges filling the area between jagged peaks rising to the south and west.

"No," Jason said.

"I was thinking the same thing," Kira said. "We have to head for that gap to the north."

They made their way along the top of a ridge that meandered between steep-sided gullies. Jason squinted at the sun, which had settled close to the tops of the peaks to the west. "At least it'll be dark again in another few hours. You know, Kira, no matter what else happens, we can be sure we threw a monkey wrench into Maxim's plans."

"You mean a manki wrench?" Kira asked.

"No, monkey." Jason laughed quietly. "On Earth they're called monkey wrenches. I don't know why. Monkeys are primates, sort of like little people," he explained. "Only with long arms, and little heads, and big feet and hands, and sometimes a tail, and they're completely covered with hair."

"That sounds revolting."

"Not really. They're sort of cute," Jason said.

"So manki wrenches are named for no known reason after what must be the strangest creature on Urth," Kira said.

"Some creatures on Earth are a lot stranger than monkeys," Jason said. "Like platypuses. They're sort of like ducks, and also like beavers, and they have poison spurs on their feet and they lay eggs but they're mammals."

Kira frowned at him, sure that Jason had to be making this up. "Paddlepuses."

"Platypuses."

"I suppose the Greek gods have pet paddlepuses."

"No," Jason said. "Platypuses don't come from Greece. They come from Australia, down south."

"Down south. Is Austraya near that Oz place?"

"It's funny you should ask that, because Australia is also called Oz," Jason said.

"So you get to Austraya by going to Kansas first, like that Dorothy of Gale you told me about?"

"Uh…"

"Jason, you told me that Oz is imaginary," Kira said.

"It is, but, uh, look, Australia is a real place with a lot of weird animals. Like kangaroos."

"Congaroos?"

"Yes," Jason said. "Kangaroos are big animals that always walk on their hind legs, but they have really big feet and big tails, so they don't actually walk or run because they jump all the time instead."

Kira shook her head as she carefully made her way down a steep drop. "Jason, stop it."

"Stop what?"

"Making up imaginary places and animals to distract me from the situation we're in. I really appreciate the effort and your intent, but stop."

"I'm not making them up!" Jason protested. "They're real!"

"Like Kansas."

"Yes! Kansas is real!"

"And Dorothy of Gale?"

"No, she's not real."

"And Oz."

Jason shook his head. "Oz is also not real."

"So Austraya isn't real," Kira said.

"Yes, it is!"

"You said Austraya is Oz, and you said Oz is imaginary. That's not a hard logic trail to follow," Kira pointed out. "That means those weird paddlepuses and congaroos are also imaginary."

He stared at her, then back down at the ground they were walking over. "You know what? You're right."

"What are you upset about?"

"I'm not upset!" Jason insisted.

"I'm sorry I didn't want to play your imaginary animals game."

"It wasn't an imaginary animals game!"

She studied him, surprised. "Why are you angry?"

He looked at her, his posture slumping with something more than weariness. "Myself, I guess. I just realized how alone I was and it made me unhappy and when I tried to pretend I wasn't unhappy I got angry."

"Alone?" Kira wrapped her arms about Jason, holding him tightly. "I'm here. Tell me."

Jason shrugged, uncomfortable. "It's really dumb."

"Why don't you tell me what it is, and we talk about it, and we decide together whether it's dumb?" Kira said. "If we're going to hopefully be married someday, maybe it'd be a good idea to practice doing that kind of thing."

He shrugged again, but this time as if he was uncertain of his own emotions. "I realized...I'm the only one on this planet who knows a lot of things. I don't mean science stuff. I mean, like what a platypus looks like. Or how someone from Australia talks. Or how the moon looks from Earth. I can't share that with anyone. I'm the only one."

"Sort of like Mother and being the daughter of Jules?" Kira asked.

"Not the same, but sort of."

"Or like the people who left Urth on the great ship? Knowing they'd never again see that world or the people they had left behind? I've thought about that. I've wondered why it didn't bother you more."

Jason spread his hands in the age old gesture of helplessness. "I guess I've been too caught up in how wonderful it is here. And it is! I mean...you!"

"Me!" Kira said with exaggerated drama, then laughed.

"And all the bad stuff I left behind!" Jason added. "But, still..."

"What about Doctor Sino? Can't you share those things with her?"

"She's busy with important stuff!"

"Sometimes she probably feels just like you do," Kira said. "When this is over, I'm going to make sure you travel to Tiaesun and have some time to just talk with Doctor Sino about Urth stuff like paddle-puses and congaroos and Kansas."

"What if Queen Sien has Doctor Sino doing something more important?"

"Then I will have a talk with the queen and make sure she understands how important this is for you, and she will listen to me and you will have time to talk to Doctor Sino."

"You can do that, huh?" Jason asked, smiling without a trace of sadness this time.

"Yeah, I can do that! I'm Lady Kira of Dematr! The daughter of the daughter! Dragon slayer! I'm not going to let my demon love from Urth be unhappy!" She grasped his hand. "Come on. We have to find a place to hide for the night. I don't like being up on this ridge. The Imperials can spot us too easily on the high parts."

"Maybe we should keep walking through the night," Jason said.

"We should, but we need to rest a while. If we walk all night we'll be completely exhausted by morning."

They walked until well after sunset before finding a spot where they could rest, huddled in a small side-canyon whose narrow entrance was almost invisible in the dark. The odds of being spotted by legionaries moving in the night were as low as they could manage, but they were far from comfortable. Their stomachs were painfully empty, their water supplies were once again dwindling, and the heat the rocks had absorbed during the day dissipated too quickly, leaving cold in its wake. Kira opened her jacket and Jason his coat so they could huddle close together, the outer garments draped over them.

"Sorry," Jason muttered as his hand brushed Kira's pistol in the holster under her arm.

"You've been very nice not to complain about that," Kira said, her head nestled against Jason's shoulder.

"Complain about what?"

"Me wearing my holster. It must really put you off."

He didn't answer for a moment. "Put me off?"

"Yeah," Kira said. "Like, it must look intimidating, right? So seeing me wearing it must make you want to stay at arm's length."

"Not exactly."

"What are you not saying?" Kira asked. "It sounds like there's something about me wearing this that bothers you. That's all right. I understand."

"It doesn't *bother* me. I, uh, like it."

She looked more closely at him. "What does that...? Wait. Are you saying that when you see me wearing my holster you like it? Or are you saying that you like it like it?"

"What?"

"You know what I'm asking, Jason. Oh, stars above! You do! You think it's exciting to see me wearing my holster!"

"What's wrong with that?" Jason asked.

"It's weird, Jason! What is wrong with guys?"

"It just makes you look...even more interesting! Don't you think you look good when you're wearing it?"

"I... This not about me!"

"You also look good in your uniform," Jason said. "With your sword and boots and all."

"Well...yeah," Kira admitted. "I do kind of like how I look in that. But you said you really liked how I looked in that Greek goddess dress."

"You look good in everything," Jason said.

"Did my father tell you to say that?" Kira asked, smiling despite the cold as she huddled against him again. "Because that was absolutely the right thing to say. *Hey.* What's with the hand?"

"That really was an accident!"

"That's all right. I'm just not…in the mood. We're cold, lying on rocks, neither one of us has had a bath in too long…" She held him, thinking. With the legionaries closing in, their chances at this point were extremely slim. This might literally be their last night together. Why keep waiting and deny herself and him something they both wanted?

Because that felt too much like giving up. Like acting out of despair instead of desire. But she had earlier told Jason of the need to share things. Kira sighed, feeling his heart beating where her head rested. "Jason," she whispered. "I'm thinking this might be our last night. So maybe we should not put off doing something. But…aside from the cold and the rocks and everything else, it'd make noise. If any Imperials came through and heard us…"

"Yeah," Jason agreed in a tentative way.

"And…that's not my real reason. It's…if we do that, it will feel to me like I'm accepting that we're doomed. Like tomorrow will be the end for certain."

"It's your decision, Kira. Are you asking me to talk you into it?"

"No. I don't want to be talked into it. I feel like talking me into it would be talking me into giving up on the idea that there would be other chances. Under much, much better circumstances. Where we could really enjoy being with each other."

"What exactly are you asking me?"

"If we die tomorrow, will you be angry with me in the next dream? Because tonight I denied you something that we both wanted?"

"If you really wanted it tonight," Jason whispered in reply, "you wouldn't be asking me that. I mean, your other reasons are good ones, but…yeah. It'd feel like okay, we're gonna die, let's get it over with. I don't want that, either. I mean, I want you," he said, fumbling with the words. "I want you so much it hurts, Kira, but I don't want you to do it because you feel guilty or scared or hopeless or like you owe me something. I'd hate to, uh, go into the next dream feeling guilty for having made you go through with something you weren't ready for."

"I love you," Kira whispered, feeling immensely safe in his arms as she fell into exhausted slumber.

She woke to a sense that something was wrong. "Jason? How long have I been asleep?"

"Most of the night."

"You were supposed to wake me for my watch!" Kira sat up, shivering in the pre-dawn cold and closing her jacket. "Did you stay up all night?"

"I catnapped," Jason said. "I really did get some good rest, and you needed as much sleep as I could give you."

"You shouldn't have." She kissed him. "Thank you. Are you going to be okay?"

"You said okay."

"Yeah. Great. I said okay. Did you get enough rest?"

"Yes," Jason said, and he did seem to be doing all right to Kira's eyes.

Breakfast was another mouthful of water for each of them. Kira's stomach only growled slightly, as if no longer believing that its protests would produce any food to fill it.

Once out of the canyon, Kira gazed around from their slightly elevated perch, watching for any signs of movement. "Did you hear anything last night?" she asked Jason.

"Yeah. Thunder. Way off in the distance."

"Thunder? Which way?"

Jason hesitated, then swung his arm through an arc from south through west and on to north. "With all the echoes from the mountains it could have come from anywhere along there."

She squinted up at the sky, where clouds gathered about the highest peaks. "Maybe it was thunder. It could have been gunfire, though. Or artillery fire. Maybe the Imperials are hitting stiffer resistance from the forces of the Free Cities."

By the time the sun rose they had reached the gap beyond the riven valley, finding that it connected to a sort of broken plateau, extending off to the west like a slanted table with a surface filled with cracks and slabs of rock jutting upwards. The obstacles were so frequent and so close together that Kira and Jason had to walk single file, Kira leading in hopes that her unreliable foresight would provide warning if any ambushes threatened.

Aside from the lonely rush of wind about the rocks, the only sound that came to them was that of an occasional distant bird mocking them with a cheery song. Still, that was something, a sign that they were drawing closer to the high valleys where the people of the Free Cities planted crops and pastured their herds.

"If we find a cow, can we eat it?" Jason asked when Kira told him.

"We'll need two cows," Kira said. "I could eat one all by myself. How are you doing?"

"Okay. And I'm following you, so the view is great."

"Try to pay attention to something besides my rear end. Legionaries could be anywhere around us."

As the sun neared its highest they drew close to where the broken plateau ended in a low ridge. Kira paused, opening the only canteen that still had water in it. "Lunch," she told Jason, before taking a swig that filled her mouth and left an equal amount for Jason.

He drank his share, gazing morosely into the nearly empty canteen. "Do you know what these mountains need?"

"What do these mountains need?" Kira asked, her eyes on the ridge ahead of them.

"Taco trucks."

"I'll talk to Mother about that," Kira said, wondering what taco trucks were. She felt her Mage powers stirring restlessly inside of her. What was causing that? Kira blinked, trying to clear a haze from her eyes as she swung her gaze across the plateau.

The haze was only there when she looked over the ridge before them.

It was dark and getting darker.

"Blazes!" Kira yanked out her pistol and scrambled toward the crest of the ridge, Jason following after a moment of surprise.

"What is it?"

"My foresight! Don't make any more noise!" When nearly at the crest, Kira dropped down and cautiously advanced a little farther until she could see down the opposite side.

Legionaries. Coming this way, their dark red uniforms standing out clearly against the landscape, armored breastplates and helms polished so they shone. Walking about a lance-length apart, perfectly spaced, their eyes sweeping the ground ahead of them, grasping rifles that looked somehow even deadlier for the skilled way they were being handled. Kira stared, taking in the details. She knew how military units moved. She had been part of the Queen's Own Lancers, the elite of Tiae's cavalry. That made it all too easy for her to assess the deadly competence with which the legionaries handled themselves, and in the way they responded quickly and surely to the hand gestures that silently conveyed orders from their centurions and officers.

They were moving so quietly that if Kira hadn't been warned by her foresight they would have come over the ridge almost face to face with her before she knew legionaries were close by. As it was, she had only a couple of minutes to act.

Her mother and father had defeated soldiers like this. Could she?

"They look tough," Jason breathed in her ear.

"They are," she barely whispered back, "and there's at least half a cohort out there." Kira studied the path of the legionaries and how fast they were approaching, then slid back a little to hide herself completely and view the terrain around her and Jason. It didn't take a military genius to see that the nearest rocks capable of hiding her and Jason were so far off that they'd never reach cover before the legionaries crested that ridge and spotted them.

"What can we do?" Jason asked, looking around frantically. He had his knife in his hand, a pathetic weapon to face the legionaries with in the open.

"We have to hide right here," Kira said. "If that doesn't work, we're dead."

"How do we hide right here?"

"There's a spell," Kira said. "Just about every Mage can do it. It makes you invisible."

"Like that guy who hit me in Kelsi?" Jason asked. "You can do that?"

"I hope so," Kira said. "Another Mage can tell where you are, but no one without Mage powers can, and I didn't see any Mages with those legionaries. I should have practiced this!"

"You never practice your Mage stuff—"

"Because everybody else freaks out every time it gets mentioned! I'm going to go to one knee, facing the crest. You come up right behind me. Wrap your arms about me! You have to be inside the bubble!"

"Bubble?"

"Just do it! If this doesn't work, if the first legionary over the crest sees us, I'll fire, and we'll charge through them to confuse their ability to fire at us, and keep running toward a rock I saw partway down the other side of the slope that'll offer us a little cover."

"How will we know if it does work?"

"The legionaries won't see us! Now please be quiet so I can concentrate! I love you!"

Kira tried to settle her frantic thoughts, her fears, and focus only on the spell. There was enough power here. All she needed to do was use it. She let loose the mental bindings on her powers.

Freed from the barriers that normally kept them tightly confined, her Mage powers swelled inside her, momentarily terrifying in their strength and intensity, like a river breaking free of a dam that had long confined it. Kira sensed other Mages in these mountains, but none of them close. They would surely sense her as well, but that was a minor worry compared to the legionaries who would come in sight any moment.

She blew out a long breath, relaxing her mind as well as her body. The world was an illusion. Everything in it an illusion, except the people. Light was an illusion. It could be changed. Not to reveal. To hide.

Kira tried to block out her knowledge that she *had* to do this, *had* to make it work. If she didn't succeed, she would be recaptured or killed, and Jason would certainly die. But that was a distraction, something that would hinder her ability to concentrate. Block it out. Forget the fear. Forget how close the legionaries must be.

Focus. Focus. Change the illusion of the way light moved, so that it didn't strike her and Jason, revealing them to all around, but flowed around to leave them unseen inside the bubble created by the spell.

She felt her mind shifting. The world changing about her. Focus on the illusion and the need to change it. Light—

Kira blinked, staring at Jason.

How had he gotten in front of her?

Why was she breathing so hard, sweat running down her face?

Where was she?

Where were the legionaries?

Where had this large rock come from that they were crouched behind?

"*Kira!*" Jason whispered, his eyes lit with fear.

"Yes." Why was he looking at her like that? "What?"

"Are you okay? You haven't answered me."

Kira took a deep breath. "I'm...I'm fine."

"But...you were acting so weird."

"What do you mean, weird?" Kira asked, trying to stay calm as she sought to figure out how she and Jason had gotten here.

"We were there while you did that spell, and I suddenly noticed that things looked a little blurry. The legionaries came over the ridge, and—" Jason swallowed convulsively. "I've never been that scared, Kira. They were right there, and walking past us, and looking at where we were, but it was like we weren't there. One almost bumped into us! I could have reached out and grabbed her rifle!"

"So the spell worked," Kira said, trying to get her breathing under control and dredge up any memory of the events Jason was describing.

"Yeah. And then they were past us, and you didn't say anything, which I understood because they were still close, but you got up and you held my arms so I stayed right behind you, against your back, and we walked as fast as we could over the crest of the ridge and down the other side and I saw the rock you'd talked about and you led us there and when we got here you pulled us both down behind it and…"

Jason shook his head, both puzzled and frightened by the memory. "You just stared at me. You didn't say anything. I kept whispering your name and you wouldn't answer. You touched my face with one hand and looked at me like…like…"

"Like what?" Kira demanded, fearing the answer.

"This is going to sound stupid," Jason said, unhappy, "but a while back I had a crush on a girl. Back on Earth. And I knew I didn't have a chance. She wasn't mean, but she made it clear it would never happen. And the way you were looking at me made me remember that. Remember how I felt about her."

Kira felt anger warring with her fears. "We're in this awful mess, we're under all kinds of strain," she whispered fiercely, "and you decide to talk about some other girl who you really liked?"

"That's not it, Kira—"

"That sounds like it! I don't need this, Jason! Why would I look at you like I could never have you when you've told me that you love me? When you've agreed to give me your promise? Do I remind you of that other girl? Is that why you like me?"

"No! You wouldn't say *anything*!" he protested, looking wounded by her attack. "You just stared at me like that! It scared me, Kira."

"I…I was tired," Kira said, contrite. "Too tired to talk. The spell took a lot out of me."

"You didn't black out again?"

"No," Kira said, appalled that she was lying to Jason but telling herself that she simply couldn't cope with discussing it right now, that she was too physically and emotionally exhausted at the moment, and that she would let him know the truth as soon as they had a chance to rest.

Seeking an excuse to change the subject, she peeked over the top of the rock, looking up toward the crest, then all around. No legionaries were visible, the line of searchers out of sight on the other side of the crest. "We need to get out of here. The Imperials always run overlapping search patterns, so there might be another unit coming through this area in a little while."

"Kira," Jason said as they stood up, obviously choosing his words carefully, "are you sure you're okay?"

"I'm fine."

He didn't believe her. And he was right not to. Kira felt ashamed of herself, wondering why she was lying to Jason but unable to tell him the truth. Something deep inside her shied away from admitting it. *Tonight. I'll tell him the truth tonight.* "Jason…"

"What?" His look at her was filled with worry.

"I'm sorry I scared you, and I'm sorry I snapped at you."

"That's okay," Jason said. "As long as you're okay."

Kira stumbled as she stood, surprised by her weakness. The spell had taken a lot out of her.

This side of the slope was not as rough, easing down toward a low area then gradually rising again. Kira walked as steadily as she could, regaining her strength, trying not to let Jason see how unnerved she was by this second blackout.

She tried again to remember anything during that time when nothing was in her memory.

Something flashed into her mind, an image as clear as if she were seeing it before her at this moment. A legionary. Dark red uniform, black boots and chest armor all showing a fine patina of dust. Her face bore the tiredness and boredom of someone who had been doing the same thing for days and seen nothing happen. She might have been twice Kira's age at most, wearing the chevron of a legion corporal on one sleeve, holding her rifle with the ease of someone to whom the weapon was a longtime and comfortable companion in the field. Dark hair drifted across her forehead. Her eyes looked directly toward Kira, but reflected no trace of recognition, no sign they saw anything but the same rocks and dirt they had viewed for days on end.

The legionary had a face. An individual stood there. A person.

"*I can't forget their faces,*" Kira's mother had told her a few months ago during one of those late-night talks when Mari had tried to unburden herself and share her experiences. *"That's the hardest part. The men and women who were trying to kill me, who were helping to keep the world enslaved. I had to stop them. I had to shoot at them. And I can't forget their faces."*

Kira shuddered, stumbling on the uneven ground, the sense of seeing the legionary at this moment vanishing from her mind but the image lingering.

"I got you," Jason said, grasping her arm to help Kira recover her balance.

"Thanks. I'm still a little weak."

Her mother had said something else, leaning in, her eyes intent. *"Life gives us choices. If someone chooses to force others, to attack others, to try to hurt others, then you have to choose to stop them. It may hurt, but you have to protect others and protect yourself."*

"All right, Mother," Kira whispered to herself.

"What?" Jason asked.

"Nothing. Let's head that way."

Nervous about the lack of cover, they maintained the best pace they could across the plateau, pausing to rest only when they reached a pass leading west. "There's just a little bit of water in this," Jason said, holding up a canteen. "That's all that's left."

"Save it for dinner," Kira said, her throat once again hurting from thirst. Her stomach was a dull, continuous ache of emptiness. She saw how gaunt Jason's face was and knew she must look the same. "How are you doing?"

"Okay," Jason said, leaning against the nearest rock face. "You said there'd be taco trucks."

"I said I'd ask Mother about getting taco trucks."

"This is a lousy game. Really. It ought to have taco trucks."

"Jason, are you sure you're all right?"

"Yeah," he said, pushing off from the rock to gesture toward the pass. "Just trying to keep my spirits up. Let's keep moving. There isn't any food or water here. Maybe there is at the other end of this pass."

The pass climbed to meet another valley, this one framed by a steep cliff to the north and the heights they had come through to the east. Kira couldn't see the far edges of the valley as it stretched off to the south and west, cheering her with the thought that they must be drawing close to land occupied by people of the Free Cities.

The valley also lacked cover. Patches of dirt offered purchase for grass, but there were only a few bushes and no trees. Kira angled their path across the rising terrain toward that northern cliff face, hoping to find fallen rock there that would offer some place to hide if necessary. The afternoon sun was dropping down, but the valley was still brightly lit by its rays.

"If there are watchers with far-seers up on those heights, we're going to be easy to spot," Kira told Jason.

"Maybe some of those watchers are friendly."

"That would be nice."

"At least this is easy walking," Jason added. "Uphill, of course, but otherwise not bad."

"When we get through with this," Kira said, her eyes fixed on the route ahead, "I'm only going to walk downhill. Toward rivers of cold, clear, fresh water. Remember when we jumped into the Glenca River?"

"You jumped," Jason said. "I got pushed."

"You're never going to let that go, are you?"

The long rise gave way to a nearly level stretch running north toward the steep cliff face, where Kira could now see the hoped-for tumble of fallen rocks at its base. The land slowly fell away to the south and west, where more distant mountains rose dramatically to mark the boundaries of the nearly barren valley.

"I think we've managed to find every vale and dell in the Northern Ramparts that have nothing in them but rocks," Kira commented as they paused to rest. "Remember the land around Kelsi? All that grass and water and…"

"Cows."

"Yeah. Cows." Kira shook her head wearily as a frigid wind off the heights staggered her and Jason. "This isn't the sort of land any farmer is going to pasture herds on."

"Kira!" a woman said from just behind her, the voice sharp and urgent.

She jerked in shock at the sound, spinning around to look.

No one stood there.

But much farther off, coming toward her and Jason at a fast trot from the south, was a line of legionaries. They were already probably just within maximum rifle range. "Run, Jason!"

They took off, veering west and north. "Shouldn't we head for the cover of those rocks to the north?" Jason gasped.

"We want to avoid being trapped there," Kira panted. "If we can get past that to the west…oh, blazes."

Coming into sight to the west, toiling up the slope, was another line of legionaries.

"Rocks?" Jason asked.

"Rocks," Kira agreed, changing her course to head straight north for the cliff face, Jason staying beside her. She had thought she was totally worn out, but fear lent strength to her legs as Kira ran.

A volley of rifle shots rang out behind. Analyze the situation, Kira told herself as she ran. Imperial rifles. Probably decent weapons made in the Empire, not cheap knockoffs of her Aunt Alli's designs, the sort of junk manufactured in Ringhmon. But even most Imperial workshops couldn't match in range and accuracy the weapons built by Master Mechanic Alli's workshops.

Standard Imperial ammunition load out was eighty rounds per rifle carried by each legionary.

It looked like the forces closing on her and Jason from the west and south added up to maybe half a cohort. Even if the Imperials had trouble getting a far-talker signal through the mountains, the sound of the rifle shots would draw more legionaries toward this spot.

The legionaries would be burdened by the weight of their armor and packs and weapons as they chased her and Jason, but they also would have been getting enough food and water for the last few days.

It all added up to a decent chance of reaching the cover of the rocks, but afterwards not much chance at all.

They ran into the shadow cast by the mountains to the west. Kira stole a glance that way, towards the setting sun. It would be a while yet before sunset and darkness fell, but maybe in the dark they'd have a chance to escape.

Another volley rang out behind them, bullets snapping past, followed by individual shots.

"It's not much farther!" Kira called to Jason as more shots filled the air.

She heard a sound like a dull thud.

Jason gave a half-cry/half-grunt, and fell.

CHAPTER FOURTEEN

Her heart almost stopping, Kira skidded to a halt and lunged back toward Jason. To her relief, he was still alive and conscious, but grimacing in agony.

"My leg!" Jason gasped. His hands were on his right thigh, just above where bright red blood was rapidly staining his trousers.

Kira stole another look toward the Imperials. The closest legionaries had ceased firing, and were now running toward her and Jason. They were too far off for a pistol shot to have much chance of a hit, so Kira didn't waste time on aiming and firing.

Her Lancer training for dealing with combat injuries in the field kicked in. She yanked one of the small med kits out of the scout backpack she was still carrying, pulling out the tourniquet. Ignoring Jason's barely suppressed grunts of pain, Kira wrapped the tourniquet tightly about his leg above the bleeding and knotted it.

She put her face close to his, trying to disregard the anguish Jason was displaying. "Can you get up, Jason? If I help you, can you move?"

He focused on her, his eyes hazed with pain. "I… I don't…"

"Then we stay here and fight here and die here."

"Kira! You can't—! Okay! Okay! Help me up!" With a groan of pain that escaped through clenched teeth, Jason rolled to his knees with Kira's help, then used his good leg to rise to his feet, leaning heavily on Kira. "That really hurts," Jason gasped.

Kira turned enough to see the legionaries running toward them, aimed as carefully as she could, and fired.

The leading legionary twisted as if someone had hit him in the shoulder, staggering.

The others slowed for a moment.

Kira got her shoulder under Jason's and got them moving toward the cliff face and the rocks that offered shelter there. Jason grunted with agony with every step, but he kept moving, doing his best to support his own weight and help their staggering run. Kira concentrated on her breathing and on her steps, trying to ensure that she didn't stumble. Even a small additional delay might well be disastrous.

The cliff face almost seemed to be receding as she tried to reach the fallen rocks littering the ground before it, mocking Kira with its closeness yet remaining out of reach. She saw a tumble of rocks that offered a good place to fort up and headed for them. A volley of shots came from the west, passing just overhead as the legionaries fired up the slope and failed to correct for it.

Kira finally reached the rocks and shoved Jason onto the lowest one forming a barrier between the cliff face and the area beyond. "Crawl behind that!"

She pivoted to face outward, her back to another boulder to steady her, her pistol coming up to aim. Several legionaries were far too close, racing to catch Kira and Jason before they could get into shelter. Kira steadied her pistol with both hands, trying to aim carefully despite the way her arms kept wavering from her recent bout of exertion.

Her sights drifted across the chest of the nearest legionary and she fired.

The legionary jerked, stumbled and fell. Kira shifted her aim to the next, fired, cursed as the shot went wide, then steadied her aim with an iron will and fired again.

The second legionary doubled over, clutching at her stomach.

Kira shifted aim to the third closest legionary, and fired a fourth time, this round spinning her target halfway around as it hit.

Two other legionaries dropped on their own, seeking cover. Kira saw their rifles coming around to aim at her.

She rolled over the rock that Jason was behind, dropping down to the dirt on the other side, then rising up again enough to level her pistol at the legionaries.

They had stayed down, though. Kira ducked as they fired, rifle bullets smashing into the rock before her and behind her.

Pulling her boxes of cartridges out of her jacket pockets, Kira hastily ejected the magazine in her pistol. Loading a full magazine, she slid cartridges into the partially empty one she had ejected until it was full.

She paused, staring at her ammunition supply. Each magazine for her pistol held fourteen rounds. There were a little more than fifty loose cartridges left in the boxes. Far, far too few for the situation they were stuck in.

A rifle shot hit the cliff face close behind her, spraying fragments of stone and dust.

She took a second to look around, seeing the rock she had leaned against was big and tall enough to protect their right side. To the left, where Jason rested, a smaller cluster of rocks provided obstacles and cover, but could be climbed over with considerable difficulty. Directly in front of her and Jason was a tilted slab of stone that rose to a bit more than waist height at the highest. The cliff face at their backs was close to vertical, a wall of rock rising behind them. It wasn't a perfect defensive position, but it could have been a lot worse.

The rifle fire had stopped. Kira raised herself up enough to look. She could see legionaries gathering out of pistol range, obviously not ready to attack immediately. For the moment, the only nearby motion was that of the closest legionaries wriggling backwards out of range.

She could finally spare some time for Jason's wound, but there hadn't been any large bandages in the packs of the Imperial scouts. Crouching down with only her eyes and the top of her head exposed so she could keep an eye out for approaching Imperials, Kira pulled off her jacket, then unstrapped her holster and yanked it free. Unbuttoning her shirt as fast as she could, Kira tugged it off, keeping her eyes on the open ground beyond the rocks sheltering her and Jason. She brought out her sailor knife, starting a cut a hand's-width above the bottom hem of the shirt, and then ripping and cutting all the way around until she had a wide strip of cloth.

"Wow," Jason said.

She spared a moment to look at him. Jason lay partially braced against the rock face behind them, his face drawn with pain, his trouser leg soaked in blood. "What?"

"You've got your shirt off. You look great."

Kira stared, frozen in disbelief for a second. Focused totally on the need for fabric for a bandage for Jason, it hadn't even occurred to her to think about what he would see. How could he care about that when he'd been shot? "Are all males insane or is it just you?"

His smile was tight with pain. "I'm just…welcoming the wonderful distraction."

"Oh. If it takes your mind off the hurt even a little, then you're welcome to it." She shrugged back into her shirt but didn't take the time to button it again. "Enjoy yourself looking. This is going to hurt worse."

Using her knife again, Kira cut away at Jason's trousers until she could access the wound, trying not to hear his grunts of pain as she worked.

The bullet's entry point looked ugly, a hole in the flesh from which blood still sluggishly welled despite the tourniquet. Kira felt around on the other side of Jason's leg, finding no matching injury. "There isn't any exit wound. The bullet's still inside you."

"Is that good?" Jason gasped.

"One less hole to bleed out of," Kira said. "I didn't see any blood spurting before I tightened the tourniquet, so I don't think the bullet nicked an artery, which is lucky, but there's enough blood that it probably got a vein. I'll need your belt," she added as she was folding the strip torn from her shirt over and over again until she had a pad of cloth. She had barely finished when Jason offered her the belt he had removed from his trousers. "Thanks. More pain coming, my love. Sorry."

Pressing the cloth pad onto the wound, Kira wrapped Jason's belt around his leg, tightening it over the pad as Jason made noises of pain again. "I'm sorry. There has to be pressure on the bandage." Pausing only for a moment to catch her breath, she carefully loosened the tourniquet higher up on his leg. "Watch the bandage," Kira told Jason as she buttoned up her shirt, then strapped the shoulder holster on over it. "We have to let blood into your leg, but if it flows heavily out of the bandage I'll have to tighten the belt and maybe the tourniquet again. Take one blue pill. Use that little bit of water we have left to wash it down."

"A blue pill? Will it knock me out?"

"It won't knock you out. It'll make you...happy, and it'll help with the pain," Kira told him. Her shirt felt weird, the tattered end fluttering around her waist when she moved. She sat back against the rock protecting their right, looking outward where the legionaries were still gathering. Hot and tired, she left her battered jacket off for the moment. "I keep ruining my clothes."

"Your pants are in better shape than mine," Jason said. He popped a single blue pill into his mouth. "This is the last of the water, Kira. I should let you—"

"I haven't been shot. Swallow the blasted pill, Jason."

Wise enough not to argue further, Jason tilted up the canteen and swallowed. "What are they doing? Are they coming at us again?"

Kira shook her head. "No. Not yet. How's the bandage doing?"

"A little blood seeping out. Not a lot. I wish I had a weapon."

"You've got that survival knife, Jason, and the daggers we took off the scouts. If they come at us in a big rush, it'll probably come down to hand-to-hand. Anyone who comes over the rocks on our left will be off-balance and having to focus on not falling, so you'll have a good chance to hit them before they can defend themselves. Bev taught you how to use a knife against people wearing steel armor, right?"

"Yeah," Jason said. "Unprotected spots, chinks in armor, that stuff. She made me practice." He tried to smile at her again. "It's a good thing you looked back when you did."

Kira shook her head once more, too tired to feel angry with herself. "I should have been looking back at intervals the whole way. I let myself get too worn out, forgot basic self-protection tactics. If somebody hadn't called my name, those legionaries would have probably been on us before I knew they were even nearby."

He frowned at her. "Somebody called your name?"

"You didn't hear? It was a woman. She said 'Kira' plain as day. It sounded like she was right behind us."

"I didn't hear anything," Jason said, grimacing as a wave of pain hit. "There wasn't anybody right behind us."

"I know," Kira said. "Maybe that was how my foresight manifested that time."

"It can make voices?"

"I guess. I'll have to ask Father when we get home." The odds of that happening seemed too small to measure, but Kira was determined to keep talking and acting as if it was a real probability.

She looked down at her hands, realizing that they were covered with Jason's blood. Kira blinked back tears, which changed to anger.

Raising both hands, Kira ran them down her cheekbones and chin, painting her face with Jason's blood.

"Why'd you do that?" Jason asked, his breathing still too shallow and too quick.

"So those Imperials will know who they're dealing with," Kira said. "They want blood? I'll give them blood."

"You're scary again, Kira," Jason said.

"That's the idea." She studied what she could see of the landscape. "I've trapped us."

"I thought the legionaries had trapped us," Jason said, his voice lower but steadier as the blue pill's effects kicked in. His eyes went a little out of focus, then centered on her. "Wow. You really are so beautiful."

Knowing that last was the effects of the blue pill talking, Kira just shook her head. "If I'd spotted the legionaries when they were farther off, I might've been able to get us to a better spot to hold them off."

She also might have been able to get them into cover before Jason was hit, but she didn't say that. "I screwed up."

"You're not perfect?"

She stole a glance his way, seeing that Jason was smiling through his pain. "That's right. I'm not perfect. You've learned my awful secret. You can call off the engagement now if you want," Kira added as she returned her gaze to the field outside their shelter.

"Nah. You're still mostly perfect."

"Mostly perfect?" Kira heard herself laugh once. "How can you make jokes right now?"

Jason's face contorted with pain again as he tried to shrug. "It beats screaming in terror, doesn't it? Which is what I'd be doing if I wasn't trying to joke about this."

"You've got a good point." Kira leaned her head against the rock wall behind her, keeping her eyes on the ground between them and the legionaries. "The Kira you first met couldn't have done this. I had the physical skills, but I couldn't have handled the pressure."

"The Jason you first met didn't have the physical skills or the ability to handle the pressure," he said. "I guess we've been good for each other."

Kira shook her head. "Says the guy with a bullet in his leg. Hold it. Somebody's coming."

Jason tensed, grasping the survival knife from the boat in one hand and an Imperial dagger in the other. "How many?"

"Just one." Kira studied the approaching figure. "Looks like they want to talk."

As was sometimes done for a parley, the legionary approaching them didn't wear a helmet, so there was no plume to help identify rank. But he had a sidearm, a pistol holstered at his belt, as well as a longer sword that identified him as an officer. He walked at a steady, unthreatening pace toward Kira, one arm extended to show an open, empty hand, and the other hand grasping a short pole bearing the traditional parley flag, white with a wide blue band around the edge. Kira watched him approach until she could make out the insignia of a major. "That's close enough!" she called, raising her pistol to emphasize her words.

The major stopped. "Your position is hopeless. If you surrender, mercy will be shown."

Worried about snipers, Kira leaned out just enough for her face to be seen as she shouted her reply so that the legionaries farther off would hear it. "This isn't the first time a woman in my family has been told her situation is hopeless! I don't have my mother's banner with me but I do have her blood in me!"

"It is senseless to throw away your life," the major called.

"The only lives being thrown away will be those of your legion," Kira yelled. "I will fight to the death, and then my mother will avenge my death! Palandur will become a crumbling, lifeless ruin just as Marandur is! The Empire will never again threaten others! Am I worth that, Major?"

The major paused before replying. "We know the boy was wounded. If you surrender, I give my word that he will be treated by healers and set free."

Kira laughed, trying not to let her fear and tension be heard in the sound. "Do you think I know nothing about the Empire? Maxim can revoke your word on a whim! Your prince is a coward and a liar! I'll make you a deal, Major. Send Maxim out here to meet me. Your brave prince against a seventeen-year-old girl. No one else has to die."

The major shouted his reply. "I'm trying to save your life, Lady Kira! As well as the life of the boy! As you said, no one else has to die!"

"I will not live a slave to the Empire!" Kira yelled. "If you want me, you'll have to take me the hard way!" She felt scared, and angry, and that inspired more words to hurl at the Imperials, because she wanted them to be scared, too. "But even if you kill me, that won't be the end of this. Once night falls I'll be coming for you, and for all of your legionaries! Are you ready for that, Major? Is your legion ready for that? Because I'm *really, really hungry!*"

Kira stood up so the legionary could see her face clearly, blood smeared on both cheeks and her chin. She imagined her eyes looked maleficent within that blood mask, and she drew back her lips in a snarl that promised more than any mere mortal threat.

The major took a step back, just as if she had struck at him with a sword.

No shots rang out before Kira dropped into cover again. Imperials could never be trusted to abide by the rules of parley, but apparently this time they were.

"Yeah," Jason said. "Scary. What's your mom going to do when she hears you did that?"

Kira shrugged, watching as the major hastened back toward the rest of the legionaries. "I've resigned myself to the fact that if the Imperials don't kill me out here, my mother will kill me when I get home."

"If I was one of those legionaries, I'd be really reluctant to attack you."

"Our lives are on the line," Kira said. "I'll use any weapon I can." She saw movement and let out a slow, calming breath. "Here they come. I'll take out as many as I can with my pistol."

"I'll take any who come over these rocks," Jason said, grimacing again as he shifted position, readying himself, his knives ready.

Kira put her jacket back on, readying for the fight. She made sure her spare magazine was close by, the boxes of extra cartridges within easy reach, as well as an imperial dagger and her sailor knife. She knelt behind the rock, steadying her pistol on it with both hands as she aimed, waiting until the Imperials came into range.

They were spread out in a line centered on her position, walking toward her, rifles at ready. About forty of them, aiming to overrun her and Jason in a mass assault that would result in casualties for the Imperials but could also end the fight quickly. "Amateurs would be running already and tired when they got to us," she said to Jason, talking to calm her nerves. "These guys won't start running until they're within pistol range."

She smiled, feeling the tightness and stress behind the grin. "But Aunt Alli personally made this pistol for me. It's like a piece of jewelry. They're going to be surprised by how far out it can hit a target."

The legionaries were in full combat uniform, which meant helmet plumes for the officers and senior enlisted. Kira could see the major at the center of the line, leading the attack. Partway to the right was a captain, and partway to the left a centurion. Master Mechanic Alli had been urging the army of the Bakre Confederation to modernize their uniforms, to reflect the changes in a world where every soldier carried a rifle, but no army in all the world had yet made such changes. Finally free to change since the fall of the Great Guilds, the militaries of the world still clung as much as possible to what had always been.

Kira aimed carefully at the major. He wasn't dodging yet, just walking forward at an even pace, an example of steadiness and courage to the legionaries following him into the attack. She hated having to shoot such a man, she hated having to shoot anyone, but he and the other Imperials had left her no choice.

She had practiced a lot, and knew how far she could hit a target, especially such an easy target.

Exhaling slowly, Kira squeezed the trigger.

The pistol bucked as it fired, the brass from the cartridge ejecting and flying off to one side of Kira.

A moment later, the major staggered, stumbled, and fell forward.

Kira was already aiming at the centurion, her second shot going off as the Imperials were still absorbing the hit on their leader.

Her pistol crashed again, and Kira shifted her aim to the captain.

The centurion spun around, falling to one side.

"If you want them to keep charging," Sergeant Bete had told her, *"take down the ones in back first. If you want to stop them, hit the ones in the lead first."*

"You got it, Sergeant," Kira breathed as her third shot fired.

The captain had just gestured for the legionaries to begin running when Kira's bullet knocked him backwards.

If she had just panicked and begun firing randomly and wildly, the Imperials would easily have swamped her. But Kira had been through drills like this a hundred times, had faced a dragon charging straight at her, so she kept aiming carefully at anyone who seemed to be a leader, anyone who was charging ahead of the others, taking them down one by one, the fall of those in the front hindering the movements of those coming on behind. The legionaries fired back as they ran, their barely aimed shots striking the rocks or the cliff face behind Kira.

Protected from the attackers' fire by the rock before her, Kira tracked her shots across the front of the assault, hitting the foremost legionaries from one end of the line to the other, then began swinging her aim back again, her mind focused totally on her targets and her task.

The slide on her pistol stayed back, the charging legionaries only a few lances away. Kira ejected the empty magazine, loaded her spare in a single movement, flipped the slide forward to load another round and fired twice, dropping two legionaries directly before her, others getting tangled in the fall of the leaders. The legionary line had tightened down into a single mass aimed at Kira's and Jason's position, making them a concentrated target impossible for Kira to miss as she stood, backing against the cliff face, firing again and again.

Out of the corner of her eye she saw a legionary clamber over the rocks on the left side and catch Jason's dagger in the throat. Another legionary followed, grappling with Jason as Jason slid his knife along one side of the legionary's breastplate until the blade slipped into the gap between the front and back armor and then into the side of the Imperial soldier. Jason yelled angrily as he stabbed the soldier again and again.

They were swarming over the rock in front as Kira switched to a one-handed grip, shooting the nearest legionary in the face as she swept up the Imperial dagger she had left ready for use and swung it at the eyes of another soldier, who flinched back. Screaming with rage and defiance, she fired again, following up with a stab that left her dagger in an Imperial neck.

Jason stabbed a third legionary in the gap under the arm, driving his blade deep into the soldier's upper body.

Their leaders gone, the legionaries before Kira reeled back. No longer thinking, just fighting for her life, she lunged after them, picking up her sailor knife, but they scrambled over the rock and ran, pausing only to grab the rifles of the fallen and carry them away. Kira fired at one of the retreating legionaries, seeing the soldier fall, then tried to shoot another.

Her pistol was empty.

Kira turned to see that Jason's opponent was being pulled to safety by two other legionaries, the pair carrying their comrade and an extra rifle each as they joined in the retreat.

She knelt to reload one of the magazines, slipping in the cartridges as fast as her fingers could move, shoved the loaded magazine into her pistol and sighted in on the last standing legionary in range of her weapon, her finger quivering on the trigger. But the legionary had paused in her retreat to reach down and help up a wounded comrade. The frenzy of battle subsiding inside her, Kira held her fire as the legionary half-carried her wounded friend to safety.

She slumped down, breathing heavily, her whole body shaking in reaction to the physical exertion and stress. After a moment, she quelled the shaking and took advantage of the pause to reload her second magazine, counting the remaining cartridges and feeling despair.

Some of the retreating legionaries had made it past where the major's body lay and were turning to fire their rifles. Kira had to keep her head down except for quick looks to see if another attack was forming.

In the quiet between Imperial gunshots, Kira heard the sounds of the wounded legionaries. Someone was crying in quick, gasping breaths. Someone else was moaning, low and continuous. Another was wheezing with wordless pain just on the other side of the rocks shielding her and Jason.

Kira waited for a gap in Imperial rifle fire, then raised herself up enough to be sure her voice would carry as she shouted, hoarse with weariness and strain. "Legionaries! Come get your wounded! I won't shoot anyone without a weapon!"

After a long pause, a reply came. "Swear it!"

"I swear on the honor of the Queen's Own Lancers of Tiae that I will not shoot anyone without a weapon who comes to retrieve your wounded!"

She used the back of one hand to wipe sweat from her brow as she waited, the perspiration mingling with the drying blood on her hand and face. "How are you doing, Jason?"

"Okay," Jason said, his own breathing once again fast and shallow. Blood was running down his chin, and also seeping from a slash in one arm of his coat where an Imperial short sword had cut through.

Kira realized he had bitten his lip from pain while fighting off the legionaries on his side of the rocks protecting them. "How bad is the cut on your arm?"

"Just a scratch," Jason said. "The coat took most of the damage. I'm okay," he repeated.

"You're amazing, my hero."

The rifle fire had stopped. Kira took a cautious look and saw legionaries approaching at a walk, their arms spread wide, their hands empty. Not trusting the Imperials to honor the truce, Kira moved herself about so that each time she looked again her head rose from another spot, keeping an eye on the legionaries as they collected the wounded. A few of the Imperials wore the ancient sign of the snake coiled around a staff that indicated they were healers, but most were soldiers pressed into saving their comrades.

Kira watched as most of the Imperials retreated with their wounded. Two were still coming, open hands clearly displayed, to recover the wounded legionary just beyond the rocks protecting Kira. She watched them, her weapon at the ready, battling an urge to rise up enough to keep them in view as the two legionaries reached the wounded one and crouched down out of her line of sight.

Kira heard the crash of at least two rifle shots, followed almost immediately by the snap of some bullets passing close above her and the sounds of bullets impacting the cliff face. If she had stood up, those shots would have caught her. Fragments of rock sprayed near her, causing Kira to duck lower.

On her back, she had her pistol pointed upward when the two

legionaries came over the rock, both holding short swords they must have had concealed at their backs.

She fired, hitting one squarely, then rolling to target the other. But Jason was there first, his knife swinging forward. The legionary twisted back, off-balance, having barely an instant to realize that Kira was sighting in. She fired again, knocking the legionary off the rock. In the momentary silence that followed, Kira heard the legionary just beyond her rocks whimper once more, the sound falling off into the final quiet that brought an end to all pain.

She closed her eyes briefly, wracked by regret that it had come to this. Jason had been right. All she was doing was trying to protect herself. They left her no choice. But she still didn't want to think about those who had died because they were following the orders of Prince Maxim.

If she miraculously survived this, she knew there were going to be nightmares.

When she opened her eyes she saw that Jason was laboriously checking over two dead legionaries inside the rocks. "They don't have food or water on them," he told Kira. "No pistols, but I got one rifle," Jason said, patting the weapon beside him.

"Good work. The legionaries must have really strong orders to ensure that no rifles were left with us." Kira checked the rifle quickly, scowling as she saw the magazine held only four cartridges. "Those two don't have any extra ammo on them?"

"No. Besides the rifle, all we have are their knives."

"All right," she muttered, looking away from the dead legionaries.

"Kira—"

"I'm fine. Let's not talk about it," she said, grasping her pistol tightly with both hands.

"Okay. What can I do?" Jason asked.

"Stay alive," Kira said, hearing the steel coming into her voice. "And keep taking care of any who get past me. Keep the rifle. You've got four shots. Don't waste any of them."

If she failed, Jason would die. She would not feel. She would not waver. Her mother had held the last wall and she would fight this fight to the death. "How's the bleeding?"

Jason looked. "Okay. I guess."

She tore her gaze from the outside long enough to kneel down and check. "You've been moving too much. Lie back." Loosening his belt, she repositioned the soaking bandage and tightened the belt over it again.

Jason let out a gasp. "Do you have any suggestions on how to not move very much while fighting hand to hand?"

"Sorry, no." She looked into his eyes, blinking back tears. "Bev would be really proud of you. You're doing great."

"Are you proud of me?" Jason asked, anxiousness as well as pain in his gaze.

"How can you wonder what the answer is?" she asked. "I'm so proud of you I can't find the words. The entire world is going to know how proud I am of you when I announce our engagement. And even Urth will know. I'll make the librarians tell Urth what an amazing man I have. Every world that Urth has colonized will know how proud Kira of Dematr is to be matched with Jason of Urth."

"And you call me delusional!" Jason said, smiling through the pain.

She eased back against the tall rock securing the right side of their position. Gazing carefully outside their sheltering rocks, she saw the ground was now littered with fallen legionaries. Kira squinted, seeing a couple of more rifles left lying. She didn't remember seeing them before and wondered how she could have missed the rifles.

Rifles lying a good three lances from the rocks where she and Jason hid.

"They left bait," she told Jason. "Rifles out there on the ground. What do you bet if I ran out to get them I'd find out they were empty of ammunition, and that every legionary left is aiming to nail me when I made the run?"

"How many legionaries are we still facing?" Jason asked.

"It doesn't matter," Kira said. "More will be coming in, drawn by the sound of battle. What matters is I nailed the leaders here. If the officers and the centurion are dead, the legionaries out there won't have much in the way of leadership until someone else arrives." She looked up at the sky, knowing that more officers could show up at any time. "If we can hold out until dark, maybe we can figure out a way to sneak through their lines, get past them and keep going west."

"Sure. We can do that." Jason sounded confident even though his voice was weak.

Kira looked back at him, seeing the blood soaking his trousers and the way he breathed. Jason wouldn't get a hundred lances on his own, and she was so exhausted that she wasn't sure how far she could help him. Nor could they sneak very well while hobbling together. "All right. I know that's a fantasy. Thanks for playing along."

She heard the faint scrape of a boot on rock behind her and gestured to Jason to say something.

"Um, maybe we can do it," Jason said.

Kira had positioned her pistol. When a legionary swung around the edge of the right-hand boulder ready to fire on her, Kira shot him before he could aim. Another legionary came right behind and also caught a bullet in the chest.

A flurry of rifle shots from the legionaries farther off drove Kira to crouch down for safety again. She faced forward, feeling rock fragments hit her back and head as bullets tore into the cliff face. "They snuck up along the cliff face to the right," Kira called to Jason. "But they have to swing out in front of us to target us."

"Can we get their rifles?" Jason asked, flinching against the hail of rock chips and dust.

"Not without rising up into that," Kira said, gesturing to the storm of bullets flying overhead. The barrage faltered, so she stole a quick glance outward before crouching behind cover again. "I saw another bunch farther off headed this way."

Jason closed his eyes, then opened them again to look at her. "Kira, I don't know how long I have left. I've lost a lot of blood. I love you."

"I love you," Kira replied, trying to keep her voice steady.

"What I mean is, I might pass out, and I don't want that to happen without being sure you know…how very happy I've been here. And with you."

"Jason, hold on. It's not over yet."

"We're trapped here, aren't we? It's just a matter of time."

Kira tried to fight back tears. "Yeah."

"How many shots do you have left?"

"Around fifty."

"Listen, Kira, when it gets dark, if I'm still…awake…I can make noise here, make them think we're both still here. And you can sneak out. Lie down out there with the dead legionaries," Jason explained, speaking quickly. "And when they swarm in here, you can run, and you can get away, and—"

"No."

"Kira, even if the Imperials leave us here and do nothing, I'm going to die before dawn, aren't I?"

She stared at him. "We don't know that."

"Don't lie to me, Kira," Jason pleaded.

"*I don't know!* I'm not a healer!"

"I can tell—"

Kira crouched near him and grasped Jason's shoulder, glaring at him, anger suddenly filling her as she thought about how little time was left to them. "You're not allowed to give up!" she told him, her voice as fierce as her expression. "I won't allow you to give up! Do you hear me? You promised me that you would live!"

"Kira—"

"Are you going to break your promise to me, Jason? *Are you?*"

"Not if I can help it! But if I die, there's no reason for you to die here! If that happens, go!"

Kira sat back on her heels, shaking her head, her anger dwindling into a tight, hard core of resolve. "I won't agree to that. Because if I do, it will be a reason for you to let go. To stop fighting. Thinking that once you're gone I can maybe escape. I won't give you that, Jason. I'm not leaving you, whether you're alive or dead. Hang on, as long as you can."

He glared at her from where he once again lay propped against the cliff face. "So it'll be my fault if you die."

"As you keep reminding me, it'll be *their* fault if that happens, Jason, but I won't give up until the end, and neither will you if I can help it!"

She noticed the barrage of rifle fire letting up and got into position again, peering over the top of the flat rock. "Here they come. Just like last time. Thirty or forty of them. Some new leaders showed up. One officer, looks like a lieutenant, and a centurion."

"World War One," Jason muttered. "Keep charging the enemy. Over and over, the same way."

"You know how to use the rifle. Have you got two daggers handy? Good. Get ready," Kira told him. She made sure her remaining loose ammunition was close at hand, another Imperial dagger and her sailor knife also within reach, and rested her pistol on the rock, steadying it as she aimed, going for the centurion first this time. A bullet struck the rock close enough to her to spray more rock fragments against her neck and ear, but Kira ignored the stings. She had pushed her anger away, keeping only the strength it gave her. Worn out, very thirsty, her stomach empty, knowing that Jason was badly injured, she had entered a Magelike state where no emotions existed, where there was only the task, and that task was to stop the Imperial soldiers no matter what it required of her.

Her first shot took out the centurion.

Her second dropped the lieutenant.

The line of legionaries paused, giving Kira time to shoot the one in the middle.

Lesser troops would have halted the attack, perhaps, but these were legionaries. They broke into a run toward the rocks protecting Kira and Jason, firing as they ran. This time some paused to aim and fire, their shots coming dangerously close to her despite her protected position behind the rock.

Kira fired methodically, without feeling, targeting the leaders, targeting those who paused to aim, ignoring the bullets snapping past her and slamming into the rock, legionaries falling silently or with cries of pain as Kira loaded a new magazine in a flash, standing up to aim with both hands on the weapon in perfect stance and firing rapidly now with the legionaries so close that she couldn't miss, the charging Imperials close enough that their frantic, barely aimed rifle shots were plucking at her jacket, the charge slowing as the bodies of the falling tripped and hindered those behind, her last shot from the second magazine knocking back a legionary trying to leap over the rock, hearing Jason's rifle fire once and then again and then rapidly two more times, hearing herself screaming again as she grabbed her dagger, feinted a stab, then slammed her empty pistol against the helmet of the next legionary.

Kira stumbled forward and fell to her knees behind the rock, breathing heavily, watching the survivors of the assault running away, once again pausing only to grab any dropped rifle.

She looked at Jason, seeing a dead legionary lying over his legs, and a second in the act of dying as Jason plunged his dagger into the legionary's neck over and over. Another legionary, shot by Jason, had fallen tangled into the rocks to the left.

Kira reloaded her magazines, using up all of her remaining loose ammunition, which was only enough to half-fill the second magazine. She felt something wet trickling down the side of her neck, touching it to feel blood welling from a shallow gouge torn by a bullet just below her jaw. Her left shoulder stung. Looking, she saw a hole sliced in her coat by an Imperial blade. It didn't hurt too badly and she couldn't see blood, so Kira decided to ignore it. Once the pistol was loaded, she crouched near Jason and helped pull the dead legionaries off of him, piling them on the left-hand rocks to further hinder anyone coming from that side. "You've got more legionary blood on your clothing than your own blood," Kira told Jason.

She stopped speaking as she saw blood from a long cut on the upper part of his lower arm running down Jason's hand, the arm of the coat split by the cut. Wordlessly, Kira yanked their other tourniquet out and using it like a length of line wrapped it around the arm of

Jason's coat to close it and hold it tightly against the injury. "That's the best I can do for that," she said when done. "I'm sorry."

He stared at her, plainly near the end of his endurance. "My rifle is empty. They didn't leave any this time. I can't keep going much longer, Kira."

"It's starting to get dark," she told him. "Hang on."

"Why?"

Jason's simple question filled her and threatened to destroy the numbness that was keeping her going. "So I won't be alone here," Kira finally said.

He looked at her with eyes full of helpless regret before finally nodding slightly. "Okay."

She settled into position to watch the area outside their rocks, wondering how long it would be before the growing darkness turned to night.

What would she do if Jason died?

"Kira?"

"Do you need something, love?"

"I just wanted to say, your mom and dad would be so proud of you. They are proud of you. You know that, right?"

Kira's smile held more sorrow than happiness. "I know that. Your mother and father will hear about this from the librarians, and they'll realize how wrong they were about you. They'll finally see what a brave, strong man you are."

Jason's short laugh was barely audible over the renewed sound of Imperial rifle fire and the impacts of bullets hitting the rocks and cliff. "No, they won't. If they hear, they'll think I was stupid. Throwing my life away instead of making a deal to save myself. I don't care what they think. All I want is for your mom and dad to know I stood by you to the end and did my best."

"Once we get married they'll be your parents, too," Kira said, pretending that there remained a chance they would survive long enough for that to happen.

"Good," Jason said. "But I don't deserve them. I don't deserve you."

"Yes, you do," Kira said, stealing a glance at him and managing a brief smile. "And we're the ones lucky to have you."

Her eyes went back to the field beyond the rocks, where stealthy figures wriggled forward in the growing darkness. "It looks like they're going to sneak close this time before rushing us," Kira said, surprised that her voice could sound so steady. "I love you, Jason."

She held her pistol, made sure she knew exactly where her knives and the spare magazine rested, and waited as the legionaries drew closer and the light faded.

CHAPTER FIFTEEN

Mari sat in the largest room in the big house in the great city of Dorcastle as the sun set outside. She stared at the map on one wall, where markers showed the march of armies and the movement of fleets. The one thing she most wanted to know—where her daughter was—remained unknown and unseen.

The day had been full of meetings and planning sessions and diplomacy and arm-twisting, all designed to kick slow-moving western governments into a major, combined effort that would knock a frantically mobilizing Empire back on its heels. In contrast to their leaders, the people of the west were too eager for a fight, welcoming an open conflict and not hesitating in their calls for all-out war, apparently oblivious to the awful human cost such an effort would produce. And in the middle she stood, a Master Mechanic who still felt way out of her depth, trying to rein in popular fervor for total war with the moral authority only the daughter of Jules could wield, a mother wishing she could race off to save her daughter but stuck here doing what no one else could.

Alain entered, coming to sit beside her, his arm about her in silent understanding and comfort.

"You've seen nothing else?" Mari finally asked him.

"I saw, briefly, a confusing mix of images," Alain said. "Something still hangs in the balance. What Kira does still matters. But I cannot grasp where she is or what is happening."

She had been with him long enough to hear something else in his voice. "And?"

He hesitated. "The images were dark. I do not know if that meant they showed events in the night, or warned of awful outcomes, or…"

"Or both," Mari finished. She leaned into him. "What will we do if Kira dies?"

"Try to continue to live as she would wish us to."

"And Jason, too. I don't think he'll leave her no matter how bad it gets. He's got that craziness in him. Just like you."

"The Empire will pay if that happens," Alain said. "Maxim will die."

"Yes," Mari agreed. "We'll ensure Maxim dies. But nothing we do to him, or to the Empire, would bring Kira back."

"Asha should already be in Alexdria. Calu has gone there as well. They intend to join the Free Cities forces searching for Kira."

"Good. I'm amazed that Bev and Alli aren't going, too."

"They have gone to Marida." Alain gestured toward the map. "The armies of the Free Cities are advancing, I see."

"Yes. Armies are advancing," Mari said, hearing the despair in her voice, feelings that she could never display to anyone else but Alain because the daughter always had to be strong, always be the one others could turn to. "Fleets are sailing. I'm not giving the orders directly, but they are answering to me. Can they save her? Would you know if Kira died, Alain? Would you feel it through your Mage powers?"

"I do not know," Alain said.

"What could I have done differently?"

"Nothing."

"What more can I do?"

"Nothing."

Mari took a deep breath, her eyes on the markers showing the world moving to war. "Please let what we have done be enough. Now it's all up to Kira. And Jason."

★

The sun had settled behind the peaks to the west, the field of shadow on the plateau gradually darkening into night. The temperature had fallen again, and despite the rocks which sheltered them from both Imperial bullets and mountain winds, enough of the breeze made it through for Kira to feel the biting cold. The Imperial rifle fire had slowed as darkness fell and they could no longer see her well enough to aim, but shots still rang out as the legionaries tried to keep her and Jason pinned down.

Jason leaned back against the cliff face, breathing raggedly, his eyes open but occasionally going out of focus. Kira cast brief looks his way, fearing that at any moment his breath would falter and stop, but Jason stayed with her as he had promised.

Kira kept a careful watch, hearing between harassing Imperial rifle fire occasional sounds which told of legionaries using the dark to sneak closer. Indistinct movements in the dark also told her the legionaries were gathering, preparing to attack once more now that the night provided some concealment. She had taught them to respect her accuracy with her pistol.

Fortunately the moon was rising, providing some illumination. That would have been a problem if she and Jason had any chance of sneaking out, but with them unable to move it was better to be able to see their enemies approaching. Kira felt a jolt of fear as dark shapes suddenly moved against the night, crouched low and coming on fast. She waited, her pistol ready. "They're coming," she told Jason.

His gaze centered on her, Jason nodded, and she saw his hands grip tightly the daggers in each one.

Not wanting to waste a single one of her remaining shots, Kira waited as the legionaries drew closer.

Her first shot sounded shockingly loud in the night, the muzzle flash lighting up her attackers and the lead legionary buckling as the bullet hit. Kira fired again and again at the shadowy figures looming up in front of their rock barricade.

One tried to vault over the low rock in front by running up the back of a falling comrade. Kira's first shot stopped that legionary in mid-leap, the second knocking the legionary back into the milling group before her rock fortress.

The slide stayed back on her pistol as she fired the last shot in that magazine. Kira slammed home her last magazine. Another legionary started to scramble forward, only to halt and fall back as Jason's thrown dagger stood out from the Imperial soldier's throat. She caught a glimpse of a legionary coming over the rocks to one side of Jason and as the slide of her pistol rocked forward to load a round Kira put a bullet into that attacker.

Facing forward again, Kira put a shot into a legionary, but the Imperial kept coming, grappling with her. She managed to twist aside to avoid a thrust from his short sword, the legionary's weapon scraping along her side under her coat instead of plunging into her upper body, the blade sliding painfully across Kira's ribs as she fired again at point blank range, the muzzle almost touching the legionary's face, the impact hurling the legionary back.

She tossed her dagger to Jason so he'd have two weapons again, then lined up and fired once more to the front as the legionaries paused in their attack, confused by the darkness and recoiling from her fierce defense, their vague figures forming indistinct targets in the night.

How many shots did she have left? Kira restrained herself from firing again, seeing the dark shapes receding into the night. Fading sounds of pain told her that the retreating Imperials were pulling their wounded comrades to safety.

Her hands had been steady when firing, but now shook as Kira rested her pistol on the rock before her. Her breathing shallow and fast, she felt incredibly tired. Her side stung painfully where the Imperial short sword had sliced it open, warm blood wetting her shirt and jacket. Without any bandages, she used her arm to press her jacket tightly against the injury and hoped that would be enough in the time remaining to them. "Jason? Are you all right?"

Jason gasped a reply, his voice quivering with pain and weakness. "I've been worse."

"Liar," Kira whispered.

"How many shots are left?"

She ejected the magazine, did a quick count, then reloaded the pistol. Two in the magazine, one in the chamber. "Three."

"Three," Jason repeated. "Okay."

He didn't have to say that the end couldn't be far off. They couldn't stop the next Imperial attack. Terror tried to tighten on Kira's throat like a merciless hand but she blocked it as ruthlessly as she could her Mage powers. At least exhaustion and cold and hunger no longer mattered. She and Jason wouldn't have much more time to suffer from those.

As if mocking their dire situation, the thread between her and Jason glowed in the night, strong and bright where it ran the short distance between them. Real love, it seemed, endured far more than fear and hopelessness. Would it survive death?

"Mage powers," Jason whispered. "Hide yourself."

"I'm too tired," Kira said. "I don't have any strength for that, even if I could manage the spell again."

He took a moment to answer. "So this is it."

"Yeah. As soon as they charge again." Kira sighed heavily. "Sorry. We should have done it last night."

"That would have been giving up," Jason said. "I'm happier knowing we kept fighting as long as we could."

"Really?"

"Yeah."

"If you'd stayed on Urth," Kira said, listening and watching for any more Imperial movements, "you would have found someone else and probably not have ended up facing death with her at the hands of an Imperial legion." The rifle fire had fallen off completely, causing her to wonder what the legionaries were up to.

"Yeah," Jason said. "I wouldn't have been happier, though. Better six months with you than a lifetime with anyone else."

"You're hopeless," Kira said, glad that her eyes were staying dry. Was she so thirsty that there was no moisture left in her for tears? Or had she simply been pushed so far that tears could no longer come?

"So you take out the first three attackers—"

"The first two," Kira said, her voice sounding unnaturally cold, matching the sense of inner ice that seemed to be freezing her soul.

"You said you had three shots left."

"I do."

Jason's voice grew louder, rougher. "No."

"There's only one way to keep them from capturing me again." Kira tried not to imagine the pain, tried not to imagine everything ending, all that she had ever wanted to be and to do coming to a finish here by her own hand.

"No," Jason repeated.

"I'm sorry, Jason," Kira said. "You know that they'll kill you. We'll go together."

"*No, we won't.*" She could hear his anger. Anger at her. "You can't quit."

"This isn't about quitting! No one else should have to die because of me!"

"Do you think you being dead would stop a war from happening?" Jason demanded. "If you're out of the way, Prince Maxim could concentrate on taking out your mother, too."

"My mother will avenge me!"

"And how many people would die because of that?"

Kira stared at him.

"Can you imagine how your parents will feel? Your mom and dad? When they hear you're gone?"

"Stop it, Jason," Kira said, her voice trembling. "That's not fair. Do you know what will happen to me if the Imperials take me? What they'll do to me in the Imperial household?"

"I know that as long as you're alive and can keep fighting and trying you have a chance," Jason said. "You have a hundred different paths forward. A hundred ways to still survive and win and get revenge. But if you end it here, you can *never* win, you can *never* influence what happens, you can *never* get another chance. Kira, you wouldn't let me give up. Don't you give up."

"You'll be dead," she said, the words barely able to leave her throat. "Because of me. You're going to die because of me, Jason, and that alone is more than I can bear."

He shook his head at her, his eyes fixed on hers. "Don't make this my fault. Don't do this because of me. Like you once said, wherever I end up, I'll know you're still alive. Please promise me that you won't stop trying, that you'll keep taking each step, that you won't leave the people who love you. You made me promise that. You do the same."

Kira heard the raggedness in her voice. "Why are you making me do this?"

"Because I love you, and I know a world with you in it is a far better world than one without you."

She bit back an angry sob. "All right. I promise. I'll keep fighting. And I will never, ever forget you. Jason, there will never be another for me."

"Don't promise me that," Jason said. "I want you to be happy, not tied to my memory like I'm a rock you're chained to."

"I don't deserve you," Kira said.

"No, I don't deserve you."

"Shut up. I can't afford to cry, and I'm about to, and if I do it'll mess up my aim."

"I'm not dead yet," Jason said. The conversation had left him with very little strength, but he still managed a smile at her.

"You're not going to die," Kira said, and she meant it, even though she knew that was nothing but an illusion she was creating. Because sometimes illusions were all that kept someone going.

Kira could again hear the faint sounds of movements and distant conversation as the legionaries prepared for another assault. Would the legionaries take her prisoner? Or would this be a fight to the death despite her promise to Jason? There might be only moments left, and so much of what she'd hoped for in this life was still undone, so many things still unsaid. "Jason, if the worst happens, I'll be looking for you in the next dream until I find you. I promise." She reached out her free hand toward him and Jason nodded in reply.

A long roll of thunder rumbled, overriding the sounds of the legionaries marshalling for the attack. Kira shook her head to clear it, then stared up at the sky, where stars were visible. "That's not a storm. Not a nearby one, anyway."

More thunder. Jason blinked. "Are you sure?"

"Yes," Kira said, not daring to hope. The thunder came again, long and low, breaking into individual crashes that went on and on. "It's rifle fire. Jason, it's a battle." More shots, the sounds clearer. "I'm hearing carbines, Jason. A lot of those shots are from cavalry carbines, not Imperial rifles. "

"You can tell by the sound?"

"It's a different barrel length and carbine ammo uses different propellant! Of course I can tell by the sound! The fight is getting closer, Jason!"

She leaned out recklessly, seeing lights sparkling along the heights to the south and where the plateau extended to the west. Muzzle flashes from firearms.

Shouts sounded from down the slope, legionary officers calling orders. The harsh notes of the brass horns that the legions still used to pass orders echoed between the sounds of battle, mingled with other faint music, the higher and sweeter notes of the cavalry bugles that Kira knew.

Figures rose up, running, and Kira's heart faltered for a moment. But as she steadied her pistol Kira realized that this time the legionaries were sprinting away from her and Jason's position. She faintly heard more orders being shouted as the flaring lights that marked muzzle flashes came closer. The thunderous crash of battle grew louder, but through it Kira heard a bugle call she recognized. "They're sounding the attack!" Kira called to Jason, her voice breaking. Tears of relief sprang to life, running down her cheeks. Bracing herself on the rock with her free hand, Kira raised the hand holding the pistol to rub the tears away.

She could barely make out the dim silhouettes of legionaries rushing into position down the slope, trying to form a line.

The bugles sounded again and suddenly the shapes of mounted cavalry appeared out of the night, charging along the slope and hitting the Imperial line in the flank. The Imperial line fell apart, the legionaries running and falling under gunfire, lance and saber.

The battle swept past along the plateau, just as if it had indeed been a violent storm, the crackle of rifle and carbine fire and sound of bugles receding down the slope but also falling off rapidly as the Imperial resistance collapsed.

Kira braced herself on the rock before her and stood up on shaky feet, seeing a small group of night-shrouded cavalry riding past. "Who are you?" she cried. "Identify yourselves!"

The riders wheeled to face her, their weapons at ready. One rode slightly forward of the others. "We're part of the Fourth Lancer Regiment. Soldiers of the Free City of Alexdria. Who are you?"

Kira couldn't speak for a moment as emotion overwhelmed her. When she attempted to answer, only a hoarse croak came out at first. She tried to wet her mouth and swallowed. "Kira. Kira of Dematr. And Jason of Urth. Friends of the Free Cities."

"Lady Kira?" The cavalry soldier's voice rose to a shout. "Colonel! We've found her! Lady Kira of Dematr! Pass the word!"

"We're coming out." Kira holstered her pistol and reached down for Jason. "Can you walk?"

"I can be carried," Jason said. "This is real? I'm not dreaming?"

"You're not dreaming. They're friends. We're safe. Come on. Help me get you up."

Jason nodded and forced himself up with Kira's help. She pulled him over the rock barricade, then with Jason leaning heavily on Kira they stumbled over the bodies littering the ground. Kira blessed the darkness that kept her from seeing those bodies clearly. She knew she'd have enough trouble living with the memories of this night. Her side was still bleeding, but she disregarded that, caught up in the euphoria of unlooked-for survival.

The Alexdrian soldiers dismounted to meet them as some of their mounted comrades raced off to spread the news. "There are columns of Free Cities soldiers all over the mountains dealing with the Imperials and looking for you!" one of the soldiers said. He stared around at the fallen legionaries. "How many are there?"

"There are more over here," another soldier said from near the rocks, her voice full of amazement. "You two did this?"

"She did, mostly," Jason said. "I just had a knife."

"They've been hitting us since late this afternoon," Kira said.

"The sounds of fighting are what drew us here," the soldier said, shaking his head. "No wonder those Imperials folded so easily when we hit them. You'd already beaten the blazes out of them. How did you do it?"

Kira shrugged selfconsciously. "I'm a Lancer, too."

Their smiles were easy to see in the night. "That's right! From the Queen's Own in Tiae! Forgive us, Lieutenant…Lady…"

"I was only an honorary lieutenant," Kira said, "and now—"

Jason slipped down, unable to keep standing and Kira no longer having the strength to hold him up. The soldiers rushed to help her lay him gently on the ground. "He's been shot," Kira said. "And cut. He's lost a lot of blood."

"Healers!" the shout went up.

"What about you, Lieutenant?" one Lancer said.

"I'm fine," she said, wanting attention to be focused on Jason.

Cavalry riders were dismounting to surround them and rush to Jason's side. A small wagon pulled by a pair of horses rattled up as well, the symbol of a snake on a staff standing out on the white canvas cover.

Kira stood watching, wobbly on her feet, knowing she was crying and laughing at the same time, so overwhelmed by events that no other words or thoughts could come to her. She felt nothing but amazed relief. For the first time since she had left the reception at the queen's palace in Tiaesun, Kira felt safe.

Another small group of cavalry rode up, their leader dismounting a little more slowly than the others.

He came forward, saluting. "Kira. Glad I could make it in time.

We've had a hard ride, but I wasn't about to let the Imperials get the daughter of my old commander."

"General Flyn!" Kira gasped as she recognized the voice of the old soldier. She straightened and returned the salute as precisely as she could, even though she felt in danger of passing out at any moment. "I don't believe it. How did you get here so fast?"

Flyn grinned. "Thank your mother for the warning that had Alexdria's forces already well along with mobilizing when the legions entered the mountains, and thank your mother's plea for me to help find her wayward daughter. I'm long past the days when I should be chasing legionaries through the Northern Ramparts, but when the daughter of Jules calls I will always answer."

He turned slightly to gesture to the west. "As to how we got *here*, thank the guidance of Lady Mage Asha, who is back there a ways and sensed your presence in this direction earlier today through means she would not explain. Then we heard the sounds of battle and figured only Lady Mari, or her daughter, could be giving a legion that much trouble on her own. You held them off for quite a while, long enough for us to get here, but that's to be expected from members of your family. Although I understand you also credit it to being a Lancer."

"The Queen's Own," Kira said, deciding to claim that even though she was no longer formally entitled. "I couldn't have done it without Jason," she added. "But he's almost a member of the family. Someday he will be."

"Oh?" Flyn asked. "Are you announcing a battlefield engagement?"

"I am," Kira said. "It's only right that you hear it first. You saved my mother and father at Dorcastle and now twenty years later you've saved me and Jason." Kira started laughing again, then took two laborious steps forward as the world seemed to tilt and sway around her. "May a lieutenant of the Lancers offer a kiss to an old cavalry general?"

"Normally not," Flyn said, "but I'll make an exception for you."

Kira kissed the old man's cheek. "How can my family ever repay you?"

"This world and I are still repaying your family," Flyn said awkwardly, then took a good close look at her in the dim light. "Stars above, girl, you're about to collapse. Is any of that blood on you your own?"

"It's mostly Jason's," Kira said, wondering why the ground felt to her as if it were trembling in a earthquake. "Or from legionaries. Some is mine." Her hand went to her side. "Oh, and that's bleeding."

"Lieutenant Kira said she was fine!" one of the nearby Lancers protested.

"She's the daughter of the daughter!" Flyn cried. "A dragon slayer, like her mother! She wouldn't complain of anything that didn't kill her! Somebody see to her injuries!"

Kira realized that she had fallen to her knees, staring blankly down at the rough surface of the plateau. Someone thrust a canteen into her hands. She started to drink, then twisted her body toward where Jason lay about two lance lengths away. "He needs…"

"He's being looked after," a voice soothed her. "Drink, Lady."

She took several swallows, halting to gasp for breath. Someone was pulling off her jacket. Kira yielded to that, but balked when hands began unstrapping her holster.

"Easy, Lieutenant," someone said. "You're in friendly hands. The healers need to look at you."

"Okay," Kira muttered.

"What did you say?"

"All right." She blinked against the darkness as someone gave her a pill that she swallowed without thinking, draining the last of the canteen this time. "I'm really tired."

"Go ahead and sleep. You've earned it."

"Wake me," Kira said, trying to focus her mind. "Midnight. My watch."

"The general says you have the night off, Lancer."

"Tell…my…mother…" She tried to say something else, but Kira couldn't keep her eyes open any longer.

CHAPTER SIXTEEN

Commodore Banda saluted Mari as she and Alain boarded the *Julesport*. The new warship, the largest ever built on Dematr, rode the waves with ponderous grace, mighty guns in turrets fore and aft poised to hurl shells farther, harder, and more accurately than any ship-mounted weapons before them. The sun had just risen, gilding the upper works of the ship as if they were adorned with gold instead of steel. "Welcome aboard, Lady," Banda said, gesturing to the uniformed woman beside him. "This is Captain Whitni, commanding officer of the *Julesport*."

"It's an honor to be aboard," Mari told her, conscious of the ranks of sailors drawn up for her arrival, the dark jackets of Mechanic specialists intermingled among them in a way that would have been unthinkable when the Mechanics Guild ruled.

"The honor is ours," Captain Whitni said. "Thank you for choosing the *Julesport* as your flagship to regain the freedom of the Sharr Isles."

Mari and Alain gazed across the steel decks as the sailors broke ranks so the *Julesport* could get under way and join the other ships waiting outside the harbor of Dorcastle. Many times the target of invasions, this time Dorcastle was launching an attack, not for conquest, but for freedom.

"Is there any word of Kira?" Commodore Banda asked as he led Mari and Alain to their stateroom on the warship.

"No," Alain said. "We have heard nothing. I have seen nothing." He looked north and paused, his eyes suddenly intent.

"What is it?" Mari asked, frightened.

"Kira. I see her face. There are bandages. She wears a uniform of the Free Cities and is riding a horse."

Mari grabbed the doorway to support herself, staring at him. "Kira is all right?"

"She will be," Alain said, breathing deeply. "But I do not see Jason, and her expression is saddened."

When Kira opened her eyes again she was looking up at the top of a canvas tent which was bright with sunlight. She stared at it, trying to remember how she could have gotten here.

"Kira?" a soft voice asked, the emotions in it muted.

She looked over and saw a beautiful and familiar face. "Aunt Asha. You won't believe the nightmare I had. Why am I—?" Kira winced as she tried to move and something pulled painfully in her side.

Where the legionary's sword had ridden along her ribs.

"It wasn't a nightmare." Kira swallowed, her heart racing. "Jason?" She frantically felt for the thread and saw it leading off to the side, strong and bright.

"Over there," Asha said.

Kira was already turning her head, feeling a large bandage beneath her jaw resisting the movement. She saw Jason lying not far away, either unconscious or sleeping, his breathing deep and regular. "He's all right?"

"Yes," Asha said. "The healers say he will recover."

"His leg… He was shot and I had to put on a tourniquet and—"

"The healers said the leg should be fine." Asha gazed at Jason. "They were surprised, saying his body handled the trauma better than it should have."

"That was probably his gene pac things," Kira said, overwhelmed with relief. "Jason's going to be okay."

"Oh-kay?"

"Ah, he's got me doing it! All right. He's going to be all right."

"Yes. Can you eat?"

Kira stared at Asha, aware again of the emptiness inside her where too little food had been for too long. "Do you have a spare cow?"

"The healers recommended that you begin with something less than an entire cow," Asha said, smiling a slight Mage smile as she offered Kira a cup filled with broth. "Do you need it heated?"

"What?" Kira mumbled around a mouthful before she swallowed. "No. It's great. The most wonderful thing I ever tasted."

Light brightened as the tent flap opened. Kira grinned at the man entering. "Uncle Calu! Where's Aunt Alli?"

"Down south, missing all the fun," he said, bending over to smile at her. "You're good with broth? I heard that your tastes have changed a bit. Something about blood?"

Kira almost choked on her latest mouthful. "Who told you that?"

"The Imperials we captured. They were terrified when they found out you were in the camp," Calu said, grinning. "What'd you do to them?"

"I just...tried to...make them less enthusiastic about attacking me," Kira said.

"Your mother is going to love hearing about it."

"Don't tell her!"

Asha gave Kira a solemn, inquisitive look. "Speaking of those things your mother will want to hear about, General Flyn told me something about you and Jason."

"We're engaged," Kira said, surprised that Asha didn't display any happiness.

Asha placed a hand over Kira's. "If you come to regret something that you agreed to in the face of great danger, no one will fault you for reconsidering."

"Why—? Oh, you're remembering me weeks ago when I was still trying to decide how I felt." Kira laughed, wincing as the movement caused her side to hurt again. "I proposed to him, Aunt Asha, when

I realized what my feelings were for him and when he stood by me like…like Father has done with Mother so many times. Jason knows he can back out at any time if he decides life with me might be a little too, um, interesting. And speaking of Father, that's how I know what I feel for Jason is real, Aunt Asha. There's a thread connecting us."

Asha finally smiled slightly and nodded. "Just as a thread ties this one to my Dav, and as a thread ties your father to your mother. That is indeed a strong proof, Kira."

"Can you sense it?" Kira asked, gesturing toward where she could see the thread. She tried to sit up a little more, grimacing at the effort and becoming aware of another bandage on her left shoulder, but Asha's hand restrained her.

"No. It is only between those who share it. But you should perhaps put on a shirt before sitting up," Asha warned.

Kira checked herself, seeing that under the sheet she was naked, a large bandage wrapped around her torso. From the feel of her side, there were fresh stitches under that bandage. "What happened to my clothes?"

Calu held up a tangled, torn, badly bloodstained mess of fabric. "You mean like this shirt?"

"That's my shirt?" The same one she had been wearing in Tiaesun, the nice shirt she had been worried might get a little blood on it if Jason accidentally stuck her with the pin on the enameled dragon. She stared at the gory remnants of the garment, one hand going to her hair. "Do I want to know what I look like?"

"Better than the shirt, and better than your mother did after Dorcastle," Calu added.

"Oh, good. So I don't look as bad as if I'd died and been brought back to life," Kira said. She touched cautiously around her head, feeling small bandages in addition to the large one under her jaw. "What are these for?"

"Small cuts," Asha said. "Except for that larger one we were told was from a bullet. That will leave a notable scar."

"Great. Another scar. I guess the small cuts are from the rock fragments knocked off by Imperial bullets," Kira realized. "There are probably some older cuts there, too, from when we fell down that cliff. Where am I going to get a shirt? And pants? And everything else?"

"I brought someone who's waiting outside who can help with that," Calu said. "You're pretty hard on clothes, you know."

"I've been through a few things the last few weeks!" Kira protested as her honorary uncle went to the entrance and beckoned a cavalry captain into the tent.

"We're about the same size," the captain said, holding out the garments in her arms, "and I understand you need something else to wear. I had this spare uniform with me. You're welcome to it."

Kira looked at the uniform, shaking her head. "I couldn't ask that of you."

The captain smiled at her. "Perhaps I should explain. I'm Diana of Alexdria. I was a young girl when my father was part of an expedition to raid the Empire. Your father was the Mage hired to assist that expedition. When my father returned home he told us that the only reason he survived was because of the heroism of your father, a Mage who had repeatedly risked his life for common people. We had a hard time believing him until we heard the stories about the daughter of Jules and her Mage. Please take this uniform of mine as a very, very small repayment for the many years since then I have had with my father, thanks to the Mage who became your father."

"Thank you," Kira said, embarrassed and pleased. "If it's offered in that spirit, I'm proud to accept. If you know any stories from your father about that fight, I'd love to hear them. My father always just says that he tried his best and leaves it at that."

Captain Diana grinned. "Of course."

Calu backed out. "I'll give you some privacy while you get dressed. We're still trying to get a far-talker message out that you've been located, Kira, but I understand one of the message Mages will be here soon."

"Where are Mother and Father?" Kira asked, suddenly realizing their absence.

"In Dorcastle. There's a war going on, you know, and the daughter was needed." Calu's smile faded into a serious expression. "It's killing Mari that she couldn't come looking for you. You know that, right?"

"I do," Kira said. "Mother is going to keep the war as short as possible?"

"She's going to try."

"Thank you, Uncle Calu. Tell her that I love her and I understand."

He paused on his way out of the tent. "You've grown up a whole lot in less than a year, Kira."

Captain Diana and Asha helped Kira sit up and struggle into the clothing. Another soldier had contributed clean underwear that Kira pulled on with a sigh of relief, having spent the time since she was kidnapped being forced to wear the same pair. Hopefully someone had burned the old pair rather than try to launder it. Alexdrian troops wore light blue shirts and dark blue trousers, which felt odd to Kira after the green and gold uniform of Tiae she was accustomed to. Someone else had provided a spare set of cavalry boots close to Kira's size to replace the badly battered boots she had been wearing. Diana hadn't brought a cuirass or helm, which Kira was grateful for since she didn't think she could handle the weight of those items in her current condition. A lightweight garrison cap would serve the needs of military protocol if she went outside.

While she was unconscious the healers must have scrubbed her down, so Kira didn't smell as bad as she had expected. She felt embarrassed by the amount of assistance she needed to get dressed, though. Those parts of her that didn't hurt from cuts and other injuries were stiff and sore. But at least the clothes hid two of the largest bandages on her as well as most of the bruises.

"You two must be made of leather and nails to have gotten so far," Captain Diana commented, glancing at Jason, who remained deeply asleep. "Your man must be tough enough to be a Lancer, too."

"Yes," Kira said, smiling proudly. "He is."

"You're a lieutenant, right?" Diana asked as Kira laboriously buttoned up the front of the uniform blouse.

"I was. Of the Queen's Own Lancers of Tiae. But only an honorary officer. And not that anymore."

Captain Diana raised her eyebrows at Kira. "If the Queen's Own Lancers of Tiae don't want you, I'm sure the Fourth Lancers of Alexdria do. I'll get you the proper insignia. One of our lieutenants is bound to have a spare set."

"I'm not—"

"Yes, you are." Diana gestured toward the outside. "Girl, there's not a Lancer out there who wouldn't follow you into the heart of the Empire. There aren't a lot of lieutenants who can say that."

Captain Diana could stay only a short time, just long enough to share a couple of stories of the battle in which Kira's future father had saved her father. Mention of the lightning Mage who had nearly killed Alain in that fight reminded her of the one who had attacked her and Jason in Kelsi six months ago. Were they the same Mage? That was a bit of unresolved family history that Kira hadn't wanted to inherit. But perhaps she had.

Afterwards, alone with Asha and Jason in the tent for a while, Kira cautiously drank some more broth, amazed that a cup seemed to fill her stomach shrunken by too many days with too little food. But other things concerned her as well. "Aunt Asha, does foresight ever manifest as a voice?"

"Sometimes," Asha said. "A voice will tell a Mage something, though as with all foresight the meaning may be far from clear."

"What about just your name?" Asha looked a question at Kira, so she explained. "Jason and I were walking, and I hadn't looked back in a while, and I suddenly heard someone say my name very clearly, as if she was right behind me. I turned that way and saw legionaries coming."

"Just your name? Did you recognize the voice?"

"No," Kira said. "It's hard to say from just one word, but the way she said my name sounded like someone from the northern Confederation."

"It said nothing else? I have not heard of any other times when foresight worked in that fashion. We will ask your father of this when we see him again," Asha said. She tilted her head slightly as she gazed at Kira. "Something else worries you."

"Not really," Kira said, not sure why she was avoiding saying more.

Mage Asha's eyes stayed on her, plainly seeing that Kira had left something important unsaid.

"I just had some trouble remembering things after doing a spell," Kira finally said.

"What does that mean?"

"It means I can't recall things," Kira said, suddenly irritable. "I mean, I was on that ship, and I hadn't eaten anything or had any water for days, and when I did the spell I must have been so tired that I couldn't remember what was happening for a little while."

"There is still something you are not saying. Using Mage powers requires strong concentration and focus. I remember every detail of casting a spell."

"You probably haven't ever done one under those conditions!"

Asha looked at Kira, her calmness somehow making it harder for Kira to handle the examination. "I have sometimes been very stressed when casting spells, Kira."

Which meant, Kira knew, that at such times Asha had been facing death while worn out from exertion. Guilt at feeling that she had denigrated Asha's own experiences made her angry, which drove her next words. "Look, I've been through a whole lot lately. Like yesterday! Do we have to go into all this?"

Asha paused before speaking. "Always you have said that you are 'fine' when using your Mage powers. I have never seen a lie in you at such times."

"There! See?" Kira insisted.

"You will speak to your father Alain of this?"

"Yes," Kira promised with a heavy sigh to make clear how badly she was being put upon.

"You used a spell yesterday, early on," Asha continued.

"Yes," Kira said. "The spell to make me and Jason invisible." Guilt tugged at her as she remembered that she had lied to Jason about blacking out during that spell as well.

Asha must have seen that, but didn't press it. "It is fortunate that you did. I sensed you using the spell, and directed General Flyn to send his forces in this direction." She smiled slightly again. "It was difficult to explain how I knew you were here without disclosing your… special talents."

"Thank you, Aunt Asha," Kira said. "I'm sorry I'm a little on edge." She felt weariness overcoming her again, perhaps triggered by the emotional turmoil inside her. She didn't remember lying down, but when she woke next the sunlight on the outside of the tent told her that it was well into the afternoon.

Fortunately, the issue of blackouts didn't arise again. But after drinking some more broth and eating some crackers, Kira felt a strange restlessness. She couldn't sit doing nothing, and once she had gotten to her feet couldn't stop pacing inside the tent even though every step hurt a little. Asha had gone off to rest, and Calu was watching Jason. "Why don't you take a walk?" Calu finally suggested.

"Because that's crazy," Kira said. "I need to rest. And it hurts to walk."

"Then how about a ride? Ask outside." He saw her glance at Jason. "I won't leave his side. Promise. He'll be all right, Kira. He just needs a lot more recovery than you do because he got hurt a lot worse. But he's not in any danger."

Reassured, Kira turned to go but paused before leaving, looking at her pistol hanging in her shoulder holster from one of the tent poles. Even though she should be perfectly safe while surrounded by Alexdrian troops, Kira still felt a need to have that protection. She couldn't wear the holster with the uniform she was in, though, so Kira drew the weapon, deciding to carry it. Her last memory of the weapon was of holstering it, but she couldn't remember making it safe. Kira ejected the magazine and worked the slide, emptying the round still in the chamber, mentally chastising herself for not having done that last night. She set the safety before loading the loose cartridge back in the magazine, pausing for a moment to gaze at the three rounds.

"Are you all right?" Calu asked.

"Yes," Kira said, looking at him. "I was just thinking how close it was. See? Three shots. That's all that was left."

He gazed back at her, solemn, before nodding in wordless agreement.

She slid the magazine back into the pistol, then cautiously stepped out of the tent, seeing a string of guards posted around it. Before she could go any farther, a sergeant confronted her with a salute.

"May I be of service, Lady?"

Kira straightened and returned the salute. "Is there any chance I could get a mount? I'd like to ride around the camp."

"Certainly, Lady. Do you prefer Lady or Lieutenant?"

"Lieutenant," Kira said.

"We'll have a mount for you in a moment, Lieutenant." The sergeant barked orders and a nearby private ran off. "And get the lieutenant a proper holster while you're at it!" the sergeant called.

Kira stood looking around at the neat rows of small tents set up on what had been an open plateau. Occasional larger tents like the one she stood by anchored the ends of rows. Horses were gathered in temporary corrals formed of rope strung between steel poles driven into the dirt. Smoke drifted upwards from wagons parked near the corrals as farriers worked on the mounts' hooves and replaced horseshoes. Pennants set at regular intervals flapped in the breeze, marking the locations of subunits of the regiment. Some of the soldiers she could see were resting, others walking about with purpose or attending to some of the horses or standing sentry. There wasn't any sense of imminent danger, or of urgent preparations for more fighting soon. "Have the Imperials been defeated?"

The sergeant nodded. "The word I have is that the legion that entered this portion of the Northern Ramparts has been destroyed, most of them taken prisoner. We caught them spread out in small units and exhausted from very rapid marches over the last few days.

The other legion has been cut up very badly, the remnants retreating toward Imperial territory. We were told to rest and regroup."

"You're not heading for Umburan?" Kira asked.

"We were hoping to," the sergeant said with a grin. "But orders came to stop. Orders from the daughter herself, Lieutenant. She has other plans for dealing with the Empire."

Kira smiled. "I have no doubt of that."

The sergeant's gaze on her grew apprehensive and fascinated. Kira wondered just what her smile had looked like, and how her voice had sounded.

The sergeant pointed downslope to the southwest, where Kira could see large groups of people gathered. "The prisoners are down there. Legionaries captured near here, and some other Imperials caught farther south."

"Sailors?" Kira asked.

"Yes, Lieutenant." The sergeant eyed her. "You sank a ship, they say."

"It blew up after I set it on fire, so it was really the ammo magazines exploding that sank it."

"I see. Here's your mount, Lieutenant."

The steed was a gelding, a little frisky but not too much to handle. Unlike the tall breeds she had worked with in Tiae, this mountain horse was of only medium height, stocky and sure-footed, perfect for use in the rocky and uncertain terrain of the mountains. Kira tried to strap on the belt holster the private had brought, her sore, battered fingers fumbling at the simple task. She paused to look at the cuts and scrapes, trying to identify the cause of any particular injury, but her mind offered up only a blur of activity over the recent past.

"May I offer assistance?" the sergeant asked in a low voice that carried real respect.

"No, thank you," Kira said. "I'll do it." Working slowly and methodically, she got the holster on her belt.

The sergeant waited, obviously prepared to help her mount, but Kira took a deep breath and swung herself up. Gritting her teeth, she made it into the saddle, feeling assorted parts of herself spasm with pain or simply protest the effort. But she wasn't about to be helped into the saddle like some new recruit straight from a pumpkin farm.

Smiling, the sergeant handed her the reins. Kira left them loose, guiding her mount with her seat and her legs. Lancers had to know how to direct their horses without the use of hands that had to be employed with weapons, and Kira wanted anyone watching to know that she really was a Lancer. The gelding was a well-trained and responsive mount, allowing her to relax and enjoy the ride.

She rode slowly through the camp, trying not to notice the stares that followed her and the pointing fingers. Soldiers she met rendered salutes, and Kira returned them. She passed a major and a captain and saluted them, earning herself bemused looks as they acknowledged the gesture.

As Kira rode, she realized why she had been restless. Being inside the tent had felt too confining, like another prison to be escaped. Even knowing how hard it was to walk had been difficult to bear, since that meant she couldn't easily get away if trouble erupted. But mounted on a fresh horse, Kira felt those fears subside. If she wanted to, she could ride off to the west, urging her mount to a gallop, all of the Northern Ramparts open to her until the mountains gave way to the great plains outside of Ihris.

She wasn't trapped. She could ride hard in any direction. It was amazing how good that felt.

Kira steadied her seat in the back of the saddle and pressed lightly with both legs, bringing her horse to a stop. She looked north, up the slope, to where the cliff face loomed. It didn't seem that far away. The bodies of the fallen had already been collected, but Kira had no trouble identifying the rocks where she and Jason had fought the legionaries. The cliff-face behind those rocks was spalled where numerous bullets had struck, giving it a rough, pockmarked appearance even from this distance. Dark stains marked the rocks where blood had been shed. Jason's blood, along with that of the legionaries who had attacked them.

Kira shivered as if a cold wind had found its way inside her uniform jacket and turned away, not wanting to view that place again.

Looking away from the north took her gaze to the southwest. The prisoners of war were gathered there, including among them the legionaries who had almost killed her and Jason.

Kira gazed down toward the prisoners, trying to sort out her thoughts and feelings. She shifted her weight in the saddle, pressing lightly with her outside leg and opening her inside leg a bit to turn the cavalry mount that way.

She rode up to the nearest mass of prisoners, confined behind the same sort of temporary corral as the horses, a heavy guard set around the perimeter with carbines at the ready. But the prisoners of war didn't appear to pose any danger. They sat closely together in the field, slumping wearily, looking both tired and beaten.

Kira stopped her horse, looking at the legionaries over the heads of the guards.

She hadn't known what she would feel when gazing on the men and women who had pursued them and nearly killed Jason. She feared to feel hatred for them, and rejected the thought of fearing them. As Kira gazed on the prisoners, she realized that she too felt tired, but also victorious, glad she had won but also regretful for those who had died.

Some of the prisoners were looking her way. They wore the uniforms of Imperial sailors, crewmembers from some of Prince Maxim's ships. Kira saw recognition blooming in their eyes, followed by something else. Fear? Awe? Disbelief? Or all of those things?

The prisoners whispered among themselves, word of who was watching them spreading rapidly among the dense group. Kira could see the results move through the prisoners like a wave as they turned to look at her.

She finally, fully understood why her mother hated so much any supposed connection with Mara, the Dark One. People like Prince Maxim probably enjoyed seeing fear in the eyes of those who looked upon them, but Kira found it painful. She had used that weapon against the Imperials out of necessity, but now wished that she had not. It was not easy having men and women look at you as if you were a monster.

The legionaries were shifting around within their confined area, but didn't seem to be moving toward the edges of their prison. The guards around the edge took note, eyes alert and weapons at ready, but none of the Imperials moved any closer to the guards. Watching them, Kira gradually realized that the women legionaries were edging toward her while pushing the males behind them, placing themselves between Kira and the men her supposed unnatural appetites might threaten.

That didn't feel very good, either.

She looked over the Imperials facing her, seeing a female centurion in the front rank. Kira gestured. "You. Come here."

The centurion walked toward Kira with the demeanor of someone walking to her execution and determined not to show a trace of fear. Behind her, the other Imperials watched with looks of dread.

Kira considered dismounting to speak with the centurion, realized how awkward she would look because of her stiff body and injuries, and instead chose to lean forward on her horse.

"There's something I want you to know," Kira said. "Something I want you to tell the others. You are prisoners now, and you will be treated with all of the respect and dignity that honorable prisoners of war deserve. Once this war is over, none of you need fear me, or my mother, or my father. Not unless the Empire once again attacks us or any of its neighbors."

"And our families?" the centurion asked, her expression unyielding. "What of our families near Umburan?"

"The Free Cities do not war on the innocent. Neither does General Flyn, who commands. You know of him from the war against the Great Guilds. You know I speak the truth."

"What of you, daughter of Mara?"

"I also do not war on the innocent," Kira said, keeping her temper by a heroic effort. "Do not ever call me that again. My name is Kira of Dematr. My mother is Master Mechanic Mari of Dematr, the daughter of Jules. The only Dark Ones in this world are those who pursue war for their own profit or benefit. *They* threaten your children, not me. How many in your legion have died in this invasion?"

The centurion remained silent, her eyes on Kira.

"In exchange for your obedience, your rulers owe you respect!" Kira said. "How many lives has Prince Maxim thrown away in pursuit of me? Look at me, Centurion! How many deaths am I worth?"

The centurion shook her head. "Such decisions are not mine to make."

"You have a right to be respected," Kira repeated. "Your lives should not be thrown away like broken toys. I do not want to fight the legions again. I will only if I have to. But if I have to, I will fight just as hard."

"I understand."

"I'm truly sorry for those who died. Will their families be looked after?"

The centurion nodded. "That is an obligation the emperor has never neglected." She studied Kira, the centurion's eyes lingering on the large bandage below Kira's jaw. "You put up a hard fight. There is no shame in our failure to defeat you."

"There is no shame," Kira said.

She was about to dismiss the centurion when the legionary spoke up. "I request to speak."

Kira nodded, quieting her mount. "Go ahead."

"It is said that you met Princess Sabrin."

"Yes," Kira said.

"Alone? She had no guards or followers?"

"Princess Sabrin was alone," Kira said, thinking of their first meeting in the passageway of Maxim's flagship.

"Why did you not harm her?"

Kira considered her answer carefully, trying to recall everything she had heard of Mara and her relationship with the first emperor, Maran, who had supposedly been the only one who could control Mara. And remembering how Sabrin had helped her escape from the harbor by providing a boat. Maxim was still out there somewhere, still enjoying the prestige and benefits of being an Imperial prince, while those he had heedlessly ordered into battle were dead or wounded or prisoners.

What would best support the position of Sabrin?

"I could not," Kira finally said. That was true enough, because she couldn't bring herself to kill or injure anyone without cause, and Sabrin had given her no cause, but the Imperials would probably interpret that very differently.

They did. The other Imperials had been listening. Kira saw the wave of reaction through them at her words. Sabrin, they now thought, could control Kira despite Kira's supposed dark powers.

She addressed the centurion once more, speaking in calm tones that made her words sound even more chilling. "But if ever I meet Prince Maxim again, I will rip his rotten heart from his chest as it still beats. He fears me. And he should."

From the look in the eyes of the centurion, her words had been taken literally. "What if the war is over?"

"My quarrel is with Maxim," Kira said. "Not with the people of the Empire. May you all return safely to your homes and families when this war has ended."

The centurion nodded. She hesitated, then saluted Kira in the Imperial fashion.

Kira returned the salute in the manner of Tiae.

As Kira turned away to ride back north, she saw that General Flyn sat his horse nearby, doubtless having been told where Kira was. "What was that about?" he asked as they rode slowly side by side through the camp.

"Facing my fears," Kira told him.

"That is something I usually advise doing," Flyn said. "But you also ventured into Imperial politics at the end. I think that your mother would want me to warn you against that. Even the sharpest and most ruthless players can find themselves in too deep when they enter that swamp."

Kira couldn't help a short laugh. "General, I respect your warning, but Imperial politics reached out and dragged me into that swamp. I came very close to drowning in it."

"Princess Sabrin is not your friend."

"I know that. But she understands loyalty, General. I can see truth or lies in people, as my father taught me. And she is smart. Smarter by far than Maxim, who thinks he's the smartest person in Palandur."

"Smart enough to realize how foolish it is to attack your family?" Flyn shrugged. "Perhaps. But you remain a pawn to her. She will sacrifice you without remorse if needed to advance her position."

"I know," Kira said, remembering the way that Sabrin had appraised her. "I heard we've beaten the legions that entered the Northern Ramparts. Can you tell me what's next?"

Flyn sighed heavily. "It's not over."

"But I heard you're not striking for Umburan."

"We're not. Your mother offered the same wise advice she did twenty years ago, and fortunately the Free Cities listened once more. But there's a major attack heading for the Sharr Isles. The Imperials are going to be ejected from those islands once and for all."

"You don't sound happy about that."

"It's necessary," the general said. "But the Sharr Isles will pay an awful price for their freedom if the Imperials dig in and fight to the last. All of those pretty cities and fine ports will be reduced to rubble, and a great many of the people of the Sharr Isles may die, as well as a great many of the soldiers from the Western Alliance and the Bakre Confederation."

"Do we have to—"

"Yes," Flyn said. "The Empire has to be pushed back within its borders, and shown that it cannot withstand the combined forces of the west. Otherwise we'll be facing this same war again in a few years, with potentially many much worse battles. But the human price of forestalling a very big war will not be small." He looked at her. "Your mother proposed the attack and got everyone in line to carry it out."

Kira closed her eyes, remembering the harbor of Caer Lyn, imagining it reduced to bloodied ruins. How could her mother be championing something that could lead to that?

Because, Kira realized, the alternative would be far worse. "There's always a choice," she said, opening her eyes again and meeting Flyn's with a somber gaze of her own. "You have to be willing to make it."

"You understand that?" Flyn asked. "That your mother hates what might happen, but is trying to prevent something far worse?"

"Yes. I know how much she sometimes hates what she has to do, General, but Mother does what she has to. She doesn't leave the job for someone else."

"Could you do it? Could you make that decision?"

Kira had to pause to think as their horses continued to pace slowly through the camp, remembering the dead legionaries in front of the rocks she had defended. Maxim had made those choices—to kidnap her, to invade the Ramparts—because he wanted to. She had fought back because she had to. What else would Maxim do if not stopped? How many more would die or kill because, like that centurion, they would follow orders without caring about who was right and who was wrong? "Yes, General," Kira said, her voice almost a whisper. "If it was my job. Someone has to."

He nodded. "Someone has to. War is insanity. You already know that. You've now seen it first-hand. But if someone begins such insanity, someone else has to stand against that, even though it means embracing the insanity."

Kira gave Flyn a sharp look. "It doesn't mean embracing deaths and destruction as a simple choice. It means finding ways to limit the insanity, to win not by becoming insane as well but by using your smarts to find the best way to win with the fewest losses possible. And while still retaining your humanity."

This time Flyn smiled at her as he nodded again. "Just so."

Their conversation paused as, along with General Flyn, Kira returned a salute from a passing lieutenant before realizing that she was still wearing captain's insignia on her borrowed uniform. "I need to get back and see if Captain Diana has found some lieutenant insignia for me."

"I'll pass word to Captain Diana not to worry about that," Flyn said. "You've received a battlefield promotion to captain."

"What? When?"

"Just now. For heroism and inspiring leadership and a keen grasp of the responsibilities of command and so on and so forth."

"You can't...can you?"

"Of course I can. And if Queen Sien doesn't confirm it for the Queen's Own Lancers, then she isn't nearly as wise as she was in the days when we rode to war together," Flyn said. "You'll be commanding the daughter's army someday, Lady. Best you get the necessary command experience now."

Kira shook her head at Flyn. "Oh, no, you don't. Don't you dare. First of all, General, I've never been 'lady' to you. And second of all, commanding the daughter's army? Where did that come from? I'm seventeen years old."

"Your mother was only twenty when—"

"She's my mother! The daughter of Jules!"

Flyn smiled at her again. "She is indeed your mother. I remember as clearly as if it happened only yesterday the expression on her face when I offered her my sword in these very mountains as your father-to-be stood by her side. Mari was eighteen then, and she looked at me just as you are looking at me now. What is the matter with him? Why is he doing such a ridiculous thing? But she graciously accepted the offer of my service. Which, I may add, I have never offered or given lightly. Only to those I believe deserve it, and will use it wisely. And you have proven yourself to me to be your mother's daughter, both in physical and moral courage, and in wisdom, at least as it applies to the command of others."

"You're not going to—" Kira began as she saw Flyn drawing his sword. "No! Don't do that!"

He rested the blade on one arm, extending the hilt toward Kira as their horses continued to walk, oblivious to the human drama of their riders. "Will you accept my service, Lady?"

Kira covered her face with both hands, then lowered them to give him a helpless look. "After your service to my mother, after your service to this world, you know there's only one thing I can do."

"I'm waiting on it," Flyn said.

She grimaced, exhaled in frustration, managed to put a solemn expression on her face, then reached to touch the hilt. "I am deeply honored by your offer and accept it, though I very much hope I will never have need of it."

Kira heard a buzz of excited conversation and knew Flyn had deliberately chosen to make the offer of his service where many would see and word of it would quickly carry.

It seemed she had escaped from several Imperial traps only to fall into a trap laid by her mother and her mother's friends.

Riding back up to the tent some time later, Kira dismounted with all the difficulty that she had expected. The cut in her side and the stitches holding it closed were particularly unhappy with the stretching of her torso required by the dismount, and let Kira know in painful terms. Before she could start to cool down her mount, the guard sergeant was there, directing a private to take the reins. "We'll take care of him, Captain Kira," the sergeant told her.

Captain Kira. Word traveled very fast in a military camp. "I rode him," Kira said. "I should handle the cooldown and rubdown."

"Yes, Captain," the sergeant said with the tone of a senior enlisted who had often had to correct officers in a respectful way, "of course. But my instructions are that you are on sick list. Regulations state that any Lancer on sick list should have their mount's care handled by others."

"It doesn't feel right," Kira grumbled, yielding the reins. She was about to tell the private to be sure to check the gelding's hooves when she caught herself. The private would know to do that, and would probably be insulted by her reminding him. "Thank you. He handled well."

"Suka's regular rider is out for a long while," the sergeant said. "Sent back to Alexdria in a healer wagon to recover from a bad wound. Would you like Suka for your usual mount?"

"Yes," Kira said. She gave Suka's neck an affectionate stroke. "He's a good horse." Suka swung his head to barely nuzzle Kira's hand in a clear sign that he approved of the arrangement.

Inside the tent, she saw Calu sitting next to where Jason lay, and that Jason was awake. They both looked at her with momentary lack of recognition, confused by the Alexdrian Lancer uniform. "Do you need something?" Calu began, then his eyes widened and he laughed. "I'd already seen you in that and it still fooled me! Look at you! I wish Alain and Mari were here!"

"Oh, hush," Kira said, embarrassed again. "They've seen me in my Queen's Own uniform plenty of times." She looked down at Jason, trying to smile as he looked back at her. Awake, his weakness and battered body were far more evident, a visible display of the price Jason had paid for her and alongside her over the last few weeks. "How are you doing, my hero?"

"Okay," Jason said, his voice frail and thin. "They say I'm going to live."

"You have to. You promised. And your leg will be all right. Did that gene pac stuff help?"

"It must have. I know there's some injury reaction stuff in there so my body can handle getting hurt a bit better. What's that uniform about? Are you a general now?"

She shook her head, smiling for real this time. "No. I had to borrow something to wear. And I'm just a captain."

"Captain?" Calu asked. "Since when? You were a lieutenant when you left this tent."

"Battlefield promotion from General Flyn," Kira explained, trying to make it sound like no big deal. "It's not real."

"It sounds real to me."

"Why don't we talk about Jason?" Kira suggested.

"I'm fine," Jason said, despite his weakness managing to mimic Kira's tone when she used the same words.

"Jason has been telling me about your adventures," Calu said, giving her a reassuring smile. "You've been pretty heroic, Kira."

"Jason has been telling you *I'm* a hero? *He's* the hero, but he's also a terrible liar," Kira said. "Has he been telling you about Kansas and the jumping congaroos and poisonous paddlepuses that live there?"

"Australia," Jason corrected, trying to be forceful, but his voice still frail. "Kangaroos and paddle…pittle…plattle…I can't even say it anymore thanks to you. They live in Australia."

"Austraya is an imaginary place on Urth," Kira told Calu. "It's also called Oz. You get there from Kansas."

"It's not— You're doing that on purpose, aren't you?" Jason said.

"Sure am," Kira said, leaning down so her face was close to his. "You'd better get used to it. We're going to have a long and happy life together. If somebody doesn't kill us." She kissed him lightly, afraid to do more when Jason was so weak.

"I've got a big reason to live," Jason said, smiling.

"Me, too. Get some more rest. You need it, and I need to talk to my honorary uncle."

Calu eyed her warily as they left the tent, waving off the attentive sergeant. "What'd I do?"

"Why did General Flyn just offer me his sword?" Kira demanded, keeping her voice low so they wouldn't be overheard.

"He did?" Calu said, looking surprised but also speaking in almost a whisper. "That's great."

"You're not answering the question, Uncle Calu. Why?"

Calu studied her before answering. "He must have thought you deserved it."

Kira laughed incredulously. "Oh, sure. Like I could do what Mother does. Look…dragon slayer? All right. I did that. *Command an army?* Not the same thing!"

"Mari lets experts handle what they're good at," Calu said. "You'd do the same. And people are going to listen to you, because you've shown how much of Mari, and your father, is in you."

"I barely survived! Has anybody noticed that?"

"That's not what everyone sees, Kira. They see you as having single-handedly frustrated the plans of Prince Maxim, destroyed nearly half of the Gray Squadron, and fought an Imperial legion to a standstill."

She shook her head, disbelieving. "That's crazy. And even if it was true, I couldn't have done it without Jason."

Calu smiled crookedly. "Your mother has spent decades telling everyone that she couldn't have done what she did without your father alongside her. The world nods and sees he's great, but they still give her the credit. Jason is going to have to accept that in the eyes of the people of Dematr, he'll always be *your* sidekick."

"How can anyone believe any of that?" Kira looked around, unable to grasp the idea that the looks of the soldiers she had seen during her ride had reflected that sort of belief in what she had done. "Uncle Calu, you know who I really am."

"I thought I did," Calu admitted. "I also thought no one but Mari could have survived what you have. Don't give me that look, Captain Kira! I'm not the only one who is happy to have seen what you've got inside you. And I know that Flyn wouldn't have done what he did unless he believed you deserved it. The symbolism of Mari's old general offering you his sword is huge."

"Why would Mother have told General Flyn to do that without telling me first? Why didn't she warn me?"

Calu shook his head. "Kira, you've known General Flyn all of your life. Do you really think that Mari could have ordered him to offer you his service? There are things even your mother can't do. Flyn did it only because he wanted to. Mari probably won't be happy when she hears about it. She didn't want this stuff thrust on you, but maybe fate has other plans."

"I knew it! Everyone wants me to be my mother. And I'm *not!*" Kira covered her face with her hands. Her physical pain and injuries were one thing, but the stresses of the previous weeks, of the previous day, still lay coiled inside her. She could feel them lashing at her, released by the strain of imagining a world depending on her decisions.

"Kira, everybody knows that. No one thinks that you're Mari."

"Then why did General Flyn offer me his sword? How I can do the same things Mother does? Because Master Mechanic Mari defeated the full might of the Great Guilds and the Empire at Dorcastle, and I managed to hide in some rocks for a few hours and not get killed?" Kira felt tears starting, born partly of frustration at the expectations of others and partly from the unresolved pressures of the day before. "It was my fault we ended up trapped there! And if General Flyn hadn't arrived when he did it would have been my fault when Jason was killed! I'm not a hero, Uncle Calu. I *survived.*"

He nodded slowly, keeping his eyes on her. "I'm sorry, Kira. I guess that's a pretty big thing to dump on somebody, especially somebody who's just been through what you have."

"Tell them the truth! Tell them I'm not who they think I am! Tell them I didn't do those things!"

"Mari used to say the same thing. They won't listen, Kira."

"My mother wouldn't have made all of the mistakes that I did," Kira added, staring to the north where the cliff wall loomed, where Jason's blood stained some of the rocks.

"Mari made a lot of mistakes," Calu said. "Kira, you of all people should know that your mother isn't perfect. Sometimes she survived by luck. I wasn't at Altis when the assassins went after your mother and father, but Alain has told me about it. Mari was beating herself up, saying that she'd trapped them, that her mistakes had doomed them."

"Mother got them out! They survived!"

"So did Jason."

Kira stared at him. "Not because of me."

"If we go in there and ask, what will Jason say?"

"You know what he'll say because his love for me will be talking! But the facts are, my decisions almost killed Jason! That's all that matters."

"No," Calu said. " 'Almost' is a very big word, Kira. What matters is, he lived. So did you. What also matters is you never gave up. Jason told me that. You wouldn't quit and you wouldn't let him quit."

"But…" Kira spread her hands helplessly. "I can fight, Uncle Calu. I can survive. I know I can do that. But being Mother, trying to measure up to the daughter of Jules, is so much more than that. This isn't the me of a year ago feeling totally worthless, this is the me of now realizing how much more it takes to be my mother. How could I ever be able to do it?"

"Don't quit."

"I…"

"Can you keep fighting even after the weapons fall silent? Can you fight the battles where no blood is shed but lives can be destroyed? Can you stand firm against wrong just as you stood against those legionaries?"

"I don't know." Kira looked out across the camp, trying to imagine all of these soldiers following her orders, their lives dependent on her…wisdom? On her? She felt suddenly dizzy and staggered, Calu catching her arm to steady her. "I'm sorry. I guess I'm still a little weak."

"It's my fault. I pushed you too hard. Why don't you get in the tent and eat and drink some more?"

He helped her inside and sat her down, pressing a canteen and another mug of broth on her. Jason was asleep again, so they talked quietly to avoid disturbing him. "Tell me if you need anything else. I should have realized you needed more time to rest and recover after the stuff that happened yesterday."

"And the days before," Kira said, forcing herself to drink slowly. "I'm sorry I freaked out. Whenever I think about what might have happened to Jason, about what did happen to him, I just… Didn't you get shot when you were with Mother?"

"Yeah, at Edinton."

"How bad does it hurt?"

He shrugged. "I think that depends on where you get hit and other stuff. It did hurt, yeah."

Kira stared down at her mug. "I shot a lot of people yesterday, Uncle Calu. And I was sure I was going to die. Among those rocks, with the legionaries coming at Jason and me again and again." She started shaking so badly that liquid spilled from the cup in her hand. "Why didn't I die?"

He held her tightly until the tremors in her subsided. "What kept you going?"

"Jason," she said, her voice muffled as she kept her face buried against his coat. "If I'd given up, he'd have died."

"What do you think kept Jason going?"

She sighed. "Me."

"So," Calu continued, his voice soft, "you lived because you had each other. That's a pretty good reason, isn't it?"

"That's not why we lived," Kira said. "It's how we survived."

"This sure brings back memories," Calu said, sitting down beside her. "After Mari was shot at Dorcastle, and Alain nearly killed himself saving her, I was in their room a lot, helping out. Your mother was really weak, especially at first, but she kept asking me why she had lived when so many other people had died in the battle. Other people like your namesake, Kira. Mari kept asking why and I kept saying I don't know. And here I am again, only with you instead of her, and I've been alive and learning things for another couple of decades since then, but I still don't know the answer."

"Maybe there isn't an answer," Kira said, darkness plucking at her spirit. "Maybe it's all random. Maybe who you are and what you're doing doesn't matter at all."

"Maybe," her honorary uncle agreed. "Maybe life is totally random. But did you ever try to calculate the odds that out of all the billions of people on Urth, Jason would be among those who came to this world? And that when he came here, you'd be here and alive and about the same age?"

"Why would the universe care that Jason and I got together?"

"I don't know. But what were the odds, Kira? And you're not alone. What were the odds that Mari and Alain would meet, and talk to each other, and become friends, and then more than friends, and survive everything to be the ones who freed this world? What were the odds that Alli and I would both be Apprentices in Caer Lyn and be close to the same age?"

Kira looked down at her hands, thinking. "Father says every person is an amazing thing, because every person is unique. There's no one else exactly like them anywhere. So everyone is sort of impossible, because the odds of them being *them*, the odds of that exact person even existing, are so very, very small."

Calu smiled. "He's right about that. If you look at the probabilities, not one single person should exist as who they are. But we do. So maybe who we are, and what we are trying to do, really does matter. Kira, you're alive. It's a priceless gift. If things start to feel dark, remember that. You survived. You've said that like it's not much of a thing. But it's a huge thing."

"It doesn't feel like it. It really doesn't."

"Try imagining a world in which you hadn't survived. Big difference, huh? You've got a lot to be happy about. And so do your parents and your friends and that guy Jason over there. Hey, did I ever tell you that when I was watching her at Dorcastle your mother insisted that I bring her some red wine and chocolate? The healers about threw a fit, but Mari insisted."

"Mother told me," Kira said, smiling despite the lingering tension inside her. "She said that chocolate did her more good than all the medicines the healers were pushing at her."

"That's why I thought I might need this," Calu added, pulling a small packet out of his coat pocket.

"Chocolate? Seriously?" Kira started to take a bite, then turned a guilty glance on Jason where he lay asleep. "I should wait until Jason and I can share it."

Calu laughed. "Now I know it's love! Not only sharing your chocolate with Jason, but being willing to wait for it!"

"What are the odds?" Kira joked. "Uncle Calu, I really am going to marry him someday. Unless he changes his mind about that."

"He's spent the last six months dreaming that one day you'd feel that way. I don't think Jason is going to be changing his mind."

"I just wish I knew who he saw when he looks at me. It doesn't seem to be any version of myself that I'd recognize."

"You're a lot like your mother that way," Calu said. "And in other ways, too. Try to listen when Jason gives you advice."

"I do." Kira looked at Calu. "There's something unsaid there that has you really tense. Is Aunt Alli all right?"

"As far as I know." He remained sitting next to her, but stared at the wall of the tent. "I just worry about people."

"People?" Kira shook her head at him. "What are you still not saying?"

"You're like your father Alain when you do that."

"I'm also like him in knowing when someone is trying to change the subject."

Calu nodded. "The truth is, I'm worried about Mari. This is threatening to be a big war, and if your mother sees any possible way to short-circuit that war, she'll pursue it. Even if…"

"Even if it's really dangerous?" Kira finished. "But Mother is in Dorcastle. She should be safe there."

"Mari was in Dorcastle the last we heard," Calu corrected her.

"Mother wouldn't—" Kira buried her face in her hands, realizing something else. "Yes, she would. She's going to keep fighting for others. The Sharr Isles. Uncle Calu, there's a big attack planned. If Mother thinks she can fix things some other way, she'll do whatever she thinks she has to."

"Alain is with her. Your father will keep her safe."

Kira looked at him. "You're not very good at saying things you don't really believe, Uncle Calu. We know that he'll do everything he can. Do you know what my father has feared the most since learning Mother was the daughter of Jules?"

"That she'd die."

The words almost stuck in her throat. "And that he wouldn't be able to save her."

From his position behind Mage Saburo, Alain watched the harbor of Caer Lyn come into view as their Roc cleared the heights leading down to Meg's Point. Not far off to his left, Mari rode on another Roc guided by Mage Alera. From above, the island displayed large swaths of greenery and a riot of color where the famous brightly painted homes and doors were visible. The skies were full of tattered storm clouds just giving way to sun.

Rocs could not land on the older sailing ships that once ruled the waters of Dematr. The masts and spars that held the sails, the rigging that supported and controlled it all, blocked the huge birds. But the new metal ships created by Mechanic arts had smaller masts, and the *Julesport* in particular boasted wide, flat tops on the "turrets" that held the massive Mechanic weapons that were called big guns. A Roc could land to perch there, if the Mage controlling the Roc had sufficient skill, and if the Roc didn't shift its illusory weight about enough to imperil the illusory stability of the ship.

When Mari had received the messages from Caer Lyn over the Mechanic far-talkers she had resolved to take the necessary chances to travel there despite the risks and despite Alain's warnings. And where Mari went, so did he. Alain had boarded his own Roc after Mari's had lifted, following across the Sea of Bakre, leaving behind the ships of the invasion fleet headed for the Sharr Isles. Looking back from above, Alain had seen the warships—mostly older ships with billowing clouds of sails as well as new Mechanic boilers and weapons—led by the mighty *Julesport*, and the transports weighted with soldiers from both the Western Alliance and Bakre Confederation. The ships painted wakes across the surface of the blue sea, looking oddly beautiful from high in the sky as they proceeded on their grim mission.

If something happened to Mari, if she and Alain were betrayed, Commodore Banda would go forward with that mission and enact an awful revenge. But that realization gave only cold comfort to Alain as he wondered yet again why Mari had to be so reckless when she had decided on a course of action.

He knew one of the things that had driven her this time. "Kira is alive," Mari had told him. "Your vision showed that. Now we have a chance to save a lot of other lives."

Alain could have argued that, but he did not want to dampen

Mari's joy. Did not want to describe how Kira's face had looked in his vision, the grimness that haunted the face of their seventeen-year-old daughter as she gazed outward. Kira must have faced terrible trials, and survived them, but traces of those trials remained in the bandages she bore and in the set of her eyes and mouth. And what had become of Jason? Was the Kira that Alain had seen grieving the death of Jason as well as any harm done to her?

When he thought of such things, Alain did not want to save lives. He wanted to destroy them. Every Imperial life, every tool of princes and emperors that was used to harm others.

Mari would not, though. Even if his worst fears about Kira and Jason were proven true, Mari would still find a way to believe in life, still insist on giving others a chance. Because that was who she was.

Alain's own thoughts sometimes fell into darkness, wondering what he might have become without Mari beside him in all things.

Bringing his thoughts back to the present, Alain looked over the city and harbor, hoping his foresight would warn of the dangers he fully expected to encounter. Like Mari, he had not been back to this island, this port, for twenty years. Unlike her, he had not grown up here. His experiences in Caer Lyn had been brief but intense. From the air, he could not identify the street where Mari's childhood home lay, or which street leading to the docks held the city government office in which he and Mari had been quickly and unceremoniously married.

His gaze went to the north, thinking again of Kira somewhere in the Northern Ramparts.

As if responding to Alain's thought, the giant birds banked, offering a clear view of the blackened, torn wreckage of a warship, most of it sunk to the bottom of the harbor, the gutted upper portions rising above the surface of the water like a scorched monument to the wrath of his daughter.

Kira did have a great deal in common with her mother.

Mage Alera brought her Roc Swift to a landing in the large square surrounding the former Mechanics Guild Hall. Mage Saburo landed his Roc named Hunter nearby. Pools of recently fallen rainwater dotted the paving of the square, the wind-driven ripples on their surfaces the only movement visible.

As promised by the Imperial officials in the Sharr Isles who had arranged this meeting, the square was empty. Alain, not comforted at all by that, looked around, searching for danger. The inhabitants of Caer Lyn, whether natives of the island or Imperial soldiers, were in their homes or their barracks, waiting to learn their fates. The resulting silence in the midst of a city felt unnatural. "I do not like this."

"You've told me that at least twenty times," Mari replied, also studying the buildings and streets leading into the square. "Alain, if this offer is legitimate, it could save a lot of lives."

"And if it is a lie, a trap, it could cost the one life I care most about."

"Swift is nervous," Mage Alera told Alain.

"Swift is not the only nervous one," he replied. "Be ready to depart quickly." Alain reached out his Mage senses to feel for other Mages nearby and to judge the amount of power available in this square to feed his own spells if necessary. The closest Mages were some distance off, probably gathered in what had once been the Mage Guild Hall. And there was power here to use. Not a large amount, but more than enough.

Three figures appeared on a broad avenue leading into the square and began walking toward Alain and Mari. Knowing that Mari would be watching those who approached, Alain kept swinging his gaze across the buildings around the square in the hopes that even if he couldn't see any danger his unreliable foresight might offer some warning.

The three came to a halt a short distance from Mari. One wore the fine suit of a high-level Imperial official, embellished with the addition of an ambassador's shield on his left breast. Another was a woman in dress uniform bearing the eagles of a full legion commander. The pistol holster and sword scabbard at her belt were empty. The last was another man, this one in the style of clothing favored in the Sharr Isles. He spoke first, his smile wide. It did not take Alain's Mage skills to see the nervousness behind that smile. "Welcome back to the Sharr Isles, Lady Mari. We are honored by your visit. I'm Councilor Glyn."

Mari's return smile was smaller and polite. "Councilor Glyn. I'm glad we're finally able to meet in person, and hopefully resolve this situation without bringing war to the streets of Caer Lyn."

"That is up to you," the Imperial ambassador said. He wasn't pretending to be happy, but was also worried. "We do not seek war here, but we have been advised that an attack on the Sharr Isles is being prepared at *your* command."

Alain's voice fell into the emotionless tones of a Mage, carrying all the greater menace because of their lack of feeling. "Do not seek to shift the blame for what will happen here. You are the aggressors."

"The Empire," Mari said, her voice as unyielding as her expression, "has conducted an unprovoked attack on the Free Cities, invading the Northern Ramparts by sea and by land. It has also progressively violated the peace agreements reached twenty years ago by adding more and more military forces to an illegal garrison in the Sharr Isles. I will add that the Empire has also personally attacked me by kidnapping my daughter. I'm not in the mood for false displays of indignation."

The legion commander spoke up, her tone professionally neutral. "You know what will happen if western forces invade these islands. The destruction and loss of life will be immense."

"What I know," Mari said, "is that Imperial forces engaging in illegal occupation of the Sharr Isles may be enough to overawe the small defense forces of the Isles, but would stand no chance against the Bakre Confederation, the Western Alliance, Tiae, and the Free Cities combining to free the Isles. I also know that blockading forces from the Confederation and the Alliance have already arrived off of Landfall and Sandurin. You're cut off, unable to receive supplies or reinforcements. Are you and all of your legionaries ready to die here?"

Councilor Glyn spoke up again with forced camaraderie. "None of us want war to come to the Sharr Isles."

"Is the offer I was told of sincere?" Mari demanded of the Imperials. "Will your forces evacuate the Sharr Isles if given safe passage through the blockade?"

The Imperial ambassador nodded, making his unhappiness clear. "I have been instructed that, if Master Mechanic Mari of Dematr herself personally guarantees such safe passage, I must accept such an arrangement. The emperor has no wish for unnecessary loss of life."

Alain, watching for any sign of deception, saw none, but that offered him little comfort. He gave the Imperials a look just short of the dead expressions that Mages could achieve. "What of Prince Maxim? He seems to wish only for war."

"Prince Maxim…is not the emperor," the ambassador said.

Mari's gaze on him sharpened. "You didn't call him Crown Prince Maxim. I know enough about diplomats to know that means something."

"I have been informed that Maxim is no longer crown prince," the ambassador admitted.

"Where is Maxim?" Alain asked, his tone severe enough to cause even the legion commander to eye him worriedly.

"I do not know, Sir Master of Mages."

"Yet you know something," Alain said, having seen the deception this time.

The ambassador was openly perspiring as he answered, clearly worried about what Alain might do. He was old enough to remember the days when Mages could behave however they wanted and common folk lived in fear of provoking or even attracting the attention of a Mage. "Prince Maxim is believed to have reached Sandurin before the Alliance blockade sealed the port. But I have no confirmation of that."

"Did you know our daughter was aboard his ship in this harbor?"

"No, Sir Mage! Not until after she had…departed."

"Escaped, you mean?" Mari asked, an edge of steel in her voice.

"Yes…Lady. No one here knew of your daughter's presence until after the ship was destroyed and Prince Maxim demanded assistance in searching the island for her." The ambassador closed his eyes for a moment, his mouth tight, then looked back at them. "I have a daughter. I understand how you feel. I am responsible for any Imperial actions here. Me, personally. I...ask that if you...intend any response for the kidnapping of your daughter, that you confine such actions to me and do not harm others."

"You speak the truth," Alain said, his anger mollified somewhat by the ambassador's bravery. "We have no wish to harm anyone who was not responsible for or aided the crimes against our daughter." He looked at the legionary commander. "Do you wish to die defending the actions of Maxim?"

The commander shook her head. "Like the ambassador, it is not my role to decide which orders from the emperor to obey. The emperor has directed that we leave these isles if the daughter of Jules guarantees that our soldiers can return to imperial territory. That is what I will do, if the daughter gives us her word."

Mari was about to reply when Alain saw Mage Alera pivot suddenly toward the buildings on one side of the square.

"There is danger!" Alera called moments before the crash of rifles broke the silence looming over the city of Caer Lyn.

CHAPTER SEVENTEEN

lain's arm, already in motion, swept Mari back as he heard the sharp snap of bullets passing near.

Mari, though surprised, yielded to the shove, dropping and rolling so that the bulk of the Roc Swift was between her and the direction of the rifle fire.

Councilor Glyn of Caer Lyn had fallen, a bright patch of red spreading on the side of his suit.

The Imperial ambassador stood as if rooted like a tree, shocked, staring toward the buildings from which the shots were coming.

The legion commander grabbed the ambassador and half-hurled him into a safer spot behind Swift before grabbing one arm of Councilor Glyn. Alain helped her drag the wounded councilor so they were all also shielded by Swift.

"Swift is hurt!" Mage Alera said, worried enough for the emotion to show in her voice. Alain could hear the thud of bullets striking the Roc, who jerked about with pain, threatening to expose them all to the fire coming at them.

"We must—" Alain looked toward Mari, then at the bulk of the Roc. If Mari and Alera tried to climb onto the Roc, they would be perfect targets for the Mechanic weapons. Glancing back at Hunter, he saw that Saburo's Roc, too, was so exposed that trying to mount the bird would be suicide.

The legion commander had crouched and yanked a far-talker from her belt, yelling into it, furious. "Get the ready force moving! No! This is not an action by the daughter! Direct no fire this way! I want whoever is firing on us from those buildings! Yes! Immediately! Kill them if necessary, but I want some prisoners who can tell us who gave them those orders!"

Swift uttered a sharp cry as the thud of another bullet hit. The Roc, in pain, leaped skyward to escape its attackers, leaving a distraught Mage Alera gazing upwards.

Alain pulled Alera down to the pavement so she wouldn't be shot. He rolled to one side to see if Mari was still safe and was startled to see the legion commander and the Imperial ambassador shielding her. As Alain watched, the ambassador let out a cry as a bullet struck him.

He finally spotted a flash that told of a Mechanic rifle firing. With the illusion of heat already glowing above his palm, Alain sent it instantly to that window.

A shriek of pain answered as the air near the sniper became intensely hot. Flames flickered at the window as the wood caught fire.

"How many are there?" Mari, her pistol out, demanded of the legionary officer.

"Five or six, I think." The legion commander listened intently to her far-talker over the sound of the shots continuing to be fired in their direction. "My forces are moving in. Sir Master of Mages, I request that you not launch any more attacks."

"It is well for you," Alain said, "that I can tell your surprise at this attack is genuine."

"My orders were to see that this arrangement was carried out! Orders from the emperor's own hand! We were also ordered to ensure that the daughter was not harmed, and you see we have followed those orders! Those who fired on us are traitors!"

Another bullet struck the pavement nearby, ricocheting back into the sky. Alain lunged to the side, placing himself as well between Mari and whoever was shooting.

"Alain!" Mari shouted angrily, but before she could berate him for risking himself to protect her, a flurry of shots erupted from the buildings.

Bracing himself for those bullets to strike nearby, or to strike him, Alain realized that the new shots had not been aimed this way. He looked toward the buildings, seeing the dark red uniforms of legionaries swarming about them.

The bell of a fire alarm began insistently clanging as someone summoned the city fire wardens to deal with the building that Alain's counterstrike had set aflame.

The legionary commander listened again to her far-talker, then turned to check the ambassador. "We need healers here," she called. "Two wounded. Get the healers here fast."

Alain saw Mari crouching beside Councilor Glyn and realized she was rendering first aid. He stood, watching as Mage Alera got up and stared into the sky. "How is Swift?"

Alera blinked rapidly as she looked up. "Hurt and scared. It is safe?"

"It is safe," Alain said.

Mage Saburo gestured to Mage Alera. "Come. We will ride Hunter to meet Swift so you may calm him."

Alera scrambled onto Hunter with Saburo, and the remaining Roc rose with a brief hurricane of wind as Hunter's huge wings pumped the air.

Which left Alain and Mari alone with the Imperials. He gave her a flat look, knowing she would understand his meaning.

"All right," Mari said. "You were right. It was dangerous."

Alain glanced at the legion commander, who betrayed to a Mage's eyes both anger and shame at the attack on those she had been ordered to protect. "You were also right," Alain said. "The offer was sincere."

Healers were running across the square, dropping down beside Councilor Glyn and the ambassador.

The legion commander stepped away to allow the healers to work, nodding to Alain and Mari. "Several of the traitors were killed, but we have three prisoners. I directed that they be brought to me."

Alain saw a squad of legionaries walking their way, among them two men and a woman in the clothing of ordinary common folk. As they drew closer, Alain saw that one of the men, the youngest of the three, had bad burns on his hands and one side of his face, the marks of Alain's heat spell. The young man was consumed by pain, trembling and stumbling, but the hardfaced legionaries herding the prisoners showed no trace of concern.

The other two presented outward attitudes of defiance, but their underlying fear was obvious to a Mage.

The legion commander, looking ready to commit murder then and there, yanked a dagger from the belt of one of her legionaries and held the naked blade up in front of the prisoners. "Start talking."

The three looked back, the burned man shaking with pain, but none of them spoke.

"Hold it." Mari stepped forward, looking over the prisoners. "I know you," she said to the woman.

The woman stared straight ahead, saying nothing, her jaw clenched.

Alain, having seen something in the prisoner's repressed reaction to Mari's words, stepped up beside Mari. "Ask her if she is a Mechanic."

"Are you a Mechanic?"

Once again, silence answered her, but Alain had seen the reactions the prisoner had not been able to suppress. "She is."

Mari frowned, turning to look back toward the old Mechanics Guild Hall, then at the prisoner again. "There. That's where I saw you. You…you were an apprentice at the same time I was."

"She's a Mechanic?" the legion commander said, her tone gone from hot to dangerously cold.

"So is he!" Mari said, pointing to the uninjured man. "Senior Mechanic Tod! He was at Caer Lyn."

"An old friend?"

"No," Mari said. "He never liked me, and the feeling was mutual. What Tod liked was lording it over apprentices and Mechanics."

Senior Mechanic Tod stared at the pavement and said nothing.

"Two Mechanics in a group of three," the imperial officer said. "And perhaps more. Once we have finished interrogating them—"

"I can tell you about your daughter!" the Mechanic first identified by Mari suddenly yelled, her fear out in the open. "You remember me, Mari! Jil of Caer Lyn! You wouldn't leave a fellow Mechanic like this! Not someone you apprenticed alongside!"

"What can you tell me?" Mari asked, trying to sound calm. Alain heard the skepticism and hostility in her voice, but he did not think any of the others here could.

"I was on Maxim's ship! Operating under his orders! Imperial orders!" Jil looked around, trying to judge the impact of her words on the legionaries. "I offered to help your daughter, but—"

"You lie," Alain said, his voice totally impassive, but powerful enough to immediately cut off the flow of words.

Mechanic Jil hesitated. "I did everything I could—"

"You lie."

"I didn't hurt her!"

Alain studied Jil for a moment. "How would Kira react if she saw you again?" The Mechanic said nothing, but the answer was obvious to the eyes of a Mage. "They did not part on friendly terms," Alain told Mari.

"Because of him!" Jil said, pointing to the prisoner who had been burnt by Alain's spell. "He was the other Mechanic on the ship and—" She realized what she had said and hesitated before plunging onward. "And he said terrible things to her. Your daughter attacked him and told him never to come back! That's true!"

"She withholds something, but that much is so," Alain told Mari.

"Another Mechanic," the legion commander said. "Three of three. And two who were recently in Imperial employ."

Mari shook her head. "You already know who must have given them their orders. The Grand Master of what remains of the Mechanics Guild. Sheltered in the Empire after the Guild's authority was shattered elsewhere. This is a viper the Empire has held close to its heart."

The legion commander shifted her gaze from the prisoners to Mari. "They attacked you because of a desire for revenge."

Alain saw the suppressed reactions in Mechanic Jil and Senior

Mechanic Tod. "That was not the only purpose. It is an old game for the Great Guilds, to play common people against each other. What would have happened had you and Mari been killed or seriously injured? A terrible battle in Caer Lyn and the rest of the Sharr Isles, sowing chaos and fueling an immense war in the hopes of perhaps causing enough damage to offer the remnants of the Guild a foothold to regain power."

The legion commander gestured for the legionaries to bring Mechanic Jil forward, stepping close to her. "If you tell us all that you know, the emperor might be forgiving of your crimes," she said to Jil in a low voice. "The emperor is merciful. Help us, and we'll help you."

"I…yes," Jil whispered in reply, her terror now easily visible. But when her eyes rested on Mari, Alain saw no sign of real remorse or friendship.

"Take those two for questioning," the commander ordered her legionaries, indicating the two male legionaries. "Take this one to the embassy. Make sure no one harms her."

The commander grinned conspiratorially at Mari and Alain as the three Mechanics were led away. "Torturing those two won't provide any useful information. It never does. But an unexpected offer of honey can make words flow." Her smile vanished. "Does our agreement stand?"

Mari nodded. "Evacuate all of your forces from the Sharr Isles, without fighting, and I will guarantee their safe passage to Landfall. Your forces will, of course, leave their weapons here."

The legion commander's eyes narrowed. "We have not been defeated."

"Yes, you have been," Mari said, her tone unyielding. "Thanks to the actions of Maxim, you are in a hopeless position. The emperor knows that, and wants your lives spared. Weapons like rifles can be easily replaced. Men and women cannot."

"Sidearms," the commander insisted after a long moment. "Officers are to retain their sidearms and swords. All other legionaries retain their swords. To surrender our swords without a fight would be unthinkable."

Mari nodded. "I agree."

"And we will undertake one more operation before leaving this island," the commander added, pointing toward the Mechanics Guild Hall. "We will clean out that place, and find any evidence of crimes against the Empire."

"Anyone inside who wishes to renounce membership in the Guild, their sincerity judged by Mages, must be allowed to remain in the Sharr Isles," Mari said.

"Very well. If you and Sir Master of Mages Alain will excuse me, I have a nest of vipers to clean out before I hear the song sung by one who wishes to save her neck." The commander gave Mari one more look. "Do you care about her fate?"

"She made her decisions a long time ago," Mari said. "We all have to live with the consequences of our decisions."

"Yes, Lady. We all do." The legionary commander saluted and walked off, calling out orders.

"You were right," Alain murmured once more to Mari.

"So were you," she murmured back. "Blast. Jil. I'd almost forgotten her."

"She clearly never forgot you."

Alain sensed another Mage approaching and turned to look, seeing an old woman in Mage robes. The woman paused before them, her Mage impassiveness giving no hint of her purpose. "This one sensed that one casting a spell. Is that one Master of Mages Alain?"

"This one is," Alain replied.

"This one has a message for that one. The one Mage Asha sends that the one Kira and the one Jason are safe. Injuries are to both, the one Jason shot by a Mechanic weapon, but that one is in no danger. The one Kira sends..." The old Mage hesitated, as if uncertain of the next word. "Love. Love to the mother and father."

Alain found himself unable to speak for a moment. Mari closed her eyes and laughed softly, then looked at the old Mage. "Can this one ask that one to send a reply message? This one will pay."

"This one accepts," the old Mage replied.

"Send to that one Mage Asha for that one Kira and that one Jason, love."

"I do not know this word love," the Mage grumbled. "Is that the message?"

"Tell them also we will meet them in Marida."

Two days later, Kira woke to hear excited conversations outside the tent. Calu soon entered, grinning. "Mari did it. The Imperials are evacuating from the Sharr Isles, and the emperor has personally promised no further aggression. Between the defeat of the legions in these mountains and the imperial retreat from the Isles, the West is celebrating a win that should satisfy popular demand for retribution. It'll take a while to work out the details, but it looks like this war got damped out long before it could peak. Flyn has received orders to bring the prisoners to Marida so they can be returned to the Imperials under a vow that they not be used outside the borders of the Empire again."

Mari sat on her cot, looking over at Jason. He had recovered fairly rapidly with enough food and water and other care, but was still weak and confined to the cot. "We're going to make it to Marida after all, my hero."

He grinned. "Next time we decide to visit the Free Cities, can we do it without being chased all over the place?"

"I'll see what I can do."

It took a while to get down out of the mountains. Kira had recovered enough to be able to ride without much discomfort, and Suka proved a reliable and affectionate mount. But Jason had to travel in a wagon for the wounded. Losses had been light enough, and most of the badly hurt already sent back to Alexdria, that Jason had the wagon to himself.

As the column of soldiers moved south toward the coast, Kira rode beside Jason's wagon, always close, and when the column made camp

Kira sat nearby while the healers checked him over. She stayed with him through the nights, sleeping near.

On the second day of travel, Kira paused as she bent to drink from a bucket of water, remembering the buckets she had drunk from on Maxim's ship. She looked at the image reflected in the water, a young woman soldier whose face bore scrapes and bruises and a large bandage under one jaw. The eyes of the soldier held a shadow deep inside, where recent memories lived. Was that really her?

"Admiring yourself?" Calu asked from nearby.

"Trying to recognize myself," Kira admitted.

"You still look like Mari. She got banged up a lot, too. Oh, bad news. Boiled bacon and beans for dinner."

Kira shook her head. "Do you know how amazing it is to have food, Uncle Calu? To be able to eat when you're hungry? I am never going to take that for granted again. Even if it is boiled bacon and beans."

As they traveled, more soldiers joined them as different units which had been fighting the legions and searching for Kira and Jason returned, many with their own prisoners in tow. By the time they wended through the pass just north of Marida and headed down toward the city, the column was an impressive thing indeed.

As they began the descent from the pass to Marida, a messenger rode back from the front of the column, saluting Kira. "Captain Kira, General Flyn has received information that he wanted passed on to you. Princess Sabrin has been declared the Crown Princess of the Empire."

"She has?" Kira smiled slightly, remembering her last sight of the princess. "Maxim must be upset."

"The same message reported that Prince Maxim is dead, Captain."

"Dead?" Kira inhaled sharply, thinking of her mother and father. "How?"

"The report says only that he had an accident while returning to Palandur."

Kira rode in silence for a moment, thinking of Maxim's assaults on her, his kidnapping of her, and how many had died because of him.

"Captain?" the messenger asked. "Do you have a reply for General Flyn?"

"Tell him I'm sorry I won't have to be the one who kills Maxim," she said.

"Yes, Captain." The messenger saluted again before riding back to the front of the column.

"Kira?"

She looked over and down to Jason on his litter on the wagon. "Are you all right, love?"

"Yeah, um…" Jason looked at her with troubled eyes as Kira rode beside the wagon. "Did you mean that? About Maxim?"

"Yes."

"But you hate killing. Kira, don't let him do that to you."

She paused, breathing slowly, thinking. "He had to be stopped."

"Yeah. That's true."

"I wonder if he's really dead?" Kira added.

"Can't your mom and dad find out for sure?"

"If anybody can, they can." She looked at him again, remembering how he had come to help her and stood by her. Those memories formed a beacon of light amid the darker ones. "Hey, Jason."

"What?"

"Will you promise yourself to me?"

"You already asked me that," Jason said, smiling.

"I just want to hear it again."

"Yes, Kira, I want to promise myself to you. You still want me, huh?"

"More than ever," Kira said.

"Will you promise yourself to me?"

"Yes, if you still want me. You do realize people are probably going to keep trying to kill me? It's kind of a family tradition, I guess."

"That's okay. I guess they'll try to kill me, too, since I'm going to be in their way when they come after you."

"Did I mention the other family traditions?" Kira said.

"What other traditions?" Jason asked.

"Nothing. No big deal. Forget I mentioned it."

"What traditions?"

"Nothing you can't handle, Jason."

"I'd still feel better if I knew what they were!"

She laughed, noticing Mage Asha and Mechanic Calu watching them and smiling. And that was good, too.

They entered Marida through a great northward-facing gate, the plains outside the city and the streets inside crowded with throngs come to see and cheer for Lady Mari and her Mage, and for the Free Cities soldiers who had once again given the Empire a harsh lesson on staying out of the Northern Ramparts.

Kira had never ridden with a victorious military force before, and she was startled by the mixture of exhilaration and relief she felt as they rode through the streets of Marida past the cheering crowds. She and Jason had survived. The world was a place of astonishing and unexpected beauty.

To her surprise, the cheers following the column of soldiers seemed to redouble around her and Jason, and then to her astonishment Kira heard her name being chanted by the crowds. "Dragon slayer! Conqueror of legions! Daughter of the sea!"

"Who do they think I am?" Kira wondered out loud.

"Just don't forget who you really are," Calu advised from close behind.

"They should be cheering for Jason, too. Jason!" Kira cried, pointing toward him in the wounded wagon. "Jason of Urth!"

Those nearest in the crowd took up the shout, and Kira grinned at Jason as he looked around, embarrassed.

Finally the head of the column reached a broad open area near the piers, normally used for transferring cargo to and from the ships that came to Marida. "Captain Kira! Jason of Urth! Forward!"

"Come on," Kira told the driver of Jason's wagon.

She rode along the column until she entered the open area and saw something that made her heart leap. Her mother and father, Alain in his Mage robes and her mother in her dark jacket, the white Mage mark in Mari's dark hair shining brightly in the sun.

"Well, Captain," General Flyn said, "what are you sitting there for?"

"Orders," Kira said.

"You are detached, Captain of Lancers. You and that young man of yours. Mind that you invite me to the wedding!"

Kira grinned and saluted Flyn, then urged Suka into a quick trot toward her parents. She dismounted in a flash, her lingering aches and the pain from the wound in her side momentarily forgotten. Her parents enfolded her in a tight embrace and for that instant she was just a seventeen-year-old girl again, grateful for all she had.

Her mother drew back and smiled, but her eyes were serious as they searched Kira's eyes. "How bad was it?"

Kira inhaled deeply. "Pretty awful at times. We survived. I…really want to talk…sometime…about some of it. But it could have been worse. A lot worse. I'm okay."

"Okay?" Her mother shook her head. "Just remember that the sun will keep rising, dearest. There is still much joy out there, much life to be lived. Keep that within you to fight the darkness when it comes."

"I will. Mother, Father," Kira said, nervous, "Jason and I are engaged."

Mari nodded. "We've already heard. Most of the population of Dematr appears to have been told about it before we were."

"I only told General Flyn! And I guess he told Aunt Asha and Uncle Calu. And…really? I'm sorry!"

Mari grinned. "That's all right. Do you really think I could be angry with you about that?"

"Father?"

Alain smiled at her. She had always valued her father's smiles. "I believe you and Jason have both shown wisdom in your choices."

"Jason is here! Oh, this is Suka, my mount. He's a good horse," Kira said, leading them to the wagon where Jason lay. The driver had parked the wagon, setting the brake, and stood off to one side to give them privacy. "Jason! Mother and Father are here!"

"Um, hi," Jason said, looking up at them with visible nervousness. "Um, Kira and I are, um…"

"Engaged," Alain said. "We are aware of this."

Mari smiled at him, grasping Jason's hand in hers. "We'll get you home. You'll have all the time you need to recover there."

Jason nodded to her, still looking anxious. "Danalee will be on your way back to Tiae, so that shouldn't put you out much."

"The only reason we'd need to go to Danalee on the way back is to drop off Calu and pick up anything of yours that's still there. Your home is in Tiae, Jason." Her mother looked at Kira. "With her, and with us."

Kira stared at Mari in amazement, then wrapped her in a tight hug that pulled at the stitches still in her side. "Thank you."

"Somebody has to try to keep you two out of trouble," Mari said, still smiling. "Is something wrong, Jason?"

"I…I just don't want to wake up," Jason said, looking stunned.

"Do you feel all right?"

"He's fine, Mother," Kira reassured her. "Jason sometimes says he thinks he's imagining all this, that none of it is real."

"Nothing is real," her father agreed.

"Did you have to give him an opening to say that?" Mari asked Kira.

"It shows that Jason understands wisdom," Alain said. "All is imaginary. Except the people. You know that, Jason, do you not? Kira is real."

"How can she be?" Jason said, smiling. "She's…mostly perfect."

Kira laughed. "You remember that? Good."

"You told your parents about the blackout, right?"

Her laughter died as Kira saw her parents giving her concerned looks. "We can talk about that later."

"Blackout?" her mother asked.

"I was really stressed," Kira said, trying to keep her voice unconcerned as her stomach tightened for reasons she didn't understand. "And I hadn't eaten or drunk anything for a few days."

"You thought it had something to do with a Mage spell," Jason pressed.

She frowned at him, unhappy that Jason kept pushing the issue. "That was a lot of extra effort. Of course it might have contributed to having trouble remembering."

"That's the only time it's happened?" Mari asked.

Kira felt a surge of her old resentment about her mother interfering in her life. Maybe that, combined with her own fears, fed what she said next. "Yes."

Her father's look on her sharpened. He knew that she had lied. When was the last time she had been stupid enough to try to lie in front of Master of Mages Alain?

But her father didn't call her on it. Instead, Alain's gaze on her altered, promising there would be more discussion of this in private. Alain spoke up, his voice calming. "We should give Kira time to rest. I am confident that she will tell us anything of importance when she has had a chance to recover."

As they finally walked up the gangway of a new steam-powered ship, Jason being carried on a stretcher ahead of them, Kira sighed.

"What's the matter?" Mari asked. "We're going home."

"But I don't have a home anymore. I don't belong in Tiae."

"What did Sien tell you? Your home is where your heart lies, and Sien will always value your presence there. So will your father and I."

Hours later, after the ship had cleared the harbor and the crowds had been left behind, the afternoon wending toward a calm evening, Kira stood by a railing looking out over the water, surprised that she had felt nervous as the ship began rolling in the swells. One more thing she would have to get past to keep her life from being bent by her recent experiences.

Mari and Alain came to stand by her. "How are you doing?" Mari asked.

"Trying to convince myself this is real," Kira said. "I finally understand why Jason has trouble accepting that at times."

"He looks really good for a guy who took a bullet," her mother said.

"Yes, but he still needs a lot of rest. I left him sleeping and came out to get some more fresh air." She rubbed her mouth nervously, which suddenly made Kira remember other things that had happened. "Mother, I have a confession to make," Kira said, nerving herself. "Something I did, more than once, and I know you won't approve, but—"

Her mother shook her head. "You're engaged. Anything that you and Jason did—"

"Mother! Jason and I didn't!"

"You didn't?"

"Why do you sound so surprised? We didn't exactly have a lot of free time!"

Mari held her hands out in surrender. "What is it then? You sound like it's something you expect me to be unhappy about."

Kira shut her eyes tightly. "I pretended to be someone to scare the Imperials."

"Someone?" Mari asked.

"The daughter of Mara." The resulting silence stretched until Kira risked opening her eyes and glancing at her mother.

"What do mean 'pretended'?" Mari asked in a voice that sounded too calm to Kira.

"I mean I…acted like I wanted…to drink…stuff…"

"Blood."

"Yes. And I told the legionaries I was…really hungry."

"Stars above."

"And Princess Sabrin caught me with blood around my mouth and thought I'd been drinking it from a guy I'd stabbed and I sort of played along with that because I wanted her to think I'd be a powerful ally and so she wouldn't try to kill me," Kira finished in a rush.

Her mother covered her face with one hand. "I was hoping the stories we'd heard were exaggerated. You deliberately pretended to be Mara."

"No, I deliberately pretended to be Mara's *daughter*," Kira said. "The daughter of the Dark One. That's different."

"The daughter of darkness," her father said. "That is what the Imperials are calling you."

"Really? That almost sounds cool." Kira saw her mother's glower deepen. "It's not that bad! So I'm the daughter of darkness. You're the daughter of Jules."

"You think that's the same thing?" Mari demanded.

"Not exactly. Mother, they think Jason's a demon! A demon that you summoned from Urth to be my boyfriend."

"Why would you need a demon boyfriend?"

"Because no normal guy could survive being my boyfriend," Kira explained.

Mari shook her head. "The Imperials might have a point in that regard. It's hard enough surviving being your mother. How does Jason feel about his demon status?"

"He thinks it's funny!"

"Good for him. But I don't think this is funny. You know how I feel about that garbage about Mara!"

Kira slumped over the rail, unhappy. "I'm sorry. I was trying to escape, and not get killed, or get taken prisoner again. I did it because it was all I could think of. I know you never would have pretended to be Mara no matter how bad things were, but I'm not you."

Kira's father cleared his throat loudly.

She gave him a puzzled look, then turned the same look on her mother. "What is Father saying?"

"Your father promised me that he would never actually say anything about it, but there was that one time—" Mari began.

Alain cleared his throat again.

"Those two times," she finished. "When it was absolutely necessary."

"You've pretended to be Mara?" Kira said.

"Yes."

"Twice? All those years I wasn't allowed to even say the name and you had pretended to be her? Twice?"

"Guilty as charged," her mother said. "When absolutely necessary. Although I drew the line at smearing blood on my mouth, unlike my daughter!"

"I had a nose bleed!" Kira paused, remembering events in the Northern Ramparts. "Did you do the seductive look and the hungry eyes and the stupid 'come here and have the night of your life' talk?"

"Yeah," Mari said. "It does feel incredibly awkward, doesn't it? Hey, young lady! Just where did you learn about that kind of thing?"

"I didn't say I was good at it!"

"Neither was I," her mother confessed, then startled Kira with a giggle. "But you should have seen the looks in their eyes."

"I know! Right? Hold on. I've been terrified of telling you about this. And it turns out you've done it, too," Kira said, her expression growing accusing. "Another secret kept from me!"

"What other secrets have we kept from you?"

"*My real name?*"

"All right, I admit you should have been told about that."

"What else haven't I been told?" Kira demanded. "What other truths haven't been revealed, what other deceptions not yet uncovered? How many other horrible family secrets are still hidden from me?"

Mari shrugged. "Your grandfather is an accountant."

"Mother, I know my grandfather is an accountant! And that is not the same thing. Most accountants are not evil."

"Are you sure?" her mother asked. "Have you ever seen your grandfather working through a ledger?"

"It is disturbing," her father said.

"I don't know why I even talk to you people," Kira grumbled, leaning on the rail.

Her mother leaned on the rail next to her. "I'm sorry, Kira. But don't you also have trouble watching my father at work with a ledger? All that red ink. Like spilled blood. Doesn't it make you thirsty, too?"

Kira stared at her mother in shock that dissolved into laughter. "*You* are making a joke about *that*? Who are you? And what have you done with my mother?"

Mari stopped laughing long enough to answer. "You should have seen your face! I've finally decided that if my daughter is going to keep feeding the flames of that story I should try to own it with mockery."

"It's not like it's ever bothered Father, has it? I mean, he wouldn't have to worry now anyway because he's so old, but when you two were first going together he was young enough to supposedly be in danger from Mara." Her mother started laughing again. "What? Father, did I say something funny?"

Alain shook his head. "No. I am certain that your mother is thinking how fortunate I am that, according to our daughter, I am *so old* I am no longer among the favored prey of Mara and her daughter of darkness. Jason, however, is much younger. I am concerned for him."

"You are, huh?" Kira said, grinning. "Are you going to warn him, Father?"

"I have already tried warning him numerous times about what he was getting into," Alain said. "But he nonetheless accepted your proposal and made his own to you. His fate has been sealed."

Kira hugged her father. "I think he's pretty happy about that."

"He should be," her father said, giving her another one of his rare smiles. "He should be the happiest man on Dematr. Except for me, for I have been fortunate enough to be the chosen companion of your mother."

Mari managed to stop laughing and rolled her eyes at Kira. "Delusions."

"You ought to hear Jason," Kira said. But that made her think of the fight against the legionaries, of her and Jason pretending there was still hope when they hadn't really believed it. Memories of the past few weeks rushed into her mind and she sobered, stepping back to look at both of her parents. "You helped me through it, you know. Through everything. Because you were there. The hardest time I went through was when I was in my prison on that ship and I thought I was alone. But then I realized that I wasn't alone, and I never would be alone. Not as long as my mother and my father and Jason are here."

"That's right," her mother said, her smile reassuring. "I felt so helpless. At least knowing I was out there helped you a little."

"It helped me a lot," Kira said. "I knew I could escape my room on Maxim's ship because you had escaped the dungeon in Ringhmon."

"Then you set the ship on fire."

"Yes. A little."

"Kira, it blew up. We saw it. There's nothing left but a burned-out hulk."

"It is a serious mistake to lock up either of you where anything flammable is present," Alain commented.

"I'm doomed to become you, aren't I, Mother?"

"If you're lucky," Mari said. "Kira, we'll figure out whatever caused that blackout. Whatever it is, we'll get through it. You, me, your father, and Jason. You do realize how happy we are that you two are engaged, right? And when we get back to Pacta Servanda there's something that Jason should be able to help us with. It could be serious, but hopefully not. For the moment, you're safe, we've short-circuited the march to a major war, and there doesn't seem to be anything awful about to fall on us."

Alain nodded. "It does not require foresight to realize that probably means something awful is about to fall."

"Yeah, probably. With any luck we'll get at least one good night's sleep before it hits. Oh, by the way, Kira, you've got a brother or a sister on the way," her mother added casually.

"*By the way?* You're—? How—?"

"How? Do I really have to explain that to you?"

"No, Mother, you don't have to explain it! Stars above!" Kira hugged her mother.

"I'm glad you're not jealous," Mari said. "We can talk more later. Are you coming in, Kira?"

She shook her head. "Not yet, Mother. Jason should still be sleeping. I want to watch the sun set."

Kira stood at the rail, the wind blowing across her, the sea running out to where the distant mountains to the north met the sky, and to the west where the sun was sinking below the horizon, the ship moving beneath her to the eternal rhythm of the waves. To the east the stars were beginning to peek out of the darkening sky. Somewhere on deck she heard sailors talking. One of them laughed. Overhead, the shape of a Roc could be seen, flying south, its feathers rendered golden by the last rays of the setting sun. "Thank you," she said to the world, and as night fell she went inside the ship to be with her family.

There would be more challenges, but tomorrow the sun would rise, and today she was free.

About the Author

"Jack Campbell" is the pseudonym for John G. Hemry, a retired Naval officer who graduated from the U.S. Naval Academy in Annapolis before serving with the surface fleet and in a variety of other assignments. He is the author of The Lost Fleet military science fiction series, as well as the Stark's War series, and the Paul Sinclair series. His short fiction appears frequently in *Analog* magazine, and many have been collected in ebook anthologies *Ad Astra*, *Borrowed Time*, and *Swords and Saddles*. He lives with his indomitable wife and three children in Maryland.

Don't miss the adventure that started
it all...

THE DRAGONS
OF DORCASTLE

PILLARS OF REALITY ❀ BOOK 1

JACK
CAMPBELL

FOR NEWS ABOUT JABBERWOCKY BOOKS AND AUTHORS

Sign up for our newsletter*: http://eepurl.com/b84tDz
visit our website: awfulagent.com/ebooks
or follow us on twitter: @awfulagent

THANKS FOR READING!

*We will never sell or giveaway your email address, nor use
it for nefarious purposes. Newsletter sent out quarterly.